Chinese Restaurants

Dan Wallace

Wylisc Press
Silver Spring, MD

Chinese Restaurants
Dan Wallace
ISBN 97817353006-8-9 Trade Paperback
ISBN 97817353006-9-6 E-Book
6 x 9
387 pages
Publication Date: August 2, 2025
Cover design by Molly A. Wallace

Wylisc Press
Silver Spring, MD 20901-1205
inthewallacemanner.com

To James Patrick O'Donnell
scholar, philanthropist
boon companion
and best friend
for all these years.

Chapter 1.

Someone's murdering a poem;
Round up the usual images.
ore]tqipg[kkkm

Will lifted his head off the keyboard and sighed, "Augh," then deleted the nonsense characters caused by his collapse. Poetry. What is a poem? A tree: the pulp of a tree, pen upon paper drawing ink, soy-based if you're of an environmental bend. Soy sauce? Did I really used to do this seriously?

The dryer next to him buzzed its noisy klaxon, then stopped, leaving the churning drone of the washer as the remaining sound. He rolled his old gray receptionist chair over to the dryer door and reached in to feel the clothes. Done, but they could wait. He spun in front of the beat-up desk, a cheap, fiberboard art-deco knockoff left over from some long-ago friend's move. As he posed his fingers above the keys, Eileen walked in.

"How's it going?" she asked as she reached into the dryer and pulled the clothes out, dumping them into a basket.

"Not well," he said, "Bad. Badly."

"Oh?" she said, looking over his shoulder.

"That's not anything," he said as her eyes scanned a sheet of paper at his elbow, "just goofing."

"Well, let me see something."

"Eileen—"

"Come on, Willy, if you can't stand me taking a look, how are you ever going to handle what critics have to say? Or the inevitable rejection letters from publishers, for that matter."

"I can handle what they have to say because I know they don't have a hidden agenda."

"Bull," she scoffed, "everyone has a hidden agenda."

"Maybe so, but I'm not married to everyone."

"Yeah, yeah, let's go. Give."

She swooped up a page from the top of the desk before he could stop her. She stood, reading intently while he watched.

She had another ten years of attractiveness ahead of her, he thought, one of those women who looked even better in middle age. Eileen had always been strikingly handsome, with her almost Mediterranean complexion and black hair, wedded wondrously to her Gaelic features. Tall and lithe, she commanded a kind of forceful sexuality now, a directness arrived from full self-knowledge and no time to waste.

She put the paper down on the desk.

"So," he said, "what do you think?"

"You're prosaic," she said.

"Well, thank you for that observation." He turned back to the keyboard, and she stooped to grab awkwardly around him.

"C'mon, Willy, what's wrong with that?"

"Nothing, if you like plain old prose."

"But I do. I like your plain old prose."

"Thanks, but no thanks."

"Now, don't pout. You're a master of expression; you can get anybody to do anything you want when you want to. So why get bent out of shape over this?"

"Because I like poetry. I've always liked it since I was a kid. Passionately."

She unwrapped her arms and stood up. "Sure. But it doesn't put food on the table."

"We've got plenty," he muttered.

"Not for long, not forever, if Harry Olssen gets his way."

"Hey. Don't start again, will you? Harry's okay."

She lifted the laundry basket waist high, saying, "I'm just telling you what the truth is. If you leave the door open, he'll walk in, okay guy or not. You know that if he gets it, he's virtually the heir apparent, the dauphin. When that happens, he won't leave any old rivals to the throne around. You'll be out. We'll both be out."

"Eileen, you think you've taken this crown-prince courtyard intrigue shit far enough? I mean, let's get a little realistic, here."

"That's how it works, really. I'm just saying."

"Yeah, yeah, yeah. Leave it alone, will you? Give me a break on Saturday, for once. We're doing fine."

She moved toward the door, circling a gaze from the walls to the low ceiling, "Unhuh. If we're doing so fine, how come we can't get a new house? How come we can't get someone to do the damn laundry?

After she left, he stared for an instant at the paper on the desk. He snatched it up, crumpled it, and dashed it into the metal trash can at his side.

Fuck.

How do you do this stuff, lamented to himself. After a twenty-year break? On weekends no less.

This wasn't the way it was supposed to turn out, this was not the way he had planned it. Instead of living in suburbia on the edge of the goddamn Beltway, he should be ensconced in the library of his elegant Tudor cottage, one hoary elm-flanked block off campus, tenure assured, quartzite beard trimmed to perfection, reading a bit of Yeats for his next critical monograph, pleasantly interrupted by one of his straight-A progeny home on hiatus before leaving to study in Europe, courtesy of the very sage Fulbright and Rhodes Scholarship committees, thank you so much.

One of his kids got A's at least, he thought. Though of course not enough to ever see any money. Mary would have had to reinvent the wheel to get a ride these days, considering his and Eileen's combined salaries. What the hell, they could afford it, which left something for kids who couldn't – though not much, thanks to the run of "education presidents" they'd had.

Mary was a good kid, even if she was a bit fresh, a bit too precociously ingenuous. She had both her mother's will power and good looks, and the combination had people of all genders falling all over themselves to give her what she wanted. Yet, she never took advantage of anyone or had a mean word to say about a soul. She just expected too much for her age, and it was those outsized expectations that worried him. He worried about her first year in college this fall, when she would go from both student council and senior class president, a first at the school, National Honor Society member, and National Merit Scholarship Honorable Mention, to being simply a first-year student. How would she handle that sort of come-down?

She'd have boyfriend Alan there to comfort her, he sighed. He hadn't been crazy about the prospect of Mary and Alan going to the same college. He had hoped that separate schools would force them to give romance a break. It wasn't like he hoped that this would delay any physical involvement, since Alan had been part of the picture for almost three years. True, he'd often wondered if the boy's testosterone levels were up to snuff. But that didn't delude him into thinking that the likely was impossible. He just did his best to avoid such discomforting, dismaying thoughts.

God. Alan. Such different concerns, Will thought, from those he'd originally had about Mary just after she'd been born. He could remember striding up and down the hospital hallway while mother and baby rested, his mind a stew of ideas, present and future. He would compose a book for his first child, his first daughter, a list of things to tell her so that he could help her avoid the pain of self-experience as much as possible.

"In winter, or on rainy days, when about to cross a street, stand one to one and a half yards back from the curb, to avoid being splashed by cars passing through puddles."

And so on, as though he could keep her from the worst things in life.

"She's such a good baby," he remembered saying to Eileen. "Do you think she's being so good now so that she can break our hearts even more when she's so rotten later?"

He smiled wryly at his naivete back then, when he supposed that when rotten things happening to good children, they naturally hurt more than bad things done to bad children. He shook his head, what a jackass he'd been. Still, he wondered how she would fare, this new Sweetheart of Sigmund Freud?

She would drive. She would assemble her dominance as she had done before. Like her mother, grain by grain, piece by piece. Like an old pol, until she had assumed her proper, higher station in life. And Alan would rise with her. Still, thought Will, here he sat again, mulling and worrying about Mary.

He focused back on the screen. Words, words, words. How to put the same words together, some half a million different ones in the English language, he remembered vaguely, so that they meant something entirely new. Lace them with exacting rhythms and tones, denotations and connotations, images and epiphanies, in order to lave with extreme pleasure and to fire leaps of imagination, thrills from trills.

So, how do you begin again after twenty years? What is the standard, the template? Yeats? Dickinson, Tennyson? Chaucer, Milton—Shakespeare, for God's sake. Heaney?

Not to mention the host of others who had surfaced since his college years, halcyon days of ivy and beer. While he had been writing endless press releases, speeches, and committee testimony, unknown peers around the world had been reading, teaching, deliberating and discussing the newest in poetic expression, names of people he'd never heard of, much less read. To take up again what constituted a life pursuit trailing by two decades with only two to four to go should be enough to bring down any flights of fancy. Especially when the wife component of the family unit damned his initial effort with faint praise, he thought. Hell, she'd damned it with no praise.

Well, to hell with that. Where to start? Anywhere.

He peered into the monitor's black screen bespeckled with yellow glow worm words. He deleted everything and keyed the cursor to center screen.

Okay, he thought, poetry. He scrunched up his face, gazed for a moment, then typed.

Love

"There," he said.

He sat back and heard a tremendous crash of glass from upstairs.

"Shit!" he heard in the distance. Will sprinted up the short steps to the first floor and ran into the kitchen. Eileen stood, holding the handle of a coffee pot attached to a star-shaped shard of glass. Beneath her feet and around her spread a glistening wreath of broken pieces of crystal.

"The coffee pot," she said. "I clipped the counter."

"Huh," he said, stooping to pick up glass. "Too bad."

Staring at the handle she said, "You think this means seven years of bad coffee?"

"What's the difference?"

"Oh, thanks a lot, Juan Valdez."

"Come on."

"Listen, you can take over anytime. You knew from the outset that I'm not into food preparation."

"Yeah, I know, Hon, but it's woman's work, right? So, . . . I couldn't possibly."

"Unhuh." She motioned an uppercut with her fist, "You and the horse that rode in on you, mister."

"Dear, Dear, Dear, Dear."

She grabbed the broom from the nook between the refrigerator and the counter. "You're just getting even because you're not doing so hot downstairs."

"Of course that's not true. I'm off to a good start."

"Not from what I read."

6

"You see? Who's being vindictive now? Did I break the coffee pot?"

"Did I break the coffee pot?" she mocked. "It's a wonder I don't break all the glasses every time I turn around in this shoebox. Say, why don't you crawl back into the basement with the rest of the bugs and spiders."

"You bet. Better company than up here."

Eighteen years he thought, and they still got along so well.

She hadn't changed a bit since her Northeastern days, fiercely single-minded even then, the only corporate law student at the nation's leading do-gooders law school. She'd explained it away to her classmates, that big business needed someone with her sensibilities working inside to keep the wheeler-dealers straight.

But most of her fellow students suspected another truth, a deeper well of attraction and longing within her for that life. So, how had he, the liberal, hippy, English major undergrad, won her over?

"You don't remember?" she'd said to him once On the way to a restaurant for dinner, he recalled, on their anniversary, though he couldn't remember which one. He remembered that he was driving.

"You said," she'd gone on, "'Okay, take your clothes off and get in the bed.'"

"I did?" he'd asked. She nodded her head, and he'd smirked. "I sure can talk some shit."

It was true, though, he had wowed her, to the amazement of his buddies, to her friends, herself, and to his own utter amazement. How could he let her go by, especially when that hard edge of hers faded when she looked at him with those big, liquid brown eyes? So deep and dark that you could drop quarters in them to lose forever. Eyes that could make him do anything, get a real job, have two kids, live in an old split-level.

She would just as soon leave the old split-level behind, no doubt about that. She'd been campaigning for some time with her big brown peepers to get him to move. The seductive stage had passed a while ago, however. Now she studied him cooly, as though privately wondering if it was time to have him committed.

The onslaught of her distancing was brutal to withstand. He countered with maxims of how this was not the time to make a move. No matter that with their combined income, they could easily afford another place. He would caution by pronouncing that people should not expend credit during a recession. They should retrench, pull cover to weather the economic storm. This was especially true, he would point out, considering the very tenuous position enjoyed by ComCon at present, a condition of potentially exponential danger to them since they both worked there.

She would riposte with the hypothesis that the delicacy of the situation at ComCon called for exactly the opposite of a defensive posture, especially with competition for the executive v.p. position coming up. The old saw that you need to spend money to make money applied to credit, too, especially personal credit. She would assert that they needed a better physical setting in which to stage events to actively pursue the new post. Also that Harry Olssen wouldn't be pulling a blanket over his head to keep his job. He will without a doubt host some serious social events for the ComCon powers that be, and he'll be sure to invite us, too. She would insist that to be a vice president you had to act vice-presidential.

Vice-presidentially, he thought. Whatever it really came down to was that she hated this old house, while he loved it. They had lived here for all these years, watching the kids grow up, planting flowers and shrubs, stretching to get a loan for the new roof. And now that they could easily pay for it, they still hadn't gotten around to having the metal casement windows replaced with energy-efficient ones. They simply ate the huge gas bills and made sure not to touch the sills during the winter.

God, he recalled that easy "two-day" job she talked him into during their first Christmas as a family. Mary was only ten months old or so, and he and Eileen both had arranged to take off the week between the Holidays. She'd wooed him into stripping the wallpaper from the master bedroom's walls and repainting them. He had to admit, the long blue, white, and gold vertical stripes of the old paper had reminded him of a hotel room in Las Vegas. As the day of the job approached, though, he'd tried to talk her into putting it off.

"But Eileen," he'd pleaded, "I'll miss the Las Vegas Bally Casino Memorial Wallpaper. And remember, it makes us look thin from every angle."

She would not relent, and the "two-day" job became a horrible six-day ordeal of steaming two-inch wet wads of paper and paste, followed by spackle and drywall mud, sandpaper and dust, oil-based primer, and two coats of light lavender paint. During the fiasco, Mary caught a cold and cried plaintively during her waking hours. Eileen caught Mary's cold two days after Christmas and spent the rest of the vacation taking care of the baby and herself. He finished the last coat at 7:00 p.m. on New Year's Eve day. At 8:00 p.m., his throat became scratchy, and he could feel the congestion building in his sinuses.

It never ended, either. When Mike was born, he'd gone through the same thing getting Mary's room ready. Then, he had to redo Mike's room to be more of a boy's room. That led to the guest room in the old laundry room, though they had gotten contractors to move the appliances to the lower basement. Naturally, his so-called office went into the laundry room, too.

And here he was, too, nascent poet at forty-two, sharing the dulcet marvels of his mind with the rhythmic tones of the Kenmores, may they never miss a beat.

God, he must have loved her insanely for her to get him to do all that kind of stuff during all these years. But he didn't want to move. The time had gone so fast. So, was he being stubborn or had love changed, too?

He looked at the screen again, and read the pale word, *Love*. He tapped out some words, then sat back to look at them.

Time flies, but love lingers.

Warm arms wrapped around him from behind.

"Hey, Longfellow, is that a sonnet for me?"

She gave him a squeeze, "What do you say? The kiddoes are out and about. How about a little snuggling and rubbing against each other?"

"I'm sorry, but I'm too prosaic."

"What's wrong with that?"

"There's no passion in prose."

"Sure there is. There's plenty."

"Oh, yeah? How do you know?"

"You've been proving it for years," she snickered as she moved her fingertips down his chest.

"I beg your pardon?"

"Sure. I thought passion equated with sex."

"You don't move me to passion."

"Oh, come on, Willy," she nibbled his ear, "let's fuck and make up."

He turned his head and stared at her. "You certainly have a way with words."

"Come on. Get up those stairs, now. Get up there, take off your clothes, and get in the bed."

So how, he thought later, could anyone expect him to do anything with all the interruptions around here? The constant din, the crashing of cymbals, symbolically speaking.

"You're awful," she'd said.

"You've made that eminently clear."

"I mean you have no shame. Anyway, why the sudden urge to do this now?"

"It's not sudden. I've always wanted to do it, but something always came up. First, we had Mary, then Mike came along, then I moved to ComCon. I just decided that if I don't do it now, I'll never do it."

She propped herself on one elbow. "You didn't want us to have Mary and Mike?"

"Hell, of course I wanted Mary and Mike. I just never wanted the rest of it. I mean, couldn't we've had them with me as a teacher and you working where you wanted? I could've taken care of them at home while you worked. I could've spent the summers with them."

"So, who are you blaming for this turn of events? You said you wanted the job. Every time you got a bonus, you sounded happy about it."

"Oh, sure. I mean, what was the alternative? No thanks? We always found a way to use the money. I mean, what was I supposed to do, what was I supposed to say?"

"Boy, Willy, it's a shame you've been so successful. My heart cries out for you."

"Unhuh, okay, okay."

"No, really, what's the alternative now? Like it or not, we have a Rube Goldberg contraption in the balance, here, called our family, you know? If you don't go after this new position, I mean really go after it, where are we going to be?"

"Why can't we just be where we are? I don't want any new responsibilities. I just want to do what I'm doing at work now. If I can do that, then maybe I'll have a little more time to write at home."

She sat up and rested her elbows on her knees. "That's naive, Willy, or is it willful ignorance? You can't stay put, it's against the laws of physics. You'll lose ground, I'm telling you. You'll risk everything."

"Yeah, yeah, I hear you."

"I'm surprised at you, Will. I thought you looked forward to the chance to run things. You complain enough about how they're run now. Is something wrong? Are you sick?"

"Sick of work."

"Or have you lost your nerve?"

Will rolled his eyes at her in exasperation, "Eileen, don't pull that macho Macbeth bullshit on me. I'm not going anywhere. I'll either get it or I won't. But all the machinations in the world or in your head aren't going to make one goddamn bit of a difference."

"Right, and in the meantime, you're going to become the great, sensitive poet. You picked a hell of a time to do it."

"Yeah," he said, jumping up to yank on his trousers, "And I'm wasting time here. I better get downstairs before Mike comes home and wants to play Nintendo."

As he ran down the stairs, he heard her voice rising, "You're running from this, Willy, you're running away," she said, finishing at a high pitch, "Mike hasn't played Nintendo for months."

Time flies, but love lingers

He couldn't think of a way to continue. He'd spent his passion, he thought, and not necessarily by making love. Of course, therein lay much of the problem, the fact that he'd been successful at everything he'd ever done despite himself. Bitching and moaning all the way, he'd always done the extra bit of business to make sure that things were just so. It didn't have anything to do with ambition, just compulsion. He was anally compulsive; Eileen possessed the ambition in the family. Of course, as hard as she'd worked, as well as she'd done, she'd missed out on opportunity after opportunity, one plum after another going to some good old boy. She'd been given the legal department more as a reward for bringing him to ComCon rather than for her own good services. Still, galling as it must have been for her throughout the past ten years, she'd never resented him for his good fortune.

His good fortune, promotion thrust upon him kicking and screaming all the way, dragging him away from his essential self, his essence. He was a victim of the opposite of the Peter Principle – the Paul Principle? The Retep Elpicnirp? The Eileen Principle.

He was tired of being eaten up by Eileen's ambition. He wished that he could fault her, but she excelled at everything, too, including family business. Hell, how could she work a long, full day the same way he did and know that Mike wasn't playing Nintendo anymore? Why hadn't he known that?

Maybe she was right about the damned promotion. Maybe he should go after it in earnest, especially with Harry neck and neck. But since when did any outfit pick the public affairs guy over R and D to be the successor? No, he thought, better to just let it happen, and stem the tide of anxiety, that about not getting it, and getting it.

Poetry; the verse's the thing. Take me away from the way things are into the magical realm of the way they should be.

Time flies, but love lingers;
I'll kiss my love, and kiss her hard—

"Will!"

"Jesus Christ!" he bellowed when he heard Eileen's cry, one of pain and rage. "What now?"

"Will!" She appeared at the door to the laundry room. "Liv Robinson just called! Joe caught Mike and Sandy screwing in the bushes in the back yard!"

Chapter 2.

Eileen drove him crazy in the morning by taking her time dressing, then insisting upon taking the wheel because he refused to drive like Mario Andretti to get to work on time. He tried reading the paper on the way, but her speed shifts and sprints in different lanes followed by abrupt downshifts sooner or later grabbed his attention.

"Eileen, slow down. What's the difference between being ten minutes late and five minutes?"

"No need to give anybody ammo for innuendo, Sweetie-pie. Five minutes late and they figure they missed us because we're in the loo. Ten minutes, and they start getting annoyed about what they're paying us for."

"We don't get paid by the hour, Eileen, so what do we care? Hell, we put in more time than anybody else anyway."

"Yeah, but appearances count. Five minutes could be critical."

"God!" he cringed as she whipped in front of a car to zip past a bus, leaving in her wake a cacophony of blaring horns.

"Shit, Eileen, if five minutes is so important, get up earlier! I'd rather be late than dead."

"I haven't killed you yet, have I? When I do, let me know."

He fretted in silence, wondering why she did things like this all of the time? He acknowledged long ago that Eileen owned more Moxy than he ever would, but did she have to prove it every day? She always struck that hardnose pose, to the extent that the casual acquaintance often thought her to be a bit abrasive. They didn't know how tender she could be, how gentle and nurturing she'd been with the kids when they were young. He remembered her holding them on her lap, humming and rocking them for hours. Naturally, as with all other wives and mothers, she'd nurtured him, too, her most complicated child.

He shook his head, thinking that in recent times she seemed to assume the tough cookie persona more often, whether at work or at home. Like the way she dealt with Mike.

"Jesus Christ, Mike, what were you thinking?"

"What? Why?" he said.

"Why? After all we talked about. What, do you think you love this girl?"

"Maybe!" Mike shouted, then said sullenly, "No. I don't know."

Eileen grabbed him by his shoulders to face her and pointed her finger like a stiletto at his chin, "Did you use a condom?"

"What? . . . ," Will trailed off. "Jesus. Eileen, what the hell is that supposed to mean?"

"Exactly what it means."

His face screwed up, Will said, "Why don't you ask him if it was good or not? He's fourteen, for Christ sake."

"I suppose you want to stand on propriety. They were caught humping in the bushes, Will, for any passing dog to see. I think his delicate sensibilities can handle the question. Michael, answer me."

"I don't know," said Mike, staring down at his feet.

"You don't know? You either did or you didn't. Which was it?"

"Eileen, what next, the cattle prod? Forty-eight hours under a bare lightbulb? Ease up!"

"I didn't use one, all right?" Mike cried, tears literally bouncing off his cheeks as he broke and darted upstairs to his room.

"Great," said Eileen. "Now what?"

"Well, Eileen, we can always take him to Kaiser, have them run up his blood serum. You know, if he's infected, we can send him to military school for his type. Type, get it?"

"That's swell, Willy, a laugh riot. You're a big help."

"What the fuck, Eileen, how do you think he feels? He's mortified. Shit, I was embarrassed to death when Mary walked in on us that time, and she was only three."

"I told you to lock the door."

He sighed, "Right. I should have."

"Listen," she said, "I asked him only because I'm terrified. He's still such a baby."

The second set of tears in the house started then, and he had comforted her in his arms. But now as they approached the turn into the park, he couldn't help giving her a sidelong glance, wondering just how calculated her emotional outburst had been?

They drove slowly through the wide, winding streets of the Fair Orchard Industrial Park toward a lot fronted by a sign proclaiming Computer Control, Inc. Eileen pulled into a reserved space in front of the long, two-story brick building, which looked so much to Will like a modern-day high school. The real estate developers called it flexible-use space, perfect for offices or research and development. ComCon used it for both.

They walked through the double glass doors, which were flanked by glass-bricks. Inside, a sky-lit atrium housed half a dozen teen-age rubber trees shooting twenty-five feet into the air. Perpendicular to the doors stood deeply varnished, cherry wood paneled walls with long hallways leading into the building's wings. Situated in front of the right wall was a round, cherry reception desk minded by two young women. A huge wall window faced the front doors, creating an overwhelming airy feel to the area.

"Good morning Ms. Day, Mr. Day," one of the women said. The other one busily chatted into her headset. "No messages for you Mr. Day."

She handed a wad to Eileen, who smiled indulgently and turned to Will.

"Okay, Hon, see you at the conference." Eileen leaned over

16

and pecked his cheek, then started down the wing opposite the reception desk.

She did that every morning, he thought, making some cursory gesture of affection to signal their long familiarity, a territorial marking "married" for the benefit of the two receptionists. She never did it anywhere else, under any other circumstances, only to serve notice to these two single gals on the prowl, miniskirted and high coifed, lips ruddy and ready for love. As if they'd have the time of day for him, he thought.

"It's nine-fifteen, Mr. Day." The receptionist, Kelly, smiled at his surprise, "Mr. Forster asked us to remind you that your meeting has been moved to nine-thirty."

"Oh, gosh, Kelly, thanks for the warning."

He feigned hurrying down the hallway, just catching a glimpse of her grin as he disappeared. The wood paneling of the lobby continued into the building's wing for forty-five feet, then gave way to fabric and metal partitions separating fifty cubicles on either side. No more than seven feet high, the short walls left a huge open-air expanse to the ceiling, effectively defeating an employee's sense of privacy or confidentiality even as the barriers affected these inalienable rights. The obvious design of the structures as portable undermined any subconscious sense of job security, too. The design ultimately exercised a subtle control over the employees, making them work just that much harder while keeping subversive talk to a minimum. Whenever he thought about it, Will appreciated his private office that much more, with its walls to the ceiling and its door that he could close.

He reached it after a dogleg left, waving to Julie as he went by her desk.

"Meeting in five, Will," she said.

"Yeah, yeah. Am I ready?"

"What's ready? Here's our fabulous schedule of awesomely influential events, plus a few clippings on which way the boys on the Hill are leaning these days, and the fifty-eighth draft of Forster's testimony. Need you say more?"

"God, I don't know, Julie. Who does?"

"Hey," she said, nudging her glasses up on her nose with both hands, "are you all right? You look hung over."

"Listen, you know I don't drink on Sundays," he said, "much. It's Mike. A neighbor caught him frolicking in the bushes with his daughter."

"What?" she said astounded. "You mean, he was . . . ."

"Making the beast with two backs? Yes he was. At least, I think he was trying to."

"Oh my God, how old is he? Twelve?"

"Fourteen."

"Oh," she said, then seeing his expression, "Still, that's too young, way too young."

"Jesus, Julie, just how avantgarde are you?"

"No, really, you're right. So, what did you do?"

"Well, we immediately grounded him and cancelled all social events." An attractive woman clearly NYC wise, Julie sat back and pulled a face. Will continued.

"What do you think we did? We confronted him, bawled him out, you know, the usual terrors of the Earth. What were we supposed to do? I would have loved getting laid at his age, or at least I thought so then. Now, we can't let them, and it doesn't have anything to do with morals or righteousness. Of course, we have to pretend that it's a moral issue, stupid as that is."

Julie nodded her head. "How did Eileen take it?"

Will rolled his eyes, "Like the storm trooper I know and love."

"Oh."

"Thing is, the kids respond to her much more than they do to me. I try that touchy-feely stuff I'm known for, and they think I'm just so lame. And when they're in a fix, they go to Eileen first."

"Oh, I don't know," said Julie, "Eileen seemed to be in the dark about Mike's doings this time."

His face brightened. "Yeah, that's true! Maybe she knew he wasn't playing Nintendo anymore but she sure didn't have a clue about why."

"Unhuh," Julie said, "the poor kid."

"Yeah," Will agreed. He looked at Julie, her frosted hair, her pretty face. She had pale skin and too round a figure, plump at best, and dumpy when she fell off her regimen.

"Okay, I better compose myself," he said as he headed to his office, thinking that Eileen was wasting her time flashing her plumage in front of the women out front while never giving Julie a thought. Of course, Eileen knew, too, that he was hopelessly lousy at being unfaithful.

The conference room for executive meetings lay behind the paneled walls adjacent to the lobby. Will hated the room because it had no windows to stare out, and the strangely shaped walnut conference table and its padded swivel chairs filled the room virtually to capacity. He always tried to sit near the door, as if some urgent phone call or a messenger bearing news of death and destruction could save him from the stultifying, banal details of these meetings immortal.

He walked into the room carrying his full clipboard and was dismayed to discover that he had arrived before everyone except Evans, the new comptroller.

"Damn, no one here?"

"Uh, no," said Evans, shifting uneasily, "except me."

"Oh, yeah. Sure," said Will. "God, I hate being first. I like showing up late and leaving early."

"Right," smiled Evans.

"Pretty unprofessional, huh?"

"Pretty unprofessional," Evans nodded, still smiling. Will watched him turn sickly as he waited for more.

"Yup, these meetings are something," said Evans.

"Yeah, like living death. Or deathly living."

Will plopped himself in the seat next to the end of the table near the door. This guy's a real live wire, he thought, gazing at him, then around the vacant seats and table, and back again. No more than five-six, he judged, and a little pudgy, he was a nice-enough looking guy, except for his thin hair. Young to be balding, in his mid-thirties, Will guessed. Evans had round, full lips and very white skin that gave the impression that he seldom spent any time outdoors or in a gym. Not that he was the great physical culturalist himself, Will admitted, but he'd always been trim, and whenever he had played games, they'd come naturally to him, much to the frustration of his opponents. The ease of sports kept him from playing much, that and the bile exercised by those he beat, usually dedicated and well-practiced friends who turned ugly in defeat.

He wondered if Evans was married. On his next idle survey of the room, he glanced at Evans' ring finger. Nope, nothing, which didn't mean anything, Will knew. Still, he bet himself that Evans was single.

Harry Olssen strolled in, a big blond man in an olive, double-breasted suit with its jacket unbuttoned and its side panels bunched over his wrists, his hands stuck in his pants pockets. He dropped into the seat opposite Will's and said "Have any aspirin, Will?"

"Only what I just took."

"Oh. How about Tylenol? Advil? Excedrin? Excedrin Plus. Bufferin? Will, I need drugs."

"I can't help you, Harry."

"How about you?" Harry said, looking at Evans.

"No, uh, just some Sinutab."

"That's good. Sinutab is good."

He took two tablets from Evans, who seemed dazed by the transaction, and swallowed them dry. Then he leaned across the table to Will and whispered, "He's a real personality kid."

"Hell, Harry, he's new. He's feeling his way."

"Sure, but look at him, Willy. He looks like he just woke up from a twenty-year trance in a doughnut shop."

Will snickered, "Harry, give him a break."

The rest of the ComCon executives trooped in and took their seats. Eileen came in trailed by Jim Forster, the president and founder of ComCon. He was as tall as Harry Olssen, but bigger in the waist, and his blond hair had turned mostly gray. He wore glasses, a Scottish tie and blue shirt in a conservative herringbone suit. His ruddy complexion set off his green-gray eyes, and his vitality remained obvious despite the common knowledge that at the age of sixty-seven, he contemplated retiring in a few years, or sooner.

Forster sat at the head seat with Eileen between him and Harry on his right. The seat next to Will on Forster's left stayed vacant.

"Morning, everyone," said Forster, "can we start? Eileen, anything we need to know?"

Eileen offered her report, followed by Harry, then the rest of the officers in turn. Like at all meetings, Forster asked the occasional question but mostly allowed the others to clarify and coordinate activities. Will imagined a window on the wall, and through it he pictured rolling hills, pine trees at either edge and a vast, blue-green ocean in the distance. He carved a path through the bluish grass, the brown, sandy loam to the water, where waves lapped languidly Still boats lay at rest between water and air as sunrays spangled off the white canvas planes of their sails.

Eileen, anything to add?" asked Forster. "All right. Will, how about you?"

Will passed around copies of the final draft of prepared testimony as he explained the upcoming Congressional committee session and the goals of the company. He watched them thumb through the briefs as they listened without comment.

"So, what about Maloney, Will?" Forster asked. "Do you think he'll hold the line?"

Shaking his head, Will said, "It's hard to tell. He's under a lot of pressure from within and without to go along with the budget cuts. We will be talking to him, but the election's imminent and his district is hurting. To be completely frank, he had a tough time just making it past the primary."

"Huh," Forster nodded grimly. He sat back in his chair, rocking it back and forth. Then he leaned forward folding his hands on the tabletop.

"People, I know that I've rattled your cages year in and year out about how tenuous our position is keeping things going. Between tough competition and past defense cutbacks, we've had to survive some pretty mean times. But never has ComCon been in a tighter bind than the one squeezing us now. The skinny is that for the first time since the World War, the Defense Department itself is staring virtual obsolescence in the face. Now, I built this company thirty years ago on one premise, one peg: computers for defense. Plain and simple, we win contracts; we sell computer expertise to the Army. But if the Army is pulling up, then we are in deep swamp water. Believe me."

He leaned in further almost out of his seat.

"On top of all of this, we're not making budget. We are running over in just about every category and I want to know the reason why. Now, I know things happen, that periodically it just becomes hard to—the money just seems to be melting away with nothing to show for it. But without the Cold War, without the Soviets scaring us, Congress is looking for ways to cut the budget. They might be eyeing us anyway as expendable, but if we can't even make budget, well, absolutely they'll cross us off the list," he said, tapping his finger hard on the table to emphasize each word of his last statement. He sat back again, feigning a relaxed pose.

"I don't know about you folks, but I want to keep my job. I like the money and I like the work." He surged forward again, "I believe in the work. We're not out of the woods in this country yet, not by a far cry, with bad guys like Quaddafi and Saddam still on the loose."

Incongruously, Will noted that Forster mispronounced the latter name exactly the same as Bush.

"And if you feel the way I do, then I suggest to you heartily to show it by doing what you can to preserve this company, and your livelihoods along with it.

"Okay," he said, straightening up, "enough passionate preamble. First, we must cut costs to make ourselves at least look worth the government's money. To do my part, I'm asking Mr. Barry Evans over there–Barry, wave your hand–our new comptroller, to tear the books apart and find what waste he can. Barry will make recommendations to me in person of how we can improve our margins. Now, I hired Barry for this very reason, and I hope that you will give him your full support and full access to any records he might need to see."

All eyes suddenly bore down on Evans, who smiled his best pasty smile. The poor tike, Will thought, I wish him luck.

"And, as far as QMIV goes, I want you to push hard in R&D, Harry. It's more important than ever now, to make it the software of choice for all service branches, to keep us unextendible. Push 'em hard, Harry, and you too, Eldon."

Harry shook his head briskly up and down, while Eldon continued his regular Sad Sack expression. Fifty-three years old, tall, with orange hair turning white, Eldon Harding looked so much like the old character actor Sterling Holloway that when he opened his mouth, people expected to hear the voice of Winnie the Pooh instead of his remarkable basso profundo. He had been the chief computer scientist and programmer at ComCon since the beginning, a whiz kid directly from Digital who had made his mark and fortune with the first Quartermaster operating system.

Since then, he'd tinkered with it, improved it, and kept it going as the Army's Material Command number one utility. Highly flexible and accurate, the Quartermaster but also extremely expensive, characteristic of intricately customized programming systems.

Eldon's current modifications had resulted in QMIV, an even faster and more versatile version than its predecessor, touted by the ComCon flaks as the first of a new generation. Forster had been so enthusiastic about its potential that he had pressed for bids on contracts not just from the Army, but also from the other branches of the Armed Forces, especially the Marine Corps, which he simplistically saw as the Army dressed in blue jackets and white slacks with red piping and other accents.

Many of his executives balked, worrying about servicing such a broad base. But Forster swore that they could handle it, that new personnel would be brought on as needed. Before needed in fact, to ensure smooth expansion by contracts signed in advance, thus allowing for funds at the ready to train new staff.

Will remembered Forster's pitch, seeing stars dancing in his eyes, a constellation of heavenly bodies made of solid brass that would permutate into gold almost overnight, QMIV the Sorcerer's Stone. Will recalled Forster's expression when he talked about his dream, a vision that chased the gray from his eyes, leaving only deep green behind.

Then, Gorbachev changed the world.

Each development that followed, heartening all nations to prospects of peace, dropped Forster and ComCon jarringly, like the ratcheted lowering of a car off a rack.

Will gazed at Eldon, reflecting how this near genius, a kind of sorrowful savant, sat throughout these varied storms of change untouched in the center, a morose man who had often expressed a desire to leave, but couldn't because he owned five percent of the company and had four college educations in the offing.

As if reading his mind, Forster said, "Will, I'd like to see you in my office. Say, in fifteen minutes?"

"Sure, Jim."

Chapter 3.

Forster's office was located at the far end of the building's north wing. On three sides, windows ran the length of the walls, starting at sternum height and extending up to the ceiling. Metal dividers took away from any penthouse office effect, instead reinforcing the school-like ambience of the building. The interior was paneled with rosewood, the same grain as the large oval table desk. Two green leather couches faced each other under the windows near the wall across from the doorway. Easy chairs with matching green leather cushions had been set on either side of a wooden coffee table topped with small tiles between the two couches. Will fancied that Forster had bought the entire set from a used office supply store thirty years ago and never saw the need to replace any since.

Forster walked into the office and motioned Jim to a chair in front of his desk.

"You really think Maloney's in trouble?"

Will rubbed his hand across the back of his head, "It's hard to say. I mean, he's in trouble, but compared to what? He's a character, unpredictable, colorful, always open to some kind of criticism."

"A loose cannon."

"I wouldn't say that, but if so, he's a howitzer, a virtuoso at working both sides of the aisle. And he's always been there for us. His constituents love him, at least until now. You know, he's like one those guys who gets reelected from prison."

"That's all we need."

"Oh, nothing like that's going on. But he is being pressed by the administration. Yet if the government contracts were to dry up in his district, well, that's serious business in Pennsylvania mining country."

"Then why is he hemming and hawing now? If we go down, he goes down. Isn't he clear on that?"

"He could go down whether he pushes more contracts or not."

"Now, how can that be? I can't believe a Republican has a chance up there, even with all the hype about throwing the bums out, especially since Maloney's always been strong on defense. What's the problem here, can't we use some influence? For God's sake, he should be a shoe-in, keeping all those outfits on that godforsaken mountain, companies from all over paying a premium for labor that they could get at half the rate in the South or in Mexico."

Will shook his head, "Defense jobs aren't where he's vulnerable in this case. And it's not Republicans who worry him, though Shenck's chances do look a little better now. Even so, neither of the party heavyweights have shown up to stump for him—"

"We've covered ourselves with a contribution, I hope?" asked Forster.

"Yeah, Julie took care of it. But Maloney's a lot more worried about the claims by the elementary school teacher who scared him in the primary. Harps that he's not looking to the future, that there's no economic development and job training going on to back up defense work. Claims that Maloney allowed this to happen because he's too busy drinking and chasing women. Maloney's problem is a question of values, morals."

"Jesus Christ."

Will nodded his agreement, "She's running as an independent, now, saying—"

"She?"

"She," Will nodded. "Carol Anne Macowiac. Thirty-one, divorced, no kids. Born and raised in Williamstown, same as

27

Maloney. She's running on the platform that denounces Maloney as typical of the good-old-boy system she says is endemic to Congress. That the country needs to make sweeping changes to keep pace with emerging Asia and the Eastern Bloc countries. She accuses Maloney of being blind to the new world afoot, that he's still pushing for more defense spending when the days of the military-industrial complex are numbered. She vows to prepare her district and the nation to meet the challenges of a world now competing strictly economically in the international marketplace."

"My God! Maloney's being bashed by a woman's libber neo-commie!" Forster said.

"Maybe so," Will said," but she's scoring points, especially among women voters. At the very least she's taking votes away from Maloney, which hurts him against Shenck. And the Republican's natural opposition to administration initiatives allows Shenck to co-opt Maloney's traditional appeal to his constituency, "Keep defense strong and defense jobs in the district." Which is why Maloney's on the fence about contract renewals in his committee." Will lifted his hand, then lowered it slowly, "And, since we don't have a facility in his district—no jobs on the line in other words—ours could be numbered among the contracts that go."

"Shit," muttered Forster. After mulling for some minutes, he said, "What can we do?"

Rubbing the back of his neck, Will said, "We can try to convince Maloney and his committee to retain QMIV on the basis of merit alone. You saw the final draft of your testimony today. But frankly, that won't be enough. I'm having lunch with Maloney this week, and, uh—"

"And?"

"I'm going to call in every chit I've got."

"Is that going to be enough?

Will shrugged, "I don't know. Maloney and I've known each other for a long time. My dad introduced us way back when he won his first term. I was just a kid. Since then, I've helped him in a few situations. But if his very survival is on the line, who knows?"

"What about the others on the committee? You know, they say a Republican might be chairing it after November."

"It'd be the first time in forty years. Patterson would be the guy then, but I'm not sure if that would change much. He'll vote consistent to his interests, according to his past records, just like the rest of them, and as the senior ranking minority member, I talk to him just as much now. I mean, we see them all, of course, but right now, as chairman, Maloney's really the key. If he delivers, we'll be off the hook for a while."

"What do you mean for a while?"

"I mean that it's only good for this vote. With the budget deficit the way it is, they'll be voting on cuts again and again. Let's face it, Jim, they can use NDI software to replace Quartermaster. We've known about the off-the-shelf threat for a good long while. We were always able to fend that concept off because of QM's reaction time and its potential in battlefield conditions as a fluid facilitator of supply-line logistics. But, considering its spotty performance during the Gulf War, the plain truth is that without the Soviets looming on the horizon, the Pentagon can get by without it."

"Until the next threat comes along, and then what? They'll be irreparably behind, and in modern warfare that can be fatal."

"That's our argument to the Committee," Will agreed.

"And QMIV will take care of that spotty performance bullshit," Forster said, almost sneering his disdain. He stood up and walked around his desk. As he passed Will to begin pacing slowly in the middle of the room, he raised his glasses up onto his forehead and rubbed his eyes.

"You know, when I started this company, I was thirty-seven years old."

Uh-oh, Will thought.

"Then, there was no question about needing a strong defense. The chance I took, along with Eldon and the others, was that the Army would adopt a sophisticated technical approach to defense organization. They did, and ComCon was on its way."

Will craned his neck to follow Forster walking around the room, wondering how long this particular deposition would last, and if it would have a point.

"Guys like me, we revolutionized the defense business. So, you know, it's a hell of a note to be on the verge of retirement and to have to deal with the possibility of seeing it all go down." He shook his head, "A hell of a thing."

Forster had made his way back to the front of the desk and propped himself on the edge. Will tried to assume a correct expression, politely attentive without being too wide-eyed.

"Things everywhere have changed so much. When I was at Big Blue, my boss Dave Brill was up for vice president. He was fifty-seven years old, and he'd been there for thirty-six years."

Good old Dave Brill thought Will.

Forster removed his glasses and began to wipe them with his hankerchief. "He didn't get it. Ed Walsh was named v.p. instead." He placed his glasses back high on his nose. Because of the reflected light, Will couldn't see his eyes.

"Brill took early retirement and opened a bookstore in Vermont." He stood up and started to make his way back behind his desk. "Oh, I think he was all right, happy with the bookstore, but, you know." Forster sat down and folded his hands on the desk. "That was the way it worked back then. You put in twenty or thirty years and you didn't screw up, you had a good chance at vice president. Even so, if you got it, you worked only for another five to seven, then retired. Nowadays, kids want vice president at thirty, thirty-five, forty, forty-five. And if they don't get it, they leave as v.p. for the competition. All it takes is some capital, not much, and a computer, or just a computer if you're really smart. Things have changed."

Will couldn't help himself from piping in, "You left shortly after Brill retired to set up ComCon, right?"

Forster laughed, "Yes, that's true. I didn't want to wait either. And I was right. Even at thirty-seven, I was ready."

How did Eileen handle these sessions, Will wondered, sitting there, physically aching to go. Or Harry: My God! 'Excuse me, Jim, I'd like to go, but I've gotta go; no, I mean I really, really gotta go—to the bathroom. Gotta run, if you get my meaning. Gotta dance!'

"So, are you ready, Will? "

A coldness seemed to pool in Will's belly. Dread? Fear? Or just surprise? Maybe it was desire and dread both. "Well, I don't know, Jim. I mean, I don't know what you mean."

"It's simple. I'm going to retire, this year or next, I don't know when. Which means I need a successor. I'm considering you."

Will felt as though his heart would burst out of his chest like the creature in *Alien*. Eileen was going to die!

"It's between you and Harry, I won't lie to you. You both have helped to keep ComCon ticking during the last ten years, even when the going got tough. Hell, normally I wouldn't even think of a public affairs guy for my job, but you're more than that, Will. You bring a lot more to the table than just a way with words."

"So, I've got the job, right?"

Forster laughed again, "Not just yet. And I can't say for now who I'm going to give the nod. You're both good men. God, I have to tell you, the decision is not first on my mind these days, the way things are going. But I must make a decision soon, especially if I pull the plug at the end of this year."

31

"Which means?"

"Which means nothing, except I wanted you to know that it will be soon, and that you are definitely in the running."

In the running. Gotta run or got the runs.

"Also, that it would be a hell of a lot easier for me to make this decision if I didn't have to worry about the immediate future of my company."

Gotta dance.

"You mean if Maloney falls the right way, you'd be in a better frame of mind to render your decision?"

Forster's face brightened, "That's true!"

"I see," said Will, wondering if Brill's bookstore was hiring and if Eileen would like Vermont.

"But what about you, Will? Do you want the job? You know, you're one hell of an original thinker, you have ideas that I have no clue about where they came from. You've done extremely well at whatever you've been asked to do. Though, to be completely straightforward, you've never seemed to have your entire spirit invested in what you do. Sometimes, you appear distracted."

Will shrugged, "I'd rather be a poet."

Forster laughed again, hard. "You certainly have a poet's soul," he said, still chuckling.

"Well, thank you."

"What about it, would you want the job?"

Will paused as if to think, then sighed, "Look, Jim, it's a wonderful opportunity, a great chance. But if we keep going the way we are, I'm not sure I want to run the place either."

"Of course, you'd cast ComCon in your own image," Forster said, "I know that. Will, when I say I'm out, I'm out. None of this chairman of the board stuff, no Paul Paley brand of succession here. It'd be your show."

"Does that mean going into the public sector, if necessary?"

Forster frowned. "Don't you think that would be difficult?"

"Sure. But it could also be our only chance."

"Hah. Defense will always be here. We go through ups and downs, sure, but each down is always followed by an up. Look to Africa, the Middle East. Trouble is out there, Will."

"Yeah, but it's tiresome, too, Jim. Even Eldon would rather design video games."

"Eldon has never been realistic," Forster said. "He's a certifiable genius, but he has no concept of how best to use it."

"I suppose so," Will said.

Gradually, the lengthening silence told him that the conversation was over.

"Okay," said Forster, "we'll talk again further on. Meanwhile, do your best with Maloney, will you? See if you can shore him up."

As he left, Will thought to himself that he would have a lot to tell Eileen on the drive home that night. And he pictured her aiming the car into an oncoming semi so that the passenger's side was sheared off. Deliberately killing him at last after prying out how he had handled Forster's overtures. He flinched at the pain as though he could feel it already.

Chapter 4.

Stretched out across his bed, head buried face down in his pillow, Mike lay clutching a tiny address book in his left hand, his right holding a felt-tipped pen. A sob rippled through him. Instead of saying it, though, he wrote it:

> I love her so much
> life is impossible.

Then he cried in pain, plain, heart-racking weeping that produced tears like a baby's. They fell onto the page, blotting the blue ink and slowly obscuring the words.

"I'm such a wuss," he cried, harder and angrier. He paused to wonder how tears could be so different, one boo to the next hoo, first a flow of flat-out misery, then a bitter mix of salt and anger at how things could be so bad, turning thin and watery at knowing he was too weak to change his life, finally returning to a steady stream of pain and hopelessness.

"Karen, I love you so much," he moaned into the bedspread.

She doesn't even know you're alive," Sandy had said. They had been sitting as usual on the porch of her house in the backyard, doing nothing. He would sigh and wonder why he spent so much time with her when it wasn't much fun, no fun at all. She lived about two blocks from his house, and they rode the bus together, she talking nonstop, he not listening. Now and then something would happen that put him in a good mood, and he would talk endlessly himself, a regular diarrhea of the mouth. She seemed to enjoy his goofing. But times like that became rarer and rarer as he felt lousier and lousier, about home, school, life, and now Karen.

Feeling so bad, which Sandy noticed and as usual wouldn't let up on him about, he'd finally told her what was wrong: Karen, Karen.

"She does too know I'm alive!" he yelled back at her.

"Oh, get real."

"She talks to me all the time."

"Sure. She's like, 'Hi, Mike,' and you're like, 'Hi, Karen,' in this little rodent voice. And she's already, 'Hi, Kirk; Hi, Jeff; Hi, Pauly; Hi, Aaron,' right down the fucking line."

He winced. Sandy made it a point to talk like a truck driver, though he didn't know why. "That's bullshit, Sandy," he said weakly. But he knew it wasn't. She was right, absolutely, which had him pouting the way that made everyone mad at him. He turned his head into his chest pocket and screw his mouth up into an incredibly pissy look, pissed at the world for treating him so badly. His long wing of straight brown hair would flop over in front of his face, exposing his buzzed sidewalls and hiding his expression. But everyone who knew him almost felt the ill will of his attitude-filled, prickly-puss face lurking underneath. He never would have believed he could look that way if his dad hadn't shown him a photograph snapped the last time he'd worn the expression. When he first saw it, Mike was stunned. Then he started laughing at how bratty he looked. Still, he couldn't help himself from acting snotty when he felt like snot.

"Why do you like her?" Sandy asked, sounding exhausted by his stubbornness. They sat a week after the new school year had started, soaking up the last of the warm weather before autumn arrived in earnest. They gazed out at the huge mix of magnolias and lilacs that her parents had planted around the perimeter of the spacious yard to hide the hurricane fence and the neighbors' view.

"I don't know," Mike said, but of course, he did. Karen was so beautiful, it hurt him to see her and still breathe.

"I know you think she's beautiful," Sandy said, "but she's not. I mean, she's okay-looking and everything, but most of that is her hair and makeup. She's really kind of scrawny." Sandy struck an aloof, hand-on-hip pose and parodied, "Face it, Babe, she's not a babe."

Mike didn't say anything. Sandy was no babe; she was not scrawny by a long shot. She could do all that she wanted to her hair and makeup and she'd still be Sandy, fat Sandy. Oh, she had a pretty face, but she was still fat. He gazed at her nice, baby blue eyes that just barely showed between her pudgy eyelids.

Then again, he was no Tom Cruise himself. The thing, though, was that he knew he was a dork and acted accordingly. But Sandy had no clue of how she really looked. She would wear the wildest clothes, the tightest tights and tube tops, for instance, as though she thought they made her look sexy instead of lumpy and dumpy.

"I mean," she continued, "she has no brains. She'll probably end up stuck here in some Beltway burg, married with a bunch of kids and a secretary job."

"So?" Mike said, "What's wrong with that?"

Sandy reached into the back pocket of her black Levi pedal pushers and pulled out a box of Marlboro Lights. She lit one, amazing Mike again with the proof that her parents allowed her to smoke. As she exhaled, she said, "Well, it's no fucking life."

She propped one foot on the porch banister, making a clunking sound on the aluminum, and said, "Now, me, I'm going to New York New York. I'm going to be the top designer in the world, Numéro One. I'll own the place before I'm twenty."

Mike finally had enough. "How do you know you're going to do that? God, you're still in junior high school and your grades suck. You get the shittiest grades in our class!"

She shook her head, smiling sorrowfully, "Mike, Mike, you're such a doofus. It doesn't matter what kind of grades you get in the fashion industry, it's who you know," she eyed him knowingly, "and who you sleep with."

He reddened deeply then behind his flop of hair. She was so full of shit. Yet, she spread it so sure of herself. Fashion designer in New York; I'll bet, he thought. And what was wrong with living here, being married and having a couple of kids? He would love to be married to Karen, to see her glorious white smile amid that golden skin framed in her burnished golden hair, looking up shyly with those big Robin's egg eyes at him, him alone, as his wife.

And when would that ever happen? The cruel truth of it burst apart his vague dream and he felt the ache welling in his chest again. How could he even think of being married to Karen when he was such a miserable failure already at only fourteen? What did he have to offer to her, he might not even pass ninth grade. He wasn't a big sports star and he was a dorky-looking wuss. It was too late, too late already.

She sat in front of him in social studies. There, his mind usually cruised above the teacher's meaningless words, the dull drone of the voice propelling the engine of his flying machine. He banked out along the wall of windows on the left and glided back into the hallway on the right, barely visible from the acute angle afforded by a first-row seat tight up against the inside wall.

More and more, though, his dreamy transport would alight upon the delicate shoulders in front of him. Her skin seemed golden all year round, almost matched by the fabulous color of her hair. He dwelled upon the metallic sheen of it, a product of her genetic makeup or hairspray, he didn't know. Sometimes she wore her hair in wild wavy layers with curved spokes spreading out and down over her brow in a strange, broadening fan. Other times she simply brushed it straight down, as straight as it could get, or she wore it in a bun. When she wore it up, he could see on the nape of her neck a thin plait of fine hair, more yellow, softer looking as it must have been when she'd been little.

She didn't wear black, either, or the weird stuff that Sandy always wore. Karen tended toward a preppy style, wearing sweaters and jeans finished off by spotless cross-trainers. Once in a while she wore a skirt, and the sight of her legs caused the air to go thin within her aura.

All of this moved him, these things and the fact that she was so nice, always saying 'Hi,' smiling at him with her eyes. At first, all he could do was grin back like some kind of doofus, mumbling back a gawky 'Hi' like a stupid parrot.

"So, why don't you talk to her?" Sandy asked.

"What am I supposed to say?"

"I don't know. Ask her out."

"Ask her out? How? Where?"

"Jesus Christ, Mikey, I don't know, you're the guy here. Ask her to meet you at the mall."

"The mall," he said, slowly envisioning it. "Then what?"

Sandy rolled her eyes in an outsized double take. "Take her to a movie."

"A movie." He mulled it over. "Which one? I don't even know what movies she likes, I never talk to her. How am I supposed to ask her to the mall and a movie if I never even talk to her in school?"

"Then talk to her!" Sandy said, bubbling laughter, "My God, you're a real rocket scientist, you know?"

"What'll I say?"

"I don't know. Say you love her and want to marry her when you both graduate. If that doesn't work, ask her to go to a movie."

"Sandy, get serious! This is important."

"Well, I don't know, just talk to her." When she saw him about to devolve into sulk mode, she said, "Be funny. You're a funny guy."

"Oh, yeah right. Like I can be funny on purpose."

"Well, I don't know," she said, trailing off, "you're always funny to me."

But he found it impossible to do more than say hello or occasionally remark how social studies sucked. Karen always agreed, her expression open, waiting for him to continue. The conversation would just lay there like a fish on a dock, gulping for air, for life.

At home, he searched for ways to break the deadlock. For, while he struggled, he witnessed the other kids flowing with ease through these treacherous straits. Popular guys such as Kirk Werley, Jeff Roth, and Pauly McArdle had no trouble meeting girls, going with them for weeks at a time, then breaking up and moving on. Mike thought that their success might have something to do with the fact that most of them had gone to the same middle school as the girls, while he had been stuck in the G & T program at Harrison.

He just didn't seem to be able to become good friends with any of them. He didn't know why. But maybe that was the problem, maybe he needed to hang with the guys who knew the girls. If he could work it right, he could go with them to the mall. He knew that meeting girls was better in a group because if one guy's line flagged, another one could pick it up and keep it going until the original dude rallied. And of course, among the girls they'd meet at the Mall would be one girl special to him, the one that because of his huge, secret feelings about her, would not be able to resist his love, whether offered to her silently or otherwise.

Yeah, he thought, this could work out! First, though, he needed to fix his image. New clothes; no more all black. He'd need a warm-up jacket, a Mavericks jacket, or maybe the Running Rebels. And new shoes. He had to get rid of these All-Stars, they were truly beat. He needed power shoes; he needed Nikes!

The warm-up jacket turned out to be no problem. His mom had been on him to get a new look for decades. He'd broken his dad's heart, though, by going for a Detriot Tigers jacket, his dad being a lifelong Red Sox fan. The choice had put him behind in securing the Nikes, too. He'd had to switch to his dad, since his mom popped for the jacket. But his dad almost stroked out at the price.

"A hundred and twenty bucks? What sneakers in the world are worth one hundred and twenty dollars!"

Mike had caught him in the rec room on Sunday, watching a football game on TV with the sound off, "so that I don't get caught up in the phony hype of the talking heads," he explained. He seemed relaxed, eating tostado chips and occasionally taking a sip of beer. Looking at him, Mike wondered how he could stay so slender when he drank beer and never exercised, or at least, not much. His dad wasn't ancient, Mike thought, but he was old. Yet, his hair still looked pretty dark except for a few gray hairs, and he didn't have a lot of wrinkles, just some around his eyes when he smiled. Sandy said that his dad was to die for, and Mike didn't get it. She explained that his dad had such a refined face, like someone from Paris. When she put it that way, Mike supposed that he could see it. Naturally, when he checked himself out in the mirror, Mike didn't see any of his dad in his own face. Sad to say, though, he couldn't see any of his mom, either, and she was truly beautiful, like a high-class model.

Wearing a suit, his sister Mary could pass for Dad, though she took after their mom in the way her mind worked. Rubbing his face as he stared at his reflection, he wondered then if he really came from this family. Then again, the way he looked, people probably wondered if he came from this planet.

"These shoes are, Dad, they're more than worth it." Mike watched his dad mimic burlesque cartoon eyes threatening to fall out of the sockets. "No, really, they are, Dad" he went on, his tone a fine-tuned mix of pleading and cajoling.

"Buddy, you are nuts, certifiably. What are they, custom made by NASA? Come on, man, you can't run this past me, I'm in the business. A hundred and twenty bucks."

"Dad, they're worth it. They'll last forever, and they'll protect my feet better. You don't want me to injure my feet, do you? Maybe permanently!"

"Doing what? Running into doors because your eyes are glued to your hundred and twenty buck sneakers?"

"That'd be my head, Dad, not my feet."

"Oh, right, no harm, no foul. Come on, Mikey, I'm not putting up that kind of money for a pair of sneakers. What's wrong with your Chucks? They were always fine for me, and I have great feet, even now. No way, Mike."

"Dad!" He was losing ground. He groped for words, for some utterly convincing arguments. "I'll pay you back."

"Right, in what century? Maybe you'll leave it to me in your will."

"No, really, I promise, Dad. I'll get a job after school."

"Get a job after school?" His father laughed, but not in a funny way. "Get a passing grade and we'll talk!"

Mike sensed the floor beginning to shift beneath him, his feet slipping and sliding toward even more dangerous ground. Desperately, he fell back, using his last resort, his final chance. "Mom!" he wailed.

"Give him the money, Willy," she said as she stepped down the stairs. She looked magnificent, like Laura Petrie only in living color and with sharper features: Mimi Rogers, maybe, or an older Mariah Carey.

"Eileen, this is outrageous, extravagant! He'll be wearing clothes worth more than his body is to science. One shoe alone would cost fifty Pakistanis their wages for a year."

"Will, give it up. It's worth it to keep him from slaughtering us in our sleep."

"Yes, yes, yes," Mike yelped, hopping up and down, "no more axe murders, I promise. Please, please, please!"

"There you are," his mom said, "give him the money and we're safe for tonight. Go on, Will, give it to him."

"Jesus in heaven, save me from these wicked, wicked times," his dad said as he stood up to go for his checkbook. He returned with the critical piece of paper in his fingers, but he held it out of reach. "Okay, go ahead and buy your Gucci sneakers. Just do me this favor. Don't get some ugly combination of colors, okay? No purple and orange, okay? Okay?"

His dad howled like a wolf when Mike returned from the outlet with his purple and maroon Nikes. But Mike didn't care because they went perfectly with the purple-patterned baggies he'd bought with his own money and the deep purple hip-hop shirt. When he examined himself in the mirror, he looked totally different, sort of strange, he thought, but cool. Yes, qualitatively and quantitatively cool, he determined, spinning back and forth, assessing every angle.

Chapter 5.

He rode the bus to the mall on Sunday, ready to debut. He headed for Waxie Maxie's where he expected to find the other kids hanging out within easy striking distance of the Cineplex and the Subway Shop. Sure enough, Kirk and the others stood in a row thumbing through CD bins.

Mike felt a bit self-conscious as he approached. He'd always hung around them at school, but on the edge rather than in the middle with Kirk and the others, the true studs in the school. Kirk was big and blond and the best athlete, but he also joked around easily, and he was pretty smart, too. He got good grades and he'd been elected class president at Woodrow Wilson Middle School and probably would win freshman class president now that they were at Spring River High. Mike got along with him well enough, though there had been some tense moments in gym class after Mike had bragged about how good he was at football. He hadn't lived up to his own billing, and Kirk had ridden him hard about it.

Kirk saw him first. "What's up Mike? How you doing?" He glanced at him again, up and down. "You look different."

"Thanks," Mike said, flushing. "I don't usually come to the mall, but I said, what the hell, why not? It's either that or watch a stupid football game with my dad, or God forbid, do my homework. God!"

"Right," said Kirk, back flipping through the CDs again.

"So, anyway," Mike said. He didn't know what to do, standing there in silence. After a moment, he walked around to his own bin and began to search, unseeing through the compact disks, saying to himself, What am I doing here?

The answer came toddling en masse up the broad thoroughfare, past the fountain at the base of the escalator, past the mall directory, past the benches where bored retirees sat opposite weary mothers and nannies rocking their charges back and forth in strollers. The gang of girls gently nudged each other to and fro like padded bumper cars as they slowly traversed the midway. Or they were a regatta of light sailboats, Mike dreamed, delicately tacking away from dangerous shoals in the middle of the floor and hugging the safe harbors of the storefront windows. As they approached, Mike could make out a few Spring River High jackets, the correct school, his school. Closer still they came, and he sensed warmth and anxiety simultaneously; they were the correct Spring River girls, a group of ninth graders with a certain little burnished blond member in their midst.

He never noticed before how short she was compared to the other girls in their class. She wore pink Bermuda shorts and a light-yellow jacket, and another pair of cross-trainers with white athletic socks. She had her hair pulled back with a red ribbon just so, making her look remarkably casual, he thought, perfectly Sunday and awesomely cute.

She walked directly up to him. "Hi, Mike, how are you? I've never seen you down here before."

"Yeah," he grinned, "Well, I never had a reason to come before."

"Oh yeah? Say, that's a really nice jacket, it looks really great on you. So, what was that?"

"What?" he said.

"The reason," she said.

"What?"

"The reason you come to the mall now."

"Oh," he said, "to see beautiful babes like you."

Jesus Christ! He wanted to die, die! He was a dork, an asshole, and now she knew it! It was all over. Blood, blood, blood everywhere.

"Oh," she said. Her mouth parted into the slightest of sly smiles. "I'll keep that in mind," she said over her shoulder as she walked by, "Hi, Kirk, Hi, Jeff."

He could have vaulted home in a single bound if he wanted to, he was so high already. He felt so good that he goofed with Kirk and the others for the rest of the afternoon. They had a great time, he'd been so funny! Sandy was right, he was funny! He just needed to loosen up a little bit.

He felt so great that night, he wanted to talk about it, to go over every detail. Sandy wasn't around, so he paced his room wondering who could he talk to about it, about everything. As he walked back and forth in front of his desk, he pondered and pondered, until he saw his books. Then, it hit him. Why not?

He grabbed his notebook and headed downstairs into the rec room. He picked up the phone and carried it into the bathroom along with the phone book. He shut the door, looked up the number, and punched it out on the phone.

"Can I speak to Kirk, please? Hey, Kirk, remember that homework I was putting off? Well, it's so far down on my priority list that I don't know what we're supposed to do for Algebra."

They spent an hour talking, talking about everything, the teachers, the other kids, the stuff they pulled at the mall, laughing a lot as they covered it.

"Yeah, man, it was unbelievable. Did you hear what I said when the girls came up to us at Waxie Maxie's? It was like, "Mike what're you doing here? And I was like, 'Dogging beautiful babes like you, Babe.'"

"No way!" Kirk said, "You never said that."

"Absolutely! I mean, let's face it, Kirk, they were looking pretty great, pretty lush."

"Yeah, yeah, they were that."

"But I'll tell you, one of them really does me in. I mean: Oh."

"Oh yeah?"

"Oh yes. She makes my heart beat. You know who I'm talking about, right? I mean, I guess it was pretty obvious."

"No, I don't know."

"Aw, man, I really like her, I thought it showed all over the place. Karen. Karen Rauch. She sits in front of me in social studies."

"Oh."

The next day Mike faced a dilemma because he didn't know what to wear. He'd already worn his purple look yesterday at the mall, which left his old black Lees and one of his black Gap shirts. Still, he had the warm-up jacket and the most wonderful pair of high-top Nikes ever made. He only wished that he had another cool shirt and pants combo to wear, or a dozen of them. Maybe he would need to get a part-time job, which meant that he'd need to get better grades if he ever expected his folks to go for it. But, why not? Life was wonderful; there was plenty of time for studying and hanging out at the mall with Kirk and the boys, and Karen. He could really start to open up to her now after yesterday.

He couldn't wait for social studies, to say 'Hi" to Karen, and a lot more. He'd told Sandy about the whole thing on the bus, both of them giggling and laughing at his incredible studliness. Sandy was a hell of a bud, he thought. Off the bus, he hurried through the double doors of the long brick building and clattered down the stairs into a hall leading to his locker. The home room bell would go off in five minutes, but if he hurried, he might be able to stash his stuff and go down to the other hall to catch a glimpse of Karen.

He turned the corner down the hall and saw Karen pressed against her locker by Kirk, who kissed her, which made her smile.

Mike stepped backward around the corner as the bell rang for home room. In social studies, she said 'Hi', and he said 'Hi' too. Throughout the day, he thought of what had happened. He ate lunch, he always ate lunch, but he couldn't taste any of it this time. The betrayal was too enormous. Karen and Kirk.

"So, what are you going to do?" Sandy asked that night. She had noticed, of course, how his mood had been completely reversed from the morning. She'd come over to his house, and his mother had insisted that he talk to her. So, this time they sat on his front stoop.

"I don't know. Die."

"Are you sure that they're going together?"

"Yes. He was telling the other guys about it at lunch. He said that he figured, 'Why not?' They went to the same church and all.'"

"Oh."

"The same church," Mike said, almost spitting the words.

"Did you talk to him about it? You know, about how you trusted him on the phone and he did this?"

"Why would I do that? Why would I remind him of what a dork I am telling him, a guy I hardly know, I like his girlfriend."

"Well, she came on to you, too, you know. She's not all that innocent either."

Mike lifted his head to give Sandy a scathing look. "Sandy, don't trash her anymore, okay? She doesn't have anything to do with this."

"Oh, she doesn't, huh? Mike, sometimes you're a total asshole, you know?"

She left then, and he sat alone in his misery. Who had he been fooling? The jacket, the clothes, the shoes, for God's sake, a hundred and twenty bucks down the toilet, and all because of that fucking Werley. He could kill him.

He sighed, looking at his shoes. Why bother wearing the dumb things now? He might as well return them, get the money back to use for something useful. Shit, he might even give it back to his dad, get on his good side. It was too late for the jacket and the other clothes, though. He'd already broken them in, getting them wrinkled and dirty. But the shoes, he could clean them up, he figured, and he still had the box and the tissue paper. What did he have to lose?

After supper, he went to his room and changed into his old Converses. He took the Nikes to the bathroom and used some wet toilet paper to rub off any dirt. He held them up to the light, trying to find any specks of dirt or grit caught in the soles. Pretty good, he thought, they looked okay. He took them back to his room and carefully wrapped them in the tissue and laid them back in the box. As an added touch, he unlaced the shoes, then tied the two sneakers together as though he'd never even tried them on.

He had to take the bus this time, since it was a clandestine operation. As the bus rumbled along, jarring him frontwards and sideways, he stared out the window at the traffic. People throughout the world found others to love and to live with, so why was he the only one who couldn't? Five billion people, two and a half billion men, and two and a half billion women, give or take a couple hundred million nuns, priests, and gay people, all with someone, and he didn't even have a cat.

The bus pulled up in front of a sidewalk bordering a parking lot of heroic size that encircled the mall. Off in the distance, the building complex looked like a small urban island surrounded by a vast, blacktop ocean, little Manhattan in the middle of a macadam sea. The sidewalk itself was edged by poles strung with phone wires and power lines, and lamp posts dotted the lot like a peg game for giants.

Mike stood up to get off. From here he would walk a long block to the shopping strip next door that housed the shoe outlet. As he began down the bus's aisle, he started to think up the story of why he was returning the shoes. Too big; no, too little; my mom already got me a pair just like them. Then it hit him; my dad blew his lid for spending the money and I gotta return them. That could work, sympathy for the disappointed kid now with no shoes. Shit, maybe they'll give me a deal on some All-Stars.

He turned the corner at the front of the bus and tumbled down the steps onto the sidewalk almost into Kirk Werley's face.

"Jesus Christ, Day," Kirk said, stepping back, "back to form, huh?"

Mike hated being called by his last name. Instinctively moving out of the way of the door, he said, "What do you mean by that, Werley?" He noticed then that Kirk wasn't alone. Jeff Roth was with him, as was Pauly McArdle, two girls Mike didn't know, and Karen. Mike felt the black cloak of despair descending over him again, unbidden.

"I mean get out of the way," Kirk said, starting to brush by.

Desperately, Mike stepped back in front of the doorway again. "No, I mean it," he said.

"What the hell?" Kirk said, "Get the fuck out of the way, shithead."

"Oh yeah?" Mike said, his voice quavering a hair, though God knew everyone could hear it, all of them, and he didn't want to do this, but what could he do?

"Hey, lighten up, Day," said Roth, "Take it easy, Kirk," said McArdle, and the two unknown girls chimed in their agreement.

But it was too late. Mike could see that Kirk was furious now, and when the bus driver called down to them to either get on or not, Kirk told him to go ahead. The others cried a chorus of anger and dismay, and Kirk said, "That's all right, there'll be another bus along. But Day, here, he has to have his day, right? Get it? Ha! Yeah, he has to show just how cool he is, even if he isn't, because he's in love. Isn't that right Mikey boy?"

"Fuck you, Werley," Mike said weakly, knowing with dread, total, enervating dread what was coming, and that he was powerless to stop it.

"Mike, here, is in love with Karen, right Mike?" Kirk flicked his head toward Karen without ever taking his eyes away, his light blue eyes as cold as ice.

Mike tore his sight away to see Karen. She stared at him without any recognition, as though gazing in wondrous horror at some madman just recaptured after an escape from the asylum. Seeing the foreignness of her expression, he began to cry.

"Yeah, that's why Mr. Studly has been hanging at the mall, wearing his cool clothes, hoping he had a chance. You asshole, you never had a chance."

Another bus rolled up, and Kirk stiff-armed Mike to the side, "Let's go people," he said, ushering them on with a wave of his hand.

The others filed past, gaping at Mike who weeped silently. As Kirk started to board the bus, Mike shouted, "You shit!" and grabbed his arm and whipped him back onto the sidewalk. Kirk regained his balance and punched Mike, shoving him at the same time to fall on the concrete, causing him to lose hold of the shoe box.

Kirk grabbed the shoe box and ripped the lid off. He pulled out the shoes and said, "New shoes won't do you any good either, fuckface," and he pivoted to throw them as high and as far as he could. The two shoes laced together pinwheeled awkwardly out of his hand straight up in the air to wrap around an electric wire. They hung there, dangling, twirling one way, knocking into each other, then untwirling the other way, perfectly suspended, perfectly balanced, and completely out of reach.

"Aw shit," said Kirk as he watched the shoes slowly spin. He rubbed his jaw, then turned and jumped onto the bus.

Mike sat in a heap, his head pointed up at the shoes. The bus horn blared, and the driver called out to ask if he was coming.

"No," he said sadly, "I'll walk."

Two weeks later, Mike lay in bed knowing that the shoes still swung in the wires. He thought that someone would have gotten them down by now. County authorities or maybe a poor black kid who figured a way to pluck them down without frying electrically. But, no, they still twisted slowly in the wind, as though a man had been executed upside down, his body rotted away, leaving the weathered Nikes all that remained swinging in the ai. What really made it bad was that the laces were made of polyester; those shoes could hang there for a thousand years.

Mike's shame seemed never ending. No one ever really brought it up when he was present, but he knew that they all talked about the whole fiasco behind his back. Most heartrending of all, Karen had asked to be moved closer to the blackboard in social studies. Of course, everyone knew the real reason, and most of the girls looked at him strangely, and kept out of his way. They didn't just think of him as a wuss, they thought he was a perverted wuss.

"I don't think you're a pervert," Sandy said, "I think what you did was romantic."

"Yeah, well, you're the only one," he said, swishing his feet back and forth from her back porch. "The rest of the school sees slasher movie written all over my face. They're all waiting for the Alien to pop out of my chest. Serve them right, too, if it did."

"Huh."

The grass beneath his feet had faded to dull green lately. Soon, it would be brown and crackly if it didn't rain. The evenings had become short too, not much help to the insanely depressed, he thought.

"So, is Karen still going with Kirk?"

"So far," Mike said bravely, but the blade turned in his heart.

"Huh." Sandy said. After a moment, she said, "You think they're doing it?"

"God, I don't know. Probably. It's been almost two weeks."
He blew out breath again and said, "That's one thing you can say;
if she was going with me instead of him, she'd still be a virgin."

"Oh, get out! You don't think she was a virgin, do you?"
Sandy exclaimed.

"Sure I do. Why not? Lots of people are. I am."

"You are not! You are? No!"

Mike turned his head down, this time to hide his pink skin.

"Why are you a virgin?" Sandy asked. "Didn't you ever want
to do it?"

"I don't know. Sure. I guess."

"Then why haven't you? Why don't you?"

"Sandy, leave me alone, will you?" he said curtly. Then,
softly, "I mean, they aren't exactly lining up at my bedroom door,
you know, saying, 'Me, me, me!'"

"Unhuh," she said distractedly. After another pause, she said,
"So, let's do it?"

"Do it? Do it how? When? Now? Here?" he said, suddenly
filled with a strange excitement mingled with foreboding and
fear.

"Sure. Right over there, under the magnolias, out of sight."

"Sandy, you're crazy! What about your parents?"

"They won't know. Come on, it's safe, I've done it before,"
she said, grabbing his hand and pulling him off of the porch.

"Before? With who?"

"Never mind. Let's go!"

She had his pants off and down around his lower legs before
he could say anything or stop her by virtue of modesty or
embarrassment. She tugged at her own tight jeans even as she
crushed his mouth with her lips and tongue, forcing her way
between his. He could taste her cigarettes, her saliva, and he
thought that this was embarrassing, stupid, he was not ready for
this! But he felt himself larger below, too, and he felt her pliant
body with no thoughts of fatness or thinness in his mind now.

She shifted above him, brushing away a magnolia branch with one hand while searching beneath her with the other; he felt himself prodded and pushed into an engulfing warm, wet pressure, and he was done.

Apparently, Sandy wasn't, as she rocked above him, sitting up between the branches and leaves, moaning in rhythm like a monk's chant, or at least how he thought a monk might chant. She groaned again, and suddenly jerked off him, leaving him naked, cold.

"You stupid little idiot, what are you doing?"

He heard the voice and froze. Sandy's father yelled at him, "Mike, get your ass out here and home before I kick you there!"

And there he laid, longing for Karen still, who had moved away from him like he had the plague, while wondering if he was a father-to-be of a child of Sandy's. Grounded for a month by his parents, he cringed at the idea that they might let him out again. And he had to face the final truth, too: He still loved Karen.

"I'll tell you one thing, Karen," he said sorrowfully, his voice full of pain and quivering with tears, "I'll never do it to you the way Sandy and I did it. It'll be for love, after we're married."

He sat upright, "And I promise I'll never do it with another girl, either, ever again," He sobbed. "Only with you, Karen."

He subsided in his pillow. Even though Karen didn't know he was alive, didn't want to know. And Kirk, that bastard.

With life so miserable, there really was only one thing to do: end it all, he thought.

Or get even.

Chapter 6.

Black Mud, a name to conjure with: O Mud
For watermelons gutted to the crust,
Mud for the mole-tide harbor, mud for the mouse, -

Will caught the change of the light in an upward glance and quickly tossed the book at the passenger seat. Nervously peering into his rear-view mirror, he jammed the gas pedal down to make up for his inattention. No one behind him blared their horn or gave him ugly looks, so the light must not have been green for long.

He hated driving into Washington, but what could he do? In the nation's capital, all the mountains traveled to Mohammed, and he represented just a little mole-hill – not a mole-hill, a mole-harbor, a muddy little mouse from a mole-tide harbor, Baltimore Harbor, maybe?

He sighed. He had been trying to work his way through Lowell's *Lord Weary's Castle* and was on his third run through *Colloquy in Black Rock*, which he thought had something to do with blood and Catholicism, though he couldn't be sure. The sad truth was that he couldn't be sure of anything. After his first few pitiful efforts, he'd decided that he had been away from the discipline of reading and writing poetry for too long and needed to retool. He hadn't relished the idea of so much extra work or, really, the intimidation that he had suspected would go along with it. But he'd thrown himself into it, a reaction typical, Eileen would say, of the anal obsessive. He used every spare moment to read, an hour stolen before bedtime, fifteen minutes on the John, when Eileen drove him to and from work, and even on trips when he drove himself, reading snatches at stoplights, traffic backups, and standing in parking garages next to his car.

To start right away, he first grabbed old texts kept from his college days, beginning at the beginning. He found a volume of *A Handbook to Literature,* dated 1960, looked up the definition of poetry and prepared to take notes.

> Poetry is a language that tells us, through a
> more or less emotional reaction, something that
> cannot be said. All poetry, great or small, does this.

He puzzled over this definition, then read the name below: Edward Arlington Robinson. Who in the heck is that? he wondered.

He read Carlyle's definition, "Poetry, therefore, we will call musical thought," Now we're getting closer, he thought. He read on.

> I would define the poetry of words as the rhythmical
> creation of beauty. Its sole arbiter is taste.
> With the intellect or with the conscience it has only
> collateral relations. Unless incidentally, it has no
> concern whatever either with duty or with truth.

Edgar Allen Poe. Okay.

He continued reading, and stumbled across a phrase by Leigh Hunt, another unknown in his poetic panoply.

> Modulating its language on the principle of variety
> in uniformity.

Variety in uniformity; was that something like planned spontaneity? It was like the play he and his buddies used to run over and over again in scores of backyard football games, "same thing, only different."

He shook his head. The entry went on for seven pages with dozens of cross-references. He jumped to a couple of them, Abstract Poetry, "poetry whose meaning results chiefly from its sound qualities." Poe, then, must have been abstract, he mused, or pre-abstract, they might call it, according to his definition of poetry, and his Tinkerbell poem, ding-dong, ding-dong.

He perused the listing for Adonic Verse, "associated with Greek and Latin PROSODY and denoting that METER which consists of a DACTYL . . .," and Aesthetic Distance, "A term applied by critics to describe the effect produced when an emotion or an experience, whether autobiographical or not, is so objectified by the proper use of FORM that it can be understood as being objectively realized . . .."

He sighed deeply, thinking about it as he drove down Pennsylvania Avenue. Suddenly, he remembered an inkling of why he hadn't stayed in literature. Who could make head or tail of critical commentary featured in a reference published back in 1960? Never mind that another thirty-plus years of explication had been added since, proving God knows what?

Not that the poetry itself was any more accessible. Is it meant to obfuscate, he wondered, to cause you to think past normal channels? Or is it meant to be accessible, familiar words put into a slightly unfamiliar order to jar you gently into other paths of discovery?

And what about the oral tradition of verse? Is poetry meant to be sounded aloud, or is there silently sounded poetry in which the words work better when heard only in the mind? For that matter, what of ideographic languages, such as Korean and Chinese? Do they have poetry that rings true only when sounds are imagined?

Haiku is among the most revered of simple poetry, yet Frost and his catty fog tip-toeing around had been dismissed summarily. Yeats is the best of accessible poets, he resolved. For all of his attenuated, Irish mythological allusions and archaic images, he still could be read with ear and eye out for beauty alone. But did Yeats, known as Willy the Spook by his fellow students before his fame, think of his impenetrable *Crazy Jane* stuff as his best work? How personal is poetry? How personal can it be and still be for others to read?

"I mean," he said out loud, "what the hell did Lowell mean by 'mud for a mole-tide harbor'?"

Maybe the muddy mouse had something to do with Frost's cat fog. Yeah, there could be a thesis somewhere in that, he thought.

He pulled into the parking garage a block away from the Capitol Club while deciding that he had set for himself an impossible task. He could add Jung and the mythology of the subconscious to the pile, and Joseph Campbell's notions about mythology. He'd sent for a book called *Hellas: A Journal of Poetry and the Humanities* that was supposed to blow up the followers of deconstructivism, and he didn't even know what deconstructivism was. He'd subscribed to *Poetics Today*, which described itself dauntingly as "the leading international journal in the theory and analysis of literature and communication." Maybe it would fill in that thirty-year gap since he plied *A Handbook to Literature.*

The latest issue of *Contemporary Literature* featured an article entitled "Collage and Pulverization in Contemporary American Poetry." *The Journal of Aesthetics and Art Criticism* countered with the treatise "Can Art Ever Be Just About Itself?" With such a plaintive title, Will wondered if the scholar who had written it kept his aesthetic distance?

There were scores of other sources and resources, Will thought as he strolled up D Street toward the restaurant, and he despaired about keeping track of them all. If he didn't back off, he decided, he would go nuts. He had to keep it simple, simple for his own sake, what worked for himself. He knew that he was reacting instinctively, but what choice did he have? He wanted to keep going, he wanted to go the distance, the aesthetic distance. He just didn't want to go crazy.

He resolved to go back to square one, the recurring terms in the Handbook's essay introducing the definitions: "rhythmic expression" and "emotional." He would go for the ear, he would go for the soul.

"Day! Over here!" Maloney sat at one of the round tables near a tall old-fashioned sash window. Will nodded his thanks to the Matre'd and headed in the congressman's direction.

Maloney was barrel large and dark, a product of the swarthy Hispanic-Hibernian gene pool initiated in the 15th century by hapless Spanish Armada sailors. Storm-driven to the Western shore, there they found succor in the arms of lonesome Irish women, and the first of the Black Irishmen were born. Maloney's giant head was covered by a morass of pure black hair, not a gray strand anywhere. And he must be past fifty, thought Will, though he would have sworn that the man did not dye.

Appearance was not Maloney's interest; his suit, though an expensive Brooks Brothers, showed wrinkles and stains that intimated more than a year between dry cleanings. His shoes, however, gleamed, testimony to his extreme pleasure at having them shined daily. During one boozy reception one, he admitted to Will that he loved sitting high on a shoe-shine chair like a great country lord. Much of his enjoyment came from his memories of being a shoe-shine when he was a boy back in Williamstown. Will believed that Maloney relished the great lord's seat, but he doubted the humble shoe-shine story as an embellishment, part and parcel of political reinvention.

He had known Maloney for a long time, back when the congressman was in his first term and Will's father had been the economist and public affairs director for Metro Ed. Maloney owed Will's father much of his success, and beyond that revered him as a mentor and model. He maintained much of his allegiance to Will in honor of his dear departed father. Although when they met, he seemed to grope for some common ground, as though he yearned for the immediate empathy he'd shared with the old man. Will suspected that Maloney didn't see him measuring up to the flint-sharp minded, hard-drinking man that was his stout father. Of course, that's what killed him, Will thought.

"Where've you been, Will? I've been waiting here for fifteen minutes."

Will eyed the empty glass rimmed with tomato juice sitting in front of Maloney and wondered if another had preceded it, maybe two.

"Struggling with your delightful Washington traffic."

"Don't call it my Washington, I'm from a mining town, remember? Anyway, you better order, I've got to get back to the office pronto."

Will lifted his eyes. "You usually have plenty of time to eat, Mike, especially here."

"I know." He cupped his mouth with his hand, "The food's better here than at the Democrats' joint, but I need to start worrying about my image." He dropped his hand, "I'm in a tough race, you know that? What would happen if they got wind of it back home that I'm eating in the enemy's beanery?"

"The Republicans aren't the enemy, Mike, they're the friendly opposition."

"Hah! You're telling me! I almost have more in common with those bastards than my own fucking party. When I think of those knife-dealing sons of bitches back home trying to dump me in the primary – I'm the goddamn incumbent, don't they know that? Those pricks wanted to give up all I've done in eighteen years, all the seniority, for Christ's sake, and now I've got to go through it all over again because of some self-righteous little school marm?"

"You don't really believe they tried to dump you, Mike," said Will, "do you?"

"How the hell should I know? People are in a feeding frenzy, the world's turned upside down. Anything could happen!" The small outburst caused Maloney's face to flush an incongruous deep crimson, making his skin look hot to the touch. "It wouldn't surprise me if a few of them didn't put her up to it, with a few greenbacks for encouragement."

"I doubt that, Mike."

"Yeah, well," Maloney said, his face resuming its usual hue, a softer ruddiness, as though sunburned all year round. He signaled to the waiter with his finger, one more.

"So, how've you been, Will? How's Eileen?"

"Stupendous as always."

"Excellent, excellent. And Mary, and the boy?"

"Knocking 'em dead. At least, Mary is. On her way to college, her freshman year. Freshperson year."

"Wonderful, that's grand. Glad to hear that the home fires are burning brightly."

"Yeah, well. And how's your gang, Mike?"

The big man shrugged as he closed his eyes, "I don't see much of them since Angie went into the home. They're all grown and launched."

"Sure," Will said.

"Out of eight kids, though, you'd think I'd see one or another now and then. Of course, most of them left Washington, and none of them would be caught dead in Williamstown. But the ones still here, you'd think they'd come see the Old Man now and again."

"They will, Mike. You know at their age they get busy."

"Yeah, doing a lot of nothing. The boys chasing the skirts, the girl anything in pants."

Will nodded, making a mental note to call Maloney's three kids still living in the District, get their asses over to see him. They'd bitch and moan about how busy they were and how boring he was, hiding the deeper truth that they'd never forgiven their father for putting their mother into a nursing home. They blamed him for their mother's deterioration, as though Alzheimer's had something to do with the philandering of one's spouse. Maybe it did though, a somatic loss of memory to repress psychic pain. Whatever, the kids had never gotten over it. For that matter, neither had Maloney.

"I guess it could be worse," the congressman said, taking a large slurp of his drink. "Katie could be after the skirts and the boys could be homos." He dabbed at the line of tomato juice above his lip, "So, are you going to order? I'm telling you, I have to run soon, Will."

"Can't eat now, no time today. Forster testifies in front of the senate committee next week and I've got to go over to the association to coordinate wavelengths."

"Huh," grunted Maloney, "Forster will have a hard sell with those guys. Things are tight these days."

"Sure, but we'll always need a strong defense, Mike. You go along with that, right?"

"Yeah, sure," said Maloney," strong, but not so expensive."

Will stared at Maloney, "Well, what are you saying, Mike?"

"I'm saying that it's getting tough, Will, to stay with you boys on this and also stay in office. People are tired of paying taxes for toilets that cost two hundred thousand bucks. I don't blame them, either."

"Come on, Mike, you know it's not that. You know that this stuff goes in cycles. Okay, we're in a down cycle right now, with this Eastern Bloc party thing. But every time we think things are fine, in a few years we end up knocking heads with some country or another. Look at what happened after the first World War, and after World War II? Korea, Vietnam, Desert Storm, plus all the wars that didn't happen because we showed that we were strong. You think that this is going to last? Mike, you know better, you nearly lost your butt in Vietnam. You want to see your sons – or your daughters, for that matter – lose theirs in some

61

jerkwater little shithole just because we stopped keeping this country ready? Do you want to risk losing another war because we weren't prepared? And I don't mean a war where we lose face and fifty thousand people, I mean lose a war that counts, really counts."

"Of course I hear you," Maloney said in an exasperated tone, "but I'm in a war myself, damn it. I'm fighting for my political life against that bitch Macowiac. The slut is crippling me with her self-righteous nah-nahs, as if she had any idea in her tiny bird brain just how things get accomplished up here. She'll ruin everything I've built, everything I've ever done for our district. All because she's a god-damn saint."

Will sat back, then said quietly, "What can we do to help you, Mike?"

"Money," he said earnestly, "I need money to campaign right. So, give me money, Willy, to operate."

"How can I do that, Mike? We're past the legal limit. What would you do with it anyway?"

"More television! I will kick her ass with TV ads. I'll see her and raise her double. Two can talk job-training, you know – I'm on one of the house subcommittees on conversion, did you know that? And I still have the defense contracts to deal. I can have it both ways, twice as much to offer than her. But I need the voters to know this, to get the message, and the only way to do that is with some really good commercials, real slick stuff, you know? That takes money, Will."

"You don't think you're overreacting a bit, Mike?" Will asked softly.

A remarkably anguished expression passed across Maloney's face. "Jesus Christ, Will, I can't take the chance that I am! This is it, this is me! Congressman Michael Andrew Maloney, period. I never wanted more than this, I never wanted governor or senator, just the House. Just my district, just Williamstown. You know, with the kids grown up and Angie in that home, what else do I have?"

Maudlin, thought Will, read two Bloody Marys before his arrival.

"I'll send out feelers at the association, Mike. We might have some friends over there who haven't gone over the limit."

"Good, Will, good."

"But you've got to stay with us on this, Mike. We're risking everything too, you know."

"I don't know, Will, what I can promise you. I just don't know until I see."

"Unhuh," Will said, "Well do me this, okay? Read Forster's testimony. I have a copyright here. Check it out before you make up your mind. We're really counting on you, Mike. Really."

"Yeah, sure, I'll take a look."

Will reached down under the table, sweeping the heavy linen tablecloth out of his way as he groped for his briefcase.

Maloney rattled the ice in his empty glass, then searched around the room for the waiter. When he couldn't find him, he dropped his shoulders and said, "Oh well."

Will put the case on the table and opened the clasps as Mike said, "So, how's Julie doing? She still with the pilot?"

"Nope," said Will distractedly, thumbing through the mess of papers and materials in the case. He couldn't find the testimony, which made him move faster, fumbling the briefs and reports now.

"What?" said Maloney sharply. "He dropped her?"

"No," Will replied, "She kind of dropped him. Had something to do with his remarks glorifying Ollie North. Julie didn't go for that, I suppose."

"No shit! Julie isn't seeing him anymore. Huh!"

Will finally pushed the water glasses to the side to make room. He wiped his damp hands on his napkin, then started piling the contents of his briefcase on the table.

"Hell, I always liked Julie," Maloney said.

"Yeah, she's a hell of a kid," said Will. Now he began to wonder if he'd forgotten the testimony completely. That would be a fine thing, the reason he asked for this lunch in the first place. Maybe he'd left it in the car.

"Say, Will," Maloney said, "How about asking Julie if it would be okay for me to call her up?"

Will stopped his fussing. He gazed up at Maloney as if looking at something familiar turned into an indescribable monster. "Mike, for Christ's sake, she's not all that much older than Katie. You don't want to call her about anything."

"Oh, come on, Will, I just want to talk to her, see how she's doing. Come on, I don't have anything in mind. I just like her."

"Mike, you just finished telling me that you're in the political fight of your life and you want to call a girl half your age? How do you think that'll read in the Williamstown Gazette?"

"Jesus Christ, Day, I didn't say I want to take her out. I just want to say hello. And even if I did, she's of age – she's over thirty, for God's sake – and if she works for you, she's discreet."

"Damn it, Mike, the Washington Post isn't. Do you want to wear Gary Hart's mantle? Listen, she's been through a rough time. She really cared for that guy and it hurt to let him go. So, why don't you let her be?"

"What is this, Day, you don't think I'm good enough? You aren't her father. I don't know why I asked you in the first place. I can call her myself; she can make up her own mind. You don't think she'd be glad to hear from me? We always got along really well."

He was right, Julie and Maloney always kidded each other like old friends the few times they met. And he wasn't her father, but if he talked to her about him, did that make him Maloney's procurer? If he refused, though, Maloney would be pissed, which could carry more weight with him than any amount of money could make up. They couldn't give him the money without

64

risking a federal indictment, either. Maloney said he would call Julie anyway, so he might as well agree. He could keep Maloney happy and tell Julie, giving her fair warning.

"All right, all right, I'll talk to her. You're right, I'm being over-protective, but I do feel like a father to her, as young as she is."

"That's wonderful, Will," gushed Maloney, a flush of pleasure filling his face. "I really am grateful. When will you talk to her?"

"Today. She's meeting me at the association. I'll mention it to her then."

"Good, then I can call her tonight," Maloney said, his eyes suddenly blank with inward concentration.

Will returned to sorting through his papers. He picked up the slim volume of Lowell and laid it on the table. Beneath it was the copy of the testimony.

"What's this?" Maloney said, picking up the book.

"Poetry."

"Poetry? You read poetry? No shit? Still waters."

"Yeah. Okay, here's the testimony. Let me know what you think. It's important, Mike, for both of us."

"Right. Hey, I know a poem."

The waiter stepped up to the table and asked if they would like anything else. "Just the check, please," Will said, handing him a credit card.

"It's not really a poem, it's a limerick," said Maloney. When the waiter returned with the credit slips, Will wrote in the tip and signed them while Maloney leaned in conspiratorially. "Actually, it's the dirtiest limerick I've ever heard," he whispered.

"Oh yeah?" Will said in a disinterested tone.

"Yeah. It's so dirty, I'll tell it to you, but I'm going to leave out the dirtiest words."

He watched the waiter walk away, then turned back to Will and recited in a low voice:

65

"Blank-blank blank-blank blank-blank,
blank blankity-blankity blank,
blank blank, blank blank,
blank blank, blank blank'
blank blankity-blankity fuck."

Maloney roared his glee, his face beet red, then said, "Well, what do you think?"

Fuck, Will thought.

Chapter 7.

Eileen tried to think back to exactly when she knew she didn't love Willy anymore. She found the moment hard to pinpoint. Things happen gradually in a twenty-year span, and the loss of love could be obscured by ongoing affection: she still liked Willy as much as she ever had.

She sat sipping coffee at the patio table in the back yard under the natural canopy provided by the elm and the beech. Toward the back of the lot stood a towering evergreen, Willy's favorite tree, he declared: "No leaves, no grass." When they first moved in, she wondered out loud what they could grow under the tree to cover an unsightly bare spot. Willy shouted, "Nothing!"

For as much as she professed loving sitting out here taking the vapors, she didn't do it very often. Personal business kept her away on weekends, while their vacations took them to other places. Even when she had the opportunity to sit outside, either on a rare free Saturday or an early evening home from work, she just lounged in the living room, paging through a magazine, or watching a news talk show. This Saturday, though, Willy was off to Washington lobbying senators, and though she had plenty of her own stuff to do, she decided to just sit. She also decided to drink coffee after the noon hour, too, though that meant she wouldn't sleep until well after midnight. So, so what?

The place was home to a full array of marginal wildlife– chipmunks, voles, rabbits, cardinals, mourning doves, and black and gray squirrels. The squirrels fought hilariously, thought their Keystone Cop chases were serious territorial survival wars. She vaguely remembered reading somewhere how red squirrels took over beat the dickens out of the larger gray and black squirrels by castrating them, a starkly effective form of genocide. Or was it internecine? Internecide? Whatever, it was nasty. She didn't know if black squirrels behaved the same way.

Willy relished the animals and their behavior, bugs and plant life too. When the kids were little, he often led them on official family nature walks on mornings before school. He showed them especially wonderful mushrooms, wild strawberries, and even the flowering blooms of what most people considered to be pernicious weeds. He marveled out loud to Mary and Mike about dandelions and ragweed flowers. He pointed to their straightforward beauty and how it belied a complexity equal to that of the foreign counterparts so cherished by suburbanites everywhere. Wide-eyed and open-mouthed, the kids listened completely without understanding. Yet they seemed to know intuitively that Daddy was sharing secrets of major importance about the pretty flowers.

Eileen shook her head, thinking while sipping her coffee. He was such a great guy, why did she feel so differently about him now after these many years? What was so different at this juncture that she chafed at what she had considered before to be the satisfying parts of their marriage. The parts that buoyed her lessening feelings for him: the kids, the house, an easy existence, and the promise of a more than comfortable retirement thanks to their careers. If she wanted to, she could summon up the exact instances in the past when she had stopped and said to herself that she loved him. Even now, objectively.

After they had taken the terrifying leap admitting to each other their love, they exalted presenting together entering a shiny new world. Like all young lovers, they traced back the minutiae of their courtship as separate souls harboring such hidden love. They proudly shared their secret, glorying in all corresponding tenderness and humor.

"So, when we first went out, what did you think? What did you really hope for?" she asked, lying happily squeezed next to him on his dorm bed, alternate from her apartment.

"To get into your pants," he said in a matter-of-fact way.

"Oh, really?" she said with mock indignation.

"Yup. Now, what you were going to wear, I don't know."

Her laughter trailed behind a cardinal banking down from the beech. The mottled red bird pulled up with a flutter of its wings, landing on top of the narrow railing of the short chain-link fence around the yard. Willy always had been a goof, she thought, and being with him had made her one, too.

"We've been married for a whole year?" he once cried in distress, "I can't believe it!"

"Yeah," she said, "it seems shorter, more like just having fun." They bumped heads together, laughing.

Then, the kids had come along. He'd been crazy about Mary, about how beautiful a baby she had been. "She has killer eyes," he'd said. "Hearts will roll."

He was crazy for Mike, too. Before Mike popped out, Willy joked about naming him. "We'll call him Onomatopoeia."

"Now, why in God's name would we name him that?"

"So, when people ask how to pronounce it, we can tell them you say it the way it sounds."

Willy even celebrated Mike's propensity for scrapes and heartaches, "Okay, so the kid's only half a genius. That means he only has halfway to go."

He spent a lot of time with the kids when they were little. She remembered him crawling around with little Mary, urging her to talk and walk, and clapping his own hands like a child when she had done something amazing. He tried to teach her to read when she was only six months old, saying solemnly when chided about it, "Teaching children to read is teaching them to see."

She sighed, thinking of how sad he had been when he realized that Mary no longer thought that the sun rose and set by her father. It had been about then that he had claimed that Mary had turned out to be more like her mother than himself. Willy, thought Eileen, you never could see it, how much more she's like you than me. But how could you, parallel lines being what they are?

"No, Eileen, you're nuts. She's exactly like you, driven. I swear, it has to do with the fact that I wasn't in on her birth like with Mike. Her Karma is totally yours."

He had no idea, she thought. Mary fretted precisely the way he did, about things that didn't matter. She obsessed over everything, all things great or small were details that counted. The world for Mary had to be just exactly so. She had Willy written all over her, including his deadening beauty.

Oh, people didn't see it in him at first, the slight build, the slightly large features, the pronounced dark eyebrows, the rich fawn skin, the overly full lips, the wiry dark hair, now touched by white, not gray, white. A mixed crowd didn't see it, most men didn't see it, and thankfully, Willy didn't see it. But women saw it. Gay men saw it, and children. Because Willy had no idea about it, he never used it as a weapon, never thought of his advantage. That probably deepened others' love for him. Most likely, it engendered envy, too. Hell, she admitted, she envied him, and he thought her to be the most beautiful woman on Earth.

She stretched her legs out, luxuriating, propping them on one of the wrought iron patio chairs. She raised her arms in the air to stretch, thinking that she was good looking, but not the way Willy thought of her. She could look in a mirror objectively and inventory her strong points, the eyes, the hair, the face that had gotten better looking, really, over the years. She also could factor in the effect of her character, the hard edge that he pointed out to her so often as something to soften. That edge added to her attractiveness, made her desirable because she seemed un-approachable, like those haughty models in the *Sunday Times Magazine* ads. Being married to Willy, the nicest guy in the world, compounded her unavailability and her beauty, she knew. But a few, a handful, always took a shot for that very reason, as though they lived for such odds. And, of course, Harry had to be one of them.

Periodically during the past fifteen years Harry had felt obligated to send a pass her way, more of a convention rather than anything serious. They both would laugh at his lame attempts, as though in on the same old joke. Yet, familiarity made for comfort she found out, and she always had admired Harry's business acumen.

"Achoo-men" Willy would say, like a sneeze. He was such a goof. Willy would never think of running around on her, he'd be appalled by the idea. Oh, he kidded about it, about the consequences of being found out.

"So, say you catch me on the couch—"

"En flagrante?" she said with a grin.

"Well, in someone, but who is beside the point—"

And her laughter cut him off.

"You see?" he said. "I'm no damn good at being unfaithful."

So, was she?

What had changed everything, really? Even as she phrased the question in her mind, she recognized that the answer had resided within her all along. The answer had engendered the entire line of inquiry in the first place. For all their years of living and working together in peaceful coexistence, she and Willy had never seen the world the same way. Actually, the fact that they had stayed together for so long constituted a minor miracle, considering the range of their philosophical differences, opposite on every level, from small particle physics to the nature of the Big Bang. And neither of them was the strong silent type.

"God is either all-powerful and not compassionate," Willy would expound, "or God is compassionate but not all-powerful. It breaks down to this, politically. The Republicans subscribe to the first God."

She smiled, saying, "You're just saying that because I voted for Bush."

"No, I'm not, but now that you mention it, how could you vote for Bush?" the last part intoned as nearly a plaintive lament.

"Because Bush seemed good for business. I'm in business, so I voted for him."

"Yup, just like I said, the first God, the 'Me God.' Look what it got you for your trouble. You really foxed yourself, didn't you, going directly for the gold."

"I beg your pardon?" she said cooly.

"I said foxed, not fucked. But that doesn't change the fact that when you voted for him you were out for yourself, not the common good. That's the Republicans for you, they steal big and right away. The Demos just cream a little over forty years, but they also spread it around."

"That's why the Democrats don't want laws limiting their terms. They're no different, just slower. And with all of them giving everything away for free, who's going to look out for me – and you, and the kids – if I don't?"

"Oh, I see. The old social triage trip, not enough to go around, so you have to do for yourself. And who deserves it more than those who work hard for what they have?"

"Yeah? So?" she'd said, "Who does?"

Every four years, she thought, like clockwork, they would hammer at each other, tongs too. They didn't pay attention to local politics; Willy was a Big Picture kind of guy. For all of his political fury, he never made the connection of how the way he lived differed from what he said, a reality that had enabled her to accommodate their union. Until now, she thought. Now, for the first time, their differing viewpoints threatened to tip the balance, at least, in her mind.

"Shit," she said out loud. Why couldn't he take this promotion seriously? And why did he have to begin this poetry thing now, of all times? She did believe in triage, and she felt in her bones that Harry would find a way to lose them if he became executive v.p. As much as Harry liked them, as well as she got along with him herself, she knew that he would be forced to get rid of them, even as she would urge Willy if he got the nod, to dump Harry. The way things were going, though, it looked like Harry would be doing the dumping.

She sighed. The coffee was gone and she was beginning to feel too warm. She noticed the sun lower in the sky and realized that she had been surprised by late afternoon. Willy would be home soon.

Harry could be intriguing in his own wicked way. She remembered the time they had worked together on the discrimination suit brought by Carol Jones after she'd been fired. Only Harry had argued along with Eileen that ComCon should not settle, that Jones' superior had documented overwhelming evidence that she plainly was a complete fuck-off, that she abused sick leave and every other kind of leave whenever she could, and that she didn't work at all when she did show up, invariably late on those rare occasions as well. "I mean, Jesus Christ, folks," Harry had said, exasperated," she isn't even black!"

What worried Forster, though, was the nature of Jones' case. Jones claimed that ComCon's had failed to promote her when she obviously deserved it, and indeed, had promoted men with less seniority from lesser positions past her. This discrimination so discouraged her, she stated, that her work performance had suffered as a consequence. When ComCon dismissed her, her reputation had been so damaged that she could not find another job. Ultimately, living on barely a subsistence level, she found herself unable to cope mentally, and was virtually housebound, afraid to venture out for fear of failure.

Eileen had despised Carol Jones for what her actions meant for other professional women. In ninety-nine out of a hundred cases, Eileen would fight arm in arm with a woman making this claim. The single exception turned out to be the one she'd actually had to face. For her position, she received flak from other attorneys she knew, both men and women, who didn't know Jones. It was like it had been in college when her classmates rode her relentlessly about studying corporate law. She'd even had to endure a cartoon in the school paper, an unmistakable caricature of her sitting in the middle of an otherwise empty lecture hall, raptly attending to a cobwebbed skeleton at the lectern wearing a sign over his ribcage labeled "Business Ethics." The goading had bothered her more than she'd ever let them know, a reaction that probably annoyed them into greater intensity. At least, it seemed more intense. Only Willy had known that she had thought about transferring. But he listened to her telling him how she felt, that she had ethics, she'd always had them, and that the other students were knocking her unfairly.

"Yeah, well, you know, to some 'ethical' is just 'ethnical' with the 'n' dropped. It's convenient so they can tell everyone else that their way's the right way. WASPs are great for this shit."

She should have been offended by the last crack, her family having converted to Episcopalian in the 1800s. But he was too cute to hold it against him, she'd decided.

So, fifteen years later Carol Jones managed to unearth all of those miserable feelings in her again with her predatory lawsuit. And even though Eileen firmly believed that Jones simply wanted to take the company for as much as she could get, Eileen'd felt uneasy about opposing her, especially since she'd experienced the same kind of invisibility regarding advancement at ComCon. The only reason that she herself had never left was her conviction that it wouldn't be any better anyplace else. And at ComCon, she did exercise some real power and influence, at least with Willy. But Willy hadn't cared much about what happened with Carol Jones. It had been Harry who had teamed up with Eileen to go after the slimy, scam artist.

With Harry's support, Forster had given the go-ahead to fight the suit. Harry and she had stayed late into the night for three months digging up everything they could find "to nail the bitch," as Harry put it. Eileen nodded her head, remembering that it was Harry siccing a private eye on Jones that had turned the trick. They had learned that she had turned down two comparable jobs, one with better pay. They also had a signed affadavit from a previous employer who admitted that her resignation had been a cooperative one, an agreement reached for a sizably increased severance check in exchange for a confidential letter promising not to pursue a discrimination case.

The kicker came when Eileen fielded a call from the detective while Harry was gone, picking up carry-out for dinner.

He strolled back into the office holding two grease-stained brown bags away from his suitcoat.

"Guess what?" Eileen said as she helped stack the white cardboard boxes on her desk. "The notoriously agora- and xenophobic Ms. Carol Jones just left for Spain two hours ago."

Harry stopped fiddling with the top of a box and looked her in the eye. "Spain, huh? Good, maybe the bitch will run with the bulls."

God, she loved that about Harry, he could be so quick and savage at work, yet funny, too, though admittedly in a lethal kind of way. She wished that Willy could be like that, if he were like that life would be perfect! Sadly, though, she knew that he would never be like Harry. She loved him for not being like Harry, and now she might have to leave him for it, too.

She sighed. Precedents did exist of office romances becoming alliances of power. Hollywood had the market cornered on that sort of thing, of course, not much of an endorsement, really. But she recalled a friend of hers who had built a publishing company with her husband, telling of how he had called her into his office to inform her that he was getting a divorce so he could marry the editor; Oh, and also, that she was fired. Eileen had counseled her to get a good contract next time. Anyway, Eileen thought, she would be in the position of the husband, or the editor, not her friend. But, Jesus Almighty, the whole idea seemed so tawdry. I mean, she thought, just how sexy is Harry Olssen?

She suspended movement for an instant as she weighed the answer. Pretty damn sexy, she decided. Oh, not for any specific physical reason. Harry cut a good figure, albeit a bit beefy; he moved well for a big, blond man. But he couldn't compete with Willy's looks, and she imagined that anyone would have a hard time matching Willy in bed, the lascivious son of a bitch.

Willy wandered into the back yard from the side of the house. He had his suit coat draped over his shoulder and his tie pulled away from his open shirt collar. He dropped into one of the iron chairs, tossing the coat on the table.

"So," said Eileen, "how did it go?"

"Like shit," he said flatly, "like clockwork in a clock made of shit."

"That well, huh?" she said.

He blew out air. "Man, they all see that ugly election staring them in the face just two months away. They're all big on cutting the budget, restoring fiscal responsibility."

"Well, that's not good," she murmured.

He stared at her and said, "Thanks for the incisive analysis."

"So, what are you going to do?"

"Hell, I don't know. Push harder. Go after Maloney to go after others. Invest in solar power, play the numbers, I don't know."

She hesitated, then said, "Have you told Forster yet?"

"It's Saturday, Eileen. Only lobbyists work on weekends. Forster's probably off on his yack-t somewhere on the Bay."

"You don't think he'd want you to call him there? You don't think he'd want to know about this development?"

"I don't know, maybe. But I sure don't want to talk to him about it. I mean, and what the fuck difference is it going to make to tell him now instead of Monday, except that he'll think of more shit for me to do. And I'm asinine enough to do it."

"Did it ever occur to you, Willy, that if you called it might show him that you are involved in what happens to ComCon, that it might be a good move on your part considering what's at stake and also that you haven't really come through, lately, with anything to shout about?"

Willy's eyes turned sharp as he gazed at her. "Well thanks, Eileen, for that vote of incompetence. Did it ever occur to you that maybe I'm not cut out to be the executive vice president, or, heaven forbid, president? I mean, especially considering that I haven't hit any long balls lately, have I, not one home run, no slam dunks, no holes in one, no TDs, rushing or passing."

"Willy, does this have to be a fight?" Eileen said sourly.

"No, really, what have I done lately, except doubt the process, the whole damn thing? I'm not sure I believe the stuff I'm telling them, Eileen. Do we really need QMIV in every Army depot? Can't we go along with Eldon and sell new, improved Marios to Nintendo? Why not?"

"You can do anything you want, Willy, when you have the power. But you have to get the power first. And you're not doing it."

"Yeah, well, I'm not all that interested. Why don't you do it?"

77

"Where are you going?" she called sharply to his back as he headed around the corner of the house.

"To the kitchen for Scotch."

The sun had left her in the midst of a dull twilight. The birds had settled for the night and the leaves on the trees had gone from a lush, wet-paint green to a dull ordnance gray. Or maybe her mood had changed everything around her. Whatever, she thought, God knows Willy was making it easier for her.

Chapter 8.

Will showed up for work on Monday completely rocked. He'd sat in the kitchen sipping Scotch for the rest of the night on Saturday, taking time only to eat some cheese and crackers. Eileen had marched in silently at around seven o'clock to fix herself some dinner. Without a word, she took her salad and a glass of white wine down to the family room where he could hear her turn on the TV. Mike strolled in later, took one look at him, and tiptoed out with some cold pizza and a Coke. Finally, at midnight, Will dragged himself up to bed, where Eileen set upon him like one of those sex-starved Amazon women in B-movies shown at drive-ins.

He called Forster on Sunday and ended up driving to Chesapeake City to be picked up for a confab on his cruiser. After an hour's worth of intense cheerleading, Forster sent him back to Washington to try and chase down senators sympathetic to the cause. When he returned home that night at eight o'clock, weary and empty-handed, Eileen greeted him with spinach tortellini in cream sauce, Caesar's salad, and a smooth Chardonnay, all ordered from their favorite restaurant. For dessert, she fed him strawberries in chocolate mousse, then took him to bed and plied him with frangipani-scented oil warmed in the microwave. As they drifted off to sleep afterwards, neither mentioning at all the fight of the day before, he wondered if she had decided to kill him with kindness. If she kept this up, he thought, he'd be happy dead. He waved to Kelly in the lobby as he walked directly back to his office. He had driven alone in the morning because Eileen had gone to a meeting in D.C. He'd arrived late, and even though she wasn't around to prod him personally, working with his wife for so long had imprinted him so that he scurried down the hall, hoping that he'd get to his desk before Forster or anyone else saw him.

He turned the last corner before reaching his door and was surprised by a strange head bobbing up from behind Julie's desk. Glassy blue eyes gazed blankly at him out of a pasty white pan of a face topped by a wreath of thin brown hair. Will's bleary vision registered first, incredibly, the reincarnation of Charles Laughton as Quasimodo. He blinked and recognized the new comptroller Barry Evans stooped to the left of the doorway in front of an open file drawer.

Will relaxed, thinking the poor guy wasn't that bad-looking, when Evans smiled and said laughing nervously, "Running kind of late today, aren't we?".

Will blinked again. "Uh, yeah. Where's Julie?"

"Gone to the storeroom. For some old files."

"Unhuh." Will shifted on his feet, then laid his briefcase on Julie's desk. "So, you've started your research. How's it going?"

"Slowly. Most of the records in this company are terribly maintained. It's very difficult to find complete and accurate information."

"I get you," said Will, then jokingly, "But mine are impeccable, right?"

"No," said Evans as he faced the files again. He turned back to Will and said, "Oh. Yeah," laughing a brittle burst of noise.

Oh boy, thought Will. Noticing Evans' smile freezing and crumbling, embarrassed self-consciousness taking over. Will quickly said, "Well, I know you have a hell of a job in front of you. I don't envy you a bit. In fact, it amazes me that you can keep track of all this stuff."

The small man stood up and put his hands in his pockets. He rocked back and forth, smiling sheepishly, "Oh, it's not so hard. Just good organization and being careful. It's pretty straight forward, really. Not the kind of interesting work that you and your wife do. You know, meeting senators and members of congress. That must be exciting."

"Exciting? No, not exciting, just crazy. It makes you nutsy, really, dealing with all those egos. Believe me, Barry, you're in a better line of work."

"Yeah," he said, "I guess. Maybe."

They faced each other in awkward silence. At length, Will said, "Well, I suppose I better get to it."

"Yeah, sure, suppose so," Barry said, grinning stiffly as he turned to the file cabinet. Will shook his head infinitesimally. He then said, "Hey, Barry, you have any plans for lunch?"

Stooped again, Barry craned his head to look back. "Lunch? No. I usually bring a sandwich."

"Want to go with me this afternoon? I'll take you to one of the ritzy places we lobbyists always go to. It'll give you a frame of reference for the expense account files you're going through." He saw him hesitating, and said, "My treat, of course," smiling broadly.

Barry smiled back and said, "Okay, sure. I can put my bag in the refrigerator for tomorrow."

They both laughed, and Will stepped into his office, casting his eyes to the heavens as he entered. Then, he stuck his head back out the door and said, "By the way, Barry, when Julie gets back, could you ask her to come here?"

"Yes. I can do that."

"Okay, thanks."

Will walked behind the large, rectangular cherry desk and laid his briefcase on the matching credenza beneath the window. He drew back the heavy drapes but left the gauzy set in place so that he could enjoy the light without being distracted or observed from outside. To the left of his desk stood his PC center, and he flicked the disk on before taking off his jacket and walking to the office door. He hung the jacket on a hanger on a hook behind the door, then closed it to a three-inch opening. He returned to the desk and fell into his chair, a leather-covered Easy Boy affair that rocked, swiveled, and also moved on wheels. He joked with Julie about his 'starship command center,' saying that it could only be improved if it was also a bed.

Will opened his briefcase and pulled out a sheaf of papers. He gazed at the first page.

Fall, 1973
(free verse)

Over the page and tome of Keats
 I steal a quick glance at her.
She is dwelling in her world,
 her book, her imaginings.
She is sweet and slow-moving in thought
 even to imperceptible measure,
     a turn of the foot
     a thumb on a page
But never with the loss of
     the concentrating eye.
 And this is the key, the sign.

I cannot presume to hold her world;
Intellect tells me this is so,
 and also to watch out, for
A vision of throwing up my hands
 fingers spread and clawed
Catching at the soft sun of night.
Ego assails me my mind knows,
 held in hand
Only by the span between the moon and man.

Dana Clough: He remembered writing the poem about her, the crush he had on her during his junior year at college, her freshman year at B.U. During the first weeks of that fall, she met him and depended upon him to squire her around, using his vast experience and knowledge to reassure her. Stately in style, she belied the small Massachusetts town that was her home with smart, conservative clothes that flattered her zaftig figure. And she practiced all the measured movements that entranced men with her long, black hair, enthralling them into the basest servitude. At intramural football games, when he caught a touchdown pass and ran off the field for a congratulatory hug and a kiss, she permitted him the slightest of pecks. When he wanted to go out during the week, she insisted upon going to the library instead, allowing him to come along if he promised to study.

Which was okay, he thought, since his grades did take an upward turn at the time. Mostly, he stared at her while she studied, which resulted in the poem. Dana finally did him in, however, when she successfully rushed a tony sorority. He asked her for a weekend date as usual, but she turned him down, saying she had to study for an exam. The following Monday he walked in on her at the snack bar, having a fake brawl with a guy, pretending to be outraged when he stood up one of her girlfriends Willy stood by, enjoying the faux brouhaha until she let slip that she had gone out that night after all Will had stood there stunned while she continued on about how the opportunity had come up, so she'd taken it. Later, after she asked him why he was so quiet, he whispered to her what he overheard her say about going out that weekend. The drama had flown high, he recalled, tears welling in her contrite eyes. But he walked. Standing outside the top of the library steps, he sighed as he surveyed the whole wide bustling world below that no longer had anything to offer him.

But he snapped out of it after a week or two, and with a poem to boot.

Will flipped the sheet and read the next one.

> Over the page and tome of Keats
>   I steal a glance at her,
> Dwelling in her imaginings deep
>   Which I cannot presume to share,
> In slow-moving thought, ever sweet,
>   To me of imperceptible measure.
>
> On disturbing her world, intellect frowns,
>   Cautioning to keep the watch tower light,
> Yet ego assails with hands up-thrown,
>   Clawing fingers at the soft sun of night.
> Temperance comes in love's cushioned palm
>   Joining two together for the higher height,
>
> Thus, my mind knows the distance and the span
>   Of the flight of evening, the moon, and man.

Huh. Like the backyard football play they ran over and over again: 'Same thing, only different.'

Looking over these poems, three stapled together, the entire exercise returned to him, vaguely. He had been studying for his comprehensive exam and found himself deeply immersed in the liquid earth of the library stacks. Pungent, ochre-hued books opened to crackling yellow pages dulled brown at the edge, full of 16th, 17th, and 18th-century poems. *The Spectator* recording nondescript verse of women caught in their dishabille—*wouldst, couldst, shouldst.*

Hours led to hours of reading rhyme without reason except they were on the list. The reading list ran six pages, single-spaced,

Piers Plowman to *Murder in the Cathedral,* current events recounted centuries apart. He couldn't tell this from that, thee from thou; he needed a break from being a Middle English *despondee.*

He smoked, supplied by a fellow student, a Vietnam vet who had revisited his training camp at Fort Bliss. The Vet had brought back the Mexican brand that he smoked then, Ovilado Delicados, the original seven-minute cigarette, though they were not any longer than the average butt. They tasted sweet, too, as if laced with sugar to soften the hack-generating, death-dealing pallor coursing down the smoker's esophagus. He cherished every one of them, smoked every hour on the hour for the three weeks that he crammed for the exam. He ran out of them on the exact day of the big ordeal. The cough lasted well past its shelf life.

He also wrote poems, emulations of what he had read on any given day. He wrote them while sitting in a small glass, fish-bowl booth at his job making change in a parking lot. That was when he had reworked the poem about Dana Clough, deciding then that he might have a sonnet on his hands.

What kind, though? That much Will could not remember after he found the poems among his old school papers. So, he would refer to his old buddies, Thrall, Hibbard, and Holman. He leaned back to the briefcase and pulled out *A Handbook to Literature* and looked up 'Sonnet.' The *Handbook* listed two kinds, Italian (Petrachan), and English (Shakespearean). Italian sonnets required an abba abba cde cde 'RIME-SCHEME in IAMBIC PENTAMETER,' though some poets experimented with 'HEXAMETER and other METERS.'

Iambic pentameter; Oh boy. The hell with it for now, he thought, and started to tick off rhymes in the first take: ababab—

Okay, it wasn't an Italian sonnet. So, Shakespearean, right? As he checked in the book, he felt a warm glow at the idea that he'd gone right to the source for his sonnet, one Will to another.

But, according to the boys, the rhyme sequence should be abab cdcd efef gg. And his was ababab—he finished counting— cdcdcd ee.

Damn. So, what did he have here?

He turned to the next page and found another version with an abaabb cdcdcd ee scheme. What the hell?

He flipped to the last page: Spenserian

> Over the page and tome of Keats
>   I steal a glance at her,
> Dwelling in her imaginings deep
> Sweet slow-moving thought, ever fair,
>   In this I cannot presume to share.
> On disturbing her world, intellect frowns
>   Yet her fancy, of imperceptible measure
> Ego assails with hands up-thrown.
>   Temperance comes in love's gentle palm
> Careful to keep the watch tower light,
>   Easing the clawed fingers together and down
> From obscuring wholly, the soft sun of night.
> Thus, my mind knows the distance and the span
>   Of the flight of evening, the moon, and man.

He picked up the book and located 'Spenserian Stanza' a few entries in back of 'Sonnet.' He found that his rhyme scheme was correct for the first nine lines, ababbcbcc. The problem rested with the fact that a Spenserian Stanza was only nine lines long, while his poem still ran the fourteen, standard for a sonnet—the next line was a 'd.' And he hadn't even touched the whole matter of METER, he thought.

Not only that, in reading the poems again, it seemed to him that every rewrite had changed the meaning of the original, which he liked pretty much the best of the bunch anyway. Although, his Sort-of-Shakespearean one on the second page wasn't all that bad. Maybe he'd invented his own sonnet form, the Will Day Sonnet, or the Willy Day Sonnet. The Dayly Sonnet? Good for what ails you, read a Sonnet Dayly. Whatever, he decided to key them in as-is and worry about editing them later.

Will pivoted to his computer and tapped in the Word-Perfect commands. He called up the directory, then took a diskette and inserted it. He named the file first, "DAYLY.POM and began to type.

Chapter 9.

"You wanted to see me?" Julie said, leaning in the doorway.

Will spun around a bit fast, feeling a little guilty. He said in a low voice, "Yeah. Is he still there?" he mouthed, pointing at the door behind the palm of his hand.

"Yes," said Julie.

"Okay." In a stentorian voice, he called out, "Julie, I want you to bring me every scrap of dirt on every congressman and senator that we have in our files."

He raised his eyes, and she glanced to her left, then came in, covering her mouth. "His head shot up like a scared deer," she said in a low tone, trying to hold back her laughter.

"Uh, good," he said, his voice as loud as before, "and bring me the secret file on the president, too. But first, take a letter."

She collapsed in a silent, laughing heap in the chair in front of his desk.

Will stepped softly to the door and closed it shut. Fifteen years later from her striking good looks, fair skin except for feint freckles in chorus with burnished red hair, she still garnered the eyes of passersby, most too daunted by her length to hit on her. Hell, even he looked up at her as though she occupied Olympus. Of course, she also stood taller than him, at least two inches. No matter, the time spent with her made him feel avuncular, not ardent.

Julie roared her laughter, "Jesus Christ you're cruel, Will. And "'Take a letter'?"

"What the hell, with him it'll establish verisimilitude."

"Oh, sure," she said, "whatever the heck that means."

"The same as it sounds. Don't play dumb with me, Julie, your résumé is still in your personnel jacket."

"All lies, damn lies. You should know that by now, working on the Hill."

"Yeah, I guess," he said, plopping back down into his chair. Casually, he hit the Page Down key on his computer, sending the first part of his free verse sonnet off the screen.

"So, what's up?" Julie said.

He looked at her and wondered if she appeared as worn out by the weekend as he felt. She had dark smears beneath her eyes, almost as if she had smudged them before a ball game to cut the sun's glare. Her face seemed a little hangdog, too, though her complexion appeared to be fresh enough. He couldn't tell, though, really, so he asked.

"How was your weekend?"

She sat back in her seat. "Good."

"Did you have any fun?"

"Yeah. It was fine." Her gleeful mood of just the moment before seemed to have faded, her emotions almost contrasting with her closing features.

Will tapped his fingers together on the desktop. "So," he said, "what did you do?"

"You mean, did I see Maloney?" she said.

Will nearly winced when she said it, though she sounded totally without rancor. Instead, he saw that wariness he first detected in her after he told her what Maloney had said. Despite all his protestations, his railing, she'd said to him, "Sure, he can call me. I always got along pretty well with the old bastard."

Will redoubled his vituperation, and she had done her best to assuage him. But, of course, he suspected that she said yes because of him, the things she intuited that he left unsaid. Ever since the whole thing had happened, he couldn't think about it

89

without feeling guilty. Naturally, whenever he felt responsible, he to try to make it better, which meant that he had to ask.

"Julie, you don't have to see Maloney. Not for this job, you don't"

"I wouldn't for this job, Will, or for any. Give me a little credit, will you?"

Will you, he thought: Will. You.

"Believe it or not, he's really not a bad guy. It's not like he comes on like a Kennedy or anything, you know."

"Unhuh. But he comes on."

"He's a boozy romantic, Will, an Irish crybaby. You ought to know all about them."

"I'm third generation," he said without thinking. "Julie, you of all people. I can't believe you went for his bullshit."

"Well, thanks a lot."

"Oh, you know what I mean," he said, lowering his hands twisting them together on the desk. He peered up, "So, you're seeing a lot of him."

She stood up and huffed a sigh, "Don't worry, Will, I'm being careful. You don't have to worry about another scandal with Maloney. I know it's an election year."

"Oh, God, Julie."

"Yeah, right. Take it easy, Will, it's not your problem, you know? Every problem is not yours to solve."

As she disappeared out the door, he cried out, "Hey, I know that."

After a fruitless moment waiting, he decided that she wouldn't be back soon, which meant that she really was angry.

Shit. She'd come around sooner or later, he thought, but the whole mess could have been avoided if he had stood up to Maloney. As it turned out, the old pol's vote hadn't made that much of a difference anyway, since the Senate committee had recommended deeper cuts, meaning that the House committee would have to go to the drawing board. The hypocritical bastards, he thought, just because a bunch of them were up for reelection, too. Maybe it was just bad luck, though, bad timing. Or maybe the timing would never be any good because the fault rested with the entire concept, as though they were feeding the sole remaining mammoth to try to keep the species from going extinct. In the meantime, he thought, he'd have to start over again.

He wondered how Harry was doing with the Army side of the equation. He'd probably hear in the next staff meeting, he thought, though it wouldn't be great news. The Army wasn't the problem, except for their lack of imagination. They hungered just as much as ComCon and all the others for continued defense funding. They merely needed inspiration to notify Congress of the newest threat to national security that required a strong defense. In this way they could include their pet programs in their poms, the plans they presented to Congress each summer for budgetary purposes. Harry provided them with epiphany after epiphany about the need for QMIV, he'd done a great job through the years, Will admitted to himself. But the guy never had to deal with the fickleness of the elected official. The Pentagon boys were lifers, seldom subject to demotion or dismissal unless they screwed up in a war, and how often did they fight any wars, really?

He had to laugh because, for all of their insistence upon more money for the best weapons and having most of the best, they were notoriously reluctant to recommend war. Look at their predictions about the Gulf War, he said to himself, though maybe those came from their experience in Vietnam. The last war always informed the next war, at least to generals. He remembered reading about Montgomery's unwillingness to engage the enemy in Africa and Italy during World War II. The scholars wrote that as a young officer in the first World War, he witnessing 60,000 close-packed Tommies machine-gunned down in two hours at the Battle of the Somme. After that, the future popinjay general swore he would never permit that to happen again. Then there existed the self-serving, such as McClellan in the Civil War, who delayed battling Robert E. Lee not for the sake of his soldiers, but because he was afraid of losing. Thereby, he was dismissed by a president whom he considered a laughable inferior, Abraham Lincoln.

So, some of those guys were okay, and some were self-serving bastards, just like people everywhere. Big revelation, he thought. Still, Harry had it easier.

Will exhaled a sigh and swiveled in his seat. He picked up his sonnets and gazed at his Spenserian poem again: . . . *the distance and the span, of the flight of evening, the moon, and man.*

He read it over . . . *the distance and the span.* What's the difference between 'distance' and 'span?' And what the does 'the flight of evening, the moon, and man' mean? He shook his head. Even if they meant something to him then, he didn't feel the same way now. What had replaced this kind of romanticism within him, such youthful passion? A sense of justice, a search for truth? Just what did he want from this regenerated impulse to put feelings on paper? What did he intend to save for posterity at this point in his life? He forced himself to ask the fundamental question: had he come to this point out of some cliché of a midlife crisis, or had he returned to where he should have been all along, the result of the true educated self? If the former, he better throw all these old verses away, get rid of the file on his computer and get back to work. In other words, get over himself.

He didn't know the answer, though. He only knew that something drove him, emotions different from those of twenty years ago, but akin. So, how was he going to handle the feelings and responsibilities accrued of the kids, Eileen, even Forster and ComCon? He knew he had an ego, but he didn't think he was an egotist. He just wanted to change his life, change it back, really, to what it once was. Was that possible? He shook his head, not really knowing.

He did know one thing, he couldn't rewrite old poems. He reached for his keyboard, entered his DAYLY.POM file, and deleted the sonnet fragment. Then he opened a file named NEWS.REL and began phrasing the weekly release: 'Quarter-Master Program Proving Fast To Army.' He looked at it, then typed over it, changing it to 'Quartermaster Proving Itself Fast to the Army.' That's better, he thought, a nice little double entendre there.

He tapped away for what seemed like only a few minutes when he heard knocking on the open door, growing louder, as though gradually rising in accord with the length of time he failed to answer it. Will gave it his full attention now, a measured pounding that must have been audible up and down the hallway.

"Yeah, yeah, I hear you," Will said, "What is it?"

Barry Evans leaned in and smiling sheepishly said, "It's noon."

Will gazed at him, slack-mouthed. "Yeah?"

"Well, uh, don't you go to lunch at twelve?" Barry said.

"Lunch? Twelve? Oh, yeah, I usually go, I don't know, whenever."

"Oh, I see. Well I, uh . . .." Barry turned to leave.

"No, no, that's okay," Will said, "It's a good time to go to lunch. I'm not getting anywhere, here, anyway. So, let's go to lunch" he said, wondering why he was going so far out of his way for this guy whom he didn't know from Adam, and who seemed to be a perfectly boring person.

"Okay," said Barry said, reviving his smile.

"Okay, then," Will said. Again, they had nothing to say to each other. Will finally said, "So. Where do you want to go?"

"Oh, well, you said you'd take me to one of those places where you run up your expense account with politicians."

"Right, right," Will said.

"Your treat, you said."

"Absolutely. Okay, let's go."

Barry didn't say a word when he drove them into the parking lot at Al's MidEast Pizza. Instead, he merely looked more and more glum, his head and shoulders dropping lower and lower as they headed for an open booth. Will smiled broadly as they sat opposite each other over the Formica table attached to the booth.

"So, what do you think?"

"This is where you have your power lunches?" Barry mumbled.

"Sure," Will said. But when he saw Barry begin to look like a high school kid teased by a bully and unable to do a thing about it, he quickly said, "Nah, I'm just kidding, Barry. We wine and dine the pols in town, they never come out here unless NASA is having a ribbon-cutting or something. I just brought you here because you need to know about this place. They have the best pizza in the area."

"Oh?" Barry replied, still skeptical and morose.

"Yeah, really. But tell you what. Next time there's a function in D.C., I'll let you know. You can come with me and rub elbows with the heavyweights, see what it's like."

"Yeah?" said Barry, brightening immediately.

"Yeah, sure," Will said, "though it's not all that fascinating, believe me. I'm telling you, this place is more interesting. The owner's from Lebanon, and his pizza is really strange and wonderful. Order some with sausage, you'll see what I mean."

"I can't imagine that," said Barry as he reached for a menu.

"No, really, try it," said Will, who began to flip through the selections on the mini-jukebox, "it's good, real spicy."

"I don't mean the pizza, I mean the insider stuff," Barry said. "I can't believe it isn't interesting. You know, deals cut behind smoke-filled rooms, kings crowned."

"Not too many smoke these days," Will said absently. Now there was a good one: 'If I Ruled the World, by Frank Sinatra. How about 'Please Release Me,' by William Keating?

They ordered from a small dark man with a light gray beard who wiped his hands on his apron before writing on his pad. He left, and Will returned to the jukebox.

"I'll bet you meet a lot of women on the Hill, too," said Barry. "A lot of good-looking aides to the senators and the congressmen."

"Oh, I don't know." How about this: 'Sympathy for the Devil' by the Ray Conniff Singers.

"I heard that the ratio in Washington is something like eight to one, women to men."

"Could be. I read it's about that. I don't pay much attention. They're so young and I'm so married, and exhausted."

"Hey," Barry said sharply, "not everyone's as old as you are. I'm not married."

Will jerked around, then pulled back as though doubting what he had just heard. Barry hurried to say, "But I'm sure a lot of girls would like to meet you. They probably see you as mature."

"Unhuh. I doubt that," Will said, shaking his head, thinking, This guy's a beaut.

"No, really, with that gray hair on your sides, women like that," he said, "they have a word for it. What is it?"

Don't say it, thought Will.

"Distinguished," he said, "That's it. You look distinguished."

Their pizza arrived. Will cradled a piece in his hands and bit off the tip. Tendrils of cheese trailed the slice as he pulled it away, drooping like the cables of a failed suspension bridge. He began to nip them up, closing in on the pizza wedge again in an effort to complete his bite.

"Enjoying today's heartburn, Mr. Day?"

He looked left, which caused the stringy cheese to drop across his cheek. Kelly from the front desk stood next to the booth with another young woman from ComCon. "Oh, woghm gohgm," Will nodded to her, chewing furiously.

"Oh, my," Kelly said, stepping back. She raised her hand to cover her mouth trying to stifle a giggle.

Will swallowed and said, "Pretty sophisticated, huh?" laughing with Kelly and the other woman.

"Yeah, real classy," Barry chimed in.

"I guess people who like pizza don't care how they look eating it," Kelly said to Will, "I know I'm that way."

"I'll bet you look great eating pizza," said Barry.

Her eyes flickered to him, then back to Will, who was saying, "It's not how I look that bothers me, it's how my shirt looks for the rest of the day. I usually like to wear powder blue when I eat pizza, it sets off the tomato sauce so well. Makes a hell of an impression at meetings."

She laughed, "I know what you mean. I'm a complete klutz, I get it all over myself every time." She patted her shoulders and waist in a Simon Says action as if checking for stains. "I wouldn't even be here, but Wendy wanted to go."

"Hi, Wendy," Will said warmly.

"Oh, excuse me, Mr. Day, this is Wendy Adams. She works for Mr. Harding in design. You know Mr. Day, in Public Affairs?" Kelly asked Wendy.

Wendy was a bigger woman than Kelly, not as pretty or as smartly dressed. She smiled with shy sweetness, so genuine, Will thought, that she could travel tariff-free throughout the world upon that beam of friendliness alone.

Wendy nodded that she knew him, "Hi, Mr. Day."

"Listen, you saw me massacre a pizza, so you better call me Will."

They started to smile as Barry leaned his head in front of Will's, "Hi, I'm Barry Evans, the new comptroller by the way, in case anyone's interested." He chuckled, "Anyone interested?"

Will winced as the women giggled politely. Kelly said, "Your pizza's getting cold, and we better order." They moved off, waving their goodbyes.

She was good-looking, Will admitted to himself, noting how short her dress was, but also that she had nice legs. Eileen still had the legs to wear a dress like that, though she never would. Kelly was bright, too, and young, forever young, forever too young. Still, the two of them were fun.

"So, you don't pay much attention to them, huh?"

He glanced at Barry, who wore a smug, canary-fed cat look. Will picked up a slice of pizza and dropped it in front of Barry. "Barry, eat your damn pizza."

Chapter 10.

Will walked through the kitchen door that night stiff in the neck and the back. Forster had collared him after lunch and congratulated him for having Maloney toe the line, then accosted him about the bad senate vote. Forster knew well enough that nothing more could be done than what was being done. Will knew that Comcon's president merely needed to vent, but it still cramped his load-bearing muscles to hear all about it again. That's the way the day had gone, a tiff with Julie, that goofy lunch with Barry Evans, and his own struggle with old poetry and new PR prose. The day was over, however, and he was home now.

He dumped his briefcase on the blond kitchen table, first pushing the pile of newspapers aside to make room. He draped his jacket and tie over the back of a matching chair and went to the refrigerator for a beer. He cracked the bottle open and strolled through the door past the dining room nook into the living room area. He halted in the middle of the high-vaulted room beneath the crystal light fixture that hung high over front door. Sitting perpendicular to each other on the French love seats, Eileen and Mike glowered in their own separate, hostile universes.

Oh shit, Will said to himself.

"What's up?" he asked as he continued toward them.

Eileen favored him with a nasty look and said, "Your wonderful genius son has gotten himself in deep at school."

"Oh yeah?" Will said. He shifted his attention to Mike, whose eyes were raised high staring into the distant ether above. "What'd you do, Mike?"

"Not much," he said.

"Not much? Not much?" Eileen cried angrily. "Your wheeler-dealer son tried to bribe his way onto the student council, that's all."

"Bribe? How'd he do that? Why?"

"God knows why, and he didn't do it, he got caught!"

"Oh, is that the bad thing, that I got caught?" Mike yelled. "I didn't do anything wrong; it wasn't a bribe."

"Well, then, what was it?" Eileen snapped.

"It was like a transaction," he said, "very much like a political contribution."

"To your own campaign?" she asked impatiently.

"What in the hell are you all talking about?" Will said loudly. "What the heck happened?"

Mike shifted his eyes back up at the ceiling while Eileen said, "Tell him, Mike." He said nothing, so she said harder, "Mike, tell your father what you did."

Mike continued to ignore them.

"What'd he do?" whined Will.

"He offered the kids in his homeroom ten bucks apiece if they would vote for him as their student council representative."

"What?" Will said. "How could he do that? Why? He never showed any interest in that stuff before."

"I don't know why. As for how, he asked the teacher and the other candidate to leave so that he could make a private address to the rest of the kids in his homeroom."

"What? They went along with that?"

"The teacher did, from what I was told. Your used-car salesman of a son talked him in to it. He said that it wasn't fair because the other kid had been on the council before where most of them had gone to middle school, except for Mike. Mike told him that because he had to go first alphabetically, the other kid could steal his ideas and say he thought of them, too. The teacher bought it."

Will gave Mike a stare. "You did this? No kidding," he said thoughtfully. "Where'd you come up with all this?"

Mike shrugged.

"In spite of the scheme's originality," Eileen said cooly, "let's not forget that Huey Long here tried to bribe his way on to the student council."

Will's face hardened, "Ten bucks a head? How many kids are in your class, twenty-five, thirty? What're we talking here, three hundred bucks?"

"Twenty-seven," Mike mumbled, "but I told them I'd pay only the first fourteen. I just needed that many to win."

"Jesus Christ," said Eileen, "how in God's name did you come up with all of this? It's like Tammany Hall all over again."

"Oh, come on, Eileen, we can get a little more current than that. How about Watergate or the Contra-Iran deal?" Will whipped his head back to Mike, "A hundred and forty bucks is still a lot of money, Mike. Where'd you get it?"

The frown on Mike's face suddenly morphed into worrisome. "I didn't lose any of it. The teacher made the kids give it back."

"Where'd you get the money?"

Will waited. Mike moved around on the couch, resting his forearms on his knees and dropping his head between them so that his parents couldn't see his face.

"Mickey, look at me," Will said quietly, sternly. "Mike," Eileen said softly, but he remained still. Will started to feel the constriction, the physical tightness caused by his restraint. From head to foot and back again, he looked at his rebellious son, loathing the long, dirty-looking hank of hair, the rumpled deep-purple shirt, the baggy Levis, the thread worn Converses. He blew out his breath slowly to control himself, and—?

"Mike, where are your shoes?"

His son tensed, then relaxed. "On my feet."

100

"Mike, you're beginning to piss me off."

"Will—"

"Never mind, Eileen. Where are your shoes, Mike, your new shoes?"

Mike raised his head to reveal himself, pale, imploring with his eyes.

"No, Mike, where are your new shoes, your new one-hundred-and-twenty-dollar shoes?" He watched the tears rise at the corners of his son's eyes, and he said, "Don't start that shit, Mike, not this time. I want to know."

But the tears ran, and Mike hiked his thorax in a huge sob.

"You sold them," Will said, "didn't you? You sold them for the money to buy your way on to the student council; is that right?"

Mike stopped crying. He seemed to think for an instance, then dropped his head out of sight again as he muttered, "Yes."

Eileen rolled her eyes and turned up her hands. Will threw himself down in the armchair opposite the couches, barking as he landed, "Shit."

He sat there clutching his arms folded tightly, wondering how things had become such a mess in so little time. His life seemed like a disaster movie at every juncture, work, home, dreams blunted wholesale. Now, here he was confronting a kid he used to like, his son, whom he still loved but was ready to kill on the spot. What more, he thought?

"I've had enough of this," Eileen said, "I'm leaving," she said as she rose and walked toward the kitchen.

"Well, thanks a lot Mother Theresa," Will said.

He brooded for a while, then turned to Mike. The kid was dry-faced, the tears done with their job. His lower lip stuck out like a nasty blue glacier, Nah-nah nah-nah-nah, Will thought. He would use a knife; no, a bludgeon, or his bare hands. But he didn't want to kill him, he was only a kid after all. Worse, he was a teenage kid. He didn't want to kill him, just his god-damn arrogance. That, he wanted to cut out of him with a big, long knife, attitude-surgery to save his life, to save both of their lives. The boy simply was troubled by becoming an adult. If they could just live together until he got over it, that's all. Maybe in separate parts of the house, he thought.

"If you'd let me get a job, I wouldn't have had to sell them," Mike said in a whiny voice.

Will darted the fingers on both hands to his temples and pressed hard. Slowly, he eased out his breath. "You're really beginning to piss me off, Mickey."

Later, Will had to admit to himself that Mike's ingenuity impressed him. Most pols on the Hill didn't operate that many moves ahead in their own campaign quests. Yet, Mike never had shown any noticeable inclination or aptitude for politics before. In wondering where this new, evidently hidden talent of Mike's had come from, Will felt himself warming up to the idea, pride mixed with a little guilt, that his son had sat at his table, had profited from his discourse on how things got done in Washington. He shook off the notion briskly. This didn't change the fact that the kid had tried to finance his way to high office. Ethics had been violated, fraud had been perpetrated; nearly perpetrated, anyway. Mike would have to pay the price, starting with the money.

"Where's the money, Mike?"

Mike's pout turned into a deeper dyspepsia, the expression of a bitter old man. Will marveled that a such a handsome youth as Mike, an assessment that he had made with complete objectivity many times in the past, could transform himself into such a mean-mouthed curmudgeon over as picayune a matter as a few hundred bucks. In fact, the uglier he became, the older he looked. Maybe he had something, here, Will thought, the key to the aging process.

"Mike, where's the money?"

Avoiding eye contact, Mike said, "Mom has it."

"Not true," singsonged Eileen from the kitchen.

Will frowned. Listening the whole time from the peanut gallery, he thought, while he dealt with it. And the little shit had lied again.

"Gimme the money," Will snapped.

"Mr. Johnson has it," said Mike.

"Gimme the goddam money before I hit you for the first time in your life, in my life." Maybe that was the problem, he fumed, even though what little rationality he had left in his brain told him, No.

Mike reached into the back pocket of his Levi's and produced a worn wallet. He opened it and handed a wad of bills to Will.

Will counted them, then stared at Mike. "One hundred and two. Where's the rest?"

Mike shrugged, "Gone."

Will gazed at his son. The gall of this kid. How had he survived for so long? He fingered through the money again, wondering what to do now. Make this a constructive thing, he decided, get something positive out of this whole mess.

"All right, you screwed up. Let's see if we can't figure out what we can salvage out of all this. First, I admire your initiative, I really do, and your willingness to sacrifice to get what you want. I know the shoes meant a lot to you. Though frankly, I thought it was pretty kid-like to, you know, want something so faddish that cost so much. They cost you too, you know what I mean? You had to use up some of your capital with your mother and myself to get the shoes. So, I think it's impressive that you made the decision to sacrifice the shoes for the council position. And,

I must admit, I like the idea that you would want to serve on the student council."

He watched Mike as he talked and was gratified to see him looking hopeful, his head up, his long wedge of hair occasionally brushed out of his eyes with his hand. Too bad the hard part had to come, now.

"But here's the thing," Will continued. "Your methods to win stink. If that's what you learned from me and your mother, then I don't know what to think. Wanting something and going after it is fine, Mickey. But going after it at all cost is not. It's wrong, Mike, plain and simple."

The boy seemed contrite. Hell, this is working out, Will thought. "So, you understand that, huh?"

"Yeah," Mike murmured.

"Okay. Now, the money. Let's try and shed some positive light on this situation. We'll take these hundred and two dollars and put them in your savings account for college later on."

Mike suddenly paled. Will blinked. What's this?

"Listen, I don't think you should be thinking about shoes at this point, do you? I know, I gave you the money, but considering everything, I think the best thing to do now is to build on some of the encouraging traits you showed, like this new interest in school and student government."

Mike was perspiring freely, now.

"Hey, the money will still be yours, technically, just on hold. You know, if you want it for something worthwhile before college, that'll be fine. Mike, I'm not even worried about the other thirty-eight bucks. We can forget that. Mike? Mickey, are you okay?"

Mike lifted his head. His face was white and shiny like Mother of Pearl inside a clam shell.

"Are you sick, Mike?"

"No," he stammered. "That's a good idea, Dad. I'll deposit the money tomorrow."

Will pulled his head back. His nose wrinkled as he pondered his sweating son with the fish-belly face. "Mike, go get your passbook. I want to see it."

The lanky boy slumped on the couch as though in one swift motion someone had yanked out all of the tendons holding his bones together.

"Mike!" Will snarled.

Mike reached into his other back pocket with the solemn deliberation of a priest presiding over a dirge. He extended the little green book to his father in a movement so graceful through its indiscernible pace that Will wondered if he wasn't witnessing an ancient funereal dance, or maybe the last walk of a political prisoner to the firing squad.

He thumbed open the book and found what he expected. One hundred, forty dollars had been withdrawn just this past Friday.

He peered up with bullet eyes and bored through his son's head. "Where are the shoes?"

Mike hesitated, then said, "At school." But it came out squeaky, almost like a question as though he was trying the idea out.

"Shall we drive down to school to get them?"

Mike started to ball, and Will said in a cutting-edge voice, "Don't cry, don't cry or I'll drown you in your own tears, I swear. Mike, God!" he shouted, grabbing the sides of his own head with both hands, "where are your shoes?"

Mike blubbered, "I lost them."

"You lost them?"

"I lost them."

"How the fuck did you do that?"

"Willy!" Eileen called, walking in from the kitchen.

"Cut it, Eileen. You left it up to me, so don't butt in now. How did you lose them, Mike?" he insisted, watching Eileen pivot back toward the kitchen. He heard the side door slam shut and thought, Great.

"I left them in the locker room. When I came back to get them, they were gone."

"Oh, no," Will said, dropping his hands to his sides as he fell against the back of the easy chair.

"I'm sorry," Mike stuttered, heaving the syllables.

"Yeah, you're sorry. So am I."

Will rubbed his face hard, trying to rearrange everything. He sighed, "Mickey, I love you so much, but you do these things that make me want to murder you. You've been on a roll, Mike, a terrible roll. And you've lied all along the way, which is unacceptable."

He wondered how this could have happened, all of it, in such short order. Was the kid going bad? He dismissed the idea immediately; no wrongful deaths had occurred, no pregnancies, thank God, no drugs, no grand larceny, at least not yet anyway. No, the real agonizing thoughts didn't center around the idea that the boy would become Vlad the Impaler, or Lucky Luciano, or even Michael Milken. The real worry was that Mike would become a complete screw-up, a guy who smokes dope then runs a train into a tree, or the ship captain of his day and age's Valdez. Or maybe he'll just sweep floors and drink cheap beer. That would be so sad, he thought. Mike was a smart kid, despite what his anemic grades might indicate. He just hadn't hit his stride yet, and being a teenager was so hard, so demoralizing. The poor kid needed help, he needed to be encouraged, not put down. He probably needed more time spent with the family doing constructive things. Of course, how much time did Eileen and himself take with Mike? Hell, they could hardly wait for him to be more independent like his older sister so that they could do

106

some of the things that they'd put off while he was growing up. But they'd abandoned him too early, it seemed. Their son was adrift. The second kid always takes it on the chin, thought Will. And Mike was really a good kid, a sweet child, who didn't deserve being alone in the world. Things would have to change, and that left it up to his old man.

Will pulled himself upright in the chair. "All right, Mike, new ball game, a new order will be established."

Mike had stopped crying except for an occasional sniffle. He wiped at his nose with his wrist as he listened, his head still down.

"First, you're grounded until further notice. That means that you come home from school, have your snack or whatever, and two hours of R and R, until I get home. Television is out. You can read, you can fool around in the backyard by yourself. No friends for any reason. No telephone."

"Dad," Mike whined.

"Quiet. You set yourself up for this, so here it is. When I get home, you and I will assemble in my office, the laundry room. Get the card table and a lamp from your room, get your books, and whatever else you might need to do your homework. Each night you will present me with your homework assignments in written form. You will inform me of your exams schedule. While we are waiting for dinner, you will do your homework while I work on the computer."

"God, Dad, you sound like the Gestapo. When did you join the Thought Police?"

"Shut up."

"Jeez!"

"On weekends, we will meet at ten in the morning to work on your homework. At noon, we will have lunch, and then do some activity together, physical or cultural, I don't know. But it will be beneficial."

"Oh, great. PBS here I come."

"That's right, buddy-boy. It's not going to be any day at the beach for me, either. But I feel partially responsible for this downward spiral that you seem to have embraced. Therefore, I'm going to do my best to give you an opportunity to right yourself. Whether or not you take advantage of it, well, that's your prerogative. But from here on in, Mickey old boy, I'm your new shadow. You and I are gonna be pals."

"Well, that's just great. You're going to wreck my life just because I made one mistake."

"You made more than one mistake, Mike, you've made it into an art form. And look to yourself, if you want to start assigning blame. It's my job to do my best at least, to see that this stuff stops. Now, go get the card table set up. Be there with your books in ten minutes. I'm going to find your mother and inform her of the way things are going to be around here from now on, so that we don't get any missed signals."

Mike trudged upstairs to his room, barely keeping his litany of complaints inaudible.

Will walked through the kitchen out the back door. Eileen's car was gone, which meant that he would have to start dinner alone. Well, the mindlessness of it might give him down time to figure out how he was going to explain all of this to her. It didn't take a genius to figure out that she would find flaws in the program, most likely centering around how this would affect his big push to win the vice presidency. He cringed at thought of the coming confrontation, but what else could he do? Mike was really floundering, and he had to do something to save him. Right or wrong, Will thought, he had to act.

Chapter 11.

At noontime the next day, Eileen sat in the garden restaurant near a fern, the autumn leaves capably blocking out the cloudy glare glowing through the large windows. The place was a favorite, a Salvadorian-Mexican eatery with reproductions of French Impressionists on the inside beige walls above waist-high mahogany paneling. The tables were covered with thick linen tablecloths and napkins, with heavy porcelain plates decorated in pastel floral patterns at each setting.

She sipped a little of her white wine, then frowned, causing an alert waiter to ask her if the vintage was off. Absent-mindedly, she shook her head, No, and gave him a glimpse of her brilliant smile to assure him that all was well. He grinned broadly himself, showing one of his front teeth full of gold, and left. She returned to her dour thoughts.

How could things get worse when they were already the worst? She leaned her head against the side of her hand propped by an elbow. Willy had gone nuts, she decided. Not only did he want to be the poet laureate of his own private little world, now he aspired to be Superdad, or Superparent, even, excluding her with infuriating disdain. The last week had been a mess, Willy urging her that they had to leave work at five-thirty sharp to get home to Mike, and Mike complaining to her constantly about what a dictator Will had become. And the quarreling, the running fight from the moment they arrived home through dinner, the dishes, and the hassling about homework. Will climbed on Mike; Mike bitched all the way down the stairs to the laundry room.

"The computer makes too much noise," Mike would say, "I can't concentrate."

"Funny, it doesn't bother you when you're doing an essay or playing a game," Will retorted.

"That's different. I don't hear it when I'm working on it."

"Yeah, well, get used to it. It's not going to change."

"So, how am I supposed to get anything done? I can't study, blah blah-blah blah-blah."

And so on, and on, and on, she sighed. They were driving her crazy and ignoring her at the same time. Mary never called anymore, either. And when they called her, she was never in.

Eileen took another sip of wine, thinking, I'm beginning to feel less like a parent than ever before; parentless.

"Eileen, you're drinking too much; look how depressed you are."

She looked up to see Harry pulling back his chair to sit down.

"Hello, Harry. Do I look depressed? I feel it."

"Sorry I'm late."

"And I can't blame it on the wine, either," she said. "This is my first glass."

"Yes, but you usually don't drink anything at lunch. Did you order?"

"Of course not. Why are you late?" she asked, seeing him for the first time. He wore a beautifully cut blue wool suit, double-breasted, highlighted by thin gold pinstripes. He sat loose-limbed in the captain's chair pushed back from the table to give his long legs more room, which played out crookedly on either side. With his suit coat open, and his hands resting on his slight paunch, he struck her as the embodiment of ease. It was a man's pose, she thought, and like nothing out of the *Fashions of The Times*. The young hunks in those ads were sharp and on the make, upwardly mobile, career-wise. Harry was too old for that image and anyway, he already had it made. He really didn't care how and he looked, he liked how he felt.

Different for women, thought Eileen, even in the nineties. Young college girls could sit like that if they were wearing pants, jeans more likely. When they entered the work force, however, they reverted to *Vogue* postures, head up, shoulders back, spine ramrod straight, legs together or crossed demurely, but with plenty of sexual signals. Unless they felt like crap, she thought. Then, they just slumped over the table, nursing their drink like everybody else.

She peered at Harry's face. His blond looks were the real thing, even his eyelashes were blond, if not white. His lids were pinkish at the edge and she expected that any mucous membrane of his would prove to be the same. Not a trace of melanin in this man's family tree, at least not for half a million years. She wondered how she liked that? What would their kids have looked like if she had married Harry twenty years ago instead of Willy?

"Are you listening to me?" he said.

"Huh?" she said.

"I said are you listening to me?"

"Yeah, sure. What did you say?"

"I said traffic."

"Traffic?"

"Yeah, traffic. The reason I was late. Traffic on the 14th Street Bridge coming back from the Pentagon. I don't know why it was jammed at this hour, but it was. Had to run up onto the sidewalk to save time. Since it was Adams Morgan, I figured it was just some bleeding-heart liberals I was mowing down. Oh, maybe I knocked over some Latin Americans, but they're a bunch of commies anyway."

"Oh."

"'Oh,' huh? Oh boy. My best P.J. O'Rourke and you're still in the dumpster."

He was a good-looking man, nice features, if a bit pudgy. No exercise, too much work. Or play. But that was why he was a success; he dedicated himself tirelessly to the work at hand without allowing distractions to interfere. Then, again, the downside did exist. He was just as extreme when partying.

"Harry," Eileen said," when you got your divorce, how did you feel about it?"

Harry pulled himself up in the chair. "Oh, you're in the domestic dumpster. How did I feel about it? What do you think? Terrible. It was a resounding failure on all fronts in every way."

"Did you think, though, after all, that it was the right thing to do? Or, maybe, to have happened?"

Harry moved his chair closer to the table. "You mean, if I'd known it was coming, would I have done anything to change it so that it wouldn't happen? Hell, I don't know; if we'd had kids, maybe." He swung his head back and forth, "I knew it was coming. I started spending more time at the office instead of less. I guess I was as happy as she was to see it over."

He shrugged his shoulders. "She's happily remarried to a guy in commercial real estate. I'm off of the alimony roller coaster, thank God. But she's still a good woman. I still like the old girl."

He reached for his water and drank, then stared into his glass. "So, why do you ask?" he said.

"Oh, it's Will," she said, "he's driving me crazy." She took a sip of her wine. "I probably shouldn't even be talking to you about this, Harry, you know. But he doesn't even seem to be trying anymore. And things are not great in his neck of the woods, believe me."

"What do you mean?"

"I mean with the senate committee hearing, and Maloney, and all the rest. He just doesn't seem to care."

"He's doing his job. The testimony he passed around for the hearing was very sharp," Harry said, "right on target. Forster loved it."

"Yeah, until the committee tore into him. Then he hated it."

"They must've had their minds made up beforehand. You can't blame Will for that."

"Sure, but he's supposed to push harder when things are tough, not back off, right? I mean, he's even got Maloney wondering what's what."

"How so?" Harry said. He leaned his elbows on the tabletop.

"Maloney's scared senseless about the election. He thinks this Macowiac chick could give him a run. He started making noises to Will that he was thinking of voting for budget cuts, and you know what that means."

"I thought Will had brought him back into the fold?"

"That's because Maloney thought he was getting more funds for his campaign." She put her head conspiratorially close to Harry's as she continued, "But the company's contribution limit is maxed out, says Will. He told Maloney that he'd go to the association, but evidently no one there's come up with any cash either. So, Maloney's griping again."

"Huh," Harry said, sitting back.

"And Willy won't do anything about it. Jesus, I shouldn't be telling you this," she said, drinking more wine, "but he's killing me on this, Harry, he really is."

"I'm getting that." Harry rubbed his chin, "Will's a good guy, a stand-up guy. He wouldn't just bag it. The association could be out of money, too, election day's only a month away. Maloney probably waited too long before getting scared by this Macowiac person."

"That doesn't change which way he's leaning on the budget talks and ComCon. And I just don't know how hard Will is going after him."

"Unhuh." Harry rolled the empty wine glass at his place by the stem between his fingers. "Well, look. Maloney's going to get it from both sides. The Army POM has QMIV in its must-have column, and you know I just saw Norton again today. He's right in line, right behind us. I'll call him when we get back to the office and have him give a jingle to the Honorable Congressman from Pennsylvania."

Eileen stared hard into his eyes, "That's really great, Harry. But don't you see, that's what Will ought to be doing."

Harry shrugged, "Maybe he is. Redundancy never hurt anything in the defense business."

"Yeah, well I doubt that he's doing anything of the sort, unless it's writing a poem, 'Ode to Maloney'." She shook her head in despair, "What kind of a vice president would Willy make compared to you?"

"Not much," Harry said. When her head snapped up, he said, "Just kidding. Will can do the job, if he wants it. Maybe he does, maybe he doesn't. One true thing, though, Eileen. Will impresses everyone at ComCon as a really nice guy, but not a pushover. He's tough, you know? So, don't sell him short."

Gazing at him, Eileen was almost startled by the realization of how serious Harry seemed to be, as if it was the most important point he'd ever made. "I'm surprised to hear you say that, Harry, considering that it's between you and Will for the promotion."

"Yeah, sure, but what's true is true. Will is no lightweight. You shouldn't lose sight of that."

"No, you're right. He's amazing when he wants to be."

She toyed with her fork, her mood interrupted by the reappearance of the waiter with the gold tooth.

"Señora," he said, "are you ready to order?"

"No, no thanks. I'm not hungry. Tell you what. I'll have another glass of wine and one of those wonderful hard rolls of yours, hot. And bring me plenty of butter."

The waiter nodded, then turned to Harry.

"I'll have the quesadilla, some fried plantain, and a couple of chimichangas, beef. Oh, and bring some sour cream with that, the low cholesterol stuff, okay? Thanks."

"Low cholesterol sour cream?" Eileen said, "As if that's going to make a difference?"

"Excess in moderation, Eileen, the motto I live by."

She laughed, "We'll see how long, Harry."

He laughed, then said soberly, "Really, Eileen, how bad is it between you and Will? At home, I mean. How far along are you two, sliding from domestic bliss to the abyss?" asking the last in a suddenly awkward, joking manner.

Eileen lifted her head and looked at Harry as though seeing him for the first time. For the first time she saw something that made her think carefully before she said, "I don't know."

"You do know, though that if there is anything I can do for you," Harry said, his eyes appearing to open wider, his expression one of clear sincerity, "and Will," he trailed off.

Again, in a reflective tone, Eileen replied, "Thanks, Harry. I'll think about that."

Chapter 12.

Can not a plain man live and think no harm
But thus, his simple truth must be abused
By silken, sly, insinuating Jacks?

Reading the verse, Mike wondered why his father had left it on the screen. The line below said 'Shakespeare' Mike thought. So, what was it supposed to mean?

He closed the file and ran the cursor up and down the directory:

POETRY.OLD, POETRY.NEW, POETRY.THE,
POETRY.REF, POETRY.JOU, PROSE.SCRAPS.

The old dork seemed obsessed by the stuff, Mike thought, the Tyrant, of all people. What did he have to complain about, he wasn't being enslaved against his will just for one little mistake. He had a lot of nerve Mike thought, pretending to be the sensitive type. How sensitive could a cop be?

He picked a file at random POETRY.NEW and opened it.

Marching with the Ants

Amid the blades of grass and
through the craggy ravines between
the flagstones of the backyard sidewalk,
Row upon row upon row
of ants

marshal up;
Warrior ants without fear
of deadly draws
that kill them just as dead
as victory in the jaws snatched,
Though perhaps not as deadening
as dreadful defeat,
Hit so hard the family dies
and alongside the Queen lies
for curious boys to pick up
the chafe of carapace, precious
bodily liquids long gone,
the product ebbed first post strife.
Still, the ants assemble
shouldering their way ahead
in loose formation, thoughtless driven
to dispute with pincer havoc
a mountain crust of bread.

A poem about ants? Mom was right, Mike nodded, the old man was losing his shit. Mike read the poem again. He thought he had figured out what 'marshal' meant, but he had no idea what 'chafe of carapace' was. He supposed that he could look it up, but what for? He knew the meaning of other words in the poem, but none of the sentences they were in made any sense to him at all. 'Nonsen-tencesical,' his English teacher would say, unless his dad really was writing about watching a bunch of ants fighting over bread crusts. Was this something that had happened in the old guy's life, Mike wondered, an old memory or something from when he was a kid? But so what? What's so great about being a bloodthirsty little twerp who likes to watch ants fight?

He shook his head, parents are weird. They all want the same thing; they want everything to stay the same. Like, if that happens, he thought, everyone will be safe. When Arnold crushes guys in *The Terminator* and *Terminator II*, who does he kill? Line up their moms and dads and see how they feel about it. He remembered watching reruns of *The A Team*, or *The Untouchables* deep into cable TV, and seeing them spray the place with bullets, a hundred million a second. Then, all these bad dudes would flinch and go for cover. But not one of them would fly apart or spit blood, not one had been hit. None of them looked like the dead people in Newsweek, some Mafia guy shot dead, lying outdoors between cafe tables, his shirt sponging up really wet, red blood, darker pools of it going out around him like spilled oil or crabapple concentrate.

He studied pictures like that, and black and white photographs of guys about to go in front of firing squads, standing before holes that they had dug for their graves. Before and after shots, standing fearful in front of the hole, then dead inside. He'd look back and forth, before and after, wondering what the difference was, alive, then dead, alive here, dead there. He thought about these guys when they were digging their own graves, how they must have felt, like maybe when they saw a worm crawl out of the side, soon to crawl all over them. Did they kill the worm, cringing at the thought of the creepy crawler sliming on their cheeks, up their noses? Or did they dig carefully around it, granting it more life than they soon would have? Did they dig as slowly as possible, hoping for some miracle to save them, did they dig deep, hoping to escape to China? Except a lot of times they were Chinese, or Asian, anyway, Vietnamese from old war pictures, or maybe Spanish-looking guys from South America. They all looked scrawny, never big football players, never blond. They looked small, dark, and scared to death of death. So, which was he supposed to believe, Arnold whacking guys left and right in his movies, or the still pictures in the news?

Parents wanted to protect their kids from that stuff, which is why they bitched about Arnold's movies, and Steven Seagal. Yet, his dad had lapped up the *Terminators*, and they really were great flicks. So, why did they try? They couldn't keep kids from stuff that was real, especially if they were into it themselves.

Like when they tried to keep him from his first drink. He remembered going around the morning after a party thrown by his parents, searching for Maraschino cherries in half-empty drinks. He found a lot of half-filled beer bottles, too. He wiped a few necks clean and took a couple of swigs, but the beer tasted warm and coarse, terrible. The mixed drinks were better if they were sweet, but he soon decided that he preferred ginger ale straight. Booze was easy to come by if he wanted it, though. His parents couldn't keep him from it any better than from drugs. It was more a question of what he wanted, not of what he could get. He only had to decide.

Maybe life had been simpler for his folks. What did they have to deal with except maybe nuclear destruction? Sex was cool, even drugs were cool back then. Life was harder for kids nowadays, he thought, too many dangerous things sitting right in the next seat. He remembered when he'd been happy, worrying only about the toys he had to play with, and when school was out, the richness of Saturdays in front of the TV watching cartoons. He could remember wonderful things, the smell of toast, the smell of fabric softener from the vent outside when the dryer was on, and honeysuckle nectar, sucking the sweet stems of honeysuckle in an endless summer vacation. He remembered his mom trying to make his bed while he was still in it, laughing and laughing. Nothing had been wrong then, everything had been right.

When had it all changed? Sometimes he would look in his closet at his old toys, even touching them, running his fingers lightly across the boxes of his favorite ones. But he never played with them anymore. Somewhere along the way he'd stopped, or kept putting it off because he didn't have time. When had things changed, when did he start noticing that not every movie was terrific, that some books weren't very good?

It all changed, of course, when he found out that he was left unloved by Karen. Oh Karen, Karen. How could his parents ever understand his devotion to her? He would be her slave if he could, even after the way she had treated him. If she gave him the chance, he would show her how much he cared, and she would change her feelings for him, she'd have to in the face of his overwhelming love. I'm so overflowing with love for you, he would say, I'm running out of love-fill. There are barges out there on the far oceans searching for a place to land to deposit their load of my love for you.

He shook his head. Until the time came when he had the chance to tell her, he would have to suffer alone. He would work until it happened, though, follow his plan and hope for the best. If not, make a new plan, and another one if necessary, forever. He would never give up, he loved her so. How could his parents know about such love? They couldn't; all they could do was get in the way. It was all so frustrating, he thought, nothing like he'd ever felt when he was a kid. The simple days of being a kid were over, he realized, and knowing it suddenly made him miss them.

He sighed, then squinted his concentration as a thought struck him. He started to look intently at his dad's poem again when he heard the screen door slam upstairs. Quickly, he exited the file and called up the Shakespeare quote. He jumped out of the secretary chair and into the folding seat in front of the card table. By the time his dad walked into the room, Mike appeared to be studiously absorbed in his history book.

"Faking again, I see," Will said.

"You got it," said Mike without looking up from the book. Out of the corner of his eye he could see that his father had come straight downstairs after entering the house. He stood there still in his raincoat, his scarf draped outside of the lapels.

"As I recall, you're supposed to be on the chapter before this one."

"Oh," said Mike, turning to the proper page.

"What were you really doing?"

"Snooping on the computer."

"Oh? Stayed out of the forbidden files I hope?" Will asked.

"You mean the porno stuff?"

"Hell, no, I don't care if you read that. It's the family finances that are off limits."

"Oh, I don't bother with those. I already know we're too poor for me to think about garroting you and Mom for the inheritance."

"Garroting? Can you spell it, even?"

"Yes," said Mike, incensed.

"Well, that's better than I can do. So, what were you looking at, Shakespeare here?"

"Yeah, that," Mike trailed off.

"Unhuh," said Will. He draped his raincoat and scarf over the back of the secretary's chair and sat down in front of the screen.

"What's it supposed to mean?" asked Mike.

"Oh, the usual, life is tough. It's from a speech by Richard himself, and it's meant to be ironic. Though, sometimes it's not."

"Why *Richard III*?"

"It's my favorite play of Shakespeare's. Though, most critics don't consider it to be one of his best. You know, the character progresses from A to A. But he's so deliciously bad, hilarious, really, in his relentless evil-doing. The play's very popular for that reason."

"Oh."

"Yeah. I suppose I'd do better reading his sonnets, though."
Will finally got up enough pluck to ask, "So, did you look at
anything else?" He dreaded his son's answer, yes or no.

"Yeah."

"Oh?"

"Yeah, one of your poems."

"Which one? How did you like it?" Why did he care what a
fourteen-year-old kid thought of what he was doing? But he did,
maybe because he thought that what he had wrought from his
hard, hard labor was only suitable for that age group.

"Ants. The one about ants." Mike wondered how he was
going to break this to him. The guy was an ogre most of the time,
but sometimes he was like a puppy ogre. "I don't get it, I think."
Shit, he thought, look at his dad's face drooping like putty. Afraid
that it might fall off completely, Mike quickly followed with, "I
don't understand poetry, I guess."

"It's not hard to understand, Mike. Here."

Will opened the file and sent the cursor skimming down the
short verse. "It's a pretty simple effort," murmured Will.

"How come it doesn't rhyme?" Mike said, trying desperately
to make his ignorance as basic-sounding as possible.

"They don't all rhyme, Mike," Will said with some irritation.
"I'd expect you to know that much after nine years of school."

"We didn't study poetry in grade school, Dad."

"Yeah. Look here, see, it's not just rhyme, it's rhythm, too,
and particularly the sound. This is supposed to sound like
something, you understand? 'Backyard sidewalk, . . . 'row upon
row upon row,' . . . even 'deadly draws' and 'deadening, dreadful
defeat,'—the repetition of all the 'ds' is a trick of sound. You
must have learned alliteration in English?"

"I don't know. Maybe."

"Come on, didn't you have to read any Dylan Thomas? 'Do
not go gentle into that night.'

"Maybe. I don't know."

"Huh. Well, he's the master of that sort of thing. This about the ants, I was trying to write a few lines like that, with the sound of a word counting as much as the meaning itself. Of course, I'm hardly any Dylan Thomas. There's a lot of precious stuff in this piece, all those 'ds.' Alliteration's pretty weak when it's overdone. The whole thing's just an experiment."

Both of them gazed at the screen for a time without saying a word. Mike finally said, "But why poetry, Dad? I mean, what for?"

"It's a way to express feelings. It's like how to make sense out of the world in an emotional way."

Peering up at Mike, Will realized that his son wasn't following him, probably because he himself felt that he was on shaky ground. "Look, it's a need I have. It helps me feel calmer."

"Mom says you're crazy for writing poetry."

"Yeah, well, mothers shouldn't tell kids that their fathers are crazy," even if they are, he thought. "You have homework to do?"

"Yes."

"How about the English paper? Did you get it done?"

"Dad, it's been done, handed in, and returned back to me."

"Oh? What'd you get?"

"I got a D+."

"What?" Will felt as though an aneurysm had blown in his brain. "How could you get a D+? You worked on that paper for two weeks!"

"The teacher said I didn't do the right assignment."

"Well, damn it, Mike, how did that happen? I saw the assignment, it was pretty straightforward, how did you screw it up?"

"I didn't!" he cried, and Will watched him retreat behind his blind of hair, with only a corner of his mouth showing, turned down in that self-pitying pout. "She said do a report on a classic book, and I did."

"Get the paper out."

Mike collapsed in a surly heap on the folding chair and began to search through his knapsack. He pulled out a pair of wrinkled pieces of paper and thrust them in the direction of his father. Will snapped them out of his hand and looked at the first page.

The big red D+ burned into his eyes, making him miss the title for an instant:

The Lowdown on Little Red—

He did a double-take, and read again:

The Lowdown on Little Red Riding Hood

For the love of—fuck!

Chapter 13.

"Mike, God-damn it! What were you doing? What were you thinking?"

"It's a classic! I read it, and I wrote the paper about it, two full pages, like she said."

"You won't quit, will you? You have to keep doing shit like this just to piss me off."

"She didn't think it was all that bad."

"Oh yeah, good enough for a D+!" Will tossed the paper at Mike, but it curled into the air before it reached him and wafted to the floor. "Get your ass into your room. I'll call when I'm over wanting to strangle you."

Mike stomped his way up out of the basement.

Will stared at the floor, his hands draped helplessly across his knees. After a few minutes of slack-jawed rumination, he focused on the rumpled paper at his feet, D+ blaring. He picked it up and began to read.

For years, kids have read Little Red Riding Hood with their parents and teachers telling them that it was a really good story. In case you haven't read it, this little girl named Little Red Riding Hood is sent into the woods by her mom to visit her grandmother. She's called Little Red Riding Hood because she wears this red cape with a hood on top. The reason she is visiting her grandmother is because her grandmother is sick, so, she's bringing her a basket of goodies (what goodies, the reader is left wondering about.) Anyway, Little meets a wolf in the woods, and he gets the idea that she would make a pretty good meal, so he hops on over to grandmother's house and eats her up, sort of an appetizer, I guess, but a pretty big one, too. And you have to wonder how he could have room for Little Red after that, but that's the way the story goes. So, he dresses up in grandmother's clothes and waits for Little Red Riding Hood to get there.

Little Red Riding Hood gets to grandma's house, and the wolf starts getting ready to eat her, but first she begins to notice that something's not right about her grandmother: big eyes, big ears, big teeth. Little kids reading this story must really think of the wolf as being cruel to play with Little Red before eatng her, which he could have done at any time. Actually, the wolf acts more like a cat than a dog-type animal, cats known to play with their victims before eating them. So maybe the story would have been better if it had been a mountain lion. But then you have to have Little Red going to grandma's over a mountain, which complicates things. Back to the story, just as the wolf is about to make his move, a woodsman bursts into the house and whacks the wolf with his axe. Grandma jumps out of the wolf alive in one piece, and they thank the woodsman, The End.

As I said at the beginning, kids are taught to love this story, the Big Bad Wolf gets his, and grandma and Little Red are reunited in love. But I say that this is a bad story for kids. For a lot of reasons. First, what mother in her right mind sends her kid off alone into the woods? She even tells her in some versions (I read four) to keep an eye out for the wolf. Yet, she sends her out there alone with a basket of goodies! To make matters worse, the kid is wearing a red cape! Any wolf with half-good eyesight could spot that cape a hundred miles away. Yet, there she is.

This brings up another point. What kind of mom names her kid Little Red Riding Hood anyway? Mother's who really like their children name them regular names, like Sally, Pete, or Betty, not after articles of clothing. I mean, even if she shortened Little Red Riding Hood to Li'l, it would sound more like a real name. But, no, it's Little Red Riding Hood all the way.

Not to mention that she's wearing this riding hood, but does she ever ride anywhere? If there's a horse or a car available, why isn't she on it? The evidence is mounting: Little Red Riding Hood could have been set up. Was it by her mother? Her grandmother? Maybe both of them were in on it, maybe for some inheritance that went directly to Little Red from her father who mysteriously never appears in the story, I might add. Neither does her grandfather. Did her mom and grandmother do away with them, too? I mean, has anyone thought to check mom and grandma's phone records?

Thinking that maybe the story has been changed over the years, I did some more research on how it used to be told originally. The only difference is that the woodsman's work is more bloody, and grandma doesn't make it. But the poor motherhood revealed in this story is still there, which makes me say again that this story, classic though it is called, is really not a very good story for little children.

Will sat back after finishing. Jesus, he thought. He read the hand-written comment by the teacher at the end:

> Your work shows talent (especially humor!), but
> it is not an appropriate response to the assignment.
> Please see me after class.

Will stood and headed upstairs. He walked down the hallway to his son's bedroom and knocked on the slightly ajar door.

"Mike, it's me."

"What do you want?"

"I want to talk to you."

He entered the room, stepping gingerly over the dirty clothes strewn across the floor. The room was a frenzy of torn and faded posters, skateboarding stars, Pink Floyd, Guns and Roses, Arnold Schwarzenegger as Conan, Dinotopia, Aliens, and of all things, The Beatles. Mike recently had tried to put up one of

Cindy Crawford, but Eileen nixed it on anti-sexist grounds. Will remembered thinking out loud that it was too bad, and Eileen almost crowned him with one of Mike's old T-ball trophies.

Books lay everywhere, science fiction, fantasy, school texts intermingled with plastic models, F16s, MIG 25s, and the Starship Enterprise: the Next Generation. Soft music played from the box on the desk situated below the only window in the room. Mike lay on the bottom of a bunkbed in the corner to the right of the desk, his face buried in his pillow. Will maneuvered over to the desk chair and carefully moved it around to face the bed. He sat and said, "Mike, I'm sorry. It's not that bad a paper. In fact, for what it is, it's really good, really a lot of fun to read."

"I know that," Mike mumbled scornfully, "Why do you think I wrote it that way? I can do this stuff, Dad, when I want to. Don't you know that by now?"

Will sat back. "Oh. Well, what did your teacher say, what's her name?"

"Harper."

"What did Ms. Harper say? I mean, after class. You did see her after class like she asked, right?"

"Yes!" he answered. "She said what you just said, that it was good, but that I didn't do the assignment right."

"Well, what were you supposed to be doing, what were you supposed to be reading."

"She gave us a list of books. I didn't like any of them, so I did this instead."

"Mike, how did you know you didn't like any of them if you never read them."

"I don't know. They sounded stupid. So I did what I wanted." He lifted his head and sneered, "I had something to say about Little Red Riding Hood."

Will had to laugh, which caused Mike to start giggling.

"God, Mike, you are funny. It is funny, and I am sorry for jumping on you. But, jeez, Mike, a D+. What can we do about that?"

"Harper said I could do another paper, and she'd change the grade if it was better."

"Well, all right!"

"All right? Dad, I'll have to read one of those stupid books, and she's given us a lot more crap to do since."

"Mike, you've got to do something about that D. Come on, Buddy, I'm trying to work with you on this. Can't you try just a little bit?"

"But Dad, it doesn't mean anything to me. School is so boring."

"How did it get so boring in only two years, Mike? You used to be a number one student until last year, and this. Shit, you were always good in English, even last year. What's going on?"

"Dad, I'm miserable in school. My life sucks. I should drop out when I'm sixteen and get a job. Pay you and Mom some rent, do something useful. School's a waste."

"Oh, Mike," Will said, rubbing his hand over his eyes. "Don't talk like that, that would be my worst nightmare. Don't you know that it gets better after high school, that it really gets great in college? I know it doesn't seem like it now, but it's true. You've got to trust me on this one, Mike, I've been there. But to get there, you have to take care of things now, even when you don't want to."

"Dad," Mike said, raising himself to lean on both hands, "I don't care about college or the future, I care about now! I want to do what I want to now, not plan for something that might never happen."

He collapsed into the pillow again, which caused Will to hold off his immediate rejoinder. Of course the kid was miserable, just like he had been at his age, just like every other kid in the world.

Except maybe for Masai warriors, he thought, who knew exactly when they were adults, after a bloody but portentous ceremony. Before he could hammer at Mike for screwing up his life, he knew that he had to recognize that immediate things were important to him now. Hell, that was true at any age. How many people really planned beyond the weekend?

He needed to find out what Mike wanted and try to work it in with his responsibilities. Equal time; even if what his son wanted sounded crazy to him, he had to at least consider it and go along with it if it wasn't madness, like joining the Marines or something. Like writing poetry, he thought ruefully.

"Mike, what could help make you less miserable right now? What could you do to make school better?"

Mike's ears pricked up. He almost couldn't believe what he was hearing. His dad was giving him an opening, one he'd never expected to get, not in a million years, and all because of a stupid paper he'd written the night before it was due. He leaped.

"I want to join the wrestling team."

Will blinked twice as involuntarily his mind neoned the word Marines, Marines, over and over again. "Wrestling?"

"Yeah. I really want to try out, Dad, I think I'd be good. The coach says I'm long and lean, a perfect build for wrestling, he says."

"Mike, wrestling? It's really tough, they run you into the ground and starve you near to death. You won't be allowed to eat, Mike, have you thought of that?"

"Ha-ha, very funny. Really, Dad, I really want to do this."

Will felt thrown for a loop. Mike never had shown any inclination whatsoever toward sports, not ever. The boy essentially spent his time lounging around like a man-size clump of noodles stuck together. As sure as the sun burned skin, Will knew that his poor, attenuated son was going to get his butt kicked. And he had to let him do it.

"Entertaining the idea that you could go out for wrestling, Mike, that still does not relieve you of your high school duties. Frankly, based upon your performance during the past two years, I shouldn't even be considering it."

"Oh, Dad, I'll study, I promise! I'll get good grades, I vow it! You won't have to worry about my schoolwork if you let me do this. Please, please, please let me wrestle."

For some bizarre reason, Will felt like a Maine farmer just about to send his only son off to the Civil War to defend the Union and the family's honor. "Okay—"

"Yes! Oh, yes!"

"Conditionally. It starts when, the third week of November? That gives us just over a month for you to get your academic act together. By the time I'm supposed to sign the parental okay, I want to see vast improvement in your grades on every front. Starting with redoing this paper."

"Gee, Dad, it'll be too tough to get all of my grades up and do that paper over, too. Can't I start clean after it?"

"Nope," Will said shaking his head. "That's the deal. Take it or leave it. By the way, the rest of the arrangement stays the same, too. You at the card table every afternoon. That doesn't change."

"God!" Mike sat on the edge of his bed, mulling over the pros and cons. Finally, he exhaled and said, "Okay, it's a deal."

"Good. Go get the book list Ms. Harper gave you."

"With one condition."

"Hey!"

"You got a condition, so I should get one, too, right? Fair's fair."

Will beetled his brows, then said, "What is it?"

"The Parent's Athletic Booster Club is having a father-son touch football game to raise money. You join the Club, and we play."

"Aw, hell, Mike, I haven't played football for twenty years."

"You have too, you play at picnics."

"Yeah, but the Booster Club's going to be serious about it, Mike. They're going to have Boosters playing!"

"That's the deal, Dad."

"Aw, nuts. All right." Mike grinned, making Will want to cut it short. "Go get the list."

The list read like a literary nerd's revenge. *Tristam Shandy* for God's sake? *Vanity Fair*? Who the hell was this Ms. Harper anyway? He searched the list up and down, finally resolving on length with interest.

"Okay, read this. It's long, but you'll like it."

"Alexander Dumas' *The Three Musketeers*. Cool. Sounds like fun."

"It is fun, but it's long. How much time did Harper give you to make this up?"

"Two weeks. A week ago."

Will looked at Mike like a trout eyeing a bad lure. "You better get to it, then. You've got your work cut out for you. One thing, though, Mike. Why wrestling?"

Mike opened his mouth, thought better of the wisecrack that immediately surfaced in his head, and said, "Because, if I'm any good, the other kids in the school will know it, too."

He stopped there, not going into the fact that Kirk wrestled, though at a higher weight, or that Kirk and his fat slob of a father would definitely be at the Booster game. He didn't say a word about the ultimate witness to all of these events, Karen.

"Oh," said Will, thinking to himself, the usual reasons.

"Okay, go get reading. I have a tough assignment of my own to prepare for."

"What's that?"

"Telling your mother of this latest development."

"Wow. Good luck, Dad."

"Yeah, pray for me."

Chapter 14.

Forster glared at the pile of onion-skin paper loosely stacked in front of him, then around the room at the other eyes watching fearfully.

"People, you are not getting the message. We are facing a serious situation." He grabbed the papers and began dealing them out like a flimsy deck of cards.

"Shit! Shit! Shit! All of them, shit! I've seen a hundred software RFPs this past year, but have I seen one new contract out of any of them? Hell no!"

Barry Evans leaned over to Will and hissed, "What's an RFP?"

Out of the side of his mouth Will whispered, "Request For Proposal, government announcements for pending contracts."

"You seem to have so much to say, Day, maybe you'd like to share your insights with the rest of us."

Shit! thought Will, seeing Eileen glower disapproval even as Forster twisted the knife, "Maybe with all of your fantastic influence on the Hill you can explain why we're being shut out?"

Will hiked his shoulders and said, "They all want to come off as being fiscally responsible in an election year. A lot of them are in tough races. With only two weeks left, their minds are not in Washington. Besides, the RFPs for the contracts you're talking about came out at least a year ago. I don't know why we didn't get them, but we still could be in the running for this year's," he finished, hoping that he didn't sound too much like a kid shifting blame to someone else. His hope seemed forlorn, though, judging by the look of disdain cast his way by Eileen.

"Oh, that makes a lot of sense, Will," Forster said, with a steely grin, "just like it did last year."

Will shrugged, holding his hands palms up, "The association's throwing a send-off tonight for the retiring director, a nonpartisan affair, so all the key M.C.s from both parties will make an appearance before they head home for the stretch run. I'll find out what I can."

"What about you, Harry, maybe you have an idea why we're nearly high and dry around here?"

Looking relaxed, Harry didn't bother to shift from his slumped posture in the conference chair, his chin barely abreast of the tabletop.

"The POM adjustments from this past summer don't look good, it's true, for the future," Harry said calmly, "but the Pentagon is still including us, according to the people I know there."

"What're poms?" Evans rasped in Will's ear.

"Program Objective Memorandums. Five-year budget plans, critical to getting military contracts," Will whispered sideways, then wondered why Evans didn't know POMs after ten years in the business.

"What's problematic, of course," Harry continued, "is just how big a role they've left ComCon."

"Well, hell, that's the problem all over this place," Forster said just short of a bellow. "Listen, folks, if things don't change around here, if we don't get into a growth mode very soon, we will start losing jobs. People will be out of work, and it'll be our fault. And let me tell you something else, if this trend continues, if the do-gooders continue to have their way, well, hell! I'll follow Anders lead; I'll roll up the welcome mat and pull up stakes. What was good enough for—"

"Who is Anders?"

Will whispered, "The former old guard heavy hitter at—"

"—General Dynamics is good enough for me, and ComCon. I'll sell, I swear, I've got my boat, I've got a nice little retirement spot picked out. Frankly, I don't need this bullshit anymore. Read the road signs, people, study the map! It's your interests at stake now. Will, I need to see you. You, too, Harry."

Forster marched out of the conference room, leaving the rest still sitting in their chairs wearing bruised expressions.

"So much for motivational speech number 86," said Harry.

"Unleash the giant within," Eldon murmured absently.

"My spirits are certainly lifted," Eileen said.

Will turned to Barry, "Look, you have questions, write them down. I'll be happy to answer them anytime except in the middle of the meeting."

"Sorry," Barry said, sounding wounded.

"Don't mind him," Harry said to Evans, "he finds it hard to be civil when he's on the rack."

"Stretches the imagination, too," Eileen joined in, "'Tough race, two weeks 'til the election,'" she mimicked, shaking her head.

"Oh yeah? Well, when this place goes down, I'll be ready to go while you're all floundering around wondering what to do. I've already laid out my contingency plans when ComCon bites the dust."

"Oh?" said Eileen, "And just what are your big plans?"

Will held up his hands as if blocking out a headline, "'It's Your Day Résumé Service'."

The others howled harsh laughter while Will protested, "Don't laugh, there'll be plenty of business around here, and you snobby specialists will be last in line."

"Do you spell 'Your' U-R?" asked Harry, causing them all to laugh again.

"Maybe it should be 'A New Day'," said Eileen, "or 'Doomsday.'"

Barry's voice broke through the laughter, "Do you really think there'll be layoffs?"

The others chatter subsided. Eileen said to the air, "Who knows? The gravy train has to hit the last stop sooner or later."

They began to stand up and file out. Harry fell into step with Will as they headed toward Forster's office.

"So, what do you think this is about?" Will asked.

"I try not to think anymore. It keeps me from feeling too sophisticated."

"What, thinking or not thinking?"

"That's right, now you're getting it" Harry looked at Will as they walked, "See, this is a simple business."

They entered Forster's office, and he almost leaped to the door to meet them.

"You two should know right now that I wasn't kidding in there. We need work to make sure that we're going to be in business next year. So, I want to hear your contingency plans."

Will and Harry traded a quick glance.

"I want to know what you think we can do to stay afloat if we are cut out. Call it a baptism of fire. You're going to inherit this place anyway, so you might as well start acting like it now, if you want a company left to inherit."

Forster moved around his desk and sat down. He folded his hands behind his neck, freed one to gesture the others to the green chairs and couch, then folded them again. He leaned back and said, "So?"

Harry had taken a seat on the couch while Will sat on an opposite chair.

Was this a test? Will wondered. He understood that things were bad, but ComCon always had muddled through somehow in the past. He'd thought it was just a matter of the company going through growing pains, a readjustment in the aftermath of the Cold War, that and the new administration. Sure, they'd had to scale back before, but he couldn't remember Forster talking such doom and gloom in the past, not continuing it behind his office door, anyway. Maybe it was a test, then, for Harry and himself. Maybe Forster wanted an idea of where each of them thought the company should be taken. So, what should he say? Which way should he jump, push for more of the same or go in an entirely new direction?

He wished that Eileen was here. He wished that he'd talked it over with her beforehand. She knew Forster a whole lot better than he did, she'd have a better idea of what he wanted to hear. But Eileen wasn't talking much these days, except for perfunctory mechanical stuff, like "the coffee's burning," things like that. This time the frost seemed to be lasting longer, turning from a nagging worry in the back of his mind to something more puzzling, more of a concern up front. If he had been on good terms with Eileen, she would have anticipated this possibility, and he would have been well-coached to deal with it. Of course, it was his very resistance to her urging such Machiavellian preparation that had him in this fix now, sitting in front of Forster without a clue of what to say to position himself as the front runner for a promotion he maybe didn't want.

So, which way? He had a fifty-fifty chance of guessing right, and he better guess now because Harry looked like he was just about to stir from his signature pose of insouciance to speak.

"Conversion," said Will, "we ought to move with a modified version of QMIV toward commercial markets as soon as we can."

Trying to suppress his puppy-dog eagerness for a reaction, Will gazed at Forster.

"That's an idea, Will," Forster said, appearing staid. "But where's the development money going to come from? ComCon itself is strapped just getting QMIV where it is today."

"The government will put it up. They've already earmarked two hundred and fifty million, and they're looking at a cool hundred and fifty million, and they're looking at a cool billion in pending legislation. We could go after a piece of that."

"But how much have they spent so far? Fifty million? A hundred? That's small change Will. Hell, I know a dozen ways that ComCon alone could use that money."

"I'm sure that's true of all the other defense outfits, too. But their problem is that they're too big. You're right, Jim, in saying that a hundred million would do the likes of TRW or the other heavyweights not much good. But it's the little guys and the midsize companies like ours that can make things happen with thirty, twenty, or even just ten million dollars."

"The public sector's tough, Will. We'd have to compete with a bunch of outfits who've been doing it forever. It would be a new thing for us. We would be behind from the very beginning, and maybe more important, we would be getting away from what we've been successful at for a quarter of a century. That's a big step you're talking about."

Will bobbed his head up and down, "All right, that's true, we would be making quite a departure from our own history. But so is the whole world, Jim. A lot of people in the Pentagon and on the Hill don't know it, yet, but the world has changed. I'm saying that it's better to compete in a market that's tough, but does exist, than it is to tie all of our fortunes to one that's dying or already dead. I don't want to see ComCon still making slide rules when everyone else is using pocket calculators, you know?"

He watched the concentration in Forster's face, doubt and worry struggling with possibility.

"Look at it this way, Jim. We can go after the money, both on the Hill and in the Pentagon while still pushing for QuarterMaster in the next budget round. We'll get the cash we need whatever the circumstances while also covering our bets, broadening our options rather than relying on selling only one product and its auxiliaries to one customer. Which is what we need to do anyway whether we go into the private sector or not."

Folding his arms in front of him, Forster pulled back so that he could look at Will from some distance. "It sounds like a viable concept, Will, I can see that you've been thinking about this."

"We're asking a lot from Eldon on this," Harry said. "He's got to come up with new modifications for QM almost at once, if not an entirely new package. It took him twenty months to complete the fourth generation. It might be impossible for him to come up with anything in any less time."

Will wanted to jump in with examples of large companies that could use the QM package virtually as is, such as GM or some of the steel giants. But Harry continued.

"I think that what Will's talking about has merit, but the timelines might be risky. I propose that we follow Will's lead and go after the government conversion funds–it'll put a hell of an extra burden on you, Will, but maybe we can import some help– I say, go with that, but we also can broaden our base in a couple of other ways, faster."

Harry leaned forward, clasping his hands between his knees to complete the classic pose of executive concentration. "As part of the commercial thrust, we should take a look at the feasibility of setting up a controlling-interest partnership with a private-sector company that could profit from such a venture. There are plenty on the West Coast still gasping for air who have good product, but no capital for distribution. Our entry into government funding could be very attractive to them, and we would have instant product while ours is brought up to speed."

The son of a bitch is smart, Will thought, nodding as Harry seamlessly welded reality to Will's fanciful notion to show how it might work. Maybe they both should run ComCon. Or maybe it should be Harry and Eileen, Will thought, admitting to himself that he'd lifted his proposal from an idle conjecture of Eileen's over breakfast some long-ago morning years before.

"Even so, Jim," Harry said, "as you pointed out, it's a risky scenario, uncharted territory." He raised an index finger in front of his face, "What we can also do to broaden our base while playing to our traditional strengths is go to new markets," he said, rolling his finger into a fist for emphasis, "overseas."

Will blinked. Forster sat up straight, but before he could speak, Harry continued, "Now, I know we've gone through this before, and we found the regulations, national security and all the other stoppers. But times have changed, and the new guys want to knock down the trade deficit, which means the rules could soften a little. From Asia to the Middle East, the Balkans, and Africa, there're plenty of potential new customers out there for what we have."

Harry leaned in, "And here's the best part. We can combine sales of our standard QM software to the defense agencies of these countries in tandem with sales of almost exactly the same package to their core industries. Korea, as an example, might want more efficient supply systems for defense and also a better management network for their auto parts operation."

Will's head drew back involuntarily, like he had been lightly smacked. No new ideas existed on Earth, he thought, all of them had been used up.

"So, we'll still be pursuing our traditional interests while expanding to increase our options and our opportunities to grow."

Forster held still as he reflected. He seemed utterly tranquil in his thoughts. "Interesting. Do you have any domestic companies in mind for such a partnership? It sounds unlikely to me that an outfit willing to be low man would have much of value to offer us."

"There are a few in New England and, as I said, some possibles on the West Coast. I have a video game producer in mind that has a topnotch line of deliverables but virtually no cash flow. They could go head-to-head with Nintendo and the others if they had the money to penetrate the market. We could help them there with conversion funds."

"And this foreign sales proposal, how sure are you that security restrictions have relaxed so much that it's suddenly become a viable alternative?"

"Colonel Norton informs me that the White House indicates that as long as it doesn't mean budget increases, they'll at least look the other way. The Pentagon is encouraging them in this posture to keep the defense industry afloat until the peace pendulum swings back again. They do not want to lose momentum as far as new development goes."

Forster grunted. "Very pretty plans, you two. No question, both of you seem to be exercising some vision for the future." He moved forward to prop his hands together on his desk, "Too bad that we need action today to keep going. You might want to put into your business models this fact; if ComCon does not capture one of the meaty contracts coming up by January 31st next year, there will be an across-the-board staff reduction, ten percent. If the situation remains status quo through June, there'll be another cut. That's the long and short of it, that's the bottom line.

"Now, I expect you two to do everything in your power to eliminate the need for these measures. That means that not only will you begin to put into execution your ideas for the future— they're all excellent concepts, and I don't consider them at all mutually exclusive—but first you will push as hard as you ever have for us doing business as usual. We are not going to abandon what our bread and butter has been for all of these years to run scared after a bunch of 'could-be's' or 'maybe ifs.' The world at war is still a reality, even if we're going through a peaceful phase right now. But we are in a state of crisis, gentlemen, and I expect you to respond accordingly.

"Will, I want you to sit on Maloney, Patterson, and the others and get them to produce for us like we've have for them in the past. Also, you can begin right away getting us to the front of the line for conversion funding. Oh, and don't count on any more staff, either, at least not permanent. I'll be damned if I'm going to risk hiring a bunch of slick lawyers or writers only to have them sue me three months later if I have to let them go. It's up to you to do it with the people you have now."

Great, thought Will. He didn't have one idea of where to start.

"On the other end, Harry, I want you to hound Norton, really make him dance to our tune. Have him help you with the foreign stuff, too. As for the private company option, get Eileen to help you with that. You and she can investigate the operations you think look good, check them out. That means you've got to come up with guarantees for the conversion money fast, Will, so that the banks will back us on a partnership at once. If these companies are teetering in the make-it break-it zone, I don't imagine they'll be around for very long or long in finding some other partner like us. Also, you might nose around some of the other boys in our business, see if they want to deal. They might be ready to pull the plug, which could put us in a position, for a little money, to take over sole number one in our area."

Will almost did a double take, wondering how much of a little money it would take to be number one.

"That's it. Look around as you leave, boys. Take a look at the things and the people who've been so familiar for all these years, and picture them gone, all of ComCon gone. That's what's at stake. And, for that matter, your chance to leave your imprint here and on the world is just as much at stake, too. So, good luck."

Again walking together down the hall, the two men gazed straight ahead while they talked.

"And you said this was a simple business," Will said.

"Simply marvelous," replied Harry as he pivoted into his office.

Chapter 15.

As Will passed through the lobby on his way to his office, he noticed Kelly standing on a short stepladder, putting up Halloween decorations passed to her by Wendy. A wave of depression hit him as he wondered if either of them would still be here at the end of January. Oblivious to the world, Kelly stretched above the doorway to hang one of those colorful cardboard cutouts so familiar in grade schools of a witch riding a broom silhouetted against a giant yellow moon. Kelly adjusted its angle by manipulating the tail of the black cat arched on the end of the broom handle. She would survive, he thought, but why allow these things to happen to people so that they had to endure such trials? Couldn't the world be managed in such a way that everyone could get work, enough to eat, a warm place to live and sleep, and the comfort and security to raise and play with their children? Then all that anyone would have to worry about is death, he sighed.

"How's it look?" Kelly murmured.

"Two-dimensional," laughed Wendy, rejoined by Kelly, "What do you expect, I got it at Woolworths."

Finally in his office, Will dropped into his chair and passed a hand over his face. He hated these funks. Nothing could console him. Of course, what could, these days, with his job turning into dog manure, his son driving him crazy, his daughter incommunicado, and his wife practicing estrangement? To top it all off, here he was feeling sorry for himself. Self-pitying slob, he thought, you're not starving in Africa. So, what could he do?

He reached into his briefcase and pulled out a small pocket notebook. He began to thumb through it, reading.

Peace moves in lovely ways.

Christopher Nolan, he read scrawled below in his own handwriting, *A Damburst of Dreams*. He read another line, *Peace naturally breeds kindness*. This from a severely crippled kid, he thought, who no one knew could think at all until they'd put him in front of a computer with a stick stuck to his head to push the keys. Poetry gushed out, stuff he'd been writing since he was three years old after learning the alphabet from the letters his mother had hung all around the kitchen walls. Thirteen years old, a kid who couldn't control the jerks of his head without some drug, and he was a master poet already. Weird, unorthodox stuff, he wrote, breaking all the rules because he was self-taught, but breaking them fantastically. And peace, he wrote about peace despite all that had befallen him, an innocent afflicted. He wrote of peace, kindness, and faith.

Plucked my last nerve, another line, but where from, what context? Will had forgotten, but the sound of it had appealed to him. Sound in poetry, so important to him, yet where was his gift for rhythmic sound, for simple thoughts and images turned into wonders of the universe, paradoxes coexisting in their plainness and their glory?

"Where da fock's da focking fork?" he said out loud.

Barry Evans stuck his head in the door. "Hello?" he murmured at first, then brightly, "Hi!"

Will frowned before he could prevent himself, and he saw Barry's face droop, a little bit like a reproached puppy. Most likely the guy was here to say that he was sorry about putting him on the spot in the staff meeting. Will decided to let him off easy if he would go away quickly.

"What's up, Barry?" he said tolerantly.

"I just stopped in to remind you of your promise," said Barry.

"Huh? What promise?"

"You know, to take me to the next bigwig political thing in Washington. Well, the, uh, party tonight is the next one." As he finished, he smiled weakly.

Will stared at Evans forever, as though plumbing the depths of the new comptroller's endless reservoir of nerve—and nerves.

"Gee, I don't know, Barry, if this is such a good idea, you know? There's going to be an awful lot of lapel-grabbing at this one, since it's just before the election. I can't imagine that you'll get much of a chance to talk to any of the interesting people. Maybe you should wait until after the election, when they're relaxed and in a bragging mode. Then they really let loose with the juicy stuff."

Barry said, "Well, I could go then, too. But tonight is the first party since when you promised I could go to the very next one."

Sweet syntax, Will observed. "Yeah, but I don't know, man, I'm going to be awfully damn busy. I won't have a chance to introduce you to anyone or anything. Maybe I should keep my promise another time, after the election."

He watched Barry's face drop in disappointment, then begin to grow petulant like a five-year old ready to unleash an outburst of tears and anger: You Promised! Maybe that's why he could stand this sad jerk at all, thought Will, because he was such a kid. People always seemed to be able to bear whatever kids did because of their natural charm in other contexts. So, when was this guy's natural charm going to surface? he wondered.

"All right, all right, you want to come along, then come." Barry lifted his eyes, beaming. Not enough, thought Will. This must be where pity enters the equation, saving grace for hammerhead adults. "The dog and pony show starts at six, so be here at five, and we'll caravan over."

Smiling broadly, Barry nodded, "Yeah, okay, great!"

"And on your way out," Will gestured to the door, "could you ask Julie to come in here?"

Barry hesitated, "Sure, but—"

"What?" Will cut in sharply.

"I found a receipt," Barry said, "I don't know what to do with it."

"What is it?" Will asked impatiently, "what's it for?"

"For the Knights of Columbus in Beltsville, Maryland," Barry said, "four thousand, five hundred dollars."

"Huh? Let me see it."

Barry handed over the thin square of paper, which was somewhat crumpled and partially stained a watery brown from coffee or tea. Will read the hand-written receipt, Four thousand, five hundred, and 00/100 dollars, public information program, Thank you so much! Ernest Best, Treasurer.

"Maybe it's a mistake, the decimal point off or something."

"No, look. The amount is written out." Barry pointed at the printing with his index finger.

"Huh. May of this year. You found it in our files? Who signed off on the check request?"

"Initials J.G."

J. G., Julie Gordon. Julie had signed off on it, so he must have known what it was for, but for the life of him he couldn't remember now.

"Okay, I'll ask Julie about it and let you know."

"Okay. See you at five."

"Yeah," mumbled Will.

He waited a full ten minutes before realizing that Evans had forgotten to tell Julie that he wanted to see her, the jerk. He leaned out of his office and said, "Julie, can you come in for a minute?"

"Sure."

He told her to take a seat as he passed behind his desk. Lounging back in his chair, he said, "So, uh, how's the Right Honorable Congressman Maloney?"

Julie stiffened and said, "Is this a work-related question?"

Will held up his hand, "All right, okay, private life off limits. But you know that it'd be better if you sort of stayed away from him at tonight's shindig, right?"

Her cheeks colored slightly, and he noticed how good she looked lately, thinner and healthier. "Of course," she said. "You really feel you need to ask that?"

"Hey, love is blind, even for pros, despite everybody's best interests. The good congressman himself sometimes has shown questionable judgement in the past when it comes to affairs of the heart."

"Will, where is this leading?"

"Aw, Julie," he said, discarding his previous measured tone, "I just don't want you to get mangled by the guy, you know? I think too much of you to see that happen."

Julie relaxed somewhat and said, "Well, thanks, Will, but I'm okay. I know who he is and where he's weak. But you have to let me deal with it myself. It's the only way, really. You understand that?"

"Yeah, yeah," he sighed, "you're right. I'm just trying to look out for you, I guess. Like a brother would."

She grinned, "Well, thanks, Bro. But knock it off, okay? That's what I'd tell my brother, too, my uncle, and my father," she laughed.

"Hey, I'm not that old."

"Okay, okay. Is that it?" she said, rising from her chair.

"No, one more thing," he said, and she slid back down. "I need a favor. Barry Evans has invited himself to the gig tonight."

"What? How did that happen?" she asked.

"Well, I sort of invited him before. Not to this one, particularly, but I did leave him an opening."

"Well, that's just peachy," said Julie. "How did you come to do that?"

"A temporary failure of foresight," he grimaced, "before I discovered what a dope he is."

"Good move, Will. I hope he doesn't get with the wrong party there."

"I wish he'd go to the wrong party," said Will, "but no chance of that. He's meeting us here at five. This is where the favor part comes in."

He watched the transformations of her features as she gradually realized what he was intimating.

"Oh, no, Will!" she cried, "Not again, not me!"

"Come on, Julie, I'm desperate here. You're the only one I can trust to keep him out of trouble. Help me out, please."

"Will, you always stick me with the shit details. Enough's enough."

"Julie, please don't make me pull rank. The guy's a train wreck before he leaves the station. I'm begging you before I'm ordering you."

"Well thanks a lot!" she said indignantly.

"Look, it won't be so bad. He's starstruck with the whole behind-closed-doors, smoked-filled room scene. Just introduce him to a couple of aides and he'll leave you completely alone. All I'm asking you to do is steer him away from the sensitive ones, the guys on the chopping block this November."

"You mean like Maloney?"

"Well," he ebbed, rubbing his chin nervously, "sure."

"Will, anyone who ever called you a nice guy didn't know your dark side," she said in a huff as she stood up.

"Julie, Julie," he implored.

"You know, you could be a nice person," she said, "but you need lessons."

She stormed out of the office.

"Julie," he said plaintively. But she was gone.

Often, at these functions, Will found himself reminded of one of Washington's eternal verities, that space was at a premium. The inflated cost of commercial real estate natural to any country's capital had been compounded by federal law prohibiting buildings constructed in Washington from being higher than the Capitol. Except for the rogue structures directly across the Potomac in Roselyn, Virginia, such as the Gannett building, the tallest edifices in the city proper could be no more than thirteen stories high.

These restrictions cramped quarters everywhere, a shock to people from places like Dallas or Minneapolis who were used to more spacious accommodations. The association's goodbye to the exiting director, really a good luck party for the six favored representatives from both parties up for reelection, took place in a room typically too small for the number of invitees. Overspill meant discreet gatherings in the main corridor, near the cloak room, and in the small auditorium.

Of course, Will knew well that the people who gravitated to these affairs didn't give a hoot about the rosewood, glass bricks, and brass frou-frou common to offices thrown up in the eighties. They'd be happy to conduct business in the Union Station men's room before renovations. Power was the architectural amenity for them. He amended the thought; make that aphrodisiac.

He stood with a flute of white wine in his left hand and in his right a plate full of doughy aperitifs made with plenty of butter and bacon. His usual procedure at these parties was to arrive early, eat a dinner's worth of hor d'ouevres while scanning

150

the room to locate those he needed to talk up, then circulate while nursing the wine, no refills.

He noticed Julie with Evans, introducing him to Stig Ebersole, Patterson's number one aide. That was good; Ebersole characteristically would regale the wide-eyed Evans with tales of the situation room during the Gulf War, Patterson being a heavyweight on National Security. For that matter, Will realized he would have to talk to Patterson himself to see how things rested at this juncture. Patterson was strong, though, a sure thing to stay in office and not one to follow any nervous nellies bolting at the first whiff of smoke. And who knew, with the Republicans threatening to take over Congress this year, Patterson might be the committee's new chair. No matter, the question with Patterson revolved around his current estimation of the value of QMIV. For Patterson, it was a simple yes or no proposition. Will merely had to poll him again, as he polled all of them continuously, over and over, week after week, year after year.

Maloney walked into the room, handing his black wool overcoat to an aide behind without looking back or breaking stride as he headed for the bar. Will watched him drain one quick drink, a double. Maloney immediately picked up another drink, which he must have ordered at the same time as the first. Grabbing it, he started toward the cheese and fruit piled high on long, linen-covered trestle tables lined up against the wood-paneled wall. He saw Will standing next to the table only at the last instant.

"Hello, Day, still writing those dirty poems?"

Will had just popped a bacon roll in his mouth, which he pushed into his cheek with his tongue to answer, "I wish I was, Congressman, but I can't think of enough obscene words that rhyme." He resumed chewing, watching the broad, dark-haired man survey the table. Maloney reminded him of a large, starving

151

cat gingerly pawing at road-kill, debating if survival was worth compromising standards of taste.

"Don't they have any real food around here?" Maloney asked, "Something that makes you feel like you ate something?"

Will offered his plate, "Try a bacon roll."

"Ah, food! Where did you get these?" he asked as he took the plate.

"At the end of the table, but I believe that's the last of them."

"Too bad. Don't expect me to save any here."

"Maybe they'll bring more."

"Nah, these shindigs are over before they need to restock, pretty much hit and run. I'll make do until I can get to dinner, anyway."

Maloney made quick work of the rolls, then began his search again. He started to build a little ziggurat on his plate with squares of cheese.

"This is the kind of shit my mother never let me do, God bless her," he said. "She'd think I was playing with my food, when all I was doing was stockpiling. I did it with the roast beef one Sunday, until my old man yelled at me to put it back." He shrugged, glancing up at Will, "I was mesmerized by all that juicy red meat, enchanted by the hot smell of it, like cast under a spell. 'Roast beast,' I used to call it when I was three. We had it every Sunday, my old man was a hell of a provider. And Yorkshire pudding, my mom got the recipe from a cookbook. Instant hit with the family. You had to grab it fast, though, in a family of eight kids. The last of those, by God. Now, everyone has one-point-five kids, or none. No wonder we all drive to work alone."

Listening, Will lowered his eyes to note Maloney's glass, empty.

"That's why there's God-little compassion in the world today, Will. You have to be around people to feel for them. You gotta live with them."

Will nodded, then said, "So, how's your campaign going, Mike?"

Maloney's eyes dropped their dreamy revery look and he answered, "It's in the bag. Macowiac the bitch is beat dead in the water. I got a TV commercial out that's killing her. It's brilliant! There I am, visiting factories, shaking workers' hands, standing on a mountaintop, gazing out over the valley where the stacks are pumping out smoke, and the voice says in solemn tones like in church: 'In times of frightening change, we can't afford to take a chance on someone who has never held public office, ever! Who has never passed laws to create jobs, who has never fought in a war, and whose radical environmental stand would shut down our factories.'

"Then, suddenly," Maloney said, spreading his hands in front of him, "the smoke from the stacks disappears! The voice comes in again and says, like death, 'Don't take a chance this November; keep experience on Capitol Hill and keep your job; keep Mike Maloney.' It's a killer!

"I got another version that spanks the Republican fall guy, Shenck. My pollsters tell me that both him and Macowiac have dropped three and two points respectively since the spot's first airing. It's costing me a bundle, but I'm going to show it a million times until they're both driven into the ground. Yeah, things are looking up."

"That's great, Mike, just super," Will said, as he wondered where Maloney had found the money.

"Hey, you guys made it all possible, Day. Believe me, I was on the ropes there for a while, all ready with a great message but no way to get it over. You guys came through in a big way, and I won't forget it."

Will stroked his lip with a finger, speculating about which outfit it might have been. When he mentioned Maloney's predicament at the association a month or so ago, he hadn't received much of a response. At this point, everyone had committed their political warchests to other people who seemed to be in bigger trouble than the lock-in Maloney. Somebody evidently had found some lose change, but who? He'd have to ask around later.

"I'm dry here, Will. Can I get you something?"

"No, I'm fine, Mike."

Julie walked up to Maloney and handed him a full glass, "Can I offer you a drink, Congressman Maloney?"

Maloney turned to her voice and light radiated through his round face. "Why, Miss Gordon, so nice to see you."

Jesus Christ thought Will.

"Nice to see you, Congressman. Can I introduce an associate of mine? Mr. Barry Evans, ComCon's Comptroller."

"Say that three times fast," Maloney said, poking at Evans' stomach.

"Huh? Oh, yeah," Barry said, giggling.

Will sighed, then tightened his mouth and scrunched down his eyebrows. He held the expression until Julie finally glanced his way. When she saw him, her warm smile turned into a disdainful sneer.

"Well, I must be off, sir. Duty calls," she said, looking Will up and down as though inventorying each of those points contributing to her disgust for him.

"That's a shame, Miss Gordon. We so seldom get to chat anymore."

"Yes," she drawled.

"I hope that we might spend more time together in the near future to go over those matters of importance that we've neglected for so long."

"I'm sure that something can be arranged," she said. "Barry, are you ready?"

"If you don't mind, Julie, I think I'll stay here, get something to eat," Barry said without his sight ever leaving Maloney's face.

"Oh," said Julie. "Fine," she said, avoiding Will's fierce glare, "Then I'll leave you all now. Have a nice evening," she said as she left.

Maloney turned to Barry and threw an arm around his shoulders as he said, "So, Mr. Evans, you know all about money. Does that include the stock market?"

"Why, no," Barry said, smiling broadly.

Will postponed his train of thought on how he intended to eviscerate Julie, and stepped in.

"Excuse me, Congressman, but I see Congressman Patterson over there, and I need to talk with him about some of the details regarding next year's budget plans."

"Okay," Maloney said, ready to continue with Barry.

"And I need Barry, here, to help with the finer fiscal points."

"Oh. Okay, I guess I don't want to get into anything, anyway, that might be misconstrued as inside trading," Maloney laughed. He lifted his head and searched the room. "Patterson, huh? He's one who'd like to get his hands on a few of our contracts to take back to Michigan."

"We're not going to give anything away, don't worry," said Will.

"Yeah," Maloney said, scowling off in the distance. He raised his glass, then said, "I'm dry. See you later, Day."

He walked off toward the bar.

"He really is a nice guy, isn't he," Barry said ingenuously.

Will gave him a look. "Let's go," he said.

Chapter 16.

Eileen sat in Harry's office looking out the window while he talked. On this side of the building the lawn outside rose gently away and up to a back service road above. She could slump low in her seat and still see the dead brown grass and the withered-looking trees outside. The trees were small, no more than ten or fifteen years old, which meant that they'd been planted as saplings, given the age of the building itself.

Harry had started to tell her about the meeting with Forster, and she hadn't gotten past the part about Will proposing conversion to the private sector. She shook her head, thinking that he probably gave it a nice try, considering he'd been surprised by the meeting, "like a pop quiz," he'd said. Of course, this was the problem, the fact that Will didn't prepare for this or any other eventuality as he should have once he heard that he was up for executive v.p. Of course, when she pointed this out to him, he closed up like a clam and ran off to hide in front of his computer.

She could have told Willy back when she first speculated about conversion, more than a year ago, that Forster would put little stock in the notion. ComCon's founder would remember too well the fate of those companies that had tried it after Vietnam. Defense companies had become too specialized after World War II and Korea. Modifying a Sherman tank transmission to fit, say, a Mack truck in 1953 was much simpler than turning an F-16 into a Lear jet today. She could have told Willy, too, that the crux of the whole notion was that it didn't matter that software application was an entirely different proposition. What mattered was what Forster believed and what he wanted to hear. Getting the job was the goal. Willy could do anything he wanted to save ComCon after he had gained control. But if he didn't get the nod, he wouldn't be able to do anything.

Yes, she thought as she examined the weave of one of the white pinstripes threaded through her blue skirt, she could tell Willy plenty if he'd listen. But he wouldn't and now they didn't talk much about it or anything else for that matter.

"So, Forster wants us to look over some prospects for this commercial venture."

She glanced up at Harry, then back at her skirt and out the window again.

"You don't seem to be very interested in this, Eileen," Harry said.

Eileen snapped her eyes to Harry's, "Well, I'd be a damned lot more interested, Harry, if you had mentioned to Forster that it was my idea to buy into one of these outfits in the first place. My enthusiasm would be overwhelming if he had just an inkling that I was the one who suggested rethinking oversea markets."

"Well, hell, Eileen," Harry said with surprise.

"Hell is right, Harry." She turned her attention back to the tree outside, which drooped a palette of varied brown leaves punctuated by a gluey wad of them marking a squirrel's nest high up in the crotch of two branches. "I mean, if you were going to use my ideas, the least you could do was get them right."

Harry rose and walked around his desk to stand between Eileen and the window. She was forced either to pretend he was not there and end up staring at his open pants zipper or raise her sight to his face.

"Eileen, I'm sorry you feel that way about it—"

"Oh, come on, Harry," she broke in, "where did you get the dope on the White House softening foreign sales regulations if not from me?"

"I thought we developed some of these concepts together," he said, "Not that they're all that revolutionary, just different spin on them."

Eileen crossed her arms and pulled her shoulders tight. She clenched her mouth, her pique now mixed with self-doubt that further fueled her anger. Dropping her head, she said bitterly, "With such a plethora of grand plans springing from you and Willy, I've got to wonder how Forster can make a choice? I mean, really, just who should he pick to steer ComCon into the 21st century?"

"Why, you, of course, Eileen," Harry said softly. She jerked her head up. "You're the natural choice," he continued.

She began to feel warmth effusing her, her arms tingling, falling away from her body. "Do you really mean that, Harry?" she said.

"Yes, I do," he said, "really. But you also know that it's never going to happen."

She slumped again. "Yeah. You're right. It's just that—it's just not fair."

Harry leaned down and held her hands. "No it isn't, Eileen. Not at all."

"Yeah, well, I appreciate your saying so." She felt a bit uncomfortable this close to him with his big hands holding hers, and excited, touched with a tinge of guilt, an added thrill. His palms were calloused, startling her. How much didn't she know about Harry? Was he a home woodworker? A weight trainer?

"What you should know, Eileen, is that whatever happens," he hesitated, "that is, if I get the job, I won't forget you."

She listened expectantly, but for what? He seemed to be searching for words, odd for the likes of a man known to be brash on any occasion.

"What I mean is, I'll stand by you."

He didn't say it again, and her eyes widened as she realized what she'd been waiting for even as he said it. Stunned, she found herself in his embrace, a strong hug, and a fierce dry kiss upon her cheek, while she thought, Willy. This time he never mentioned Willy.

He pulled back, obviously self-conscious, and she said softly, "Harry. Jesus."

"You're shocked," he said.

"Well, yes. I guess so, I think," she murmured, thn suddenly realizing what he had done had been completely predictable. She should have known it all along. Men don't sit still in relationships, they either move ahead or leave you behind, she thought. All the signs had been there, but she merely had assumed that they'd been friends, the usual fallback defense position of women, so many pointed out. Maybe they were right.

"I guess I blew it," he said, smiling sickly.

"No," she said unthinking. "I mean, I don't know. It's . . . it would be such a change between us."

"That would be my assessment," he laughed.

She laughed too, and felt light, light on her feet. "Now what?" she said, almost to herself.

"Well," he said, quickly sober, "Will."

"Willy," she breathed, and a shroud of sadness descended upon her, instantly dampening her breezy spirit. Her eyes turned sorrowful as she thought of Willy, poor, poor Willy. Out of his element, she thought. "I don't know," she said staring down at nothingness, "I don't know. . .Willy . . . what to say, I don't know."

She raised her eyes to Harry, "I'm not sure, Harry, what to say to you. It's just not clear."

"Of course, Eileen," Harry said, again grasping her hands. "I didn't expect anything else from you. To tell you the truth," he laughed, "I didn't expect anything like this from myself. At least, not right at this moment."

"Yeah," she said. Then, almost plaintively, "Oh, Harry, I've never done anything like this before, I've never even thought about it, not in real terms. I mean, Willy, the kids; how could I?"

"I know," he said tenderly.

"You're divorced, Harry, you know about these things. I don't. I mean, I must tell you, I always looked down upon people who did things like this before, got divorced and things. Even you," she said, peering up at him sheepishly. "Carol Jones, for God's sake."

"Oh, thanks for grouping me with that paragon of virtue," he said.

"Well," she moaned, "you know what I mean."

"Yeah, yeah," he sighed. He looked at her for a moment, then at length said, "Listen, I didn't do this to make you unhappier. Whatever you decide is fine. I'm still going to be behind you, professionally. I'll put other dreams on hold."

"Thanks, Harry."

"And look at it this way, Eileen. Whoever Forster picks now, you've got it covered."

"Harry!"

"No, really, you're in the catbird's seat now," he teased.

"Boy, doesn't that make me sound like a sweet little opportunist."

"Oh, come on, Eileen, who isn't an opportunist when a chance comes along? Besides, it could be worse, you could be a common gold digger. You reached the pinnacle of cynical business competition through hard, efficient work. You should be proud of yourself!"

"You do have a way with words, Harry."

He shrugged his shoulders. "As Steve Martin says, 'Some not have way.'"

She laughed and he smiled, "So, listen. Think about it, whatever you want. Take your time. This offer is open-ended, okay?"

"Even if I decide to close it from my side?" she asked.

He flashed a grim smile, "The professional part is permanent."

"Thanks, again, Harry."

He leaned to her and gave her a quick kiss on the mouth, saying, "Had to do it."

He dropped her hands and returned behind his desk. Eileen stood in the middle of his office, still feeling the impression of his dry lips upon hers, noticing the slightest smell of tobacco. Was Harry a secret smoker, she wondered, or did it come from sitting in a meeting with people who smoke? Will sometimes came home reeking of the stale, acrid scent, as though he had indeed been captive in a smoke-filled room. Willy: automatic to her thoughts.

"In the meantime, we're supposed to go to Massachusetts to check out Dencor, Inc, and to California for some other possibilities. I'll make the arrangements for a week from Monday, if that suits you."

She stood still, not answering immediately. "Schedule it," she said evenly, "I'll let you know if we need to change plans."

Harr nodded his head solemnly, "All right."

Chapter 17.

Will pondered the receipt lying in the middle of his desktop. Four thousand, five hundred, and 00/100 dollars, Thank you so much! Ernest Best, Treasurer.

Why did Julie sign off on a forty-five hundred dollar check for the Beltsville Knights of Columbus? For some sort of public information thing, the receipt indicated, but what? Julie handled foundation contributions for ComCon, but she usually ran anything out of the ordinary past him to see if he wanted to build some publicity around it. Local club events normally wouldn't qualify, but the amount should have piqued his interest. Julie could sign off for up to five thousand, contributions that usually went to tax-sheltered groups and the like. They discussed those kinds of commitments beforehand when preparing their annual budget. The smaller giveaways fell into a discretionary fund that she doled out as she saw fit. But forty-five hundred to the Beltsville Knights of Columbus?

He sighed. He would have asked her if she had come in, but she was home sick. Sick of him, he suspected, still angry about last night. Whatever, he ought to find out what was what before Barry Evans made a bigger pest out of himself. He reached for the phone.

"Ernie Best." The voice sounded flat, business-like, with a hint of forbearance.

"Mr. Best, this is Will Day of Computer Control Incorporated calling."

"Oh, yeah. What can I do for you?"

The voice on the other end of the phone seemed warmer now, as though making the connection that they were old friends.

"I'm looking for some information about a contribution that ComCon made to the Beltsville Knights of Columbus back in May."

"May?" Best said.

"Yessir, four thousand, five hundred dollars."

"Forty-five hundred dollars?" said Best.

"That's correct." Will waited, but the line seemed dead.

"Mr. Best?"

"Yes?"

"I'm just trying to complete our records," Will continued quickly, "since we're coming on the close of the year." He waited for a response that didn't materialize, so he continued, "We don't want the money back or anything." He followed with a self-conscious laugh, but Best didn't join in.

"May, huh?"

"That's right."

"Well, I don't know about May, but that probably would be for a forum."

"A forum?" said Will. "What kind of forum?"

"Yeah, one of those information forums. I don't remember exactly which one this was, but that's what it'd be for. That's the only thing I know you guys for. ComCon, right?"

"That's right, Mr. Best."

"Yeah. Then that would be it."

An information forum? Will asked himself. What was that, and who did it involve?

"I hate to trouble you anymore than this, Mr. Best, but the auditors need more specific information than that, and we sponsor so many forums. Could you tell me who was invited on that day? May 15th, I believe."

"Well," Best said dubiously, "I could make a guess. But to be sure, I'd have to go look it up."

"I would be very appreciative if you would, sir."

"That means I need to go to the Club and look at the book. You're calling me at my office number."

"Oh," Will said, disappointment and concern obviously riding in his voice.

"Say, that's not a problem," Best said. "It's only around the corner and I was heading over there anyway for lunch. I'll just go a little earlier and call you from there."

"Mr. Best, you're a hero."

"Oh, gosh," Best said.

"No, really."

"Well, okay, I'll call you soon."

Will stretched, not really ready to dig into the piles of paper strewn around his desk and on the credenzas against the walls. One of his worst work habits, he knew, was that he found it torture to get down to work at all. Thank God that when he finally did bite the bullet, he was fast because he usually started only at the penultimate moment. No matter how far in advance he planned, he always found ways to procrastinate. He'd read the newspapers, part of his job, true, but not the style and living sections, or the sports page, for God's sake, – he didn't even care that much for sports.

Mike was the big sports fan in the family, so maybe he read to keep up with him. But they never talked sports. Really, they didn't talk much about anything at all, at least not until lately, after they'd started their new regimen together. Now they talked, Will nodded to himself, but mostly they just argued about Mike's homework, schoolwork, and household duties, Mike furiously dodging all of them in turn. When Will quizzed him on these matters, Mike labored over his display of indignation, as though claiming to be some kind of political dissident objecting to his treatment as a criminal prisoner. This attitude, of course, annoyed Will to no end. They both would turn to their desks in silent anger.

Well, maybe the Booster game will thaw the ice a bit, Will thought, though he admitted to himself that he wasn't looking forward to it. He'd gone out one morning early to do some running, trying to get into some sort of shape to keep from embarrassing himself. Wheezing and gasping, he'd made it a mile out from the house, then had to stop to rest a vicious side stitch. He walked-jogged back home and hadn't been out since. For the first time in his life, he wondered if his natural athletic ability would desert him due to bad conditioning and his age. That would be a hard message to accept, one in which no satisfaction could be gained from killing the messenger, his own decrepit body.

He breathed a sigh. Maybe they could hide him, a decoy receiver or something. Whatever, he would just have to try his best not to humiliate himself and hope that Mike wasn't too disappointed in the Old Man. The Old Man.

He stood up and stretched more vigorously, arching his back and reaching for the low ceiling with his hands clenched together. He'd take a little walk before he started in, he decided. As he headed out the door and passed Julie's empty desk, he noted how men were always finding ways to goof off while women never even thought of wasting time on the job. Studies had proven it; men worked about half the time compared to women, who performed their duties for some phenomenally high percentage of hours during the day.

"Boy, statistics like that really make men look bad," Eileen said after reading a story about it in the paper. Months ago.

"Nah," said Will, "it all evens out in the end."

"Oh, really?" said Eileen "How do you come to that conclusion?"

"Simple," he'd said, "That story doesn't say anything about how many days babes take off from work."

"Babes?" Eileen said dryly.

"Yeah, babes are forever taking a day off here, a day there, for congestion or headaches, cramps."

"Oh, brother."

"So, it all evens out: babes take days off, men fuck off daily."

"Boy, is this illuminating. I can see it on the cover of *Scientific American*: 'Babes and Guys at Work: An Incredible Approach'." He smiled wryly, "You don't think I can quantify my data?"

"I don't think you can say it with a straight face."

He loved jerking her chain about that kind of stuff, she left herself wide open for it. She had one of those coffee mugs with the saying on it "In order to receive half the credit as men for doing the same job, women must do twice as much work. Fortunately, this isn't difficult."

After reading it again on one occasion while sitting in her office, he finally had said, "You know, I absolutely agree with the sentiment on this mug. Women do have to do twice as much as men to get the same credit."

"Yes?" she said guardedly.

"And you know what I say? I say, 'Go to it!'" He pumped his fist in a flourish of encouragement. Then he leaned back with his hands clasped behind his head, saying, "I believe that you should do twice the work for the same credit, you gals deserve it. I think I speak for all of us guys when I say that we're happy to step aside to give all of you the opportunities that you've truly earned." He stopped only to duck the wadded napkin she threw at him, thinking he was glad that he held the mug, not her.

As he strolled down the broad hallway, he felt sad again that they didn't seem to have much to joke about anymore. He reached the kitchen area in this wing of the building, the usual array of refrigerator, counter space, range, and oven, but sandwiched between two rest rooms and open to the hallway, an arrangement that often reminded him of an exhibit at a home appliance convention. He pushed the door open to the Men's room, thinking that he really missed teasing her that way. Since he had been leaving work promptly at five-thirty to study with Mike, he and Eileen had driven separately. He realized as he stood staring at the painted concrete block above the urinal that he missed squabbling with her on their morning drive to work.

Hell, he thought, washing his hands, he just plain missed her.

Chapter 18.

He walked back toward his office slowly, his hands deep in his pants pockets, which made his shoulders slump. He passed the cubicles where the engineering team endlessly played with their programs, and happened to glance in. Eldon Harding sat in a secretarial chair, his long legs and arms folded tight as he calmly stared at a shifting pattern of figures rippling down a monitor's screen like fluorescent glow worms fleeing a bat in a cave.

"Eldon." Will uttered the name more like he was identifying the man rather than greeting him.

Eldon glanced up and back at the screen without saying a word until the figures froze. "That's something," he said, his voice so deep it seemed to sound like it echoed itself. "Now, if we just do this," he slapped the keyboard furiously, making the computer sound like a percolating coffee pot, "then, we should get a little of this," and he sat back, folding his legs and arms again to wait patiently.

"You seem surprised to see me, Will," he said without taking his eyes off the screen. On it, the worms began to wiggle and squirm again.

"No. Well, surprised to see you out here, not in your office."

"Yeah. On my way back from lunch, I had a thought," Eldon said, as if that explained everything.

"I see," said Will, "that's great."

Eldon turned his head. "You don't say that like it sounds great."

"Oh, yeah, well. I guess I'm a bit distracted."

"Unhuh," Eldon said, intent upon the display again.

For a time, Will rocked back and forth on his feet. He stopped and took his hands out of his pockets. "Well," he said. He turned to go, then said, "Say, how's your family? How're the kids?"

"Growing fast," Eldon said. He tapped out another rapid tattoo on the keys, saying as he finished, "I wish some of them would move out. There, that should do it. Now, let's run this thing."

He tapped in a code sequence, then turned his head to Will. "Don't get me wrong, I love my kids. But the two oldest should get out into the world. They're doing themselves a disservice staying at home. They love their mother, though."

He swiveled the secretarial chair around to face Will fully.

"So, how's your bid for the vice presidency coming along?"

The question startled Will, but he quickly realized that word would have gone around the company by now one way or another. Forster himself might even have "leaked" the information, a dynamic, maybe, of one of his arcane machinations. Still, Will found himself embarrassed to be asked about it by Eldon, one of the original founders of the business and by all criteria a logical candidate for the post in his own right.

"Uh, fine, I guess." Will suddenly exhaled as he sat in the visitor's chair in the cubicle. "Gee, I don't know, Eldon. Would you understand if I told you that I'm not sure I even want the job if it's offered?"

Eldon smirked, "A proper modicum of modesty expressed, or should I take it at face value and believe you?"

"Huh. People vying for these positions even gauge the correct quotient of humility, huh?" said Will.

"For someone in public affairs, I'm surprised that this comes as a revelation to you. But, if you are genuine, I will tell you that I'm not surprised by your doubts."

"You're not. Well, let me ask you straight out, then. Are you pissed that your name hasn't come up for this?"

"What makes you think that Forster didn't offer it to me already, but I turned it down?"

Will moved back, feeling really embarrassed now. Eldon raised his hand palm out and said, "He didn't. Let me be the first to say that I'm not the man for this job. Also, it's the last thing I'd want to do."

He said the last a bit offhandedly, taking his glasses off as he spoke. He rubbed them clean with a handkerchief from his pocket, and as he held them up to the light, he murmured, "Maybe that's one reason why I'm not suitable to succeed Forster." He rubbed the left lens again and put them back on, "It doesn't suit me."

"Hell, Eldon, that's what I'm afraid of myself. Why would I want all of these headaches, and why would anyone think that I could handle them? To be truthful, I'm not sure I even support the whole Cold War scenario anymore, now that things have changed wholesale internationally. I mean, if I ever did support it." Will opened his eyes ingenuously, "Would you believe it, I was an anti-war protestor back in the early seventies."

Eldon cocked and tossed his head, "So was Jerry Rubin. People change throughout their lives. It's all right to change back again once in a while. I suppose it is, anyway."

"Okay, but what about you, Eldon? Everyone here talks about how you wouldn't even be at ComCon if it wasn't for your five percent share, that and the kids going to college. You complain about it enough, for Christ's sake. Is that just bullshit, just a smoke screen, or are you really unhappy here?"

The computer scientist frowned annoyance. "That would make me quite a spoiled skinny little shit, wouldn't it?"

Will immediately began to hem and haw about it being none of his business, apologizing as he started to get up to leave. Eldon stopped him with a big bony hand on his arm.

"Sit down, sit down. If it weren't you asking me this Will, I wouldn't bother telling you. But you're a good enough guy. Actually, you really are a good guy, an honest guy. I know we don't talk that much, but I enjoy it when we do. I get a kick out of you in the meetings, too, you're so sincere. You're like a boy scout, or, no, no, no," he said, searching in the back of his mind, "What would one say? An altar boy, that's it! You're a real altar boy."

"Well, thanks a lot, Eldon," Will said, irritated himself, now.

"Oh, don't get mad at me. Episcopalians have altar boys too, you know. Of course, we have altar girls as well, we're just that much more enlightened. Anyway, about what you asked; naturally, I'm sick of this place, of Forster and his affectations, his 'crises.' I'm tired of being tied to it by money, too. Oh, yes," he said with a roll of his eyes, "the kids have to go to school and the money is too good to pass up, though calculatedly not enough to retire."

Eldon assumed his characteristic pose, closing his body by crossing one thigh tightly over the other and folding his arms with his hands tucked in his armpits. "Mostly, I'm enervated by the years I've spent exhausting my God-given talent so that nineteen-year-old skinheads can keep track of a division's dirty green underwear without the Army having to worry about them losing count on their fingers and toes!"

Will blinked at the bitterness of Eldon's tone. He suddenly recognized the frustration that he'd been feeling himself during the past decade magnified in Eldon by a factor of three. He'd been aware of the man's complaints peripherally before and always had dismissed them as eccentricities that went along with being a computer science genius. It'd been convenient to pay no attention. Will had plenty of his own problems to keep him from really hearing Eldon talk about his.

"Hell, Eldon," he said softly, "I had no idea." He stumbled over the words, "What else would you rather do than this?"

"What else?" Eldon said sharply, "What else? I'm going to assume that you don't mean that rhetorically. You really want to know?"

The sting in his voice told that he teetered on the brink of completely misunderstanding the question. Flustered, Will hurried to say, "Why, sure. Sure I do, Eldon," he finished fervently.

"Okay then. I'll show you." Eldon rose abruptly and led the way deep to the back of the clustered cubicles to an office like Will's, enclosed with the far wall a row of windows that looked out on the the lawn. Eldon's office housed a half-dozen different PCs all wired together as though evidence of a megalomaniacal demand upon the reigning computer priest to have his own personal network. In fact, Will knew that he needed all of the different models, CD-ROM setups, and the rest to mirror the various arrays and systems in use by the Army from depot to depot marking the respective stage of computer requisition that each had reached. Despite the numerous pieces of hardware and manuals and the scores of plastic file boxes full of diskettes, Eldon's office was bare of anything not in use. No dusty hard drives or obsolete keyboards cluttered his windowsill, no piles of used computer paper could be seen beneath the long table that he had substituted for a desk.

Even personal belongings had been kept to a minimum. One photograph of the family stood propped on the only file cabinet in the office, showing a much younger Eldon, his hair almost completely orange without a trace of the gray seeping down his sideburns now. The children looked to be five or ten years younger than Will knew them to be, and the color of the photo had faded, its hue now making it seem as though the picture had been taken under the sea. One other nonwork-related item hung from the wall, a poster from an old movie, *The Time Travelers*, starring Preston Foster aging even then, John Hoyt, and a bunch of others who Will had never seen before. Despite the age of the poster, Eldon apparently didn't value it as a collector's item. He had hung it from the wall unframed, using masking tape that over time had pulled away, causing the image of the mutant-terrified, fleeing men and women to sag in the middle.

Sitting on his own secretary chair, Eldon crouched over the keyboard and rifled a series of commands into the station. The screen burst into a nebula of color, radiating a three-dimensional shower of fragments that caused Will to flinch back out of the way. The falling fluorescents refracted different hues before they settled into gigantic letters:

PARAL-LIEGE
The Ultimate Power of the Multiverse

Eldon hit Enter, and another sequence of colors splashed, coalescing into a window that showed a fanciful scene of large plants and giant dinosaur-type creatures lumbering through; the scene within the window shifted, and row upon row of soldiers vaguely reminiscent of 16th-century Japanese samurais cried a joined chorus of "Ho Chai! Ho Chai! Ho Chai!;" a scene shift, and laser beams picked off quick-silver needle ships darting at the screen; another shift, and leviathans bumped into each other beneath raspberry murk, exuding lime green bodily fluids as they thudded together; the scene shifted—

"So, what do you think?" asked Eldon eagerly.

Will did not take his eyes from the scrolling myriads of flora, fauna, topography, meteorology, life, death, and space, as he said, "Remarkable."

Eventually, he turned to Eldon and said, "How did you do it?"

Eldon grinned and grinned as he answered, "A lot of work."

"But how can so much be there?" asked Will.

"Memory, and lots of it."

"You mean CD-ROM?"

"Well, sure, to put it simply. It's a 66-bit system in which several CDs multiphase, which really jacks up the capability."

"Amazing," said Will, staring again at the moving panoply of beings and environs. "It's so real. So, what's it for?"

"What is it for?" Eldon echoed. "Why it's a game! The greatest game ever created!"

Will looked perplexed and doubtful, which sent Eldon out of his seat, "Wait here."

He returned with a small colorful booklet that displayed a dramatic painting of two fists encased in metal-studded gloves. The fists bent a studded bar of gray metal from which a blast of searing light flowed to split in half a planet that hung in black space. Above the picture in molten letters were the words "STARSEER."

Will paged through the booklet and discovered page after page of rules, scenarios, and illustrations. He flipped back to the inside cover and read a bit of the instructions, which described how to conquer six planet systems, each graduating in difficulty. The book also outlined what the player would need in computer strength to be able to play the game at all.

"Do you understand now?" asked Eldon.

"It's a computer game," said Will.

"Right! STARSEER is one of the most popular computer games out right now, but it's nothing compared to PARAL-LIEGE. STARSEER offers only six levels, but I've got my PARAL-LIEGE up to twenty-three and counting. The random select I've written really lends verisimilitude to the whole thing, though the virtual reality version will really take care of that in the future. Need a lot more from R&D before that becomes viable, though." Eldon then shook his head, "Doesn't matter, my liege traveling from universe to universe will blow their minds, and all of the other games right out of the water!"

He sat back down in his chair and folded himself up, smiling smugly. "So, now you know."

Will rubbed his jaw as he slowly nodded, "You do want to do computer games."

"Exactly!" shouted Eldon. He leaned forward spreading his hands wide, "I don't want to be a Cold Warrior, I want to be the Road Warrior!" He grinned, "Throughout all the universes!"

Will nodded again, then scratched the top of his head. "I never had a clue, Eldon. This is all amazing. Does anyone else know about this? Have you shown it to Forster?"

"Absolutely not!" He turned to the side slightly as he said it as if he had half a thought of shielding the flashing screen with his body. "This is my game, my program, one hundred percent this time. Besides, Forster doesn't have the imagination to see the potential of something like this. He thinks they're impractical."

Will gestured, "I guess so."

Neither of them said anything for a time. Eldon turned to the keyboard and exited the program.

"I suppose you think I'm crazy, a real stereotypical computer nerd," Eldon said, "dreaming up a thing like this."

"No, Eldon, not at all. I've had my own daydreams lately, writing poetry."

Eldon looked up at him with a puzzled expression. "Poetry? Really?"

"Yeah," Will said, somewhat self-conscious. "I used to write some in college. I've been trying to get back to it."

Eldon glanced at the screen, empty except for the cursor, and said, "Man, that is weird." Then, back at Will, "Why would you want to spend your time doing something like that?"

Before Will could react, Eldon pointed his finger at him and flicked his thumb like a gun hammer, "Gotcha."

Chapter 19.

Sitting on top of a pile of boxes stacked on a scaffold twenty feet in the air, Will tried to make sense out of what he'd found in the worn manila file folders strewn around him. In his left hand he clutched a dozen blue check request carbons while he clawed with his right hand through another file balanced on his thigh. The file, old with bent corners, bore the label P.A.–Misc., 1983-84. That's where he'd found the other copies, made out to a potpourri of community organizations, the Centreville Lions Club in Virginia, the Annapolis Odd Fellows, the Masons, for God's sake, in Charlottesville, and more for different Knights of Columbus chapters. He recognized the style of the forms as the same as ComCon's, but the legend at the top said Security Information Foundation. The amount of each check wasn't staggering by itself – $2,500 here, $3,000 there – the overall total could easily go into six figures. And that was only what he'd come across just by poking around. God knew how much he'd find if he performed a methodical search. And Julie had signed off on them.

He dangled his feet wondering what to do next, wishing that he'd never heard the name Ernie Best, or at least that the guy had blown him off and had not called him back. But he had.

"Yeah, this is Ernie Best, Mr. Day, from the Knights of Columbus, about the information forum here back in May?"

"Oh, yes, Mr. Best, thanks for calling back."

"Call me Ernie. Okay, I was right when I thought it was him, but I wanted to be sure. The record book says I was right; the moderator was a Mr. Thomas Voldani, Chief Aide to Senator Alan Beatty."

Voldani? thought Will. Forty-five hundred dollars was paid to Tom Voldani.

"Mr. Voldani subbed for the Senator," Best continued, "who had to cancel at the last minute. But everybody was happy. He did a great job."

"He did," Will said. Beatty was supposed to be the scheduled "moderator."

"Yeah, he really gave us the skinny on defense. When you get somebody like that who really knows what he's talking about, we don't mind that the principal guy scheduled doesn't show." Best laughed, "Of course, it's foundations like yours footing the bill that makes it work. So, if the main draw can't make it, no one blinks."

Will shook his head. "Let me get this straight. The foundation, that is, our foundation gave you four thousand, five hundred dollars for this forum?"

"Yeah, your security information foundation," Best replied, sounding a little bit puzzled that he needed to explain.

"And Mr. Voldani collected the full forty-five hundred on behalf of the senator?"

"No," said Best, and Will started to relax. "We keep five hundred for holding the forum.

"You keep five hundred," Will repeated.

"Well, sure. We have to make something out of the deal, you know, to pay for electricity, rent. I figure it's a win-win situation all around."

"And the rest, the four thousand—"

"Is donated by us to the senator's choice of organizations. You know that; you arranged the program."

"I did know that," Will said "of course. I'm sorry if I seem dense, Mr. Best, I'm picking up someone else's work. It's just a function of finding out which funds go where, for taxes."

"Yeah, yeah, look I've got to go."

"Sure Mr. Best, thanks for clearing this up. We really do have to establish a better record-keeping system, absolutely. Thank you again and, oh, if you don't mind; do you have another forum scheduled soon?"

"No, nothing until next month. Usually, we have one a month, no more. We did have Mike Maloney scheduled for this past month, but he didn't show. When that happens, we turn it into a party, so no one goes home mad."

Will said. "You spent the forum fee on a party?"

"Oh, hell no, just our share. That'd be a hell of a party, three or four grand."

"In that case, you refund the money or save it for future forums."

"Well, the money was already sent. I admit, it was unusual that he couldn't find a substitute, but his office said that he had a family emergency. His wife has Alzheimer's, you know? With that and his staff being busy and all, we understood. The overall program is so great, we have no complaints. Over the years, we've had some fantastic people, Justice Rabinold, Senator Burchart from Louisiana, lots of other people. It's been great."

Over the years? How many years had this been going on, he wondered. But he couldn't ask because he already was supposed to know.

"They've really given us a perspective, you know? We really appreciate the opportunity, and we think the forums are even better than the lectures you used to do. More give and take, you know? We think you people are doing a hell of a job, let me tell you, in a lot of different ways."

"Well, thank you for saying so," Will said automatically.

"Not at all. Hey, listen, I really got to go. I'm way over my lunch hour."

"Yes, well thank you very much, Mr. Best, for jogging my memory."

"Ernie. No problem at all. If you need anything else, just call me anytime."

"Thanks, Ernie. I might take you up on that."

"No problem."

Of course, there was a problem, but how big Will didn't know. At the very least he could be looking at systematic illegal campaign contributions, and that by itself could mean prosecution. The one he'd stumbled on had come out of his office, Julie signed off on them, for God's sake. Ultimately, the finger would point at him, and he didn't know a thing about it. They used to do lectures, now forums. Of course, the 1989 ethics legislation made honoraria illegal. So, they'd switched to local information forums, a neat way to get a heavyweight's undivided attention privately. Very neat, but ethical? He doubted it.

Will couldn't believe it; he didn't even want to entertain the notion at all. But the logic of such a worst-case scenario demanded that the money involved be invisible. The press of carbons in his hand already stacked up to an amount that he knew was not recorded in his budget. He continued to poke through the files, pulling the old check requests faster as the pattern became more familiar. He felt queasy every time the loop of logic running through his head reached the same juncture, the starting point for the whole train of thought.

Who came up with this scheme? Who ran it, and who had okayed it? Julie? He found the idea preposterous. Besides, other names appeared on forms dated before she had started at ComCon. Various scribbled initials had signed off on them, but he couldn't make out any of them. So, how had the old comptroller, Aaron Miller, read them? Or were these his initials? He couldn't be asked because he was gone, retired to West Palm Beach, quite a wealthy man.

Will sat back. He was getting ahead of himself, here, he reasoned. There was no call for going completely paranoid until he found out more. One step at a time, he said to himself, calming himself even as the thought crossed his mind that Forster might have hired Barry Evans counting on the new comptroller to be stupid. Will shook his head, Back up, think messy illegal campaign funding first, conspiracy to defraud and bribery later, when he had more—more what, he thought, more evidence?

He slapped his leg with the wadded papers and rubbed his eyes with the back of his hand. He was going crazy, everything in his life was driving him closer around that curve in the road, the Bend. He should take this one step at a time, and the first step was to make calls to some of these other clubs to find out who sat at the head of their speakers table on those nights.

He returned the manila folders to their storage boxes and worked his way down the scaffolding, holding the carbon copies tucked beneath his chin. Gloomily, he walked back to his office. How could this be going on all around him for so long without him knowing about it? Did everyone else know it was going on? Forster, Harry, maybe Eileen, too, though she'd never mentioned anything about it. Even Julie was involved, though how much he couldn't imagine. Maybe they all assumed that he knew, it was such common practice, they all thought, business as usual. If so, then he felt even more left out, more like a high school kid who wasn't with it. He and Barry Evans, he thought, out of it.

He reached his office to find Barry sitting in Julie's chair. Shit, thought Will. Seeing him approach, the pudgy comptroller jumped slightly, looking somewhat guilty.

"What's up, Barry?" Will said as he passed by into his office.

Barry followed him in, "I didn't want to bother you, Will."

"I'm pretty busy," Will said. He rounded his desk, opened the top file drawer and stuffed the carbons inside in the same motion as he sat down. "I have to make some calls right away. You know, the election's just days away and we have quite a lot to do, a lot at stake."

"Yeah, I know it's a bad time for you, and everything," Barry trailed off. He sat without thinking in the chair facing the desk, hunched over, twisting his hands.

"What is it?" asked Will, alert now. "What's bothering you?"

"Well," said Barry. He smiled a pasty grin, then frowned, unable to continue. He stared at the office floor.

"Is it that check request? I'm working on it Barry, trying to track it down. But with Julie out today, well . . .," he trailed off.

Barry raised his eyes, hopefully.

"Barry?" asked Will gently.

"It's this," Barry said, "I need a favor."

He halted again, until Will prompted, "Yeah? What can I do to help?"

Barry wrung his hands again, making them appear even whiter from the pressure. "It's," he said, "it's Julie."

Will sank back into his chair.

"I can't stop thinking about her," Barry gasped, "and I don't know what to do." He lowered his eyes, "I think I love her, I think. So, anyway . . . I thought, maybe . . . I thought that maybe you could . . . talk to her."

Oh my God.

Chapter 20.

The USAir Arena typified the new entertainment forums that had shot up throughout the country during the past quarter century. Fans from all over drove to the center for several reasons, not just sports, though plenty of basketball and ice hockey held court much of the year. So did closed-circuit broadcasts of the big fights, and track meets also brought in their small cadre of afficionados. But rock concerts vied with sports as drawing cards to the Arena, and junk events like truck pulls and World Wrestling Federation matches packed them in. Will could remember an occasion when a popular drivetime disk jockey bragged that he could bench-press Big John Slaughter, a 300-pound pro monster at some Grand Slam of Wrestling. The shock jock only managed to wrench his back, ending up in the hospital in traction and off the air for a week.

That kind of thing marked the new driving force behind multipurpose arenas, the entertainment quotient. Instead of flocking to a dirt field with a few wooden bleachers to witness the heroic efforts of a Jim Thorpe or a Jim Brown, people gathered at the Forums, the Omni Centers, the Cow Palaces. There they ate two-dollar slices of pizza and drank three-dollar beers with a four-dollar Dove bar for dessert while they gazed at the spandex cheerleaders aerobicizing and the electronic pyrotechnics of the giant computerized scoreboard above. Rock had replaced organ music, and auxiliary acts had become de rigueur to back up athletic displays that sometimes tested fans loyalty. Put bluntly, if you didn't have these sideshows, how could you charge twenty bucks a seat for a 13 – 30 team? On his way with Mike from the sprawling parking lot to the Arena, Will remembered hearing TV wags call sports complexes the new churches in America. It made him wonder if the denominations that went along with the analogy were the NFL, the NBA, and the NHL. So, did that make the NCAA the church youth group? Were the star players the prophets, or maybe even gods? That would explain their salaries, he thought wryly. Of course, if they were deities, they were minor ones compared to the owners, who sat above the contests in their aptly named aeries, the sky suites.

"Are we sitting in the sky suite again?" asked Mike.

"You bet."

"But, Dad, you can't see the game from there," Mike whined. "The players all look like little shrimps. Little sea shrimps in little tank shirts jumping and snapping at an orange ping-pong ball."

"I don't know what to tell you, Mike, except that this is what we got. It's the sky suite or nothing."

Even though he wasn't much of a sports fan, Will had to admit that Mike was right. He shook his head at the illogic of sky suites. Many times he'd sat in one looming above the rafters and wondered at how small a seven-foot center could look from that distance. He would hold up a forefinger and close one eye; the giant and his digit were exactly the same size. And you couldn't watch the game on the scoreboard screen because the suites sat too high; the dip of the curved roof blocked the upper half of the picture.

For those who cared to look in on the action, a 19-inch television was suspended over the glass partition between the suite's seats and the long swooping drop to the floor. The TV could be run out on a rail so that the fans could look down at a play, then up at the screen for the replay. Of course, if the cameras happened to be on the other side of the arena, the players on TV would be running in the opposite direction from those down below even though they were the same people. This became so disconcerting that the viewer usually chose one way or the other to watch the game. The fact that the television plainly offered a better view brought the absurdity full circle: Any real sports fan was better off watching at home than sitting in the so-so luxury of a $100,000 per year sky suite.

With his hand on his son's back, Will gently nudged him through the tower door and handed the tickets to the tall black man at the turnstile.

"Yes, sir, thank you, please go to your left."

He sensed genuine respect in the man's formal manner, probably for no other reason than that Will had tickets admitting him to the exclusive sky suite entrance. He had to smile as he and Mike walked into the elevator that would shoot them up to the top of the Centre. Other people stepped in, and a bubbling conversation full of camaraderie broke out, with plenty of lighthearted jokes about the game, the weather, life. They arrived at the suite level and walked down a narrow corridor where attendants greeted them warmly but business-like, asking to see their ticket stubs. Then, they separated and head down to the row of doors leading into the two-level suites, cheerily saying goodbye as they peeled off.

Of course, everything changed when two parties found themselves going into the same suite, all guests of the same absentee owner. He remembered it happening once with a young couple who had chatted him up on the elevator ride. As they walked into the suite behind him, Will said, "So, you're not rich, either, huh?"

They burst out laughing, "No, we're just happy to be here."

He and Mike were the first to arrive on this Thursday, two days after the election. The association owned the suite, and he had reserved it for a pre-season Bullets game as either a celebration of the poll results or as a salve. He had invited Maloney once he learned that he had won reelection, a miracle considering the fate of most other Democrats.

Even with all of the early indications of the groundswell that was about to occur, the results had stunned everyone. After forty years of Democrats owning Congress, no one really thought that the Republicans posed any kind of serious threat of taking control. But they had, thanks to the turnout of throngs of silently smoldering, middle-age, white males. Now, things would be different.

The Republicans crowed like Peter Pan, and the administration cowered like lost boys left out of Never Land, never say never. Newt Gingrich was everywhere in the media, and every talk show in Washington analyzed what had happened over and over again. A jubilant Forster joked at Republican victory bashes that the press wags would be asking that question for another forty years. Will, Harry, and Eileen had stayed up late, separately traversing the winners' party trail, marveling at the monumental change, potentially anyway, yet deciding to tread lightly to see how the pieces would fall.

Maloney had lost his committee chair, true, but he still knew how to work things his way. A lot of the opposition party members owed him, and if they didn't come across, he knew how to punish. But the same went for Patterson, the new chair, so Will made sure to stop in at both parties for the staff still in town.

Will had told Maloney to bring some of his kids or some friends if he liked, secretly hoping that he wouldn't ask Julie. Will also invited a few other people who he knew liked sports, some of his neighbors and some "gofers" from the association.

He always tried to include people who otherwise might never get a chance to see a sky suite. He knew that they might be surprised at the lousy view of the game, but they were never disappointed by the environs themselves, the photographs on the walls of past association directors standing next to a string of presidents: Kennedy, Johnson, Nixon, Reagan, Bush, Clinton. They spotted the senators and congressmen later: Dole, O'Neill,

Byrd, Ted Kennedy, Wright, and a host of others pressing the flesh in other faded color shots hanging above and below the chief executives. The visitors gawked at the easy chairs and tables on the lower level, which had no view of the court, remarking on the fact that people who paid the steep price for these accommodations might sometimes come and never watch the game. They murmured about the wet bar on the second floor with its ice machine and refrigerator, and the posh stools and seats stacked above the glass partition overlooking the playing area beneath them.

In a way, a visit to a sky suite was worth it whether they thought the seats or the game were any good. To most, the sky suite was a real-life ticket to "Lifestyles of the Rich and Famous." They realized right away that the suite's terrible vantage point didn't matter to people who were so far removed from any emotional stake in the sport already. Diehard fans were the first to recognize, for example, that if Jack Kent Cooke could sell the Rams and buy the Redskins without missing a beat, what did he care about how well he could see a game from his box seats? So, it came as no surprise to the various disparate guests that they could be invited to an event in a box or suite and never see their hosts. The only wonder left to them was imagining what the owners were doing instead that was so much more fascinating? Pointing out to guests that the sky suites mostly were used for business entertainment, Will noticed again and again their indifferent shrugs, as if saying, So? So who owns the businesses? They don't own themselves.

Mike immediately headed for one of the seats in front of the plexiglass to watch the teams warm up. Will checked around the bar to be sure that all of the provisions had been delivered. He found a full case of beer cooling in the small refrigerator and a pile of deli sandwiches on a shelf above. Plenty of ice in the maker, and a selection of soft drinks and mineral water, and where were the chips? He spotted them next to several stacks of plastic cups over on a credenza. Everything seemed to be ready, so he grabbed a beer and sat in one of the easy chairs in the back to wait for people to show up.

He sipped his beer quietly and decided not to worry about the security forum contributions anymore, at least until he knew more. That might take some doing, though. When he finally asked Julie, she said in a snit that she couldn't remember signing the check request, and that she didn't know what it was for. He told her what he had learned from Ernie Best, but it didn't seem to make much of an impression upon her, so he dropped it. Since the election was history, the odds were against the matter popping up.

He still would have to find some answer for Barry Evans, but even if it turned out to fall into the gray area regarding political donation legalities, for a lousy few thousand bucks maybe they'd only be slapped on the wrist, fined, and forced to promise never to do it again. As for the rest of the receipts, most of them were so old that he imagined that no one would care about running them down now.

He didn't bother saying anything to Julie about Barry's newfound ardor, either. Good Lord, he thought, shaking his head, I'm living in a political soap opera. Either that or a high school drama, Beverly Hills 909090.

The guests started filing in downstairs. Before they could reach his seat, he rose to meet them, genuinely glad to see each one of them. He introduced Mike and urged them to get a sandwich, some chips, and a drink: Find a seat, enjoy the game.

The visiting team was just returning to the floor, half-circling one basket to practice some more shots. The game would begin soon, Will noted, and Maloney hadn't shown up yet. But that was about par for the course.

Neither had Eileen. He left her a ticket, and she mumbled something about coming later if she could, after she told him that she couldn't go early with Mike. She'd been busy that way a lot these days. She said that with this trip to New England finally coming up on Monday, after being postponed twice, and another later on to the West Coast, she had to tie up loose ends now.

It saddened him, though, because he sensed a feeling of relief on her part that she was too busy to spend much time at home, or with him. They hadn't made love for a long time, not since she jumped all over him after the big fight. When was that, a month ago or more? He didn't feel so horny as he did lonely.

Eileen's libido drove her quicker to settle quarrels, sometimes before the dissolution of her anger. It made for interesting sex. This time, though, she hadn't come around, and as it lasted longer and longer, he found it to be more and more worrisome. Sooner or later, he would have to talk to her about it, and he really didn't know how to do it. He clenched his teeth as he realized again that everything causing this mess seemed to be getting worse, not better. And now with this thing about campaign money, Eileen would be the logical one to ask regarding the law. But if he did, he'd have to admit that he hadn't known about the contributions beforehand, another reason for her to lose respect for him. So, what could he do?

The overhead lights outside of the sky suite went out, and kliegs began to flash back and forth. The announcer used his best stentorian style to incite the home crowd, "Ladies and gentlemen, the Washington Bullets!" The fans roared their approval, placing hope before experience in this preseason game, this is the year for the new Bullets, this year they'll surprise everyone. The game started and they immediately fell behind by ten points.

"Jesus Christ, Day, they started on time again? Oh, well, it's a long season. How about a beer?"

Maloney shook himself out of his overcoat, then doffed his jacket. He loosened his tie as he headed back behind the bar and stooped before the refrigerator door.

A young woman following him had stopped in the middle of the room. She stood uncertainly, and Will moved up to her, taking in her fresh makeup, her black hair styled in a short, wavy cut, and the edge of a black evening dress peeking out from the collar of a long wool coat.

"Hi, I'm Will Day, from ComCon," he said, reaching to shake her hand. Her palm was cold and very small; he eased his grip in automatic fear of crushing bones.

"That's Amy Carhart, she directed my commercial," said Maloney, who had risen with a beer and sandwich in his hands.

"You know Nellie," he dipped his head toward the man behind Amy, Larry Nelson, his chief aide.

"Nice to meet you," Will said, wondering about her and where Julie was. He waved to Nelson, "Help yourself to the spread, Larry."

Will redirected his eyes to Amy, "I heard that was a fantastic spot you did for the Congressman."

"Oh, it wasn't all that difficult," she said, smiling with her eyes. "He's an amazing man. He just needed to get his message across, that's all. We were happy to be able to help."

"I'm sure there was more to it than that," he said, figuring her to be thirty or so, maybe twenty-nine. He offered to take her coat, but she said that she was still cold.

Maloney came over and said, "What do you say, let's get a seat. The first quarter's almost over."

The two ascended the short set of steps up to the stools situated on a platform behind the front row of seats looking down on the court. Will turned to Nelson, who was folding his coat and laying it over a chair.

"So, what's the deal, Larry?"

Nelson assumed a neutral expression and said, "The congressman has a very active social life. What can I say?"

"What about Julie?"

"He's still seeing Julie. Look, Will," he said, resting a hand on his shoulder, "this is nothing. Her idea, you know? She flatters the hell out of him, so he invited her to the game to hear some more."

"Really?"

"Really. She's not his type. Too pushy, you know what I mean? Oh, he likes them smart, all right, but in the background. Trust me on this, Will."

"Can I, Larry?"

"Believe me, I'll end up driving her home tonight. And that's fine with me."

"It is?" Will said, surprised now.

"Yeah. I suggested that he invite her in the first place."

"Huh. No kidding?"

"No, I'm not. I like them pushy."

"Well, okay."

Mike approached him at halftime for some money to go downstairs.

"Why do you need to do that? We have plenty to eat up here."

"Pizza? I don't see any pizza. Dove bars? Is there a secret stash of Dove bars here that I don't know about? Peanuts, popcorn– face it, Dad, we don't have any bare essentials up here in the ivory tower."

"All right, all right, here, here's the money for your college education. Don't come around in three years looking for it. Sorry, but it's your choice."

Maloney dropped into a chair near a coffee table and said, "You're spoiling that kid, Will. Let him do whatever he wants whenever, and he'll lose respect for you. Pay attention to what I say."

"Unhuh, which reminds me, Mike, where are your kids? I thought they were coming."

Maloney winced, "That's heartless, Will. They couldn't make it. I think they had to wash each other's hair."

"Yeah, I can imagine." He bent his head toward the stools, "I see you managed to get a substitute about the right age."

Maloney wrinkled his nose, "She's a favor. Good-looking, though, I'll give you that. Lots of leg. But I'm being good like you told me. Hey, Nellie, toss me another beer, will you?"

He snatched the can one-handed out of the air, "Thanks." He snapped it open, and a spray of foam shrouded his head and shoulders. He dabbed at his shirt with a napkin. "Man, I'm a real slob."

He raised his eyes, "My wife hated that about me, you know? She learned to live with it, I guess, or around it, anyway. She did a lot to maintain my image in spite of the messes I made. When I was just coming up, she used to spot my suits every morning before I left the house. She bought me twice as many shirts as a man needed and insisted that I take an extra one with me every day, sometimes two if I had a long night ahead of me. That's why I had to lug around that oversize briefcase all those years. I got a lot of unnecessary flak for that, too, I'll tell you. The newspaper boys would say 'Here comes Maloney with his bag full of deals.' Believe me, I was glad to get rid of that thing after I'd earned a little seniority. I got smart, had a stock of clean shirts laid in at the office, in the car. After she went into the hospital, though, I kind of lost the habit. But, you know, to her it wasn't really the image thing. She was so fixed on being neat, she would have had me carrying extra shirts if I was a trash man, you know?"

For a while, he dwelled on the beer can in memory. Will said, "Yeah, well, your image doesn't seem to be suffering much. You're still winning elections."

Maloney's eyes flicked up, "Yeah, but did you see them fall around me? The carnage," he said, swinging his head in sympathy "and I lost my chair, God damn it. Yeah, maybe I won, but it was close. No, I don't want to have to go through that again," he said, swinging his head back and forth like a muskox shaking off a stunning head butt. "Things have changed out there, believe me, people are not thinking the same way they used to. I've got to adjust my sights, too, I have to hear what they're saying. I mean, if a measly little schoolmarm can strike the fear of God in me, what do you think might happen when the Republicans put up someone, stealing in Macowiac's song about my competency to go along their contract bullshit and enough money for ten, hell, twenty commercials?"

"Shenck didn't do all that well."

Maloney made a clownish face, "That stiff? I wish they'd run him again, I'd cut his balls off blindfolded, I'd beat him silly. Macowiac made it a race. Hell, our party was split and he had my position, the position that won in every other district in the country, and he blew it. No, he was my only good luck this time. But they know I'm vulnerable, now, and in two years they'll find a real candidate and pound away at me, with Dole and all the others showing up to say that their guy is the best guy since Abraham Lincoln, or worse, Ronald Reagan. And, who knows? Maybe their presidential candidate will win and sweep the guy in on his coattails no matter what I do."

He shook his head again, dourly, "No, I'm going to have to change my tune." He looked into Will's eyes, "I guess this is a lousy time to tell you," he said, gesturing around the sky suite, "but this session I'll be amending my position on defense in a pretty dramatic way."

Will eased back against his seat for more support. "What do you mean, Mike?"

"I'm going to have to shift focus, Will, and make some alternative recommendations."

"I'm not sure I understand you. Just what recommendations are you talking about?"

"Now, Will, you know that the Republicans are planning on beefing up defense, part of their contract with the devil. I can't let them do that, Will, I can't let them steal my thunder. I need to help them be unsuccessful in this by pointing out how they're going to waste money on contracts that we don't need, especially considering the peaceful state of the world."

Will couldn't believe what he was hearing; he didn't want to know what he might hear next. "So, I'm going to counter with some proposals calling for more selective defense funding, and, uh, one of the areas we've targeted as excessive is in the area of computer software support."

Will concentrated fiercely, as if bearing down in his mind could alter the words that he had just heard. "Mike, you can't be serious."

Maloney leaned to meet Will's eyes sharply, "I'm in earnest about this, Will. Everyone's going to have to sacrifice some for the good of all."

"My God, Mike, it'll murder us!"

Maloney motioned a calming quiet gesture with his hand, "I know, I know that's how you feel right now, I knew you'd take it this way, but think of it in the long run—"

"There won't be any long run for ComCon! Mike, you're killing us, you're announcing our death sentence."

"Wait a minute, Will, it's not going to be that bad—"

"Mike, you don't know. We haven't won a contract all year long. Forster's making noises about layoffs right now! If you suggest that they start rolling back, we'll be out of business by the end of the next quarter."

"Will, don't you think you're being a little melodramatic, here?"

"No, I'm not. These are the facts. We backed you, Mike, all the way when others wanted to bail out, especially with Macowiac on your case. But we were there. Now we need you. You've got to find a way to exclude us from these cuts."

Maloney sat back and grunted. "I can't do that, Will. It's got to be an even-handed approach. I can't show ComCon any consideration at all because of the very fact that you've been behind me. If I put you at the head of the list, no one can hound me either way for any favoritism, while the others looking for a break will see that they have to bite the bullet, too. I'm sorry, Will, but that's the way it's got to be; that's the way it's going to be. Damn it, Will I want my committee chair back in two years and no later."

Will slumped back in his chair. "That's just great. We're dead. I'm dead. You killed me, Mike."

An expression of remorse flew across Maloney's face. He leaned forward and patted one of Will's kneecaps.

"Come on, Will, you'll get through this."

"No, I won't, Mike, not at ComCon. For me, ComCon is over."

Maloney pulled his hand back, "That's too bad. But you should have seen it coming, Will, the sign was on a long time ago. I'm just lucky enough to have seen it before it was too late. You should do the same. If ComCon is no good for you, then I suggest that you find a new work venue."

The burly congressman stood up and made his way back to his stool next to Amy.

Chapter 21.

After the game, Will slowly followed Mike out to the parking lot, now a vast desolate expanse empty of the thousands of cars that had parked on it for the evening's event. He always tried to arrive early and leave late to avoid the long queues of cars inching their way in and out of the complex. At this late hour, the barren macadam was a sparse landscape of regularly spaced light poles that reminded him of some kind of nuclear testing ground, or worse, the no-man's land surrounding a concentration camp. The brooding dark mass of the sports complex itself added to the effect, making him nod silently, thinking of the practice during South American coups of rounding up political dissidents and herding them into soccer stadiums where they disappeared by the thousands forever.

He would have to tell Eileen and everyone else about this development right away. Forster was somewhere in Florida for a long weekend. He would have to be informed, too, and he'd probably fly back to preside over an emergency meeting, as if that would help.

During the long drive home Will tried to put Maloney's announcement in perspective. It didn't have to mean the end of the world, and he really overreacted, probably due to the distractions, the stress of everything happening. Politics always presented volatile situations, like an active volcano, subject to eruption at any time after long periods of relative stability. Maloney might be persuaded to change his position again, or modify it, or at least delay it. Other powers could be brought into play, like Patterson. The new chair of the committee certainly would have a substantially different agenda than Maloney, and he'd been a shoo-in in his district for twenty years. Many things could happen and much could be done, but Forster and Eileen wouldn't see it that way. Both would read Maloney's plans as a defection at the highest level, and both would hold the Director of Public Affairs responsible – they blame me, thought Will, me alone. He shook his head in disgust.

"Man, do they stink," said Mike.

"Huh? Who?"

"The Bullets. They're really lousy."

Will glanced at his son, "Just because they lost an exhibition game? The season hasn't even begun yet, how can you be sure? They played their rookies tonight. They could be all right when their starters play."

"Come on, Dad, even you could see that they don't have anyone who can deal with Shaq or Sir Charles. They lost to the Clippers!"

"So, aren't they any good?"

"They weren't last year."

"Well, maybe they've gotten better, too."

"Yeah, dream on. I don't know why we bothered going," Mike said in a sardonic tone. "I don't know why the players bothered showing. All they get is a bad case of embarrassment."

That's all he'd get in a special meeting of the officers, Will realized. He stole a glance at Mike again, then looked back at the road.

His young son with the long blade of hair falling into his eyes stared straight ahead, clear-eyed, innocent to the whirlwind around him. He expected to see his father out playing football with the other fathers and sons. He still carried high the hope that they would not stink, that they would prevail, that honor would be served and glory won. If so, they would be Number One, simple as that. If not, life would be intolerable for that day and maybe the day after, until the next challenge appeared. But his teenage son would not be able to reconcile his father's no-show because of some fuzzy emergency work meeting called at the last minute. Will tightened his grip on the steering wheel, sure in his knowledge of Forster that he would schedule the meeting as soon as he got back, Friday night to continue through Saturday and into Sunday "if necessary."

To do what? Will asked himself, except humiliate him. Right now, if he had to choose his humiliation, he'd rather take his chances at the hands of the Booster Club than leave himself at the mercy of ComCon's officers, including his wife. And if Forster or Eileen didn't like it, they could sue him.

"Don't worry, Dad," Mike said, "The Bullets stink. But we'll get ours tomorrow at the game."

"Game?" Will said, frowning with the effort to remember.

"Yeah," said Mike. The father-son Thanksgiving football game. Tomorrow. Us Wolves against the Springfield Silver Knights. We're gonna kick their butts, right? Right?"

Oh, shit, Will silently cursed. He thought the game was next Saturday. He'd hope to run some this week. Instead, he was in no shape to play any kind of ball. But seeing his lanky little teenage boy looking at him so hopefully, he could only say, "Absolutely. We're gonna kick their butts."

He found that he had no breathing time, no time for breath. The motion nonstop as the sky met silhouettes of figures crossing in the air, body parts, arms, hands, fingers grasping, clutching. Ball geometry, air sound rushing past his ears, and he extending both arms in extremis, feeling their strange, pointed leather cups in the palms of his hands. Unnaturally he rolled his arms in with the ball, flopping forward to hold on, rolling onto the ground, as the others rolled over him, impact.

"Wonderful catch, great grab!" he heard distantly, coughing, earth air from his O-mouth to the brown ground as they told

him what to do, "No, wait – do this," and he was off his hands
from his knees out to the turf riding wet on a late season swamp.
Strangers opposing him he heard, distant dull huffs of air that
sent him powering by abreast of the stark-eyed, then away and
back again, opposite the last time, down, down, falling down on
the run but keeping going until he saw in the brooding sky air the
brown Voit again spinning, losing attitude. Hands curled out
beneath his shoulders, fixated on the burrowing vortex, abrading
fingerprints that held on, knuckles slipping between ball and dirt.

"Yes! Yes! Yes!' bellowed the coach for a day, "where have
you been hiding?"

Slaps on back, "Man, I was just getting rid of it. You got
hands, pal, that's for sure." Life was hard to grasp as oxygen,
voice calling, crying from the side, who is that? Mike. Shouting,
screaming, proud Poppa. Again, the heaving play calling,
wandering out straight line ridiculous, different place. Running in
place, too hard, turn, see ball, sit down and find it stuck in his
groin.

"All right! All right. Let's put it over."

Not hearing, breaking to the position, blood metal taste in
the throat, no blood. Rushing air in ears, run a twist to the corner,
turn feel five guys pushing hands at face, shoulders, falling
backwards, head over heels, ass over teacups, turf shoes for
earmuffs, bodies, bodies, everywhere, whistle shrilling, about
God-damn time!

"Touchdown! Jesus that was great! Jesus!"
Weary, bone, Tie, back-running, eye on tension, ball released, go
to ball, run, run, run, knock down, fall down, rest, take a nap.

Will hit the ground and lolled, with only enough strength left
to watch the tall angular end from the other team prance his way
across the imaginary line into the end zone.

God, I'm tired, he thought. And we lost.

He lay on the damp ground, breathing, and breathing again, hard. He'd had his hands on the ball but couldn't get up one more millimeter. He couldn't rise the fraction more that he had in the first quarter to knock down a long pass on exactly the same play. At the end, he'd been too tired, and they'd lost on the last play of the game.

"Tough luck, there, Will. You played one hell of a game."

"Thanks, Gary." Will stared up at the tall, heavy shouldered man standing over him. The quarterback for their team, he was a nice guy, although a bit traditionally macho. Gary's son trotted over, the spitting image of his dad, albeit without laugh wrinkles around the eyes or any gray peeking from beneath his blond hair.

"Good game, Mr. Day. You played pretty good."
"Thanks a lot, Kirk. You were good yourself."

"Yeah, well — Dad, we going soon? Some of the other kids want to meet later for something to eat."

"Yeah, sure. Take care, Will. See you next year."

Will laughed, "Ha! Don't sit any players on that bet, Gary."

Laughing, the other two strolled off.

Will looked down at his jeans, wet and muddy at the knees from falling down so many times. A collar of sweat curved beneath his neck as further evidence of his all-out effort. At least, he thought it had been all out. Too bad they'd lost, though. He hadn't felt this bone tired since he'd been a kid after playing in the back yard, all afternoon long until dark.

"Man, I'm tired," he uttered as he stood up in stages. He strolled slowly to the sidelines where Mike waited. As he drew closer, he could see a funny grin on Mike's face. He reached him and began to say, "Well, Mike—"

Mike started to laugh, high and loud, rolling his stomach as he leaned back, pointing his finger at Will, accusing, laughing, laughing hysterically.

"Mike?"

Mike laughed harder, forcing it now to sound like laughter, his eyes completely serious.

"Mike, what the hell?"

Mike still laughed, still pointing. Will finally swept past him, and muttered, "Come on. We're going, now."

At home, Mike disappeared upstairs, and Will threw himself into a kitchen chair. He was too tired to crack a beer, too tired to go up for a shower. He leaned his chin in his hands, his elbows barely able to keep him upright. Finally, he lowered his head between his arms on the tabletop to rest.

Poor Mike, he thought. Obviously, he was disappointed in the severe way possible only to fourteen-year olds. But man, that hyena act of his wears thin fast. Will told himself that he tried as hard as he could, for God's sake, and he did pretty well, considering. Poor Mike, though, had to be offsides in the last important drive and what did they do? They benched him as if the stupid game really mattered. And who remembers how good anyone was when they all played on the losers' team?

Well, it's over. Time to forget it, time would close the new fissure between Mike and him, he hoped. Right now, he didn't care. He just wanted to recover, maybe doze off a little bit.

"So, I hope you're satisfied."

A disembodied voice, he sensed; a Valkyrie or a siren? "The meeting's over?" he asked.

"What do you think?" Eileen snapped. "Without you, there wasn't much to talk about, now, was there?"

"That's supposed to make me feel bad about not showing?" Will said.

"Oh, isn't that funny," she said.

"It's not my A stuff, but it'll have to do. So, am I fired?"

And she shouted, "Damn it, Will, can't you take this seriously? Will you ever take anything I say seriously?"

"Why should I start now?"

"Because it's important to me!" she snapped.

"What, ComCon? It's a job, Eileen, just a job. There are plenty of other jobs."

"Not for me! Don't you know that? Hasn't it sunk in with you yet that I think it's important? Doesn't what I think count with you at all?"

Will straightened up. "What are you talking about Eileen? What does this have to do with you and me? It's where we work, it doesn't have anything to do with our lives."

"That's just it, Willy," she said, almost imploring him, "It's always meant more to me than to you. Only you've never understood that. Because things come so easy to you, you don't value any of it. It's harder for me to do well, so it means more to me. But you don't see that."

Will placed his hands palm down on the table, and sighed. "Eileen, I'm sorry that I'm up for the promotion—was up. I'm sorry that you aren't. You should have been; you know it and I know it. But you can't make me feel the way you do about it, about ComCon. You can't blame me for Maloney, either, nobody can, even if they want to. And we can't let these differences get between us or we're lost."

"That's right, Will," she said.

Will blinked. Something more rested in that reply other than agreement. "Eileen, what's going on?"

She sighed now, exhaling as if she was expelling months-old submerged air.

"I'm thinking of a change, Will. I don't think we're working too well anymore. Together."

He felt time wash over him, the time before she said what she just said, the time of the words registering in his mind again and again, then the endless time that began after he understood what they meant.

"Are you going to leave me?"

She didn't answer, but tears collected in her eyes. She's crying and she's leaving me. Why?

"Is there someone else?" he asked, not even knowing why.

She moved across the kitchen from the counter to the oven. "I don't know," she said, hoarsely. "I don't know what I'm going to do."

"Oh. Good."

He couldn't talk to her now. He couldn't say any of the things that flooded through him, the anger, the hurt, ego, he thought, the sympathy for her for what she must feel, the agony, the anger. He was furious. Twenty years almost, down the goddamn drain. How could he love her at a time like this, he asked himself, laughing at himself. How could he go on living, not dying right away? People live dreading these moments all their lives, the final dread a fear of a lover's death. But there was some conciliation in death, comfort in knowing that the lover who died would have stayed if there'd been a choice. But abandonment, betrayal — what an indictment, he thought, and the person who normally gave relief from such self-inflicted pain was handing it down, and leaving.

He was furious with her and curious that she looked the same as she had five minutes ago when things had been different. Now that he possessed this new knowledge about her, he didn't know what to do, just like she. Shall they go to bed together tonight? Will she sleep in the guest room? My God, he thought.

The phone rang. He leaped up, beating her to it before she could move, his fatigue, a memory long gone.

"Daddy?" a voice asked, one he couldn't recognize.

"Mary?" he said, "Is that you?"

"Yes," she said.

"Hi, Honey, what a nice surprise," he said fervently. "How are you?"

"Well," she said, her voice quavering.

"Mary?" he said, suddenly alert. "What's wrong?"

"Daddy," she said, and the word dissolved into tears a million miles away, "Alan left me."

She cried and cried, broken-hearted sobs, and he said softly, "Oh, Mary, Mary, I'm sorry. Oh, Mary," he said, but he had nothing else to say.

"Daddy, what am I going to do?" she said.

"Oh, Mary," and he jerked his head at Eileen to come over.

"Daddy, I love him so," she wept.

"Oh, Mary, here, here's Momma," and he handed the phone to Eileen.

"Hi, Baby, what's wrong?" Eileen said, then, "Oh, no. I'm sorry, Honey, that's so sad."

Without thinking, she sat down and crossed her legs, settling in to listen and console her baby, her oldest child.

Will watched her do what she did best, what he had always admired her for, her natural accord with their children. Not a woman's thing, he knew, it was an Eileen thing. With five words she could seal a broken heart while he spent weeks, months mired in an awkward, stumbling enforced bond with his son. And what was the result? Peals of neurotic laughter ridiculing his hapless efforts. He couldn't do anything right.

Eileen had done everything right, and now she was moving on, making a change. He hated her for it, and loved her, and wondered how he would ever get over losing her?

Chapter 22.

There is no disorder but the heart's
For in every place but love
the imagination lies in its limits.

He closed the volume, a collection by Mona Van Duyn, the nation's former poet laureate. The title sounded so strange for an American poet, such an affectation for a country that promoted itself as having no class distinctions. Yet, they'd created this fancy honorary post as if it meant something. He supposed that it came out of the same vein of denial in the U.S. in which people swore that they had no interest in royalty even while they fell all over each other kowtowing to England's Queen, Prince Charles, Princess Di, and the rest.

They did pick a fair country poet in Van Duyn, he admitted. He had turned to poetry to escape from his multimillion problems, and what did he end up reading but "The Gardener to His God." She was good, direct, the way he liked it. But she cut too close to the bone, this emotional expert on marital affairs. Marital affairs; haha.

He placed the book in the bottom drawer of his desk and closed it. Since Eileen had unloaded on him, he hadn't been able to concentrate much on work at the office or his own poetical meanderings, for that matter. How could he wax lyrical when he felt so wan? Haha.

Every time he tried to do something constructive, part of it, a detail would bring back an association, a memory of Eileen before her announcement. With simple-minded ease he could range back and forth through their twenty years together, decades that had sped by like spring snow, or a straw sent by a tornado dead center through the trunk of a tree. The science fiction of his recollections transported him instantly to two weeks ago when, jokingly, he'd declared to Julie that "Eileen is the antihistamine to my histamine." Just as suddenly he would find himself in the seventies, just months after their wedding, in the middle of mock-railing at her for being late.

"If I had known this before we got married—" he started.

"Yeah, what would you have done?" she pulled him up short, challenging him gleefully with her eyes.

"I would have married you a year earlier," he yelled, "then, we might've had a chance of being on time tonight!"

God, he used to joke with her about divorce; "Divorce! Divorce! My kingdom for a divorce!"

He recalled telling friends while she stood by, Yes, they were going to divorce but not separate. The line usually earned him a good shot to the shoulder. "Ouch!" he'd cry, "You're so physical."

So, what was their status now, separated but living together?

His chin almost nudged his breast as he blew out air, a release. This was hard, hard. He reached into his desk for the bottle of ibuprofen he kept there when his back acted up from sitting too long. His body still ached from the Booster game, even though it was nearly a week past. As he gripped the top, pressed down and unscrewed, he thought of Eileen walking into his office once, reaching into his drawer for the bottle and walking out with it without saying a word.

"Take the whole bottle," he'd called to her retreating back, then in an aside to the surprised people sitting in his office, "It's a pain-free form of suicide, though I have to admit, I didn't know being married to me was that bad."

And, he hadn't, either. God, he said to himself, gripping his head with both hands, I've got to stop this. Instead, he thought of her lying next to him at night this week, hearing the deep breathing of her slumber and wondering how she could sleep after doing what she had done. No, he resented that she could sleep when he knew that he would be awake in the night for the rest of his life. He'd lay there, too, sensing her figure next to him, the long legs, still taut from daily exercise, the hip turned up, covered by the oversize t-shirt that she wore as a night gown, her breasts obvious even in this relaxed posture. And he felt desire for her, different from that during twenty years of married life. Suddenly, her body had become foreign to him. Amazingly, he'd felt an urge for her now that he hadn't felt since he'd first seen her before they'd even met, when physical fulfillment had been a very remote possibility. Now, it was remote again, he thought, for a sadder reason, desire driven by sorrow.

"What a terrible time in life for this to happen," he said to himself. Then, he reframed it in his mind; A lyric of grief, a sorrow so great. So, was it worthy of Poet Laureate Van Duyn?

He heaved his chest again, another cliche of pain, self-pity. So, when will this pain that's so delicious ever become delicious? He glanced around his office, but it remained the same, same furniture, same papers piled here and there, same family photos. Nothing rushed out of its familiarity to distract him from this relentlessly dull misery. Nothing was going to change for him, ever again. He might as well continue with the usual.

He rubbed his eyes with his fists, then picked up the phone and speed-dialed a number.

"Will Day for Congressman Maloney," he said in a tired voice.

"Hi, Will." Will recognized Larry Nelson's voice on the other end. "He's out at a breakfast meeting, then there's a closed subcommittee meeting. Then he has a fund-raiser luncheon at twelve-thirty. He should be back afterwards, say three o'clock. Can I do anything?" he asked.

"I need to know if he's moved any on this cost-cutting proposal of his since we last met." When he dropped his bombshell, Will added silently to himself.

"Aw, shit," Nelson muttered. "I'm sorrier than hell about that whole thing, Will. I wish he wouldn't do that, you know, talk out of school, off the top of his head before he's made any real decision. It's really unfortunate."

"Yeah, I know, but he did it and it places us in kind of a bind, Larry. I admit, I was a bit over-dramatic myself saying what I did about its effect on ComCon. But if he gets a chance to think about the ramifications of what he's considering, the ripple-down effect of that kind of cut. It doesn't just mean that ComCon takes a major hit, it also means that a whole lot of other people will be out of work. We'll be handing this kind of R and D work to Asia, and with every high-tech job that goes to Japan or India, eighty other jobs drop out of the picture here as well. That's not even considering what this means to the defense of this country. The players might have new names, but they have the same old nuclear arsenals. And there are more of them joining the party every day. Quick strike capacity is paramount, and that means supply lines in place instantaneously. You sacrifice software support; you can severely mitigate that supply line model."

He could almost sense Nelson nodding on the phone as he heard him answer, "You're right, you're right, Will. I'm sure that the Congressman will take these factors into account before he does anything."

"I'd like to think that he'll do that."

"Look, I'll tell him you called and I'll push him to call you back at three as soon as he returns from lunch. I promise, I'll do my best."

"Yeah." Will paused, then said, "Off the record, Larry, you and me. Is he really behind closed doors all day? Julie's out of the office again."

He didn't hear anything for a short time.

"I won't bullshit you, Will, I know he's scheduled for the AACA lunch this afternoon. As for breakfast and the hearing, he wrote them on the calendar himself, not anyone here. But my honest best guess is that he's not seeing her right now. The close call of this election has given him pause, Will."

"All right. Thanks, Larry. And listen, if he can't call me this afternoon, please, before he makes any decisions or announcements, ask him to talk to Patterson, okay? Have him discuss it with other members of the committee, too, will you? I think that he might see the issue differently, you know?"

"He's talking to a lot of people, Will, before he does anything, I can assure you of that. I take it, you've discussed this with Patterson?"

"Yeah, I have, and with Stig. They're strong on this, Larry, they're behind a strong defense. Your congressman should know this firsthand from them."

"That's important to know," Nelson said, his response heavy with the weight of unspoken understanding. "I'll be sure to inform him."

"Okay, thanks a lot, Larry. I'll be waiting for him to call."

The same old crap, he thought, building a coalition to rope a stray bull and lead him back into the pen. A weekly event, he thought, that was wearing him out. Forster had been right; Maloney was a loose cannon. But damn it, he was a damn powerful cannon and hard to maneuver. Well, maybe the threat of Patterson could make a difference. But if Maloney's concern about losing his chair ran deep, no one could change his mind, not the Pope himself, not even the Second Coming, not if it happened for that purpose alone.

He sighed. He was doing what he could, though Forster couldn't see it, wouldn't see him, literally. Of course, since he'd missed the emergency meeting last Saturday, he'd become persona non grata to Forster. Will wasn't sure how much damage he'd sustained, whether or not Forster avoided him as one of his games, sort of tacit punishment through ostracization, or that he really couldn't stand the sight of him. Maybe he'd been fired after all. Will remembered the old story of how one guy had been fired for incompetence, and how he had refused to leave. He showed up day after day in his office despite repeatedly being told that his services were no longer required, that he'd been terminated, fired, Get out! The poor fellow ignored every announcement, each stronger than the last, and continued to come to work. Then, one day he walked into his office to find that his desk, chair, and the rest of his furniture had been removed. A small box with his personal effects lay in the middle of the bare floor, no more. He left carrying his box, never to return.

Will wondered if tomorrow his furniture would be gone. Forster would eliminate the interim formalities, the niceties, and cut to the chase, cut to the quick. Maybe he was so furious, he not only wanted Will out, he wanted him to suffer in the process. Truly, such behavior epitomized the highest form of barbarianism, Will thought, not just killing your victim, but making them suffer as much as possible before the dispatch. Well, if Forster removed his furniture overnight, he would march right up into his office and say, "I suppose the promotion is out of the question?"

He laughed a brittle laugh.

"I'm glad to see your spirits are soaring."

Will raised his eyes to the source of the voice and found Harry leaning in the doorway.

"I came by to see how you're doing," Harry said.

"What, do I look like I'm not doing well?" Will responded.

"Funereal is an appropriate descriptive."

"Yeah, well, I guess it's my funeral since I no-showed at the infamous weekend strategy meeting. I suppose you can afford to be generous to the vanquished now that I'm out of the promotion picture. Or is it I'm out of the company family portrait altogether?"

Harry entered the room and sat down, wrinkling his nose as he said, "You're not out of any picture, if there is one. Forster's too clever to include anybody out of anything if there's a hint of usefulness to consider. Anyway, even if he wanted to, he couldn't replace you right now."

"Yeah, sure. There're a million lobbyists out there ready to shill for ComCon."

"Better than you? As good as you?"

"No worse. Call them, aim them, and let 'em loose."

"Yeah, for five times the money. How do you think Forster would go for that, especially given the serious need of capital around here? You know Forster, he demands singleness of purpose, complete loyalty, and he's not going to get that for what he pays you."

"Yeah," Will grunted, "I come cheap."

"And you're the best."

"You mean for the money."

Harry snorted. "You know what happened at the vital ComCon meeting on Saturday? You know, the one you missed? We all sat around and asked each other what we should do. And no one had an answer that didn't start and end with your name. No one."

"You're kidding?"

"I'm not kidding. Didn't Eileen tell you about this?"

"No," Will murmured, "She's pretty pissed I didn't show up in the first place."

"Oh."

"She thinks I should have pushed harder on the promotion. I guess it doesn't matter, me telling you this now."

"Go on," Harry trailed off softly, waving Will's words away with his hand.

"So, I was the center of attention, indispensable even in absentia. I'll bet that stuck in Forster's craw."

"Forster's too smart to hold grudges, remember. If he finds that he needs you, that you're best for the job, he'll eat his own feelings about you, if he has any. His love affair is with ComCon."

Subdued, Will said, "He isn't the only one."

He gazed down at his desktop, unthinkingly tracing with his eyes the parallel scratches he'd caused a few years ago by dragging a full brief case off the surface. The scratches in the otherwise sleek, smooth mahogany burl always bothered him when he noticed them, not often enough to have the desk refinished. Gradually, the silence brought his attention back to Harry.

"Anyway, thanks for trying to pick me up, Harry. I appreciate it."

Harry opened his hands in dismissal, "Only the truth, sir."

"Yeah, one of many," Will sighed. He sat back in his chair and propped a knee on the desk's edge. "So, how did your New England trip turn out?"

"Not as I expected," Harry said quickly, starting to rise.

"Oh? You didn't find the perfect commercial venture that we need?"

"It wasn't just that. We found two possibilities, but they all wanted the same thing; money, lots of it, and right away.

"Huh," said Will.

"Yeah, if they're interested in this kind of joint action, it's usually because they're right on the edge themselves. The problem is that we can't produce instant cash, not until you shake down some of that federal conversion dough."

"I'm not sure it'll be that fast coming, Harry, if we can get it at all. Especially with the Republicans' new take on things."

"Well, if it is doable, you're the guy who can do it," Harry said as he headed for the door.

"Yeah, thanks. Anyway, maybe you'll find things more promising when you go to the West Coast."

"Hope so," Harry said as he left.

He's a good guy, Will thought sitting by himself. He felt a bit better. Maybe he wasn't in such bad shape here after all. If he could turn this around, snatch victory out of the jaws of defeat, maybe Forster would be impressed enough to put him back in the running for the promotion.

Everyone liked a comeback, sometimes even better than when the favorite won. If he could just get back into consideration for the top spot, he'd go after it hard. For the first time in his life, he wouldn't wait for matters to happen of their own accord. He would do anything to get this promotion now because he would do anything to get Eileen back.

He started to pick up the telephone to begin making calls.

"Hello?" said a voice on the other end.

"Hello?" Will replied. The phone hadn't rung, the voice was just there, a man's, familiar. Even as he realized that someone must have been calling him just as he picked up the receiver, the other said sharply, "Who is this?"

"This is Will, Mike," he said, saying to himself, I can name that congressman in three notes.

"Will, it's you. Did the phone ring?"

"Not exactly."

"Well, never mind. Listen, there's a problem." Maloney sounded strained, as though in a hurry but somehow stuck.

"What's the matter, Mike?"

"All right, I'm at Julie's. But I can't leave. Paul Sloan is standing outside with a photographer."

214

Sloan from the *Post*, Will registered, outside, ready to nail Congressman Maloney up to his old womanizing tricks, photo and all. A problem, no question, and Will suddenly had every expectation that it was about to become his.

"Did you try the back door?"

"No, I didn't try the back door!" Maloney shouted. "There's no way, her yard's surrounded by a six-foot fence. Even if I could get over it, the noise might bring those guys around anyway. Hell, they might have another guy posted there, ready to shoot me with one leg over the fucking fence. How the fuck did they get wind of this anyway?" he yelled.

"Okay, okay," Will said evenly, "You're right, we'll have to think of something else. I don't know who tipped them off." Though I'm the guy who has good reason to hang you out to dry, Will said to himself. I'm the can-do guy no longer needed, remember, and you call me?

He took a deep breath and said, "All right. Let's slow down, see what we can do."

Will drew his head back quickly from the noise, and he saw in his mind Maloney's face flushing crimson, almost as if an artery had burst beneath his skin. He wondered who had tipped Sloan off? The election was past, but House terms were short and voter memories long, especially if the opposition kept such matters alive. Once again, Maloney was at risk.

Chapter 23.

Will recalled that Julie's house, an old Victorian on Capitol Hill, had a small backyard leading to a narrow alleyway. So the old warhorse couldn't get out that way. In fact, his options looked thin on the face of it. But maybe if he couldn't get out, he might concoct a reasonable explanation for being in Julie's house besides tickling her fancy.

"Mike, it sounds like you're going to have to keep your head down for a while, maybe even all day. I don't think you want to chance Sloan getting hold of this. You'll have to wait him out."

"I can't wait him out," Maloney spit, "I've got to get out of here. I have a critical meeting at ten-thirty and a fund-raiser at lunch. I've got to get my ass out of here!"

Well, you should have thought of that before, Will thought. He mulled for a moment, then said, "Okay, did you call your office? Does Nelson know where you are?"

"Yeah, he told me to call you," Maloney said, trailing off quietly, "since you're Julie's boss. She's, uh, – we're not getting along all that well now."

Will's upper lip curled. But he had no time to wonder what was going on. For whatever reason, Nelson had thrown him an opportunity, and he had to act fast or lose it. The fundraiser struck a chord.

"Okay, what time is your lunch this afternoon?"

"Twelve-thirty. But I have a ten-thirty committee meeting."

"You're going to have to miss that," said Will.

"It's imperative that I be there!" Maloney cried out.

"All right Mike, then you might as well ask Sloan to give you a lift."

Will waited for a response but heard nothing. He could imagine Maloney silently stewing in his frustration, begrudgingly allowing reason to subsume desire. "Call Nelson and have him go," Will said, "or see if he can have it postponed. You must stay put for now, okay? You understand?"

"Yes," the congressman said sullenly, reminding Will of his son when he was in a snit. He felt the same way, too, again barely keeping a lid on his own resentment of Maloney calling him for a bail-out after announcing that he was abandoning ComCon. But Will knew that he had to control himself just as much as Maloney to get what he wanted.

"I suppose it'll be all right to miss the meeting," Maloney continued, "but I've got to make that fundraiser."

"Did Sloan see you go into the house?"

"How the hell should I know," Maloney said, "I don't have any idea how long he's been out there." He paused, then murmured, "For all I know he could've been lurking there all night, the bastard."

Will winced. As he feared, Maloney had spent the night. If Sloan had staked out Julie's place since the night before, then it didn't matter when or how Maloney came out this morning, he was screwed. Ha ha.

"It was shit-ass luck that I spotted him at all," Maloney went on, "I was looking out to see if it was raining, and there he was across the street, leaning against a car. The guy wasn't even trying to hide himself or anything. It's like he knew I was here and that I can't get out any other way but the front door, the cocksucker! Someone must have informed, goddamn 'em. When I find out who it was, I'll kill him, I'll string him up by his balls with piano wire!" Maloney paused, then said, "Hey. It wasn't you, was it?"

Ready to kill, Will calmly said, "No, it wasn't me. But yes, it's likely somebody tipped him off. Or he might just be following you. But we'll have to worry about that later. For now, you better call Larry about the committee meeting. I'll let you know about the fundraiser. Who's running it, anyway?"

"Ted Newhouse of AACA."

"AACA?"

"The American Association of Commercial Appraisers, a small outfit that's after some tax breaks in real estate. They're not the only group sponsoring the lunch, AALA's involved, CiCore, a couple more. Newhouse organized the affair, though, a hundred bucks a plate, with one-fifty sold. I've got to be there; I need to put a dent in my campaign debt."

For a cool fifteen grand, Will didn't wonder that Maloney was agitated. Of course, fundraising was a year-round activity for most pols, but he still was amazed that Maloney talked about the dinner to pay off the last election run. He must have dug deep to beat Macowiac, deeper than he had to in a long time. He was ranging far and wide to pay the tab. Will never heard of the appraisers' group before, or the others. The knowledge gave him what he needed, however, for what he had in mind to deal with Maloney's present fix.

"Okay, sit tight, Mike. I need to make some calls, then I'll get right back to you."

"All right, but make it fast, will you? I've got to get moving."

"Yeah, hold on. One more thing. Do you have a change of clothes there?"

Will waited for Maloney's answer. Finally, the congressman said, "No. I was going to stop off at my apartment before heading to the meeting."

Shit, thought Will. "Okay, don't worry about it. I'll take care of it. Is there a spare key at your office?"

"Larry has one."

"Okay, I'll have him get the duds. I'll be in touch soon."

Will called Larry at once and filled him in quickly. Then he called the AACA and asked for Newhouse. When the receptionist asked who was calling, he said, "Will Day for Congressman Maloney."

"Ted Newhouse here." The voice sounded young to Will, maybe a decade younger than himself.

"This is Will Day from Computer Control, Inc."

"Yes, what can I do for you, Mr. Day?"

"I understand that you're hosting a testimonial luncheon for Congressman Maloney this afternoon?"

"That's right, Mr. Day, but if you're interested in tickets, I'm afraid we're completely sold out."

"That's not why I called, but I'm happy to hear that you're going to have such a fantastic turnout. One hundred and fifty?"

"That's correct," Newhouse said, sounding a bit smug.

"That's excellent, excellent," Will said. "And AACA is the only sponsor, right?"

"No, there are a number of organizations involved."

"I see," Will said, trailing off as if almost troubled, murmuring quietly, "And each and every one of them with a separate agenda for the congressman." He said nothing for a heartbeat, letting the remark sink in. Then he said crisply, "Let me ask you a question, Mr. Newhouse. How would you like to have your key AACA members meet Congressman Maloney at a private breakfast before the lunch?"

"Why, that would be incredible!" Newhouse blurted, stunned by the proposal. Then, he said doubtfully, "Is it possible?"

"Completely, but you must act fast. I'm going to give you an address on Capitol Hill. You pick out twelve people whom you would like to offer this opportunity and have them be there at ten sharp."

"This is fantastic!" Newhouse said breathlessly.

"Yes, it's a unique situation. Here's the address." He rattled off Julie's address.

"I'm just blown away, Mr. Day, you know what I mean? I mean, I thought the congressman agreeing to the lunch was large. But this! How can I thank you?"

"Well, maybe someday you'll be able to. But right now, get those guys lined up, okay? Oh, and tell them not to forget their checkbooks."

A white cloudy sky curved over the morning horizon like a whipped egg custard. Although the weather mavens had predicted a warm sunny afternoon, the early cast at dawn marked a chill in the air, one of the reminders these days that winter would arrive soon.

Will waited in his car around the corner from Julie's house until the caterer's van showed up. Then, he got out and made a big scene of walking up and giving him instructions to the kitchen door yet trying not to sound too officious to the two guys unloading. One wore a standard uniform, the driver. The other wore black slacks and a formal dress shirt, with a bright red sash around his waist. Will whispered in his ear, and the young man nodded as he disappeared around back. Then, Will turned as if casually surveying the street and feigned surprise when he spied Paul Sloan.

About forty, Sloan struck the mean of men across America, average height, average build, neither pudgy nor cast iron. His hair was sandy blond, a little long and a little rumpled. He would win no more hearts than his due with his regular features, mostly looking dour, a stereotype of his profession. But his eyes changed the impression enormously, piercingly bright blue sapphires that burned like cobalt. Seeing those eyes for the first time, Will thought to himself that if they belonged to a woman, she would be considered a striking beauty. However, eyes were only eyes, and except for his better than average writing style, Sloan's resoundingly average personality brought him back to the middle of the human mean.

"Why, Paul, what a surprise!" Will called out as he approached, "What brings you here?"

"More like why are you here, Day? This is a little out of your way, isn't it?" Sloan said.

"No, not at all. My colleague, Julie Gordon, lives here. We're about to have a small breakfast party for Congressman Maloney. Are you here to cover it? Seems like a rather mundane event for the *Post*."

"Yeah, well, that's not what I heard. From what I've been told, the party's a lot smaller than you'd like me to believe."

"And who told you that, Paul?"

Sloan smiled sickly, "That's not even close to a good try, Day."

Will shrugged his shoulders, "Whoever, they've misled you."

The kitchen porter appeared from the back balancing two trays, one with two cups of coffee on top, the other with petite Danishes. "Anyway," Will continued, "if you're going to stand out in the cold, you might as well have some breakfast yourself. Ciao."

Will headed for the front door and Sloan called to his back, "Thanks, Day, don't mind if I do, 'cause I intend to stay here and see just who shows up. Anyone can call a caterer, you know?"

That's right, asshole, Will thought. He rang the bell, and Maloney let him into the small hallway.

"Hello, Will, how you doing?" He had a tumbler full of ice and what looked like tomato juice in his free hand. He closed the door and ushered Will into the small living room where the waiter continued to set up a small breakfast buffet.

"A stroke of genius, Day, you are fucking clever. I never doubted it before, and I will never doubt it again."

"Yeah, right." This close to Maloney, Will could smell that he was drinking more than just tomato juice. "Where's Julie, Mike?"

Maloney's face dimmed, "Upstairs. She's been there all morning."

Without comment, Will gazed around. Julie's house had been built at the turn of the century, and it had suffered several bad renovations. Julie had fallen in love with it despite its cramped space and the fact that it was on the margin of a "good" block in Washington.

She used a small inheritance for a down payment and her life savings to tear away all the bad fix-it jobs done over the years. After a decade of work, she could showcase a set of rooms restored with exquisitely carved plaster ceilings and real plaster walls. She put in a beautiful Italian-marble fireplace in the living room and, in the hallway, stylish black and white tiles that ran all the way into the kitchen. The wooden floors glowed from a new finish, covered only by the best factory-made oriental rugs from North Carolina. Her furniture, a mix of French Provincial and Early American replicas, had been reupholstered with beautiful floral fabrics, which she paid for with a bonus received during the go-go eighties.

The pieces de resistance were two chandeliers, one a totally unique plaster bowl that matched the ceiling and wall carvings in the living room. The other, a delicate cascade of crystal, hung in the foyer. For her troubles, she now owned the most expensive house on her block, one that if she ever decided to sell, would never yield the money that she put into it. Far from regretting her investment, however, her house was her pride and joy, the masterpiece of her personality fully expressed.

Right now, though, the place was a pig sty. Newspapers lay everywhere and almost every tabletop bore two or three glasses, dirty, some half-empty. In the kitchen, plates were piled high and the garbage overflowed the can. Will shook his head, thinking that she'd called in sick the past few days, true, but also knowing that Julie on her deathbed would never allow things to get this bad. So, she was worse off than dying, he thought.

He walked back to the caterer and said, "Hi Timmy. Is your buddy still here?"

"Yeah, out back, getting the last trays."

Will nodded, then said, "Look, there's an extra fifty apiece for you and him if you hustle and pick up around here. The caterer rolled his eyes, and Will said, "Come on, Tim, it's an emergency. Help a guy out."

Timmy sighed, then said, "I'll do my best. Jeremy!" he yelled out the kitchen door, "Get your sweet ass in here!"

"Thanks, pal."

Will walked to the front and climbed the narrow stairs up to the second floor. The door to Julie's bedroom was ajar. He knocked softly, saying, "Julie? You there?"

Chapter 24.

The door swung open upon the light touch of his knuckle. Julie lay stretched out on her unmade bed, wearing a housecoat over her nightgown. He could see that she wasn't asleep. Her eyes were open, but she didn't move even after hearing his voice. She seemed to stare at the edge of the night table instead, something that she could have been doing for hours, he imagined.

Her bedroom also sported the splintered remains of a bombed-out shell. Like lichen over so many rocks, clothes covered every piece of furniture, the dresser, an easy chair, a valet stand, the small portable television and its table. To get to the edge of her bed he picked his way across the floor, avoiding overturned shoes and strewn belts, clumped pantyhose, and rumpled, stale towels.

"Julie, what's up? What's happening?"

"You told me so," she mumbled, "So, so what?"

Up closer, now, Will could see that she looked pretty beat. Her eyes were red and puffy, either from crying or not sleeping, or both. Her skin appeared dull, too, waxy, as though she had been out of the sunlight for too long and her body hungered for vitamin D. The slackness of her muscle tone, her listless posture completed the startling, sad transformation of the bright, happy woman he'd taken note of just a few weeks before.

"He's working his way up to leaving me," she said, still gazing at the white wooden table. "He's doing a lot of hemming and hawing, telling me he's worried about his wife, about being loyal to her. He says he's worried about the media finding out. He tells me that he really loves me," she said, catching a sob in her throat that erupted inadvertently when she said the words, "but that he's not sure this is the right thing to continue doing."

Will slowly lowered himself to sit on the bed. "Oh," he said, stymied by the pain that she so plainly felt. "I'm really sorry to hear it," he said, "it's so sad." Then, unable to help himself, he said ingenuously, "You really fell in love with him, Julie? I mean, even knowing about the others?"

She sobbed plainly this time, "He said that with me it was different. He said he really loved me." She began to cry hard, without making a sound.

"Oh, Julie," Will said, and he pulled her up to embrace her, hugging her and patting the back of her head. She lifted her head and said, "He's seeing someone else, you know?"

Will froze. "You're kidding?"

"No, the bastard. He's seeing that bitch who helped him make the commercial."

"Amy Carhart?"

"You know her?" Julie said in surprise. Her eyes hooded with suspicion.

"Yeah," he said quickly, "she came with him to the Bullets game last week. Larry said she was with him, not Maloney," he replied, thinking Nelson you son of a bitch. Then he said, "You don't know this for sure, do you?"

She swung her head up and down vigorously, "Sure I'm sure. He called her from here! I listened to him on my bedroom phone, he thought I was asleep. He told her that he couldn't come over this morning, he was running late. Running late! The fucking bastard!"

"My God, what a shit," Will said with absolute amazement. "You mean, he spent the night with you, and then go directly to her place?"

Julie pulled away from him, twisting her back to him. "He didn't sleep with me last night," she said.

225

"What?" Will said.

"It's a little honor thing of his. He won't fuck someone he's about to dump."

Will flinched at the bitter words.

Julie sighed, "I know I should have seen it coming, I knew the way he is, and you tried to tell me. You knew it'd be no different with me?"

"Aw, Julie, what do I know?"

"Enough. But I had to go fall for him. Figure that out, will you?"

"Yeah, it's a screwed-up world," he thought, remembering his own troubles with Eileen. He sighed and patted her shoulder.

They sat quietly for a time. Then Will said, "So, when did you call Sloan?"

She said, "Right after he hung up with that Carhart bitch. I called the paper, and Sloan was on the night desk. So, he got lucky."

Then Sloan hadn't seen Maloney enter Julie's house last night, Will thought. Although after all of this, he wondered now why he was still covering for the no-good son of a bitch. But allowing Maloney to go down the drain wouldn't do Julie any good, not professionally or romantically. That's the way lobbying went mostly, he thought. There always seemed to be a good reason that helped everyone else do what you wanted done for their own interests.

"Okay, Julie, so you want to get Maloney, but that's no good. First, he's not worth it."

"I don't care."

"Listen, if Sloan does nail him, where does that put you? Your reputation in this town will be over. Forster will cut you loose and nobody else will touch you with a ten-foot pole. Your career is not worth destroying just to lay one on Maloney."

"I don't care."

I don't care, I don't care, he mocked in his thoughts. Isn't anyone around here a grownup? He exhaled slowly, trying to maintain his grasp upon things. Then he said, "All right, what is it you want? I mean, really want?"

She turned her head to see him over her shoulder. Her mouth quivered, "I want him back."

He stopped surprised. Then, he said, "Well, okay, then this is not the way to do it. One thing for sure, Maloney values his job more than anything on the planet, more than you, his wife, or some smart-ass woman from an ad agency. He'd give his life to stay a congressman."

"Don't you think I know that?" she shouted, and he glanced nervously out the door toward the staircase. "Maybe that bitch made his big fucking commercial, but I got him the goddamn money for it."

Will nodded, completely understanding how proportions are distorted when viewed through the facets of love.

"I know," he said, "I found the receipts."

"You know?" she said in surprise, "You found the receipts?"

"Yeah. I had to, Barry Evans tumbled upon one of them, so I had to do a little digging." While he spoke, red slowly effused Julie's face. She smiled that peculiar little smile of the thoroughly mortified, as if hoping to be relieved of the enormity of her transgression by good humor. Oddly, he noted that her smile was like the Mona Lisa's, and he wondered if by chance that he'd fallen upon the explanation of her mystery at last. He shook free of the thought as she started to speak.

"So, you know," she said. "Jesus, Will."

"Yeah," he said reassuringly, "but what I'd really like to know, Julie, is who authorized the money? It doesn't show up in our budget. Is Forster behind this? Is he running a special fund?"

While he was still talking, Julie swung her head back and forth, "No, not Forster, Harry Olssen."

The information stung him. Harry?

"He had me set up those information forums, and lectures before that. I've been doing it and making other special arrangements for Harry for years, now, even before you came."

Harry? Will blinked, trying to grab hold of the idea.

"Harry picked it up from Miller, who started it years ago to, you know, make some friends on the Hill and at the Pentagon. When the media started crying about the Iron Triangle and Forster hired you, Harry decided to keep his hand in."

She finished with a shrug.

Will said, "I can't believe this. Harry," he lowered his eyes, "and you. Man, Julie."

"I'm sorry, Will. When he asked me to keep it private, I didn't know you then. By the time I felt comfortable with you, I'd kept it to myself for so long, I didn't know how to tell you. So, I didn't."

Oblivious to her now, his mind rushed ahead, leaping from thought to thought. Julie had initialed the receipts, and she worked for him as far as any auditor could tell. That meant that he might be the one held responsible for a pile of illegal contributions that he hadn't known a thing about for ten years. At the very least it was embarrassing, moving right on up to incompetence on the brink of indictment. What to do, what to do? He ran his hand through his hair, thinking hard.

"I'm really sorry, Will. This puts you in a bad spot."

"Huh? Yeah, well, never mind about that right now. Let me tell you what you have to do. You've got to pull yourself together and be the perfect hostess for this breakfast. I mean you have to be the life of the party, Julie, if you want any chance to salvage this situation."

She dropped her head in a pout, "I can't do it, Will. I'm not feeling well, and I don't feel like it."

"Yeah, well, maybe so, Julie, but you don't have any choice. Because they're coming whether you're ready or not. I'm telling you, maybe it's over with Maloney, maybe not. But if you don't stand up for him now, it will be over, and so will your job. If you act strong now, though, at least you'll have a chance later to see how things go. But you've got to come through today."

She perked up a bit during his pep talk, the tone of defeat in her voice replaced by a whine, "But I can't have anybody over here, the house is a disaster. I can't get it straightened in time."

"I've taken care of that. All you have to do is get yourself together. Julie, show him the you that grabbed him in the first place. Show him how much you don't care if he walks. Be yourself again, and maybe he'll stick around to see more."

He saw a tiny shaft of light, of hope, in her eyes. "Come on," he said, "Go shower. I'll send up some coffee."

Will headed downstairs and looked around. The house appeared immaculate, as though just visited by an Army cleaning service. He turned to the caterer putting the finishing touches to a small breakfast buffet in the dining room and nodded his respect. The thin young man shrugged and said, "I use to work for a cleaning service. I was a hair too compulsive for them, ate up their profit margin, so they canned me. But," he sighed, "I guess it helped here."

"It sure did," Will said, "Thanks a lot."

He stood up to leave, then stopped. "What's your name?"

Surprised, the young porter straightened up. "Jeremy. Jeremy Helmsworth."

"Jeremy," Will said. He held out his hand, "Nice to meet you, Jeremy."

The young man's face reddened as he shook Will's hand, "Thanks Mr. Day."

"Sure, Jer'. You know, you're tall."

Jeremy grinned, "About six-one. Maybe two."

"Unhuh. Play any ball?"

He shrugged, "Intramural in college. I'm on a break now. Working for next year's tuition."

"Oh. You're lean, man."

"Oh, not that much. Thirty-four around my waist."

"Yeah, of course. Listen, Jeremy, how'd you like to earn a C-note on top of your fifty?"

Jeremy blinked. "Wow! What do I have to do?"

"Let me borrow your clothes."

"Huh?"

"No, nothing like that. You'll simply occupy the downstairs loo in your skivvies for an hour or so. Restroom temporarily off limits."

Jeremy grinned, then frowned. "What about my boss? I really need to keep this job."

"Yeah, don't worry about that. Timmy and I go way back."

Chapter 25.

Will wandered into the living room and found Maloney sitting on a couch holding his Bloody Mary in both hands. Most of the ice had melted, and the slice of lime floated in the watery juice like a derelict ship waiting for salvage.

"You better make that your last. You still have to take care of the people coming over this morning."

"Huh," grunted Maloney, seeming to inspect the liquid with his gaze, "It's just to take the edge off of last night." He looked up, "Besides, when did I ever have trouble holding my booze?" He sipped, staring again into his glass. "Of course, it's an insidious thing, booze is" he said. "It creeps up on you after forty years or so. I've seen guys who could really drink when they were young, you know, act like they were fresh-washed for the morning even though they hadn't been to bed the night before. Sooner or later, though, the long-term sets in. They'd stop communicating. Oh, they talked, God, would they talk. But they didn't hear anybody else, just themselves."

He looked up, "Women marry these guys, thinking nothing is wrong, that their husbands go off now and then, you know, really let loose at parties, not all that unusual. They realize later that there's nothing left but the drinking. The brain cells shut down, one by one. These guys become full-time boozers without even knowing it. And because the brain cells that tell them to stop are gone, they don't stop. Then, they're gone."

Contemplatively, he took another sip. Then he raised his sight to Will. "How's Julie?"

Will clamped down on his anger. "Not good."

Maloney nodded his head several times. "We've hit a few rough spots."

"You're messing up her life, Mike. She's missing work and doesn't seem to care. Her job is really important to her, as important as yours is to you."

Maloney nodded again, "I know, I know. I've got to make things right. I'll work it out, it'll be better, I promise you that."

He paused, concentrating, Will supposed, though the big man's florid features didn't seem to change through the process. No revelation appeared to light his face with an emotional epiphany. But then he looked up and said in a quavering voice, "I love Julie, you know. I really love her, as much as anyone, as much as I love my wife."

Will winced at Maloney's latest heartfelt declaration, though the poll's obvious sincerity startled him somewhat. At length Will said, "If that's so, then you have to treat her better."

"Yeah, yeah, I know," Maloney said. "But look at this shit I'm in now. It's hard, Day, damn hard." He dropped his head again.

Will didn't know whether to believe him and wondered if it made a difference one way or the other. Probably not, he thought, although a corner of his mind entertained the fantasy of Maloney quitting the Hill and running off with Julie to Pennsylvania, or to her home in Ohio. Madness, he thought to himself. Look at your own life and find the romance.

Maloney stirred. "I guess, after this," he said, "I owe you."

Will didn't respond, keeping his expression neutral.

"Once, I had this girlfriend," Maloney said. "She was tough, more self-centered than me, even," he said, laughing at his own self-deprecation. "I never really knew where I stood with her, I was never sure that she gave a damn. Anyway, one morning she calls me and tells me that her car is stalled, just a few blocks from my place. So, I drive over and give her a start, it's the battery, see.

232

She follows me back to my place and we go inside. So, she looks at me and says, 'I guess I owe you now.' And I said, 'I guess you do.' Well, before you know it, we're going at it on the living room floor. And I don't know what it was, that she was a knockout—she was a fitness nut, you know? Or maybe it was because she was so stingy about doing it at all that I got over-excited. Or maybe it was the position, I had her from behind, not my best for staying power. Whatever, I finished in a matter of half a minute. She looks around at me and says, 'You're done? Great, I still have time to go out and run.'"

Maloney shifted to Will. "And she did," he said, an amazed look upon his face, "Off she went jogging as if nothing had happened, full of me and everything." Then, he smiled sheepishly and said, "She owed me, and I guess she paid me. But, for the life of me, I don't know how she, on her hands and knees with her bare ass sticking up in the air, how she could make me feel like I was the one fucked like a dog."

Will listened impassively. When Maloney fell into silence, he said, "Okay. You better get dressed. Use the downstairs bathroom. Do you want a cup of coffee?"

Malone shook his head no, Will nodded and pivoted to the front room. Nelson arrived with the change of clothes, and as he passed by in the narrow hallway, Will murmured harshly out of the side of his mouth, "I need to talk to you later, alone."

Nelson started slightly, then lowered his chin in assent.

Will kept watch at the front window, eyeing every move by Sloan and his camera man. Nothing disturbed the quiet morning in Georgetown until Timmy backed the van out of the driveway and sped down the street opposite Julie's house and Sloan on the corner. With the street's peace restored, Will straightened up smiling grimly as he turned to get coffee.

A half-hour later, two limousines pulled up in front of the house, filling both lanes of the small side street. Six men stepped out of the cars and waited as a seventh emerged from the passenger's side of the lead car. Nelson bounded down the front steps to meet Maloney, gripping his elbow as he pivoted to assess the men crowded around them. After introducing the representative, he deftly slipped around to Ted Newhouse who grinned broadly, almost triumphantly in fact.

Will watched Newhouse act the peacock among his fellow appraisers. He was young, as Will had originally imagined. Just thirty, he estimated, though surprisingly so, as he was almost totally bald on top. The ring of reddish hair around his head looked like a tonsure, the monkish effect heightened by his innocent, open features and creamy complexion.

He saw Will looking his way and walked over. "Ted Newhouse," he said, putting out his hand.

"Nice to meet you, Ted, I'm Will Day."

The young man beamed his gratitude. "I can't tell you, Mr. Day, how marvelous this is. If you ever . . . I mean—"

"Don't think about it, Ted. And it's Will. You're helping me out, too, you know? I think it's important that people with common interests work together."

Newhouse's face instantly turned solemn, as though swearing an oath, "Absolutely, Will."

He entered, and Will brought him to Maloney and Nelson. Julie appeared at the top of the stairs. Her hair shone lustrously, a fantastic contrast to the stylish blue of her suit, the jacket a professional statement that demurely deflected the sensual effect of her short skirt and black hose. Her unhappiness had caused her to lose weight, he noted, which ironically made her look more attractive. She descended the stairs and took over, the old Julie, kidding the awkward businessmen and association flaks into feeling comfortable. And Maloney noticed, Will noted.

Maloney charmed all of them himself, one by one and as a group. The old campaign warrior lived again, sipping coffee as he listened, telling stories as he presided. Will nodded to himself, it seemed about as good as it could get.

The doorbell rang, and he said, "I've got it."

He opened the door and greeted a tall man standing on the porch in front of another man with a TV camcorder on his shoulder.

"Paul Sloan, how the Helsinki are you?" Will asked, grasping the tall man by the shoulders.

"I'm good, Will, just fine. How are you, how's Eileen and the kids?"

"Good, good, all's well. How's Paul Junior? Does he like college?"

"Yeah, he does," Sloan said, "You were right about Maryland, he loves it. Though I kind of wish he went some place a little further from home." He grinned, "Anyway, thanks for getting 'Maloney' to write the letter. I'm sure it sealed the deal."

"Ah, bullshit, he got himself in. So, ready to take the congressman's

"Yeah," Sloan said, then in an anxious tone following with, "but I can't guarantee they'll use it at all, Will. You know that, right?"

"Of course." He looked over Sloan shoulder at the WUSA van parked in front of the house, then over to where Sloan had been standing just five minutes before. The sidewalk was empty.

"I think you've done a great job already, Pauly Boy. Do you need to set up any lights?"

He ushered the two men in, and as they set up to tape, Ted Newhouse ran over to him, gushing, "Will, I don't get it, but I love it. I owe you big time! What can I do, what can I do, now and forever?"

Will watched Maloney broadcast his ad hoc stump speech, pontificating about the need for real estate tax reform and other vital issues, with Julie standing to his right and slightly behind, smiling, really smiling.

"Ted, you don't owe me anything," Will said. Then, he looked around the house. "Well, you could do me one favor."

"Name it."

"The waiter over there," he gestured with his head at the buffet, "he has the invoice for the breakfast."

"No problem," said Ted, already starting to walk over.

"Oh, and—," Will said.

Ted pulled up, flashing a brief expression of concern.

"I promised the two guys each an extra fifty bucks," Will finished, "but the tall one should get seventy-five."

Ted blinked, then said, as if he'd expected more, "Fine."

Yeah, everything's fine, Will thought, laughing silently as he pictured Timmy walking out the kitchen door, trying to front Maloney on the short distance on the driveway to the van. Dressed in Jeremy's patriotic outfit, the so, so honorable congressman held a bulky box of clothes wedged on his shoulder to block his head from view. At the same time, he could barely hold up his too-tight catering trousers from tripping him. Amazing how just half an hour later he strutted back in his usual dapper duds. But that was Maloney.

The end of that kind of fun, too, Will recognized. Now, all left to think of was Julie and Maloney, of Harry and the campaign money, and eventually, finally, of Eileen and himself.

Chapter 26.

Eileen draped the garment bag over a kitchen chair and dropped her small overnight suitcase on the floor next to it. She filled a glass with ice and mineral water, then sat down at the table and flicked on C-SPAN. She felt tired, exhausted, drained of the ability to think. Yet, all she did was run over again and over again the things she didn't want to think about, looping through her mind out of control. That was it, her life, out of control.

She stared down at her legs and splayed feet, half out of her half heels, her skirt, a bit short in the first place to show off her good legs, now high on her thighs spread shapeless and weary on the edge of the chair. She imagined herself a spent boxer slumped on his stool, waiting for the next round to start, dreading the repeated blows to come. As she yanked at her hosiery, she realized that the image was laughable, consistent to one of the trendy yuppie professional women who had "discovered" boxing. But the dread was serious enough.

She didn't want to leave the kitchen to go to the bedroom because that would take her past the stairs down to the laundry room where Mike would be studying next to Will. They might hear her and come up to say hello, Mike leading the way, Will following grudgingly him. She wasn't sure she could face Mike in his innocence, or Will, dark-faced and brooding. She could picture the terrible imaginations going through his mind, to which she was forced now to add the actual secret facts of her betrayal.

She felt guilty. But did she feel regret? She bit her upper lip, thinking. Harry had laid it on in New England, that was for sure, but she'd also lapped it up with a spoon. Waving her hand in front of her face self-mockingly as if for air, she'd really been beckoning to Harry, "More, more!"

And he'd given it.

The time with Harry had been a relief, fun, something different. It had been easy to be knocked over by him, the big golden bear, after twenty years of half-hearted recognition by others, her colleagues, her children, even Willy, though inside she always knew he respected her deeply. Was that the same as love, respect?

Maybe she put Harry off because of that, because she owed Will that much. Or had she demurred this time as a step in the dance? Harry had retired graciously, and she felt a little bit foolish for being so coquettish at this point in her life, married twenty years with two children. Except, they were the same exact reasons why she held back. The idea of going to bed with Harry didn't faze her. She could admit to herself objectively that she wanted to, that she found herself thinking about him more and more in that way, what it would be like to feel his big blond body above her, crushing her deliciously. In her younger days, she might have given into a moment's headiness and taken her chances that it would last longer than a short romantic interlude. If it ended quickly, she would have felt lousy but still ready to chance it again, love.

All that, of course, was before she met Willy. Twenty years since had taught her well, as with most adults, especially ones who'd become parents, the tried-and-true old saw that sex wasn't love. So, was she holding Harry off because she wanted to be sure of his love, or of her own?

The nagging question had kept her in check, but for how long? When she looked into the future, she could see matters only growing worse between herself and Willy, while she grew closer to Harry. The horrible truth to her, the real betrayal of Willy and their marriage wasn't that she almost went to bed with

Harry, but knowing that she could, that most likely she would. If things continued to deteriorate between herself and Willy, she knew that sooner or later she'd fall into bed with Harry. Even if she tried to persuade herself that it was simply a physical activity, a pleasurable release that had nothing to do with their troubles, she knew the lie of it beforehand, at the very least as far as Willy was concerned. So, she grieved now for their loss even before it had been lost.

A rumble of feet on the stairs below coming up to the living room caused her to cringe until Mike barreled headlong into the kitchen. He braked abruptly before hitting the back door.

"Oh," he said, surprised. "You're back. I didn't hear you come in."

"Hi, Mike, how are you? I just got in, so I thought I'd get a sip of something cold before dragging myself upstairs. How are you?"

"Eh," he said, shrugging and pursing his lips in a grimace of forbearance. He said, "Nothing's knew. Life sucks and I want to die."

"Unhuh," she said, "So, where are you going?"

"Oh, uh," he said, turning back from the door, "out."

"Yeah? Where?"

"I don't know. Just out," he said sullenly until he saw her face begin to pull together tightly. His voice then shifted higher verging on a whine, "To take a break. I'm sick of studying."

"Oh? I'm surprised your father is letting you," Eileen said, peering around the edge of the door frame.

"He's not here. He called to tell me that he wouldn't be home until later. He has some meetings or something."

"Oh." Eileen blinked at the news. Since Mike had been caught trying to bribe his classmates, Willy had been religious about getting home early and shutting himself in with his son.

They spent three hours a night together in the laundry room, one and a half before dinner, and one and a half after.

Eileen could see Mike bolting at any opportunity, and she didn't blame him one bit.

"So, you're taking off?"

Mike lowered his head, ready to be bitter at having his near escape unexpectedly thwarted.

"Don't worry," Eileen said, "You can go—"

He pivoted and started for the back door.

"—in a minute! Sit down for a second and talk to your mother."

"Oh, Mom!"

"Sit! No, sit here, next to me."

Mike clambered onto the kitchen chair next to her, hanging one long arm around her shoulder and stretching his legs on the floor. He weighed a lot, Eileen thought, though after moving around a bit, she managed to redistribute the load to make them both comfortable.

Mike lowered his head into the crook of her neck and shoulder. He nestled in, and she pressed back with her hand on his brow, slowly caressing, saying, "How's my baby? How's my baby boy?"

"Oh, Mom," he sighed, "why do things have to be so hard?"

Continuing to pat him, she said, "I don't know, Honey. Maybe because we're only human. You understand?"

"No," he said sadly.

"I mean," she said, "because we're not perfect, we make things hard for ourselves. If we really tried more, think more about what we're trying to do, we might not have these problems."

"Yeah," he said, "but knowing that doesn't make it any easier."

"No," she admitted, "but maybe it could make us easier on other people knowing that they're human, too. If we all think this way, maybe we all would be kinder, and things would get better for everyone."

Even as she floated these bromides, she realized that she could never say them to another adult with any conviction. She hoped that they would comfort her young son, that was all.

"You see what I mean?" she said.

"I suppose," he said, "but not a lot of other people are doing it."

"No, I guess not," she said, "But you have to try."

He didn't respond. She patted him a bit longer, then said, "What is it, a girl?"

"Yeah," he said at length. "She likes some other guy."

"Oh, that's too bad."

"Yeah," he said, raising his voice, "and don't tell me that there's something wrong with her if she doesn't like me, because I know better. There's something wrong with me. To her, anyway."

"Oh, no," Eileen said in a hushed voice, "What is it? Is it fatal? Is that why she's avoiding you? You have a dread disease? Would you mind moving over a little bit right now?"

"Mom!"

He tried to get up, but she grabbed him in a neck lock. "Don't leave me," she said, "I'll miss you so. Besides, I'm probably already infected."

"Mom, this is not funny!" he said, keeping a stern face, "This is my life!"

"Oh, come on, don't make me laugh," she said.

He struggled harder but she held on until he gave up. After a moment's quiet, she said, "Don't you know that you're irresistible to real women?"

"No."

"Sure you are. You're irresistible to me," she said, nuzzling his neck.

"But you're not a real woman, you're my mom. Ugh!"

She pulled back. "Well, thanks a lot."

"Oh, you know what I mean. I'm a geek. I'm no good at anything. My life is over, or it might as well be."

"Now don't say that. You're good at plenty of wonderful things, oodles."

"Yeah? Name three."

"Okay," she said, pausing to think. The pause grew longer, until they both burst out laughing.

"See? I'm a dork."

"You are not. Remember, Sandy liked you." She could have bitten her own tongue off as soon as she said it.

"Sandy? I thought both of us were on the shithouse list—"

"Watch your language."

"Yeah, okay, sure. But since when did Sandy become okay again?"

"Since she went away to school," Eileen said, following quickly with, "Listen, it wasn't so much that you did something bad as that you did it too soon, and the fact that doing it at all these days can be dangerous. I don't have anything against Sandy, I just don't want you to get hurt or ruin your life."

Mike jumped to his feet and said, "My life is already ruined, Mom! I suck in school, I suck at sports, and everyone laughs at me when I try to do anything. Can't you see this?"

"No. Because things can change for the better. They really will, Mike, really. You have to possess that kind of hope, or you'll never find out that it's true."

"Mom, this is strange coming from you. I'd expect it from Dad, but you?"

She sat back. She never realized that Mike thought of her like that. Skeptical, even cynical? She never thought of herself like that and even so, she thought she kept any such impulses away from the kids. Was she that transparent? They knew her better than she knew herself.

She shook her head and continued, "Your father wasn't always good at doing things, which is why he believes in working hard to improve."

"Mom, you've got to be kidding. Dad's a natural, he's been one all his life. He can play sports without ever practicing, he's drop-dead goodlooking, all the girls in school say so whenever he shows up. And he can talk to anybody no matter who they are. Face it, he's a stud, and amazing that he's such a nice guy about it, you know?"

He stood looking down at Eileen while she marshalled more arguments to persuade him that life was good. A familiar voice broke over the lull from the TV. She glanced and said unconsciously, "Maloney. Look, it's Maloney, the congressman your father is always chasing."

They both watched the set as the big, dark-haired representative expounded on the need for commercial real estate tax reform. The camera drew back to show Maloney's aide Nelson and a few others affecting rapt attention.

"My God," Eileen said, "it's Will. Look, Mike, it's your dad."

They stared at the small black and white screen as his nose and mouth bobbed in and out at the edge of the picture frame.

"And that's Julie behind Maloney," Eileen said softly.

Maloney finished his strident comments, then shook hands with a small balding man who grinned broadly. Maloney grabbed the man around the shoulders with one arm and Julie with the other and squeezed, triumphant.

"Huh," Eileen mumbled, "Willy on TV."

"You see what I have to deal with?" Mike said waving his arm at the screen. "How am I supposed to match that?"

In two steps he was through the kitchen door.

"Mike," Eileen called to the empty space, but he was gone.

She swung her head, still mildly astonished to see her husband on television. He had been on now and then through the years, popping up in the wings of various video news bites. But today's appearance surprised her seeing that he had caught up with Maloney once again. She wondered if Forster had seen the clip.

The kitchen door opened as Will walked in.

"Hello, Willy."

He glanced at her and said cooly, "Hello Eileen."

"You just missed yourself on TV, with Maloney and Julie."

"What? Oh, Maloney? What station is this? C-Span." He gazed at the screen, identified the newscast as one on Iran, and turned back to Eileen. "What did he talk about, real estate taxes?"

She nodded, "Yeah, he seemed to be standing in front of a fireplace in a small house. We saw you to the side, your nose and mouth, anyway."

"Yup, they shot it at Julie's house during breakfast. Did you see the time?" She shook her head no. "So, we got a little bonus," he said. "No shit. That's great. I'll get a clip tomorrow and send it over to Maloney's office."

"What happened?" she asked. "How come it was at Julie's place?"

Will sat down and told her about Maloney's peccadillo and his escape. "So, he might get a favorable recommendation from the ethics committee after all, if he can keep his nose clean for a while. Which seems like a remote possibility. When I got there, he was working on a Bloody

Mary. This is at nine in the morning, mind you. But" he sighed, "his ass is safe for one more day."

244

"That's great, Willy," Eileen said, genuinely impressed, "how you did what you did was amazing."

"Yeah, thanks," he said, smiling wanly. She could see his enthusiasm ebb away as he returned to what was happening between them.

"So, how was New England?" Will asked. "Are we now proudly part of the free market system?"

She pressed her mouth together skeptically, saying, "No. Too much debt to absorb, not enough cash flow. They tried to make it look more attractive with six-month figures showing a steady incline in sales, but a little digging turned up too many deep discounts given at the same time. Kind of like a fire sale."

"Oh. Well, maybe California will be more fruitful."

"Maybe," she said, "but they're in bad shape, too. We have to be really careful."

"Yeah. Maybe conversion isn't such a good idea. I mean, this way, taking this route."

"Ah, it's hard to say," Eileen said in a tired voice. "The perfect match might just fall out of the sky."

"Yeah."

They looked at each other searching for something to say. Finally, Will made a move to rise. "Well," he trailed off.

"You're home late," Eileen said hurriedly.

"Yeah," Will said, sitting back. He turning his head to the basement door. "Is Mike downstairs? I called to tell him I wouldn't be home on time."

"He went out," Eileen said.

"Out? Just out? You don't know where he went?"

"No, I don't, but I'm not worried. He just needed to take a break."

"Oh," Will said. He leaned forward in the chair and clasped his hands loosely between his knees. "I told him he had to keep studying as if I was there, but I guess it's okay for him to go out for a while."

A tassel of hair fell curling across his brow, making Eileen wonder at how he still could look so boyish, even with gray racing strands intertwined. After so many years together, sometimes the realization of how striking he was came to her as a surprise. It saddened her now.

"That kid is a piece of work, boy," Will said, "a real pistol. I don't know if this new regimen is working, but it makes me cringe to think of what might happen if I didn't have him on a tight leash."

"You're joking," she said.

"Well, maybe," he said, "but you have to admit he's a lot different than Mary."

"Oh, well, Mary," Eileen said. "You can't compare Mike to Mary. You can't compare Mary to anyone, there's no one else like her."

"Yeah, I guess that's for sure. I'm not surprised that old Alan left her. Who could ever meet her standards? Where did she get them from anyway? We certainly never had any standards that high."

She laughed, "Oh, come on."

"No, I'm serious. Remember when we were urging her to try some different things, experiment in life. You remember?"

"Sort of," Eileen replied.

"And she came back at us asking why she should experiment when she knew what was important and what wasn't, what was right and what was wrong. I remember it now; 'what's right and what's wrong,' her exact words. 'Why should I try different things and end up like you two – you don't even go to church!'"

Eileen did recall the incident now. She remembered vividly exchanging looks with Will, both consumed with guilt. She felt guilty even now and wondered if there was truth in what Mary said, given their horrific present state of affairs. State of affairs. Ha. That's how Will would joke if he could read her mind.

"Man, that was a stopper," Will said. "I still don't have an answer, not good enough for Mary, anyway. Funny, though, she never elected to go to church on her own. And now Alan has bailed out on her, the poor kid."

Eileen watched Will gazing at the kitchen tiles, struck by his sweet selflessness again. His own misery couldn't prevent him from feeling sorry for his daughter losing her first love. This was becoming so sad, she thought.

He caught her staring when he looked up.

"I was out late, Eileen, working. Not just Maloney, but Patterson and all the rest. I'm going after them, I'm going to save ComCon's ass. I'm going to give Harry a run for his money."

She flinched at the name, but he didn't seem to notice.

"I don't want you to go, Eileen, that's the reason. I love you too much to let this happen meekly. I might get the promotion, I might not. But it won't be for lack of trying."

He hesitated before going on, "I know, it's weak of me to ask you this, but I'm weak. If you can, can you tell me if this might make a difference?"

He hung on for her answer, she saw plainly, which made her feel worse. She shook her head miserably, saying, "I'm not sure, Willy, that it's not too late. I don't know."

He sat back deflated against the chair.

"All right. All right," he said, a tinge of bitterness in his voice, "I know it's a sudden transformation, tough to believe. But I'm still going to do it."

He stood up and headed toward the living room, throwing over his shoulder, "Send Mike down when he gets back, okay?"

Even though he'd left, the air seemed heavy with his presence. For God's sake, she thought, he hasn't died. If she craned her head, she could hear him rustling about downstairs, settling down in front of his computer, ready to start in on his poetry.

He'd always been one in love with words. At any idle moment, waiting in a bank line or for a train, he would pass the time trying out the sound of them, ruminating over their meanings. He liked to play off them, and he'd come up with some God-awful creations, too. Years ago, visiting Washington with Mary, eight, and Mike, five, he kept teasing the kids while on their way to the National Cathedral. "I sure hope we don't get too close to the garlic-goyles."

"Garlic-goyles? You mean gargoyles, don't you?"

"Oh, sure, they're bad, too," he said, "but the garlic-goyles, they don't just look horrible – you should smell their breath!"

She'd winced, but the kids had howled. They'd been very disappointed to discover that the National Cathedral's gargoyles were placed well beyond the range of their noses.

She shook her head, smiling, thinking of how he'd force two together that never had a chance of working, sounding goofy even to himself.

"You think 'indigenous' could have come from a root word like 'indian-genous?' Or maybe 'indian-genous' should be used when referring to Native Americans."

"You mean East Indians, don't you, from India?"

He rubbed his chin, "Yeah. It's something that looks right on paper, but doesn't sound quite exactly right when you say it, you know?"

"Believe me," she'd said, "I know."

Oh, Willy, Willy, she thought, you were always funny with words, but are you any good with them? How could she judge, she was hardly a writing virtuoso herself, except for legal briefs, for which she was renowned. But that was just grind work, good research and logic. How could she compare that and the promotional kind of writing Will did daily to what it takes to be a successful poet? For that matter, did any successful poet ever make a decent living?

But she had to ask herself if that should be the criterion, money. Oh, sure, they had to have it to keep the family going, but she couldn't fault Will in that area ever. He'd always brought home his share of the family income; he had never been without a job. When she stayed home with the kids for those first few years, he'd never uttered one complaint, not one gripe about her lousy housekeeping or so-so cooking. Oh, occasionally, if she fed the kids late, then serve their meal afterwards, he'd bitch about eating at ten. And she grinned, the son of a bitch always did do the laundry.

She sighed. Mike was right, Will was a hard act to follow. Maybe she wasn't giving him a chance to be good or bad at what he wanted to do. Like the old pop-psych cliche, she had her time at home with her babies; maybe Will was looking for time at home with babies he could have. Maybe she owed him that much.

She dropped her head, her hand balled beneath one cheek, her elbow propped in the cup of her other hand across her waist. Why was she thinking these things now, so late? What about Harry? If Will really did fight for the promotion, does that mean that was what it's all been about? Was she supposed to choose whoever won?

Her stomach roiled as she saw the image. This wasn't what she wanted; this wasn't it at all. She stood up and went to the refrigerator. She uncorked a half-full bottle of white wine and poured herself a glass. After a sip, she returned to the table and threw her garment bag over her shoulder. She stooped and grabbed her overnight bag, careful at the same time not to spill the wine. I'm too tired to be thinking like this, she said to herself. Just too damned tired.

She left the kitchen to climb the stairs to the bedroom.

Chapter 27.

Will sat at his computer wondering what to do next, poetry, laundry, or suicide. He wanted to kill himself, not to be dead but to punish himself. One day at full throttle and he bragged about it universally, shamelessly, to Eileen. God help me, I'm stupid!

He placed his palms into the hollows on either side of his skull and pressed. He used to be able to talk to her without sounding like an idiot or a stranger. The more he listened to himself, the worse he sounded. And the stranger he acted, the more remote the possibility of ever being able to talk to her again.

She probably saw right through him. Oh, sure, he talked a good game about going after the promotion, now, but she knew him. The first thing that came up that he didn't like about the job, or Forster, or whatever, he would pull back and rethink what he was doing. What a fucking prima donna I am, he thought – prima don? Primo don? Prime rib overdone. How about asshole?

"How can you sit around joking when you're about to lose her?" he mumbled out loud, self-mockingly, in a schoolmarm's nasal voice. Because I have the time.

The rush of busyness among contented marrieds marked by their wistful yearning for more time together contrasted sharply, brutally, to the temporal wasteland they occupied when on the outs. Then, they asked themselves what had happened, why, and what could they have done to avoid it? They pondered the past and the dreary present, he thought, but never the future. The future seemed too apocalyptic to envision, too unknown.

He could analyze these things endlessly. He had before, in a clinical fashion as he watched and supported friends during the dissolution of their marriages, always an awkward situation. Did you choose sides? Did you try to keep them both as friends, or just the one you knew first? Or the one you liked the best? Would you change friends because your wife had? Suddenly, your opinion of "one of the boys" must turn sour because of the mental cruelty reported by his wife through yours. Or she's found out having an affair with a neighbor, but your wife forgives her. Then what?

All their friends might be facing these questions soon. What would they do, who would they choose? He saw a vision of Eileen showing up at a friend's party with someone new. Who could that be?

She hadn't mentioned anyone, and she'd been vague when he had asked her if there was someone else. He couldn't conceive of it, after twenty years of knowing each other to the point of unconsciousness. How could there be anyone else? Where did she find the time to even think of it?

He pressed his lips flatly as he realized that he was rounding the same curve again on the loop. Time, of course. Time weighed heavily when a person was unhappy, and he would he have known that Eileen was unhappy if his knowledge of her hadn't been unconscious. It was his fault again for not knowing. Ignorance is no excuse, especially at home.

He breathed out and shook his head. After staring at the keyboard for an instant, he switched on the computer and opened a file, CHINESE.RST.

Chinese restaurants
somehow are
dirty and neat at the same time;
it's the floors, I think,
cracks ingrained with black grime
between redwood planks
stone cleaned

by tenants inclined to work.

The odor, too
tastes more like cooking at home
than attempts I've made
to reproduce
Mother and Sister's dishes.
I like Chinese food
though sour eggrolls
too often in the past
have made Canton cuisine
adventures in eating.

I like French food,
dealt out for special occasions,
learning to hold a viola bow
over coffee with a spoon
held "just so"
by a girl from a symphony
And those subtle New Yorkers
kitty-corner to us
have got to know
just what we're doing?

Greek food strikes me
with the violence of emotions,
juice, drink, and dance
mark such mortal feasts;
"How's Papannous?"
one friend about another,
"Dead," the waiter said.
Before his time, we know,
we know it's not so.

He started the poem years ago when he had been hired by Ventura Associates to do public relations. During his first job out of college, he found himself meeting successful clients over lunches in Baltimore's best restaurants. Before that, he figured that he'd eaten out maybe a dozen times with his parents, on a few dates, and with Eileen.

At Ventura, he enjoyed himself trying out new ethnic foods almost once a week. He had discovered pig heaven.

Through the years, his slowing metabolism and the sheer repetitiveness of business lunches and dinners jaded him to the culinary marvels. Searching back to bring youthful inspiration to his new writing, he had discovered "Chinese Restaurants," his callow paen to exotic food.

He reread the poem again and laughed when he remembered his pal Charlie asking the waiter about an old Greek friend of his father's. The waiter obviously didn't know Papannous from Adam, so out of the side of his mouth, he said flatly, "Dead." Shocked at first, Charlie said it couldn't be because his father had just mentioned talking with his friend only a week ago. After the waiter had left the table, Charlie and he had laughed hysterically at the waiter's lie and their own presumption that he would know the guy.

Will also recalled the New York trip, of awkwardly trying to grasp the spoon with his fingers in the fashion that Melanie had showed him. They had been at dinner in a French restaurant in the upper fifties, Georges Reys was the name. An associate at another P.R. firm doing a joint campaign with Ventura, Melanie also played in an amateur orchestra, possible only in the Big Apple. They laughed over his inept efforts, and a middle-age couple sitting tight next to them finally butted in, almost demanding to know what he was doing with the spoon. When he told them, they seemed disappointed that it was something so pedestrian.

Melanie and he had exchanged sparks at dinner, but he remembered Eileen. He introduced her into the natural course of the conversation, and Melanie picked it up without dropping a stitch. He bit his lower lip when he thought of how he had liked her even more for thatThe restaurant had been long closed, now.

Since he had found the poem, below the first few verses he had added another, thinking he needed to round it out with something Latino.

> Quesadilla during the daytime
> A multimedia event
> when the law of diminishing returns
> kicks in, and taste ebbs
> as heat flows.

He reviewed it and sighed. Lousy. He deleted the four lines.

Will rubbed his face, wishing that he could think, wishing that he could bring back some enthusiasm and hope to his life. He gazed at the poem and then began to write.

> These are the romantic gifts,
> God's repasts
> for lovers lingering.
> I'm curious now
> if I'll ever return to such
> complicit gleaning,
> if children will follow
> who usurp the time
> for all gracious dining,
> or if I'll dine alone.

Chapter 28.

Will pulled into the ComCon parking lot in a bitter mood. The trees barely grasping their brown, puckered leaves seemed to be suffering from some sort of vegetative emphysema, paying now with agonizing shortness of life for the long excesses of spring and summer. Good for them, he thought, why should I be the only one dying around here? Climbing out of the old Chevy station wagon, he bit his lower lip sullenly like a schoolboy after a scolding he knew he deserved but still hadn't liked. He rued his mean thought about the trees, never ever really wanting anything bad to happen to a living thing, plant, animal, or rock star. Mentally patting himself on the back for his magnanimity, he then asked the Universe why he had to be the one dealing with such all-encompassing misery? At once he felt guilty again, picturing in his mind the truly unfortunate people in three quarters of the world – when told, as a kid who refused to clean his plate, to think of the starving people in Asia, he did. Yet, when his righteous father had used the same hokey homily on his smart-ass younger brother, his brother had said, "Name three." Their father couldn't help laughing.

See, Will chided himself, you're even lousy at self-pity.

He strolled into the lobby, expecting business as usual until Kelly substituted her usual warm greeting with a drawn-back pose of respect and a knowing gleam in her eye.

"Well, hello, Mr. Day. I hear you were a big star on TV last night. Wow," she said playfully.

"Oh yeah?" he said, "who told you that?"

"Wendy," she said, "you know, from the pizza place. She saw you on CNN. I am impressed."

"Oh," he replied, remembering Wendy, the tall woman with the winning smile. "Yeah, well I'm amazed she recognized me. I have it that only my nose showed. Must be a unique schnoz for Wendy to I.D. me from it alone."

"Oh, no," Kelly scoffed, "I'm sure she saw more than your nose."

He started back toward his office and Eldon passed him in the hall.

"Aces, Will," he said, holding his thumbs up awkwardly, "Quite a display."

"Aces, yeah," Will said, thinking, this is getting strange. But he was beginning to enjoy it, like being a BMOC, for once. People at ComCon were giving him sidelong glances of admiration and he liked it. His blue mood lifted somewhat, though he knew that with just a hair's breadth change in circumstances he could bring it back down around him like a shroud instantaneously.

He cut left toward his office and frowned sourly when he saw that Julie wasn't in yet. He wondered if she would show up at all or if she was merely late. Whatever, they would have to talk, he resolved, heart-broken or not.

He walked into his office, dropped-kicked his briefcase under the desk, and slid into his chair. He swiveled to crank up his computer when he heard a noise outside like someone knocking into Julie's desk.

Barry Evans lurched into his office, bending at every step to rub his shin. He startled Will with wildness in his eyes and without looking he threw himself over the desk, leaning on the knuckles of his clenched hands.

"You dirty rat," he shouted, "you betrayed me!"

Will snatched his head back, blinking twice. "Say what?"

"I said, you betrayed me, you rotten rat!"

Barry pounded the desktop at the last epithet with one of his pudgy white fists. Color effused his neck, his face, climbing to his hairline to the very crown of his head.

"I saw her on TV, Julie and that sleazy Maloney. I saw him put his arm around her!"

Jesus Christ thought Will. "Is that what this is about?"

"You're damn right it is!" yelled Evans. Surprising himself with his own volume, he pulled back from the desk. "What happened?" he cried, almost a lament.

What happened, thought Will, closing his eyes to send the hidden behind his lids on a barrel roll from the ceiling to the floor. He opened them and said calmly, "Barry, what do you mean, 'What happened?' What do you want me to say?"

"You said that you would talk to her for me! You promised!"

"Yeah, all right, I promised to talk to her and I did, but it isn't like promising you lunch. I talked to her, I told her how you felt, and that's all I could do. The rest was up to her and you."

"But she's seeing that Maloney," Evans said, bewilderment teetering on madness honing a sharp edge to his eyes again, "He's married, and he's so – Oh, God, I don't know what."

Sleazy, Will prompted silently, you said it before.

Evans collapsed against the back of the chair, overcome by his distress, suddenly distracted by a terrible inner vision.

This is unbelievable, thought Will. I must endure this on top of everything else? He wanted to toss the little twerp out on his soft rump telling him as he bounced that he didn't have time for his adolescent fantasies. Go get on the Dating Game, or the Love Connection, or whatever the fuck they have on TV for self-helpless little jackasses like you.

Evans was crying. Will stiffened as he thought he saw tears, what could be tears. But they weren't, were they? No; lifting his head, Evans showed a bone-dry face. Still, the small comptroller sniffed and swallowed in a heavy way to clear his passages, and he touched his cheeks with his fingertips as if checking for moisture. Maybe he didn't have tear ducts, Will thought.

Evans sniffed again and said, "I suppose you think this is stupid."

Pathetic, more like.

"How I could love Julie this way, you probably think because I'm not very goodlooking or good at talking to people. Because I'm not good at sports. I'm not good at making people like me, girls especially. That doesn't mean they're better than me, any of them. I have feelings, too, you know, I want to get married and have children. The good things aren't just for people like you, you know."

In the middle of Evans' mournful life litany, Will began to shake his head from side to side. Why do you think I spent time with you if I didn't know this?

"Oh, sure, you probably pitied me, let me hang out with you. People sometimes do that. Then, they get tired and go back to their great lives. I want a great life, too, you know? So I asked you to do one thing for me, one. And did you do it?"

"I'm sorry," said Will, hoping he could hide his impatience and trying hard to remain sympathetic.

"You knew she was seeing Maloney," Evans said, agitated again. "You knew all along and didn't tell me."

How was I supposed to tell you? Will said to himself.

"Everyone at ComCon knew. They all think I'm an idiot!"

Will shifted uneasily, suddenly speculating on just how secret Julie and Maloney were around here. If it was common knowledge at ComCon, then maybe the rest of the world knew, too.

"That's why Julie gave him all that money," Evans said thoughtfully, "for his campaign." He turned piercing eyes on Will, "And you let her. You okayed it."

"No, now hold on, Barry. That's not true. She did it on her own, for the most part. She's allowed to, anyway. It's part of her job."

"You authorized the money for her, you knew about her romance with Maloney the whole time," Evans went on, pointing at Will now, "And I asked you to help me with her. I'm such a jerk."

"Look, Barry—"

"That's why you put me off when I asked about the money. You were in with her on it, illegal campaign contributions. You probably agreed to talk to her to distract me, keep me off base so that I wouldn't check further."

"What are you talking about, Barry?" Will said, suddenly attentive. "I only found out about it when you told me. Anyway, she gave him a couple extra thousand. We'll report it as a mistake and pay a fine. Maloney can give the money back, he doesn't care. He can afford it now, he won."

"Fifty thousand dollars?" said Evans. "You think he can just pay a little fine on that?"

"Fifty thousand dollars?" Will said, "What are you talking about?"

"Julie gave Maloney more than fifty thousand dollars. So, don't try to feed me this bunk about paying a fine like a parking ticket. The Attorney General will want more out of Maloney and you than a slap on the wrist. And your little miss helpmate couldn't get that kind of money without authorization."

"I don't know what you're talking about, fifty thousand dollars. I checked the receipts. Total, they amounted to around seven thousand," Will said, sensing that something was wrong even while saying that nothing was.

"You saw the receipts?" Evans said, "the ones in her desk? The ones hidden behind the bottom drawer?"

"In her desk? Behind the drawer?"

Evans leaped up and rushed out of the office. When Will followed, he found him hunched over Julie's bottom drawer, which he had yanked off its metal runners and out of the desk. He stuck a handful of receipts in Will's hands.

"Seventeen receipts and vouchers, ranging from twenty-five hundred to five thousand a piece, all for some so-called information forums the week of October 18th. All paid out of that phony Security Information Foundation. The grand total: fifty-one thousand, five hundred dollars. A quarter of these events were scheduled for the same day and at the same time in places hundreds of miles apart. There is no way Maloney could get to all of them."

Will tried to read the receipts and listen to Evans at the same time but failed. The race of information coming and going through his mind silenced him, even though his thoughts were anything but quiet.

"Ipso facto, illegal campaign contributions, maybe with a little bit of fraud thrown in."

"This is not real," muttered Will.

"Yeah, I found it hard to believe, too, when I stumbled upon it. But I cared so for Julie, I thought there might be an explanation. Since you'd been so nice to me, too, I was going to wait until you straightened it out. Boy, was I dumb."

He said the last with a vicious sneer.

"Listen, Barry, you're right," Will said quickly, "there must be an explanation. Look, none of these receipts have been initialed, see? I didn't sign off on them and neither did anyone else here with the authority. So, it might be a mistake."

"Come on, Day, don't expect me to be stupid forever."

"I'm not, I don't know what's going on either. Julie's not here, so I can't ask her. At least let's talk to her first. Maybe she has a simple explanation."

Barry nodded his head slowly, wearing a sickly smile that slowly evolved into a severe death head grin. "Oh, sure. If she can tear herself away from her congressman, Day, you can talk to her. You're so good at that. But don't think I'm going to get stuck holding the bag for any of you when the feds show up. That would be stupid."

"I know, Barry, but no one is going to get stuck holding any bag," Will said, hoping to God he was telling the truth. "Let's see if we can straighten this out. Julie will be in today, I'm sure she's late for good reason. When she comes in, I'll find out about the receipts, and I'll let you know about the mix up."

Barry shook his head frowning, "Not this time, Day. I'm going to Forster on this mess. I'm not going to let you fool with me again."

Will raised his hands palms out in front of him and pressed the air in front of Evans twice, forestalling him. "If you really care about Julie—" he stopped when he saw Evans' fierce glare. "If you ever cared for her, you'll give her a chance to straighten this out."

Evans paused, thinking, but his face remained darkly sinister, foreboding. Finally, he said, "Okay, let her explain. If she can, fine. If not, it doesn't matter what song and dance you do, you'll all go down. And I won't wait for forever on this, Day. I'm not going to sit around until the agents arrive."

He turned and marched down the hall.

Holy shit thought Will. He watched Evans' back disappear, then bolted back into his office to his desk. He slapped the phone into his hand and hit the programmed number for Julie's home. No answer. He rummaged through his rolodex until he found Maloney's apartment phone number and called that. As the phone rang, Julie popped her head through the door and said, "Hi, Will, I'm here. Late, but here."

Her smile fled when she saw his troubled look. "What's wrong, what's the matter?" she asked.

"Jesus Christ, Julie, did you give Maloney fifty thousand dollars? Jesus Christ!" he said before she could answer.

"Yes, no, but—" she stumbled.

"God – how could you? No, don't tell me, I know how."

"—you knew about it, you told me at my house that you knew."

"Knew? I knew about a few thousand here and there. I thought that was stupid, but this!" He whipped the receipts up from his desk and brandished them like a handful of arrows. "Fifty thousand dollars – more than that – in a week! You set him up with a bunch of bogus group meetings for only one week? What were you thinking?"

She fell without looking into the seat in front of his desk, resting her head on her breast. Barely in a voice he could hear, she said, "I love him."

"Oh, God," Will exhaled as he dropped into his own chair. He rubbed his face hard as if trying to wipe away his own features so that nobody could recognize him, no one could find him.

Julie spoke softly to the floor, "He needed it for the commercial. He told me he was dying inside, that Macowiac was beating him for no good reason. The money would save him, he said. So, I gave it to him. I did it because I love him–loved him. Love him."

She slumped back in the chair, "So what does he do? He screws the bitch who made the ad."

Will froze, his mouth open, the bitter words of rebuke suspended. He watched her laid out on the chair, crying silently without tears, and he remembered who she was and saw how sad she was now.

"Well," he said, "I guess we're the ones screwed now."

Julie raised her eyes to him hopefully. "It's my problem, Will, not yours. I knew what I was doing, I knew what would happen to me if it came out."

"Yeah, well, it looks like it's going to come out soon because your secret admirer Barry Evans intends to tell Forster all about it. That's how deep his love for you runs."

"My God," she said listlessly. "I could understand if it were someone I really had something going with, like my old flyboy heartthrob Major Woods. But to be done in by a lovesick nerd, that's hard to take. Even if I did it to myself out of a jealous rage to get back at Maloney, I could understand. But this," she turned a hand in the air, then let it drop in her lap.

"As long as you brought it up, how could you go for Maloney? I mean, after dumping the Marine for political reasons, how could you fall for someone as ethics-less as he is?"

Julie tightened her lips, then relaxed them as though realizing that defending her privacy and independence would be superfluous given the circumstances of her disgrace.

"I don't know, Will, I can't explain it. It started out with a lot of wicked jokes at each other's expense. Somehow, we felt respect for each other out of it, maybe because we both laughed at ourselves. We both admired that we could take it. I don't know. But it changed, we started joking about the others so we could laugh together. Then, he started telling me the serious stuff, about his kids, his wife, his fear of losing his job," she glanced up at Will, "that's why he exists, he thinks. He doesn't really know that he's a character, you know?"

"Yeah, but Julie, you knew."

"Yeah, yeah, I knew, and I know you tried to tell me and I wouldn't listen to you. But didn't you ever fall in love with someone you weren't supposed to, someone you had no business falling in love with? Really off the wall?"

Will nodded, "When I was about seventeen, I fell for the next-door neighbor's kid – she was only twelve. One night over dinner the whole family teased me about it, and all I could do was grin and say, 'I can't help it!'"

"Yeah, well," Julie murmured, trailing off for a moment. Then she said, "Twelve?"

"Hey!" Will said, "I didn't do anything with her, not even a kiss. We just talked. She was so articulate. She seemed like an adult trapped in a child's body."

"Unhuh," Julie said, "when they're twelve, it's usually the other way around."

"Nevermind that," Will sighed, "we have to deal with this money problem, Julie."

Raising a hand, she said, "What's to deal? I'm a dead duck."

"No, no, it isn't all that simple. You don't have the authority to just give away fifty thousand dollars to anybody, even Maloney or any other congressman. I'm just amazed that Harry went along with this."

"He didn't sign off on it."

"What?" said Will. "I thought you told me he wanted to keep his hand in. He didn't know about this?"

"Oh, sure, I told him, and he said to go ahead with it, but I didn't have time to get him to initial every chit. It had to be done right away, Will, in a week, to do Maloney any good."

"Man," Will said. "So, there's no written sign-off by Harry for fifty thousand dollars."

The room grew silent as the two paused, each thinking separate thoughts, he supposed, though not that much different. Here Julie had performed for love this grand indiscretion that could cost her everything. He could imagine the emotions tumbling in her head, of Maloney and how he would react to this newest crisis, of her fragile feelings wondering if the congressman cared for her at all anymore. In his own thoughts he found himself picturing how Eileen would react to this development, his ignorance of what was happening in his department and the potential disaster to everyone and everything at ComCon. Suddenly, Eileen had more reason to disdain him, even despise him. She was ready to walk out on him now simply for insufficient ambition. That his failure was much more general would crush any wistful hope he might have of keeping her, once she found out. The discovery would propel her out of his life like a bullet. Then what was the use, he thought, of anything?

How could it have escaped him for ten years? What had he been doing in all that time, what good was he? He found the anguish almost overwhelming. He sighed, then said, "Why did Harry do it? Fifty thousand dollars. Why?"

Julie gazed up at him in surprise. "This isn't the only time Harry's put out that kind of money, Will. He's given the okay for a lot more than that over the years, a lot more."

"I can't believe it. Why was I never told?"

Julie rolled her eyes, "I don't know, maybe because you're so straight. Besides, it wasn't such a big deal until lately, with the new administration and all."

"Yeah, but hell, Julie, there are plenty of legal ways to get all the money out there that anybody needs. You know that."

Julie lifted her eyes to him, hesitated, then shrugged.

Chapter 29.

When his father led him out to the station wagon, Mike sat in the back seat. He was long past complaining openly about the control his father had clamped down on his life. Instead, he submitted silently, resignedly, when told that they were going to the mall to find a birthday present for his mom. Arguments never surfaced that her birthday was a full week off, that he and his dad had never gone together to get her a present before, or that she always said that she didn't even care if she got a present from them, just hugs and kisses. Instead, without a word, Mike stood up from the card table, got his winter coat on, and headed out to the driveway, his head downcast in a perfect study of long-suffering forbearance.

He'd been sitting at the card table frozen in limbo again by his father's law: No goofing off until the homework was finished. That included weekends – Fridays, Saturdays, and Sundays. He could finish what he had to do in a few hours, he supposed. But he couldn't bring himself to start. Except for reading stories for English, the work seemed so awful and there was so much of it that he just couldn't do it. The longer he waited, the more awful in his mind it seemed, so that instead of getting it done, he found himself sitting, waiting, his mind wandering everywhere except to any good place. His father endlessly pointed out how he was wasting time, his own time to have fun, and it was true, a plain fact. He couldn't help it, though, he just kept putting it off, wasting time, wasting it until he felt that he himself might waste away in time. When he thought about why, he had to face another truth, that his life wasn't worth living. If something had no value, how could it be wasted? he asked.

A question he couldn't put to his dad, he knew, or his mom either. After reading sixty-two Newsweek articles about teenage suicide, they'd rush him right off to some shrink to find out what was wrong with him, how could they make him better? It's too late to make him better, the doctor would say looking down at him through thick glasses, This kid is so messed up, his defects are defecting.

His dad pulled the car out of the driveway and slowly maneuvered through the suburb's side streets. Mike pulled his coat closer around himself against the bone-cutting cold. Why didn't cars have heaters that worked right away? They've had a hundred years to figure it out. Another gripe that would stay buried in his bitter soul along with all the others that got him nothing but scorn from his parents, even though they complained about the same things. It was as though they felt that as grown-ups they earned the right to bitch. They were so lame. They ordered kids around all the time, told them not to do stuff, then went ahead and did it themselves. If you pointed it out to them, they would say that it was different. Right, and they thought the Evil Empire was history, he sighed.

They turned on to Raritan Road, a main thoroughfare that would take them the couple of miles to 695. From there they would go another mile or so to the exit that spilled into the mall. Mike stared out the side window as they drove, peering over the lower section not steamed opaque by his breath to observe the grim gray sky and its promise of freezing weather. He imagined the steely cold enveloping everything living and otherwise and wondered why falling in the winter hurt so much more than in warmer months. Some law of physics explained it, he supposed, but he preferred to think of it as the balance of earthly powers. Like in myths, winter always tried to kill you, while spring and summer fattened you up. And fall, fall became this slow slide toward the dead of winter. Then trees and other growing things showed their sadness by losing their green colors, fading into dullness, weeping about their loss of life that came with winter.

He stirred, noticing that they rode along in complete silence. Usually, his dad would turn on the radio to play some pretty old music from the sixties. Pretty bad, too, except for Pink Floyd and the Beatles. If they were talking to each other, Mike would beg hard to have him change it to a good station, one with some serious rock, like Nirvana or Pearl Jam, maybe some rap with Ice-T. His dad didn't mind if it was a band like U2, but mostly he didn't like good music, new music. If they argued about it, the old man would say that all of it had been done before by Jimi Hendrix, and that Aerosmith was still around. It was a matter of taste, not age, he'd say. Maybe, Mike said, but he still thought that old guys like the Rolling Stones looked weird up there trying to be young, even if some of their songs sounded okay. To his amazement, his dad agreed with him.

Mike could see from the look of him though, that his dad wasn't enjoying this trip either. Weird, since it was his idea, Mike thought. But what was the big deal? His dad had been getting presents for his mom for a hundred years. Of course, that didn't mean he ever liked it. His dad was not the kind of guy who relished hanging around malls under any circum-stances. It wasn't just a generational difference either, he said. whatever that meant.

Mike had to admit to himself too, that aside from the deadening dullness of shopping for his mom, he wasn't looking forward to going to the mall either. He hadn't been back since Kirk ruined him in front of Karen. He didn't need any reminders of the devastating loss he had suffered; it was bad enough that his bus passed by the place every day. For the past two months solid, he had to deal with the dread that built in his body as they approached the mall, twice a day. Every morning, he tried to find a seat on the left, as far away as possible from the side that gave the best view of the site of his abject humiliation. Every afternoon he planned on sitting on the right, when the bus traveled in the opposite direction going home. If all those seats were taken, he would sit where he had to, but as the bus neared the mall, he would strike up a lively conversation with someone across the aisle so that he faced inward, away from the windows. He would talk louder as they passed, keeping his eyes averted until they drove by.

For the most part, his strategy worked, and the incident didn't come up in the daily chatter full of the usual offhanded cruelties common to high school kids. Mike knew that only time could distance him from the miserable event, the time it took for someone else to replace him as the big joke around school for whatever terrible thing happened to that poor doofus. But he also knew that his own shame lurked barely beneath the surface, and that out of sheer boredom, one smart-ass could revive the entire mess simply by pointing and laughing as they rode by. Then, his disgrace would be fresh again, the evidence plain and everywhere, inside and out, especially his own expression. His loss of face would be made larger when he didn't try to punch out the new punk tormentor. When it happened, he couldn't do it, faltering again, half out of fear, the other half knowing then that the asshole was right, he was a complete chickenshit.

Gratefully, Mike sighed his relief when his father parked close to Nordstrom's, far away from the bus stop.

"Let's go," his dad said in a flat voice.

Mike trailed him as they entered the double glass doors. They passed through another set of doors into the department store and made their way between rows of women's underwear to head for the main causeway of the mall. As they ambled past the wispy garments, Mike eyed the mannequin torsos marveling at their pointy nipples, as if the artist who designed them held ice on real women models. The eyes of the dummies stared into the distance beyond any real guys who might be staring at them, drooling. He found them sexy, too, even though he knew that they were nothing but elaborate plexiglass. It had something to do with what they could be and the fact that they were right there, close enough to be looked at when real women like them could never be so available. They confused him, their bold nakedness mixed with their cold, far-off gazes. Yet, seeing the flimsy, filmy shorts and tops they wore made him wonder why his dad didn't stop right here for mom's gift. But his dad never gave them a glance.

Entering the broad passage transversing the mall, they walked to the right of a fountain flanked by benches with a bookstore and a clothing store on opposite sides. Next to them stood shoe stores, household appliances, sporting goods, a Gap, a Brookstone, and a pretzel shop promoting genuine Philadelphia soft pretzels. They came upon a directory and searched its multi-colored map for the hexagon, "You are here."

"So," said Will, "where are we?"

"Here," pointed Mike. "Where do you want to go?"

Will shook his head, "I haven't a clue." He turned to Mike, "What do you think of jewelry?"

Mike looked back in surprise, "I don't know. What's our price range?"

"That's a good question," his father replied.

They scanned the map again, but neither could suggest a destination.

"Well, maybe we should just stroll," said Will.

They started off at a halting pace, and Mike sighed to himself thinking that they could be here for years if they didn't know where they were going. They turned into one branch and dead-ended at a Door Store, then meandered down the main drag past a designer cookie store and a Tower CD store. While they walked, Mike savored the different fragrances suffusing the enclosed arena, the aroma of buttered popcorn from a cart mingling with perfumes jetted out into the midway by the haut boutiques. Architectural figures in the distance gradually drew closer, transforming into people in perfect accord with established weekend demographics. Several middle-age couples wandered here and there with no particular place to go except where their fancy took them. Harried mothers swept young children before them, intent upon some vital social mission with buying the proper present as the overriding imperative. On stone and wooden benches near the fountains next to the food court, single oldsters sat, politely leaving breathing space between themselves and other seniors, sufficient room for privacy, yet close enough to talk if they could make that connection. Mike had sat with them now and then in the past, and was struck by how ordinary their chats were, with a lot of time spent upon children and grandchildren, where they lived and what they did, and so on. For as boring as it all seemed to him, he found himself drawn into listening and watching by the growing liveliness that the talks seemed to spark in these otherwise gray-haired, gray-skinned old folks. Amazingly, he could see their complexions turn pink as they talked and laughed cordially.

"Come on," his dad said, "let's try in here."

They went into a jewelry store and began surveying the contents of the glass cases. Mike noticed that they both walked around the jewelry with their hands stuck into their pants pockets, as though they wanted to look like casual shoppers, not worthy of a salesperson's attention. Of course, the stratagem was doomed to failure.

"Can I help you?" a young man said. Decked out in a striped shirt, tie, and suspenders beneath his double-breasted suit, he looked like a throwback to *L.A. Law* or some other knock-off show, Mike thought. His hair had that clipped, slick look of the thirties and forties, too, although much more streamlined through the well-practiced use of mousse.

"No thanks, we're just looking," Will said.

"Well, if you need something, I'll be right over there. My name is Rudy."

"Yeah, thanks."

They stared down at a spread of expensive-looking gold pins elaborately encrusted with red and green gems accented by folds of silver. Except for slight differences, the pins all seemed the same.

Will cleared his voice. "What do you think?"

"Gee, Dad, I don't know. What about you?"

"I think that Rudy hanging over our shoulders is annoying. I get the sense that he knows a lot more about what's 'in' than I do, and I don't like the idea of making a mistake in front of him."

He faced Mike and grinned wanly, "Weird, huh? Why should I give a damn what he thinks?"

Mike sighed in relief, "Yeah. But I know what you mean."

"So, let's get out of here."

They lapped the hangar-like complex several times, popping into one store or another, but never seeing anything that struck them as just right. They drifted slowly, scanning the showcases for something that might work. Mike stopped at the front display of a combination art gallery/print shop to look at a gray canvas with a long triangle of white paint thickly layered in the center.

"I guess this is what they call minimalist art," he said.

His dad shook his head, "Of course, true minimalists are called minimists."

They meandered on, going into an occasional store, but hardly spending any time looking at all. Mike was about to suggest the lingerie back in Nordstrom's when his father said, "Let's sit for a minute, okay?"

They drifted over to a bench beneath the escalators and slumped down, leaning over their hands clasped between their spread knees.

"You know, you need to be in the mood for this kind of thing. I guess I'm just not in the mood."

They sat quietly for a few minutes. Mike pondered why they were there if neither of them wanted to be there. Maybe now was a good time to ask to go home, he thought.

"Look there," Will said.

Mike raised his head and froze. Coming down the vast walkway toward them tripped a group of girls, familiar, from his school. Mike frantically scanned each one's features, trying to recognize 'the one' as he desperately sought a place to hide.

His father continued, "Now that, that's a tribute to modern orthodontics–that and fluorinated water. I've never seen so many sets of straight, white teeth. You can bet never seeing such perfect bites back when I was in school. Of course, now many of my former classmates are wearing braces, too."

The young women sauntered by. She wasn't with them.

"Still, natural perfection has its own appeal," Will said. He clacked his teeth together and spread his lips, baring perfect, straight teeth though somewhat yellowed by time and coffee.

One of the girls trailing in the rear turned and said slyly, "Hi, Michael. How are you?"

She trotted on without waiting for a response.

"A friend?" his dad asked.

"Not really," Mike said, "just another reporter for *Tiger Beat*."

"Oh," Will said, "A rumorer. Unlike you, a murmurer."

"Huh?" Mike said.

"Sure. People who murmur say things unclearly on purpose because they're talking about things the way they'd like them to be. when they really suspect that they might not be that way. People who rumor say things that don't sound clear because they think they're telling the truth when they're not. Simple, murmurs and rumors."

"Sounds like a Woody Allen movie to me," Mike said. "So, how is anyone supposed to know what's true and what isn't?"

"That's hard," his father said with a grimace. "Truth changes."

They sat quietly for a moment longer, until Will said, "Well, let's get a move on, what do you say? Let's try The Nature Store. I always liked their stuff even if your mom isn't that keen on it."

Mike croaked, "But if we get something, and she doesn't like it, then what?"

"Then we go unshopping – de-shopping. Hey, I bet half the people here are de-shopping something."

Mike groaned silently and lagged behind. They walked up the stairs to the second level. His father huffed up the last few steps, Mike observing that he seemed slighter than before and smaller, maybe older, too. Standing side by side, he could see that his dad was still as tall, but not as large for some reason. Mike felt his mood suddenly lighten as he realized that in talking to him now, he could almost look him in the eye. Things were changing, even if only a little.

They walked inside the store and gazed around at the different items. His father peered into a case suspended from a pillar. Inside, earrings hung, painted like birds or shaped like dolphins and whales. Ceramic pins of green exotic frogs showed next to rough-finished, silver full moons with matching quarter-moon earrings next to them.

Will rubbed his jaw, saying, "I don't think this is your mother. Let's press on."

They moved to the back part and examined plate tectonic maps and paleontological posters, even though they knew they were wasting time. Circling around to the front again, they found a case of minerals, breathtaking gem-like crystals in colors akin to the splendors of tropical sea life.

"Wow!" said Will, "Can you imagine that?"

Mike stared at the glorious fuchsia, crimson and azure pieces, some encased in rough semi spheres of dull rock, like coconuts cracked open. "I can't believe that all of these colors were found under ground." He glanced up at his dad, "What's the point of hiding beautiful things like this forever in the dark?"

Will gave him a strange look, then smiled. "Well, whatever. How much are they?"

Mike twisted his head to see the price tag. "Jeeze, Dad, this one's three hundred dollars!"

"Whoa!" His father pulled back. "That's steep for any rock."

"Yeah."

"Can I help you?" a voice said behind them. They both turned at the same time and in unison dropped their jaws.

"Alan!"

Chapter 30.

Alan Scarpatti, Mary's boyfriend, now ex-boyfriend, stood in front of them just as surprised to see them as they were seeing him. The three pulled back after their immediate effusive greeting as they recognized Alan's new status.

"Why, hello Mr. Day, nice to see you. And how you doing, B.D.?"

B.D. Mike remembered, Brain-Dead. Even though he knew that his dad wasn't crazy about him, Mike always liked Alan. Unlike the stereotypical boyfriend who wished all little brothers dead, Alan really seemed to enjoy spending time with him, kidding him, wrestling with him, talking to him. "I'm good, D.B." Mike said with feeling. Old Dumb Butt, he thought, he really missed him.

"Yeah? That's great. You look good."

But it was Alan who looked good, Mike thought, great, completely changed. Instead of wearing the preppy stuff that he used to wear with Mary – the stuff she helped him pick out – he looked cool in jeans and a black shirt. He even had on a pair of Dr. Marten's engineer boots, and his hair covered his ears and curled over his shirt collar. But what really stunned Mike was the sparkling aquamarine stone peeking out dead center from Alan's earlobe.

"Alan, you've changed," Mike said, awed, "you're completely different."

Alan ran his hand through his brown hair as he said, "Yeah, well, I've done some different things," and he said, shifting his attention to Will.

Mike cringed, wondering what his dad would say heavy with the knowledge that Alan had dumped Mary. An outlandish image flurried through his mind of his father bending Alan over the mineral case, breaking the glass with his fist, grabbing one of the three-hundred-dollar crystals inside, then proceeding to beat the shit out of the former preppie who dumped his beloved daughter.

"You do look well," Will said, "college seems to suit you. Are you home for Thanksgiving?"

"Yeah, I came home a little early so I could work this weekend. I'll go fulltime here Christmas break and in the summer."

"That's terrific."

The conversation lapsed. Not fooled by his father's opening friendliness, Mike tried to grow smaller. Here it comes, he thought.

"Uh, Mr. Day, about Mary and me," Alan started.

"Alan, this kind of thing happens. You're both going through big changes, so it's natural that the two of you might need to, you know, move on. It's not easy or happy, but it's true."

Mike raised his head like a turtle testing the outside of his shell. What is this? he thought. Then, he strung it together; Dad never liked Alan anyway, so he's beyond happy. He can afford to be kind and supportive, especially since it reinforces what he wants, Mary and Alan crashed and burned.

"That's very nice of you to say, Mr. Day."

"Yeah, well, I have to admit, looking at you now, Alan, I'm kind of sorry that you and Mary aren't seeing each other anymore. I think she could learn a lot from you about being open to new things."

"Hey, Mr. Day, thank you so much. I try to tell her that myself."

"Oh, you still see her now and then?"

"Well, sure. Mary means a lot to me, you know, even though we don't go out anymore. We've been through a lot together, and I try to see her now and then anyway."

Will grabbed Alan's hand to shake it, "That's wonderful, Alan. I really appreciate it, I mean it. And, you know, I wasn't always your biggest fan around our house."

"Yeah," Alan chuckled, "I picked that up a few times."

They both laughed together, shaking hands in rhythm, and Mike shook his head to clear his senses. Was this happening? he asked himself.

"So, can I help you with anything?" Alan asked.

"Yeah, we're interested in that beautiful piece of quartzite there."

"Oh, that is spectacular. A special occasion?"

"Yup. Eileen's birthday is coming up."

"Well, I'll bet that Mrs. Day will enjoy this. It's quite an unusual gift."

"Yeah, that's what makes us nervous," Will said, elbowing Mike as he spoke.

"Oh, I'm sure she'll love it."

"Okay, wrap it up, and put it on my Blockbuster card."

They shared another hearty laugh, and Mike thought that he was going to be sick. How could they move so easily from saying what they really felt to such incredible phoniness? Why did they do it?

They left the store and as they reached the lower level, his father said, "You hungry? Want to get a sandwich?"

"Sure."

They chose a deli and ate without speaking. Mike pushed his pickle around waiting for his dad to finish.

"Do you think your mother will like the crystal?"

"How should I know?" Mike said. "I doubt it. Don't you think it's a little different for her?"

"Yeah, well, maybe she could use something a little different in her life." Will continued, "Like Alan, he's really making the most of what college has to offer. I wish Mary would do the same."

"I don't get it, Dad. You never liked him. You were always making cracks about him when he wasn't around."

Will shrugged, "So, maybe I was wrong. I was wrong anyway to make cracks. How are you supposed to know what people are like if you don't talk to them? And even if you do, people change. You just have to hope that when they change, they don't include you out. That is, if it's important to you."

Mike squinted, trying to understand. "But if people change all the time, how can anyone count on anyone else for life?"

Will glanced up sternly, "Now you're getting it. Your best bet is to find someone close enough to your interests and feelings to keep going together. Of course, that's damn near impossible, especially when you introduce chemistry into the formula."

He picked up his pickle and brandished it like a pointer, "Be sure of one thing, though, that the hormones come after the interests and feelings part of it." He bit off the top of the pickle as a punctuation point.

Mike flinched, "I guess the stone is a better gift than silk undies," he mumbled.

"What was that?" Will asked.

"Nothing."

"All right. Shall we go?"

They started back toward the Nordstrom end of the Mall. Will stopped suddenly and dragged him into a drugstore. Mike objected, "What do we need in here?"

"Creams, lotions, nostrums, exotic elixirs," his dad said, scanning the shelves as he led them to the back of the store, "and chewing gum."

He grabbed a pack of Trident and, to Mike's alarm, opened it, unwrapped a piece and popped it in his mouth. He held the pack out to his son who reluctantly took one.

"Will you look at that!" Will exclaimed, pointing over Mike's shoulder. He moved past him, and Mike turned to find them in front of the condom display rack.

"'Magnum Large,' for God's sake. What happened to one size fits all? Do you think they have a 'Magnum Small?' Maybe it's like laundry detergent packaging, the 'Large' is average, and for big guys they sell the 'Magnum Humongous.'"

Mike could feel his skin burning red. Will noticed and said quickly, "Sorry. Let's move on."

As he paid for the gum, he started chewing like Bugs Bunny, and said to the young woman behind the counter, "Hey, there're two pieces missing. Do we get a discount?"

Mike felt himself wilting again. Without looking up, the clerk said flatly, "Only on Wednesdays, sir." His dad laughed, and she dimpled a slight smile.

"Want a stick?" Will said, extending the pack.

"Sure," she said.

As he handed it to her, he said, "Also, my son here wants to know when you get off."

Mike felt his head go into a barrel roll rushing toward the ground.

She looked up, gazed at him cooly, then said, "Six. But you're the kind that never calls back, aren't you."

Mike grinned shyly, and they left.

They stepped outside and hustled to the station wagon to avoid the cold. Mike sat in the back again as his father turned on the ignition. Nothing happened.

"Uh oh," he said. He tried again. "Damn. This is not good." After another try, he sat back and glimpsed behind him. "The battery is dead."

"Aw," Mike moaned.

"Yeah, I know. I could call a garage I suppose, for a boost. But I hate to spend the money."

Yet, you're ready to spend loads of it on a rock that Mom isn't going to like one bit, thought Mike.

"Come on," Will said, climbing out of the car, "We'll take the bus home and get our good neighbor Ritchie to bring us back with some cables."

Mike flattened both hands on either side of the car seat. The bus? No!

"Come on, buddy, let's hike."

"Dad, can't we ask someone inside," Mike said in a panic.

"Why bother? Ritchie's got jumper cables. Let's hurry, though, it's cold and a bus might be along any minute."

Mike couldn't believe this was happening, it was impossible. Life was cruel enough for it not to be this ridiculous, he thought, like sending World War II vets back to die in Korea. But they jogged to the bus stop anyway and stood at the sign exactly where he had lost everything.

"Damn, it's cold," his dad mumbled.

Mike stared straight ahead for as long as he could, not daring to look around or up. He was dead, he thought, with a sickness inside of him that rivaled any bad feeling he'd ever had. Maybe their bus would arrive right away, right now, and he would be saved. His father wouldn't know. He hoped, but he also knew that hoping was hopeless.

Finally, he couldn't resist any longer. Slowly, he rotated his head around, around again, and up.

They still hung there, motionless, as quiet as the air.

Mike snapped his eyes down, wondering why they were still there, why the elements hadn't rotted the laces after two months, more than two months! Why hadn't someone called the electric company, weren't they a safety hazard? Or why hadn't some kid figured out a way to get them down, kids in New York and L.A. shot people to steal them. He sneaked another glance; they twisted slightly in tandem to the rustle of a gentle breeze.

"Man, maybe you were right," Will said. "We could go inside and call Ritchie from there. Or for that matter, buy a new battery. It's cold enough, as far as I'm concerned, to warrant drastic measures."

Mike didn't reply. His head was straight, but his eyes peeked above.

"Hey, suddenly you don't have an opinion? What's the matter?"

Mike started and saw his father's expression change from staring at him to gazing around, and up.

"What's that?" He squeezed his eyes harder. "Those are shoes, sneakers." He continued craning, "They look like"— and he lowered his eyes.

Mike pulled his shoulders inward and leaned away from his father as he heard him bellow, "Mike! What's this? They're your shoes. Aren't they? I'm right, right? They're yours, right?"

Mike started to edge away, slipping down from the bus stand to the parking lot macadam.

"Mike—stand right there, buster! How did your shoes get up there? Mike, turn around and answer me, now!"

Against his will, Mike felt slowly drawn around to the furious voice. He tucked his face hard against his chest as his father said sharply, "Look at me and tell me what happened! Why did you lie?"

Mike lifted his face streaked with tears. He saw his father's fierce expression soften at once, but the voice was still harsh, "What happened?"

Mike told him. He recounted only the facts, about Karen, about Kirk's betrayal, without offering how he had felt, and the facts of his ultimate defeat and humiliation. He didn't bother trying to explain why he had wanted the shoes and the jacket in the first place, as he might have to his mom, or even Alan. He just laid it out as quickly as possible and waited for the final condemnation from his dad. After he finished, he sat down on the curb in a heap.

Will squatted down next to him. "Jesus, Mike, I wish you'd told me sooner. I wish I could have helped you with this somehow." He put his arm around his son, and Mike turned into his chest and cried as hard as he ever had in his life. Will held him and rocked him like the little baby he once had been, now a giant boy or a small giant, but crying just the same in his old dad's arms.

He felt the sobs slowing down and Mike resting against him. He said softly into his ear, "Don't worry about it. You'll always be my son; I love you, and I will forever."

Mike clutched Will desperately, hugging him hard enough to thrill him with an unreasoned scare. "Hey, you're going to kill me with all this affection."

Mike laughed coarsely, "I've been looking for how to do you and get away with it."

They both roared hard at each other, laughing new tears. Their howls trailed off and they sat quietly again with their hands between their knees, nearly around their ears because of the low curb. After a moment, Will spoke.

"Man, I could disembowel that little shit Kirk—"

"Kirk's pretty big, Dad."

"—and his old man, the son of a bitch, for raising such a turd of a kid. Hey, let me at them. No one shits on my kid."

Mike grinned at the notion of his father fighting Kirk and his old man.

"So, that's what all the shenanigans were about, huh? The student council scam, the Booster football game, the wrestling, all that."

"Yeah," said Mike, "only, I'm not going out for wrestling."

"Oh, no?"

Mike shook his head, "Nah. One reality check finally worked, anyway."

"Well, thank God for that." Wi stumbled slightly over his next words, "So, I guess this Karen meant a lot to you?"

"Like the earth and the sky, Dad. I don't know why, but that's how I feel. It's painful, you know?"

Will said, "I know it well, Mike." He shook his head, "She probably doesn't deserve you."

"Oh, I'm sure of that, Dad. Afterall, she goes out with Kirk." They laughed, then he said, "But I still think about her all the time. The exact opposite of what you were saying in the deli, you know? She isn't interested in any of my things, she absolutely doesn't share my feelings, yet the chemistry of the situation is killing me."

"Aw, Mike—"

"Hey, Dad, remember, I'm only fourteen; it's my job."

Will laughed and said, "Yeah, well, I hope you survive your age. And I know a lot of guys in their forties who never got past fourteen. Listen, pal, it's still cold out here. Let's go in and get a new battery and go home."

"Okay."

They stood up, and Will hugged Mike to him one more time, kissing him on the neck before they ambled back into the mall.

Chapter 31.

Whenever he drove back from a tedious task, Will played music, then allowed the music to play him. He would think of things impossible outside the usual world of time, then hope to bring them back with him. On this trip, though, in the aftermath of the catharsis with Mike, he had nothing to bring back.

He glanced over at Mike, who sat trancelike gazing out the windshield. For all that had been found in the mall parking lot, they still had to face their ongoing personal trials. Mike was still screwing up in school, which meant that he would have to bear down on him, a sure way to reestablish some distance between them. And Mike would have to live in the shadow, or the presence at least, of Kirk parading around with Karen, the Dream Girl.

As for himself, Will thought, on Monday he would have to meet with Maloney, to try and stave off the House Ethics Committee, not to mention Sloan and all the other media ghouls tossing the congressman around on TV. Forster would be chewing on him again, too, as he'd done all last week. On top of all this, Eileen was leaving this week for California to rendezvous with Harry or whomever else, maybe. Not a word about Thanksgiving, either. And Mary had missed out on Alan. For all of that, though, he was worried now about his second kid. He had to admit that the ruined shoes hanging from the power line still burned him, a hundred and twenty bucks worth. But he also felt desperate to do something for his kid whom he loved right now more than any person on the planet. All right, he still loved Eileen desperately, and he had a soft spot for Mary that would never go away, and he could name a host of other people for whom he would do anything at any time. But Mike needed him now, and he wanted to tame the world for him.

It struck him as ironic that Mike's woes seemed to have gone on for the same length of time as his own problems, two months. To a fourteen-year-old, that was like a lifetime. The big difference, Will divined, was that Mike didn't deserve any of it, whereas he could blame himself for his problems with Eileen, Forster, and Maloney. Mike was just a kid, for Christ's sake.

He wanted to murder Kirk, or at least be murderous to the shithead, and he wanted to kick that girl Karen's silly little ass— Doesn't she see what she's missing? But he was tied up, he couldn't do anything except maybe give Mike advice. Yeah, sure, to do what?

They turned into the side road that eventually would lead to their street. As they passed through the twilight beneath the large maples common to the tract, Mike stirred.

"Man, Fall's just about over. See? All the trees are giving up their leaves."

Will slowly swung his head to view his son. Mike stared with fixed eyes out the window.

"Say, Mike, have you ever thought of a different approach with this Karen?"

"Huh? Like what?"

"Well, did you ever try to tell her how you felt?"

"What; 'Karen, I know I'm a dweeb to you, but I love you?'"

"No, no, not like that. Like telling her that her very breath is where you suspend your dreams."

"Huh?"

"That's paraphrasing Fitzgerald, I think. What I mean is, you might consider trying to tell her your feelings for her by writing them down."

"You're kidding."

"No, I'm not. I think you could do it. I think you'd be great at it. And, let me tell you something, Buster Brown, that's how I won your mother's love."

"You're not serious? You won Mom's love with poetry? Now she says she doesn't know why you're trying to write it now."

A frown fled briefly across Will's face. "Yeah, well, take my word for it, she liked it back then. Young women do, you know. Karen might."

"Yeah, and she might not. She might share it with Kirk and all the rest as another fabulous joke."

"So what? You're already the laughingstock of the school. What have you got to lose?"

Mike laughed despite himself, "Well, thanks a lot, Dad. But I don't know the first thing about writing poetry."

"Ah, but you do," Will said as they pulled into the driveway. "'The trees are giving up their leaves.' That's a fair country image, I'd say."

"Oh, come on, Dad."

"No, listen. Let's go downstairs and fool around on the computer. If you like what you do, fine. If not, we certainly can delete it for posterity's sake."

"Dad," Mike intoned the plea flatly.

"Come on, give it a try.

"What'll I write?"

"Write what you feel. Say what comes easy, then move some things around. Come on, we're here, let's give it a shot."

Will followed Mike downstairs and sat him in front of the computer. He watched him set up a file, then waited.

Mike sat. He lifted his fingers, then dropped them. "I don't know where to begin."

"Begin anywhere. Try something with the thing you said about fall. Or something else."

Mike still couldn't begin. Finally, he said, "I'm blocked."

"Mike, how can you be blocked when you never wrote anything before?"

"Well, maybe that's the problem. Anyway, I can't do anything with you hanging over my shoulder."

"Oh. Okay, okay, I get it. I'll be in the kitchen."

He sat in the kitchen sipping a beer. Eileen was nowhere to be found. She disappeared often on weekends these days. Couldn't stand being in the house, he supposed. He breathed a sigh. How much longer would this go on? he wondered. How much longer could it go on?

An hour later, he heard Mike call from downstairs. He ran down, and Mike said, "Okay, it's not finished, yet, but here it is."

Will leaned over to read the screen.

The trees
are giving up their leaves.
My thoughts of life
are like a leaf
dying silently
falling, fading
from a tree,
death as drift
without pain
for them or for me,
A natural act
unlike, Karen,
when I lost your love.

Will pulled back.

"Well?" Mike said.

"You're not prosaic," Will said.

"Huh?"

"It's okay, Mike, it's good." Will read it again. "Really good."

Mike brightened, "It's just my first shot at it."

"Yeah, you might want to add an analogy of what winning her love back might be like, like the new life of spring leaves or something. But, really, it's not bad. Why don't you print it out and show it to her?"

"Oh, I don't know. Print it, and I'll think about showing it to her."

"Sure. I'll print it, and I'll save this file for you. 'MIKES.POE'. How's that?"

"Great!"

After printing a copy, he handed it to his son. Then, he said, "Go ahead, Mike, you're off. It's been a tough day."

Mike grinned broadly, "Thanks, Dad. Thanks for, you know, the stuff at the mall and everything."

"Yeah, sure. See you."

After Mike left, Will sat and gazed at the screen for a while. He saved the file, but didn't close it. Instead, he stared at the poem, reading it once again. Finally, he tapped a few keys, then sat back.

The phone rang. He went upstairs to answer it.

Eileen arrived in the late afternoon to an empty house. She felt that familiar mix of relief and disappointment again, a signal that she didn't know how she felt really. Weighed down, she thought, growing heavier each day, but why? Because soon she would leave for California, and maybe this life forever. The idea chilled her. Yet, what choice did she have?

She poured herself a glass of wine from a bottle in the refrigerator, sat down at the kitchen table, and began to finger through the mail without really reading it.

She'd been cycling memories again, odd, passing thoughts of their past together recurring out of nowhere for no reason – Willy watching her change baby Mike who peed in her eye. "The little dickens!" she'd cried, and Will saying, "An apropos characterization. But now maybe you'll appreciate me for what I don't do."

Willy preening when Carter was elected president, saying "What do you think he'll make me in his Cabinet?"

"Potpourri," she said.

"What?"

"Mothballs."

"Where are you getting all this disrespect from?" he huffed.

"Well, where did you get such grand illusions?"

"In the Grand Illusion Islands, of course," he said, and she winced all over again remembering.

Willy telling her to drive carefully just as she was going out the door, then stopping her abruptly, "Wait."

He reached under the sink and pulled out a plastic Safeway bag, blew it up, and tied a knot to the end. He handed it to her, saying, "Here. An airbag."

She cried out a short, painful laugh, he was so shameless. And relentless! Without a doubt, the Henny Youngman of married life, one after another, bad followed by worse. And she missed it.

Harry was funny too, hilarious sometimes, like that crack about Carol Jones in Spain, or the time Forster skipped giving bonuses one year in the early eighties, claiming the recession. When everyone griped knowing that the defense industry was fatter than ever, Harry said in that dry way of his, "You could say that his generosity knows bounds."

Harry was funny, all right, but he wasn't goofy. Willy lived to be goofy, he filled idle time with goofiness, waiting in line, driving in traffic. He spent every spare moment dreaming about crazy stuff, the kind of guy who noted a near-empty page in a computer manual and its single sentence that read, "This page left blank on purpose." Or driving her to a bed and breakfast called The Waddling Dog Inn. And miles later, while waiting for a ferry, noticing an old dog that looked like a sea lion with fur, lying in a heap licking the bricks. "Look, the Inn's namesake. You think he waddled all the way here?"

People went through their entire lives talking about today's weather until they died. Willy refused to allow a boring moment to prevail. The rest of the world had no idea of what they were missing. And now she could look forward to joining them, the ranks of the terminally bored.

Except that Willy had stopped being funny, ever since she had told him what she felt, or no longer felt. Suddenly, Willy had become serious about things, at least things he'd never been serious about before. She sipped some wine as she recognized that in many ways, he was more like what she'd been after him to be for all these months. He'd been remarkable at work under impossible conditions – Maloney for God's sake. Who could deal with him but Will? She had to admit that he had at least put himself into position for promotion in the sense that Forster had to acknowledge his effectiveness. But how Forster would react only God knew. And Maloney's latest hijinks didn't help a bit. But if anyone could contain Maloney and this illegal contribution flap, Will could. Fifty thousand dollars? She shook her head free of the amazing thought, back to Willy. Yes, his attitude had changed all right, and she understood plainly why. For her.

Too late. She breathed in and out heavily. She'd gotten what she wanted from Will, but at what cost? He'd changed for her, and she didn't know if she liked it. An old story, the Chinese admonition about getting what you wish for, watch out. Willy had changed and she was almost out the door. She could see it all in front of her; first, she would have to tell Mary and Mike. Mary would be crushed. In spite of all her bravado and achievements, she was the most vulnerable, the most insecure. Mike would handle it better, but she also knew that she risked losing him. Mike nurtured a hard kernel within him that didn't forgive or forget.

She would tell people at work incrementally, over a discreet period of time. Oh, how could they continue working together afterwards? Maybe she better start looking for another job. She'd be able to find one easier than Willy, and ComCon didn't mean that much to her anymore. Forster had no intention of ever giving her what she deserved. Harry said he would, but she wasn't sure. How could they be involved romantically while he was her boss? And that would really push Will out. No, she better leave, giving both situations a better chance.

She would move out. Willy had always loved the house more than she, although leaving it altogether struck her as a dismal prospect now. So, where would she live, an apartment to start, or maybe a condo? Condos would give her a tax break, but their resale value in this market amounted to nil. Maybe she'd get her own house someday, a townhouse, or a small single-family place. Only, would the kids come with her? Mary, probably, but Mike was doubtful. Except that Willy would encourage him to live with her, even though it would kill him, he would miss them so much.

She shook her head, So sad, she thought. She stood up and walked into the dining room, looking at the familiar paintings, the breakfront full of Mom's china and his grandmother's silverware. The table itself with the scratches Mike had put into it that galled her to this day. She passed through the living room down the short staircase to the rec room, Willy called it the family wreck room where they all went down to be dysfunctional. It needed new carpet so desperately, she thought.

She wandered into the laundry room and sat in his old secretarial chair at the computer. He'd left it on, and she pushed closer to read the handful of yellow words displayed.

The trees
are giving up their leaves;
my thoughts of life
are like a leaf
dying silently
falling, fading
from a tree,
death as drift
without pain
for them, for me,
a natural act
unlike, Eileen,
when I lost your love.

She caught her breath in a sob and quickly swallowed the rest of her wine. Her cool calculations were swept away by the awful truth: She missed him, she missed him for the future, but now it was the future and Willy was gone.

"Honey, you married an old man," he said, surveying his body in front of the bathroom mirror.

"You're not that old, I'm older, remember?"

"Yeah, but I've got a lot more mileage on me."

"You look great to me."

"Oh? So, I was your perfect choice, huh?"

"Perfect for me," she said.

"Yup," he said, looking and spinning around, "Plenty of hair on the chest and none on the back."

"Perfect," she laughed.

Perfect, she thought. She shuddered, What chance do I have now? What possibly could be left?

Chapter 32.

Maloney leaned close in as he spoke, his eyes full of a wild sort of seriousness, Will noticed, something akin to that worn by combat troops just ambushed and surrounded. They sat in the Pisces Club, a small bistro with black furniture and maroon walls favored by the local rainmakers for its obscurity, tucked away as it was in a Georgetown alley. On a weekend afternoon even fewer of the anonymous decision makers could be found, which suited the two at the table, though for different reasons, Will suspected.

"They're all over me," Maloney said, "The Ethics Committee, the media punks, everyone! They're pushing hard, and I don't like it."

He sat back sullenly like a teenager, angry and powerless. He lifted his glass and drew long before putting it down, then hunched over the table again. "These guys better back off, I tell you. I can hurt them bad, each and every one of them. And I will, too, if they don't drop this shit."

"You should try to take it easy, Congressman. Nothing's happened yet."

"Take it easy? Take it easy?" he replied, almost in a cry. "Why are you saying that? Every time we get together, you always say take it easy. You're never on the spot like I am, you know? You don't have the whole goddamn world falling in on your head."

"Forster doesn't count?"

"Forster? What do I give a fuck about Forster? You can handle him, for Christ sake, and even if you don't, there's plenty for you to do somewhere else."

Will winced, wondering if Maloney was aware of the insult, and if he was, whether he even cared. The real pain, of course, lay in its truth. He was someone's nursemaid, Maloney's. And Forster's. And whoever else came along that could make any kind of difference to ComCon's fortune.

He lifted his glass and took a sip, feeling a fleeting sense of guilt at breaking his own cardinal rule. Never drink during business, and this was business even if it was a Saturday. He followed the guilt quickly with self-scorn and another sip. What difference did it make now?

"But this is it for me," Maloney went on, "the last stop. I never had a chance at being a senator or president, God forbid, before all this shit. Now, no way. This is as good as it's going to get for me. If I go down over this piddling bullshit, what am I gonna do? Be a consultant? Be some P.R. flak somewhere? Make big bucks, but so what? Who the hell wants to end up like that? I'm the tail that wags this dog, pal, I sure as hell don't want to wind up wiping its ass — as if any outfit'd have me after the disgrace of it all."

Maloney rattled the ice around in his glass as he tipped it up. He put it down and motioned to a waiter standing behind Will.

"The thing that pisses me off," Maloney muttered quietly, "is that I've given all of my life to this goddamn country, to my state and my district. To the people, for Christ sake! You know, I wasn't always a fuck-up."

Will made a show of widening his eyes at the statement, but Maloney stopped him with a raised hand and continued, "Oh, I admit it, I know I drink too much, and I've had too many girl friends. But damn it, that's away from what I do. I've gotten a lot of jobs for people back home, and I kept a lot of them in work despite the best efforts of every president in the last twenty years to write them off. I was behind Kennedy every step of the way on health care, way before it became popular, and I stood strong, tall behind O'Neill when those other name-only Democrats were slobbering all over Reagan and his supply-side bullshit. And these are only my headlines. I've done good work! And what has it gotten me? Some smarmy little tabloid fuck trying to tear me down as though I never accomplished a thing! Jesus Christ, I'm not the only one who scrounged a few extra bucks in a tight race. And I'll tell you this, I'm one of the few who used it strictly to keep my job. You won't find any new swimming pools or putting greens in my backyard, or new air conditioning, or any thousand-dollar suits in my closets. I live in the same house I did thirty years ago!"

It was true, Will admitted to himself, he'd been to Maloney's house, a little split-level leaning off a hillside above Williamstown, Pennsylvania. The place smelled of every meal ever cooked there, although hardly a soul could be found there, now, with Maloney in Washington and his wife in a nursing home for the past ten years. But it still served as hard evidence that Malony was a throwback to ward healer politics, an anomaly even in his own generation.

"So, why are they stringing me up?" he asked, almost imploring an answer. "Because I've done evil things in office or because I have a bad image? It's not my fault that the system dictates against allowing poor people in Congress, good or bad. Only the rich or those connected to them stay in office, the good along with the bad. So you tell me, is this protecting the interests of the people? What the fuck does Joe Blow have to say to the likes of those assholes? But guys like him have always been able to talk to me, always. I'm one of the few who continue to listen to guys with dirty necks. That's why I'm on the way out!"

He slammed his fist on the tabletop, shaking the glasses. He quickly steadied the full one that had been dropped off by the waiter during his tirade. Once sure the liquid had stabilized, he swept up the glass, took a long draught, then slammed it down again. "This is not fair, I tell you, and, if it comes to it, I'm not going to fight fair. I will crucify them up-side-down! I'll dynamite myself if I have to, but I'll spill plenty of their blood, too, everywhere!"

He moved away, snarling his serious intent, and Will wondered uneasily just how much of this was rhetoric? How far would Maloney really go?

"Listen, Mike, you're way ahead of yourself here. If Packwood can survive his mess, you can breast this. I mean, what are you talking here, are you going to take everyone down with you when it might not even be necessary? It's certainly not called for. If you go off half-cocked like this, what happens to Julie? What about your kids? How would Angie feel about it if she knew? What if she weren't sick, do you think she'd want you to do this?"

"Jesus, Angie," Maloney said mournfully. "God, I miss her, Will. If she hadn't gotten sick, I wouldn't be like this. Oh, God."

He dropped his head into his hands, causing his long black hair to fall in front of his face like a shroud. "You know," he mumbled, "when it was first diagnosed, she used to joke about it, called it her Old-Timer's Disease.' Christ, it's not funny anymore." He lifted his head and wiped back his hair, "I never would have gotten this way, the booze, the broads. She was my rock. If she'd been around, it wouldn't have happened. If it had she would've known what to do. If there was nothing to do, I wouldn't care because I'd still have her."

Will listened, his mouth slightly set in rictus. Before Angie had gotten sick, Maloney had spent most of his time railing against her interference. His drinking and womanizing had predated her illness as well. Yet, he sounded deeply remorseful now, or was it a boozy mood swing? Will sighed, figuring that he had to give him the benefit of the doubt.

"It's not too late, you know," he said, "to change. For the sake of Angie's memory. I mean, not that she's gone, God forbid, but for when she was able to understand. You could cut down on the drinking," he trailed off softly, "maybe even quit altogether."

"For Angie," Maloney said. "This could be my last drink, for her."

He picked up the glass, held it aloft to catch the burnish of the whiskey in light, then drained it.

"I could spend more time with her, too. Maybe she'd get better, maybe she'd have a remission."

"I don't think it's the kind of disease that works that way," Will mumbled.

"Oh, don't say that, Day. Don't be the voice of doom and gloom on the very day I turn over a new leaf. I'm changing. I don't care what happens to me, now. I just want to go home and take care of my Angie. My God, I couldn't live if I thought that she'd never see me again as myself. That would be too cruel a fate to continue walking the face of the Earth."

God, he was far gone, thought Will. He could feel the kernel of hope that he'd had for the man just an instant ago crumple from the weight of their history together. The best he could aim for now was damage control, minimizing the destruction as always, forever.

"I'm happy for you Mike, and I'm no doctor. Angie might give you a big bear hug the minute you walk in the door. This stuff happens all the time. The physicians can't explain it so they keep quiet about it."

"Do you really think so, Will?"

"Sure. You just have to keep faith."

"You're right. I'm getting out of here. I'm going home and see her right away." He started to stand, signaling for his coat at the same time.

"Wait, wait, wait, wait," said Will, "you're pretty shaky. Hold off until tomorrow. She'll still be there."

"Oh, I don't know, Will. I want to see her, I want out of this hell hole."

"Yeah, but you've had a lot. It's a long trip."

"Don't you worry about it, Day, I can take care of myself. I've driven further in a lot worse shape."

He shrugged into his overcoat held by the waiter.

"Wait a minute!" Will shouted, which froze everyone. Grasping, he leaped with the first thing that popped into his mind, "What about Julie?"

Maloney's stern outrage melted. "Julie. I forgot–you're right, I'm going to have to tell her."

Shit, thought Will. "Don't do that, can't you wait on that overnight? It'll give you a better chance to think through what you want to tell her, how you want to say it."

The waiter took the pause between them as his chance to quietly slip away.

"No," said Maloney, "I want to get this done, tabla rasa, a clean slate. I can think of a way to tell her in the car."

Will felt close to bursting, frantic with frustration. "Mike, you must trust me on this. You don't want to tell Julie anything right away. You'll risk breaking her heart if you do. Can't you let it rest until tomorrow?"

"Break her heart?" Maloney said. "Hearts get broken all the time. If it isn't hers this time, she'll break mine eventually."

"Well, let her do that, then. Now that you have your mind made up, what difference does it make to you if you tell her or not?"

"You mean string her along?"

"Jesus Christ, no. I mean pick a better moment! One when you're not loaded to the gills so that you can try to exercise a little compassion for once. For once you could think of Julie instead of yourself."

Maloney drew himself up to royal height, and Will knew he'd made a mistake, a fundamental one. He'd spoken too frankly.

"Thank you for your kind concern," Maloney said cooly, sounding absolutely sober. "I'll take it under advisement."

Will hurried, "All right, you're mad at me and for good reason. I should mind my own business, but this is a general warning about keeping your seat in the House. Come on, get over my nastiness now, because this is your job I'm talking about. That's why you dragged me down here on a Saturday, right? To help you hold on to your job, right?"

Begrudgingly, Maloney relaxed. "What sage words do you have to offer in this area?"

"Don't do or say anything no matter what the newspapers or TV guys report this week. Let them take their best shot before you respond. Remember, the details connecting you to any alleged illegal activity are tenuous at best. If they're proven inconclusive, the ethics part of it goes away too."

"Say nothing."

"Utterly nothing."

"Thank you, Day. You've been enlightening as usual. I won't forget your unwavering support."

Maloney turned and stalked away. Will watched him leave the dark club. Maloney tried to appear in full control of his senses, although a nudge of a chair on the right, a brush of a table to the left told the truth. He was drunk, drunk as a skunk, Will thought, as his father would say, though now he wondered why he used the word skunk? Did skunks have a propensity for drinking, or was it just the rhyme? How about drunk as a monk? It rhymed, he thought, and medieval history warranted the image as more accurate. But it didn't seem to work as well. Probably he liked the familiarity of the phrase in relation to his father's memory, even if it didn't make sense. An acquired affection, like Australians raised on Vegemite. They loved the stuff despite its noxious odor and taste. Maybe though drunk as a skunk worked for him because of the reputation most drunks and skunks share. His problem with this explanation, though, rested in admitting to himself that he kind of liked skunks.

Chapter 33.

He walked through the kitchen door and found Eileen sitting at the table, a cup of tea in front of her and the newspaper. She folded the paper carefully and put it to one side. Then she clasped her hands and waited.

"Hello," he said, disquieted.

"Hello," she replied in a measured, even tone, "How are you?"

"How am I? You mean am I like the guy falling off the ten-story building said while passing the eighth floor, 'So far so good?' Or like the reporter who said, 'Other than that, Mrs. Lincoln, how did you like the play?' If you meant something like that, then I could say that I had quite a day, Ms. Day."

She nodded slightly, "Glad I asked."

He started to pass through to the dining room when she said, "Perhaps you would like to tell me about it."

Her words brought him up short in front of the doorway. "I'm surprised that you have any interest. Or are you just being polite?"

She sighed, hardening a little, then appeared to exercise patience. He felt his teeth clenching involuntarily.

"Yes, I am interested," she said. "Of course I am interested. I thought that maybe," she said hesitantly, "that I could help, if you needed any."

"Oh. Thanks. In that case, I will tell you."

"Fine," she said. "Have a seat. I'll get you a drink."

Somewhat startled by the gesture, he sat down in the chair near the door. She came back from the breakfront in the dining room with a tumbler of Scotch, went to the freezer to add a few ice cubes, then handed it to him. She took her own seat, shifted to a comfortable position crossing her legs, then said, "Okay. Regale me."

He took a long sip. "Where shall I begin?"

"In another galaxy."

"How about Far Fig Newton?"

"Ah, a distant cookie."

He began by telling her about Julie's affair with Maloney. Watching her shock from that bombshell, he couldn't help going on about it, describing it in overly sordid detail that he made up on the spot. Wondering why he did it, he imagined that he was exacting some revenge by channeling the smarminess of such matters in her direction. He noticed her tightening as he went on, so he shifted to Barry Evans' infatuation with Julie. Her jaw dropped another fraction of an inch in disbelief.

Will told her of how he had tried to head Evans off, then being distracted by Maloney's crisis with the Post. He ran over again his face-off with Sloan, this time laying out how Julie had tipped off the reporter in the first place because Maloney had dropped hints to her about breaking up. And just when he thought he'd had that dam plugged, Evans had come to him outraged at learning that Julie and Maloney were together and threatening to tear them down along with everything else.

"Wait a minute, what did he mean by that?" Eileen asked, "Was he going to go to the media with Maloney's affair? Would he tell Sloan?"

"Maybe," Will said, brushing past the question by moving on to his meeting with Maloney that afternoon. He relived for her the congressman's furious raging, his sudden shift into lugubrious histrionics, and their final icy parting.

"So, now," Will said, "Maloney's decided to dry out, dump Julie all over again, then go home to Williamstown to be with his wife the Vegamatic. Tomorrow, I must report all of this to our fearless leader Forster, who is royally pissed anyway for being dragged back from his boat in the Bahamas over this campaign contribution mess during what's supposed to be quiet time around this town."

"So, how did Sloan get the story about ComCon giving Maloney all this money, fifty thousand dollars?"

Will gazed straight into her eyes as he said, "I wish I could tell you."

He had tried to watch her dispassionately throughout his story, but he couldn't. Her reaction to Maloney and Julie's affair, enough in itself to damn him, the idea that he would allow his number one manager to consort with a congressman, was more than polite. She'd been enraptured. Maybe it was her proclivity for office politics, or maybe just her big heart responding, with empathy only, to his troubles. Whatever, while speaking, he'd seen every little movement in her body as an evocation of her feelings, lifting and falling at the various points of his story. He saw bared for him again that vivacious soul of hers, the flames of which licked at his own, consuming him, eating his spirit away at the rate that she receded from him. He couldn't tell her what he knew about the campaign money, not now, even though she must have her suspicions, unless she actually knew. Whatever, the truth would come out anyway, and soon. He didn't want to jeopardize this moment rare of late, when they sat together talking and listening to each other.

"So, what do you think of all this, Eileen?" he said. "You think I'm still in the running for the vice president job?"

Eileen uncrossed her legs and sat up straight, somehow bringing to his mind a good schoolgirl who had momentarily lapsed into a daydream and was now composing herself after being called upon to answer a question. She opened her mouth, then closed it. She moistened her lips as if carefully preparing what she had to say. "It's hard for me to fathom," she began, "how you could learn of all these things, have them happening, and still be able to function as well as you have."

Another surprise, he thought. What restraint, and what was going on?

"I'm happy you think so. But it doesn't improve my chances of getting that promotion, does it? Not by a long shot, right? How about by a short shot?"

"It's not fair."

"Oh, come on Eileen, what's fair about anything? You of all people know that."

"No," she murmured, "but maybe it will work out. If Maloney follows your advice, maybe he can weather this one like he has before."

Will shook his head with a tight grin. "Not likely, not after the phone call I received from Congressman Patterson. He called up to warn me about the five o'clock news. I was in the car, so I missed it. Did you see it?"

"No," she said.

"Well, we can watch the rerun at six, or we can find it on C-SPAN." He flipped on the television and tuned in the station as he said, "A *Post* story alleging improprieties by Maloney during the election is supposed to run tomorrow, but the House Ethics Committee isn't waiting. They've announced that they intend to conduct a full investigation of Maloney's campaign finances and any other matters that might impinge upon issues of his conduct."

"You're not serious? They called a press conference for this?"

"Oh, yes," Will said sardonically, "It's the right thing to do when most of the nation has been shouting 'throw the bums out.' They're proving their mettle and sincerity by initiating a hunt for one of their own, a big one, I might add, someone who's been around for a long time. It also deflects attention from their own affairs. Very neat, you might say."

"So, Patterson's in on this?"

"He's on the Ethics Committee," Will said. He sipped, then said, "He was doing me a favor calling me beforehand. Of course, he couldn't find Nelson or Maloney. I think I have an idea where the congressman is, though."

"Oh," Eileen said, "did you try Julie?"

"Not yet. To tell you the plain truth, I don't have much heart for it anymore. I'm sorry, Eileen, I've been trying, but it's hard keeping it all together. If Sloan's story bears out, there'll be no place for me to go."

She shook her head up and down, in sympathy again, he supposed. She looked wonderful, still wearing a forest-green business suit and skirt from going out somewhere or another this morning. Or maybe it had been brunch with her new lover. Her hair wreathed her face's stony, dramatic features somewhat wildly, a gorgeous black cloud accented by touches of gray here and there. He found it tough to look at her and feel desire for her while he felt anger bordering upon hatred. Wait until she learns about Julie and the money, he thought.

"Willy," she said soberly, "I want to help if you'll let me."

Thrown for another loop, he thought. Had it gotten so bad between them, the distance, that she could feel sorry for him in an abstract way and come to his aid like CARE for some impoverished third-world country?

"What for, Eileen? What's this all about, sympathy?"

"No," she said, drawing out the word, "not sympathy. Because you deserve help. You've earned it."

"Ah, the old-fashioned way? Constance makes the heart grow fonder, right?"

She sighed, "This is hard, Willy. I want to help."

"Why?"

"Can't we just say," she said, "that I owe you that much?"

He didn't know what to think. "What is this, guilt, Eileen?"

She grimaced, then sighed a breath. "All right. It's guilt. Just let me do what I can for you, okay?"

"Well, for Christ's sake, sure. Help me if you want, do whatever you want, only leave me out of it. I don't think I can stand any more switchbacks, you know? Do what you will, only let me be."

"Okay, okay," she said. She sipped her tea and he knocked back his Scotch, sullen and resentful that he was, feeling guilty now, about being so surly to her.

"So," she said, "do you want some dinner?"

"Dinner? You're cooking? Do you hope to poison me?"

She smiled slightly, "The notion has crossed my mind now and then—"

"Unhuh."

"—a few thousand times."

"Well, once you do decide, if you cook you won't have to make any special effort. Fortunately, over the years I've built up an immunity."

"Fortunate when you don't cook yourself."

"It's not manly work."

"Oh no? But laundry is."

"Allow me to correct you; I do the lion's laundry share. The only time you come down to do laundry is when you want to eavesdrop on me. So, to your objections of the laundry end game, I shall continue doing so if you assert that you don't mind a lot of new colors in your clothes. What about Mike? Is he here?"

"No. You don't know where he is?"

"I sprung him for the day. He's had problems of his own."

"Oh?"

"I'll tell you about them later, but he's not back, huh?" He sighed, "Man, give the kid an inch and he's at Inchon."

"Maybe he'll show up just in time. What would you like?"

"How about your specialty? A Hungry Man Dinner?"

"Accompanied by a cheeky, amusing little vintage?"

"Laughable in its pretention, yes, that would be marvelous."

"Coming right up."

They used to kid around this way all the time, he thought. The lines about the wine had become a standard routine whenever they opened a bottle, originating years ago on a European trip they took before the kids had been born. He was guardedly happy about it now, but also bitter that it had been two months since they last traded jokes. This time could be the last time ever. A remnant, he thought, no more than that.

While they waited for the dinners to cook, they watched the Ethics Committee press conference on the news. As the Chairman droned on, Will pointed out Patterson in the back row.

"Look, he's almost hiding. Who could blame him? Listen to them pontificate, will you? The self-righteous bastards. There, the back of Sloan's head. I'd know that peabrain anywhere."

"God, this must be tough on Maloney."

"If he's seen it."

Mike strolled through the door, stopped to look at the table, then said, "Mom! You cooked!"

"Very funny, Mister Smartass. Go wash your hands and I'll put one in the oven for you."

"Listen to that," Will cried out, "they're already hinting at censuring Maloney. And not a damn thing has been proven. What a bunch of goddamn ghouls." He swung his head sadly, "Even if they don't get him, I'm not sure he can survive. It was a tight race with Macowiac without any of this."

"Voters have short memories," Eileen said.

"Yeah. Well, what will be will be. I'm going to go to bed and not think about it."

"No dessert?"

"No stomach."

Later in the night, he felt her climb into bed next to him. He felt her turn over, brushing his back with the electric silk of her nightgown. He was wide awake immediately. Though they'd never stopped sleeping in the same bed, this was the first time in two months that they had touched each other. Had she meant it? Or, was it a mistake, he wondered. Again, was it one of those signs of past affection that women could make, the ones that men took so earnestly to mean something totally different? She'd been so nice tonight, so engaged. Was it because she no longer felt threatened by her feelings for him? Or was something else happening?

He bit his pillow hard. How was he to know, and even if something was changing, how was he supposed to react after the way she'd treated him? If by some miracle she was moving back toward him, what kind of man would he be if he allowed it? Would that mean that he'd have to accept the ebb and flow of her affections from here on and forever? According to some state laws, if a spouse was aware of a mate's infidelity and did not move out immediately, the court saw this as tacit approval and would refuse divorce on those grounds. If he and Eileen ever reconciled, would he be consigning himself to that part of the law written about such weaklings? How was he to know that he wouldn't be winning her affection back for now, but not without creating a deeper current of disregard within her for allowing her treat him this way? He wouldn't know, he couldn't know. He would have to choose between his pride and the consequent misery of losing her, or the sacrifice of his pride and the misery of having her but with a new disrespect for him. Some choice. Enough to keep him up for the rest of the night, he thought, reason itself to strangle her in her sleep and spend the rest of his life in jail, sleeping peacefully.

Of course, the whole thing was a phantasmic hope in the dark. Whatever reason would there be for her to stay with him once the illegal contribution came to light, especially when she found out that he'd had no idea that any money had been going out under the table? Even if he didn't go to jail and was fired only, why would she keep her string tied to his kite, nose-diving as it was straight into the hard sand?

The phone ringing for the fifth time brought him back from his drifting sleep.

"Yeah, I'm here. What is it?"

"Will!" A woman's voice shrilled at him. Involuntarily he pulled the receiver away. "Will!" the voice cried again, and he answered.

"Yes, what is it? Julie?"

"Will," she cried, "Mike is dead! My God, Will, he's dead, gone!"

He shook the sleep away, realizing what he'd heard. "What? What? When? What happened?"

"My God, Will, he came over, he was drinking, then he left to drive home. He was killed on the way."

Jesus Christ, thought Will, Maloney, dead.

"What's the matter, what is it?" Eileen asked drowsily.

"Maloney's dead. Jesus Christ!"

"Dead! What? What happened?"

"Car accident. Hello, Julie?"

She was crying uncontrollably, hardly understandable.

"How did you find out?"

"Nelson called me," she said. "The Pennsylvania State Police called him to find out what to do. He was so drunk, Will, so unhappy. The news just killed him."

"Yeah, yeah, I see, Julie, I see. Jesus, Julie, I'm so sorry, it's terrible."

"What am I going to do, Will? I loved him so and now he's gone!"

"Yeah, I know, honey, I know. Look, I'm coming right over, okay? You just hang on until I get there, all right? Just hold on, Julie, and I'll be there real soon."

He hung up the phone. He stared into the darkness.

"My God."

He felt Eileen grope for his arm, touch it, and hold on to it. "I know, Will. Maloney. I can't believe it!"

"My God, Eileen. He's gone, dead. I always thought it would happen this way, the way he drank, but I never believed it would, either. Holy shit."

"It's just unbelievable."

"Yeah. Listen, I've got to get over to Julie's place."

"Sure, sure. Do you want me to do anything?"

"Yeah, get Nelson on the phone. Tell him to call me, or you call me with the details. I want to know what he told the state cops, you know. Monitor the news and find out what they're saying. I'll call you when I get to Julie's."

He drove fast and carefully with his side window open. Snow had dusted the streets, and he wondered absently if it had caused Maloney's accident. His eyes peered out on the road searching for some grounding of his feelings. As irritating and frustrating as Maloney had been through all their years together, he couldn't imagine him dead, he never could think of wishing him that. Maloney was bigger than life! How could he be dead? Jesus, the memories, he thought. Until recently, he had enjoyed the bearish man's excesses. He was hilarious to observe, not to mention his comments about himself. After so many years on the Hill, Maloney had traveled that spiral down into petty self-indulgence, but he'd been an amazing force in his time. He never lied about his interest in the poor working stiffs, he was a stalwart for them even when the good of the nation at large had been in question. Now, times had changed, and he was dead. He'd been near political expiration anyway, whether he could have made it through this most recent scandal or not. Now the physical had caught up with his political epitaph. For all of it, though, what really bothered Will was the hole he felt inside personally, left there by the passing of Mike Maloney. He never would have believed it.

How Julie must be grieving if he felt this way himself. What could he say to her, how could he make the pain go away? She really loved Maloney, he thought, enough to try to save him, to destroy him, then try to rescue him again. Love was inexplicable and, for Julie, now hopeless except in memory. So, which was worse, he thought, loving the dead or loving one who lived but might as well be dead to you? Or worse, thought of you as dead?

Julie met him at the door of the little townhouse, which was still neat and clean after the news conference just days ago. The disorder of mourning hadn't yet lapped over onto the premises. Only Julie herself bore the marks of such a loss, a terrible maiming, he thought. All the good rest and health in the world couldn't preserve a person's well-being in the aftermath of a lover's death. Julie's face was torn apart with wracking grief and bewilderment at the incomprehensible permanence of it. He hugged her and guided her to the couch in the living room while she continued to cry.

"Why, Will, why?" she wailed.

"Ah, Julie," he said, "I don't know."

"I miss him so already," she said, choking.

"I know, I know."

"God, I wish he'd listened to what I said! I told him to quit drinking, I told him a dozen times."

"You did?" Will was surprised, never suspecting that Maloney would have given her equal footing to hound him, as he would've put it, as Angie always had.

"Yes, but he wouldn't listen to me. Now, he's dead."

"Yes. It's so sad."

She quieted in his arms, exhausted by it all, he supposed. Soon, though, she started heaving again.

"We fought before he left. He kept talking about going back to his wife, the son of a bitch. She's a fucking basket case, but he prefers her to me. So, he goes off, and I'm left with telling him to fuck off as the memory of our last words. Great."

"Did he see the news conference?"

"Did he ever! God, he roared. He was furious, calling each one by name a no-good fucking motherfucker. But I think he was also scared, too, you know? I think he really thought the jig was up. He felt his days on the Hill were numbered, that he was essentially through, you know?"

"I don't think he was far off the truth, Julie."

"Yeah. Well, he ducked out on us all, didn't he."

"I guess so," Will said wistfully.

"Though maybe it gets us all of the hook, too."

Will looked at her. "What? How?"

"Well," she said, "who's going to bother investigating him now?"

In his distress, Will hadn't thought of that. The crisis about the campaign money might be over. But he'd lost Maloney, his main connection to the power of the House.

She started crying heavily again, silent howls that caused her face to form a hovering, open-mouthed expression of horror. "How will I live without him, Will?"

"I don't know, Julie. I guess you have to think of him as being there, not here."

"What?" She stared at him, looking unsure of whether he was being sincere or just sending up meaningless smoke.

"Really, think of him there, not here. Like, you have a fifty-fifty chance of ever seeing him again. If he's somewhere out there, then we'll see him again sometime when we're there, too. If not, then we're close enough to the event ourselves to know that our pain won't last long. There, not here. Not here, there."

She looked at him in total incomprehension. Her face started to whither again in anguish. "What am I going to do now?" she keened.

"Cry," he said, holding her tight to him. "Cry, cry, cry. We all die, and the best thing to do is to cry."

Chapter 34.

Will drained the dregs of his cup, his third, and still felt hollow from being up all night. He'd been up with Julie, and stayed with her through Sunday, making phone calls to Eileen, Nelson, and whoever else he could reach. He'd left at four in the morning, after Julie had fallen asleep, exhausted and dreamless, he hoped, her emotions spent for that day, anyway. Only ten thousand more to go, he thought. He arrived home at five and tossed in his bed for an hour before dropping off. The alarm jangled him awake at seven.

He stood leaning against the counter brooding over having a fourth cup when Eileen walked into the kitchen.

"Are you about to leave?" she said.

He stared into the pot, deliberated for a moment, then said, "I guess so."

"Come on," she said, "I'll drive you. You can catch a nap on the way."

More amazement, he thought warily as he shambled after her. He supposed her intention to be conciliatory, but he found the trip itself anything but soothing. After riding to work alone for the past couple of months, he'd forgotten about her white-knuckle driving style. He felt himself bracing his elbows against the door and the console, flinching at every down shift into a curve and shutting his eyes at the blind speed shift that inevitably followed. She roared up to the back end of a BMW maintaining the speed limit.

"Come on, you're in the ultimate driving machine," she said, "so, drive!"

She revved her engine and blinked her lights. The BMW continued along at the same pace.

"The son of a bitch," she said, "I'll rear-end him, I'll end his rear!"

Abruptly, she clutched and shifted, jamming the pedal down as she pulled out and blew by him, zipping in front just before an oncoming truck went screeching past, horn blaring.

"Jesus Christ, Eileen, slow down! This isn't Indy, you know?"

"All right, all right," she replied, and he could see that sullen look descend upon her, but he couldn't leave it alone, he was too tired to be patient. "No, I mean it. Why you have to drive like a Formula One just to go to the store escapes me, but if you could save it for when you're alone, I'd be a lot happier."

"Look," she said, "you aren't dead yet, are you?"

"No, but you'd think you'd tone it down at least considering what happened last night."

"I'm not Maloney," she said, then mumbling, "I'm not drunk."

He turned to face the side window. Great, he thought. So much for rapprochement. Really, what was the use, things would never change between them now. He might as well get used to it.

When they walked into the lobby, Kelly called them immediately.

"Mr. Forster has scheduled a meeting this morning in the conference room. He told me to tell you as soon as you got in."

Shit, thought Will. "Can we take our coats off first?"

Kelly stammered, "Yeah, sure. I mean, I guess so."

"Thanks."

This was going to be a wonderful day, he thought as he walked to his office. He hung up his coat, then headed to the men's room. Three cups, he said to himself as he stood at the urinal, I'll be back here every fifteen minutes.

He stalked down the long hall through the lobby past the reception desk into the conference room. He was the first to arrive. Shit, he said to himself as he fell into a seat. He tried closing his eyes, to rest, to shut out time. No good.

A few of the others dragged themselves in, cutting short their conversation when they saw him, averting their eyes as if he really cared, he mused. Eileen walked in and sat in the opposite chair. Harry, Eldon, and Barry Evans soon followed.

They all waited, disquieted by the awkward silence, unusual before meetings, even those when they expected Forster to savage them.

Will searched each of them for some kind of exchange other than a shift away to hide their mortification.

Finally, he said, "Hey, folks, the funeral's not until tomorrow," and waited. He continued, "I heard he knocked thirteen mailboxes flat, like dominoes in a row. Nothing but post stubs sticking in the air," he said, finishing with a mumble, "I guess that's one way to deliver the mail."

Harry and Eldon erupted a short burst of laughter. Startled, Will looked up. "Yeah, he said wryly, watching them, "I guess he got the message," then joined them as they laughed again.

"I wonder what the Coroner put down as the cause of death?" Harry said.

"Cadillac arrest," Will blurted.

This time everyone roared, hard, even the young managers who had been uneasy before. Will winced inside, asking himself why he was doing this as he went on, "Cutty Sark express might be apt, though Maloney was more of a Dewar's man, or single malt if someone else was buying. Anyway, he died with his booze on."

The roar in the room built with each joke, tears squeezing out of eyes in red faces.

"Yeah," said Barry, brightening, "the undertaker won't have to embalm him, he was already pickled!"

The laughter dipped as everyone eyed him. Harry said, "Whatever, it's the old rule: you live by the asshole, you die by the asshole," and the laughter soared again, redoubling as Eldon offered, "Maybe they call it recticide, death of an asshole."

Among the teary-eyed audience, Will could see that Eileen no longer laughed behind her faint smile. Her eyes looked troubled, cautioning him, and he hated himself for starting this feeding frenzy, but he couldn't help himself, either. Was he just trying to survive, or was this payback to the man who'd run him ragged through all these years? Although, he thought, in those same years Maloney had sponsored ComCon the entire time and helped them all keep their jobs and their swell, middle-class American way of life. Except for Evans, who hadn't been here long enough, though Will wasn't sure that even Maloney, had he lived, could have saved that little rat's ass.

Forster walked into the room, quelling the noisy group at once. "Well," he said sternly, "I'm happy to see such good cheer among you all, considering the friend this company just lost. Is this some sort of Eastern Buddhist way of dealing with grief?" He paused, still standing, wearing a Polo shirt and slacks, deeply tanned with a fresh, red glow on the surface showing that he'd just left the sun. "I'm delighted to be here myself, especially since the reason I'm back seems to have suddenly dissipated."

Evans barked a laugh, cut short by Forster's eyes knifing into him. "Nice sense of gallows humor, Evans. Remind me not to invite you to my funeral. You might wake up the dead."

Will dropped his head into one hand propped up on his elbow.

"So, can I assume that this crisis involving us and the late congressman is no more? Will?"

Will raised his head, "It's early to tell. C-Span caught a few House members this morning, including the head of the Ethics Committee. Mostly, he talked about his shock, etcetera, and what a fine congressman and good, personal friend Maloney had been. When they asked if the investigation would continue, he said he couldn't say now until the committee met. There wasn't anything in the morning *Post*."

"I picked up a later edition," said Harry, "and it only has a couple of graphs. It does mention the allegations against Maloney, but the rest is pretty sketchy, a lot of archive stuff."

"So what do you think's going to happen?" asked Forster.

Will paused, then said, "I think it might fade. My guess is that Maloney's sins will be forgiven by his colleagues in the House if they've half a chance. I don't think it's going to take much encouragement to get them to recall his good deeds in their eulogies rather than his faults. The latter might look too much like their own. Maloney's premature passing might have wiped away all of his troubles, unless the media keep pushing it. The *Post* might, especially Sloan, who started the whole thing. He's probably one person who's truly sorry that Maloney's gone, though not for the usual reasons."

The other one was Julie, Will thought, and me. Beyond that, he couldn't think of anyone else in Washington.

"Okay," said Forster, who had seated himself during Will's report, "let's stay on it. He was a great American and a great congressman, and that's what people should remember. When's the funeral?"

"Tomorrow, so it won't interfere with Thanksgiving," said Will, "in Williamsport. His kids insisted that he be buried where he came from, not in Arlington or anything like that. I think he would have agreed wholeheartedly with them, not that he'd get a spot in Arlington. I don't think he was eligible for the Army. Genuinely, I mean. He wasn't trying to duck Vietnam or anything. Too old. He would have loved going. Every old-guard politician wante a war record, and they all think they're immortal," he finished wistfully.

"All right," Forster said, "ComCon should keep a low profile regarding the funeral. We don't need to remind any media hounds of our past relationship with him."

Will stared at him, "I'm going."

Forster flicked his eyes to Will, "Of course you are. I expected you to. Anyone who wants to go should, of course. Just don't talk to the media. They'll use anything you say as the official word from ComCon. I don't want to see any surprises in the morning news. Now, as long as I am here, I want to catch up on our regular affairs."

No one else, of course, offered to go with him to Williamstown. Despite his overriding exhaustion during the past two days, Will dragged himself out of bed Tuesday at four in the morning to drive to Maloney's funeral, which was at ten. As predicted, suddenly the whole town's attitude changed about the long-term Representative from PA. It was like a Mafia funeral. The House Ethics Committee solemnly dropped their investigation. The elegies and eulogies ran thick and deep in the papers and on television. As Will suspected, only a handful of people in Washington were not secretly relieved or guilty happy that the problem had gone away. Paul Sloan did try to keep the story going, hinting his follow-up piece at suicide because of the pressure of the investigation. But without the colorful presence of the late congressman, the story looked like it would simply peter out.

"Yeah, Mike," Will said as he drove, "looks like you suffered a timely death."

He had tried to persuade Julie to come with him to the funeral, but she had refused. He wasn't sure if it was the notoriety of her romance with Maloney or that she just couldn't stand the pain. Whatever the reason, he drove by himself this morning, not that he'd have any of the other bastards he thought, burning at the fresh memory of their reaction, their glee as they watched him humiliate himself. Except for Eileen. And Eldon, of all people, coming up to him afterward.

"I'm sorry, Will," he'd said, "it must have been hard for you to hear."

Eldon, he thought, shaking his head. But Eldon wasn't here either. It was understandable, though. And, naturally, Eileen wouldn't come.

He'd been on the road for four hours and still had another hour and a half to go. Williamstown lay in the northern center of the state, triangulated between the towns of Lock Haven, Bellefonte, and Lewisburg, not far from the minimum-security facility at Allenwood. He drove the interstate, which in some places in Pennsylvania cut through the heart of the low mountains, rare occasions in which human intervention seemed to enhance nature's majesty. At these points, the giant sliced-open escarpments suddenly surprised him with every syncline and anticline bared, rolling up and down in glorious loops of earthen colors, topped by the original concealing matt of dark soil and trees. The vast fissures filled him with a vaulting sense of awe at being part of such a wide-screen wonder. At the end of this fall, though, Will felt heart-ache at the sight of a sprinkled snow frozen on the rounded peaks softening the edges of their larger-than-life exposed beauty.

Maloney would miss all this from now on, he thought. So would we all someday, and maybe on that same day these dynamite cuts would be filled again with dirt, dust, and humus.

Grass and trees would grow over them, and they'd be as they were before, quiet, and hidden from human sight.

The son of a bitch stopped me in my tracks, Will spoke out loud as he drove. I thought he couldn't surprise me anymore, and here he has me surprising myself, denying him three times at the fountain – Cadillac arrest, for Christ sake.

Will started laughing at the same time trying to blink back a few tears in his eyes. Christ, Maloney, you're dead and you're still raising hell with me. The old warhorse would have laughed, too, he thought, sobbing a breath of air. He sighed to himself, God, I'm tired.

He dropped through one last pass halfway down the mountainside where the buildings of Williamstown clung from different elevations. The newest ones, the manufacturing plants that Maloney had steered here, sat overhead atop the highest aeries as befitted the saviors of the region. The structures closest to the old center of town showed their age as relics from the defunct mining era. Will cruised past them down to the main street where he found St. Anthony's Holy Roman Catholic Church. He parked his car a few feet away from the front doorsteps and walked quickly in, nodding and smiling to familiar faces, but not saying anything.

The church wasn't large, but it emulated the classic gothic cathedral on a smaller scale with its vaulted ceiling and intricate, ornate plaster fleur-de-les and reliefs of minor saints. The original craftsmanship bore witness to the firm belief of the first parishioners, though the dullness of the chipped goldleaf reflected the church's recent waning fortunes, whether economic or spiritual he couldn't tell. Old P.A. speakers hanging from the support columns further interrupted the illusion of timeless faith. Their curved wooden boxes with round black fabric screens in the middle suggested that they, too, were original equipment, from the fifties, forties, or even thirties, he imagined.

He sat with strangers in a pew three-quarters to the rear of the church so that he could barely see Maloney's coffin resting on a gurney in the center of the aisle. As the mass began, he thought of Maloney lying inside the box, with the satiny lid of the casket no more than a quarter inch from his mouth sewn tightly shut, his lips stretched down by the hidden sutures. Will begged off attending the viewing, claiming that too much work had to be done in the aftermath. It was true, but Will really had been to enough viewings, his grandparents, his mother, his father. After his father had died, Will's brother had said, "We're orphans now," then kissed him hard straight on the mouth, a thrilling, heartbreaking surprise.

He'd been to wakes before, friends dead early for one reason or another. Bob Toohey, kidney disease. "Gee, he lost a lot of weight," one friend said, and another, "He looks asleep. Wake up, Bob."

To Will, though, he looked completely different, and not just because of his ravished body. Will had seen him a week before he died, and he looked sick to death, though still alive. But in his coffin, he appeared nothing like himself, an effigy, vacant. He looked like he was . . . dead. Bob in his box. Bob in a Box— here we go again, he thought.

Maloney must have done no better, so far gone from his body that everyone noticed. So why do they do it? He could imagine all of them milling around, the family members in a daze of grief, but the others quietly standing aside the corpse, socializing. Eventually, the new body becomes familiar and secondary, almost like a piece of furniture. Maybe that's how people start getting used to the change.

He often thought that Jews dealt with death the best way, cry hard but stick them in the ground fast. But they hang around bodies day and night, too, sitting shiva. In some societies, the people dry out the remains of loved ones and decorate their houses with them. Death for them is more intimate, almost ordinary perhaps, which makes sense since it visits them sooner and more often. Like the inner city black kid he heard on the radio that time, talking about a funeral of a young friend killed in a gang shooting. Another kid had said to him, "I can't see myself lying in a box like that." The young narrator then said that the other kid was killed that night. Will shook his head, another society foreign to him, lying in a box. Bob in a Box, Mike in a box, and, someday, me in a box.

Maloney's was made of beautifully burnished oak, with bronze handles. A simple, splendid piece of woodwork, soon it would be put into the ground for no eyes to see, eventually to warp and disintegrate. A true act of faith, Will supposed.

He remembered being told, once, by someone whose name he couldn't recall, of being a boy fascinated with the art of fine gun-making. A master gunsmith lived next-door, and when the friend asked to be taught how, as an exercise he was given a lump of metal and told to use the gunsmith's tools to fashion it by hand into a perfect sphere. The boy labored ceaselessly over the metal ball, honing and shaving, inspecting, then slicing here and there again, until after several weeks he proudly presented the ball to the master.

The gunsmith examined the metal ball carefully, turning it over in his hands back and forth. Finally, he nodded, placed the sphere on his table, and smashed it into a pancake with a ballpeen hammer. The master gunsmith then proceeded to state to the shocked, disbelieving boy some homily about craftsmanship, objectivity, and distance, or something like it that Will had forgotten completely. Apparently, it had been one of those nuggets that had made the friend nod his head in understanding and think enough of the experience as an adult to tell it as a parable. For the life of him, though, Will couldn't remember why, except that it must have been something sage since the story still recurred regularly to him. The reason he found it worthy of memory though, he had to admit, was his astonishment at the friend for thinking the crushing of his perfect ball to smithereens was a priceless learning experience. All Will could think of was the time the friend had spent carving the ball. He did know that he hadn't become a gunsmith, either.

Will stood and kneeled on cue, mumbling the prayers rote-learned thirty years ago as his mind wandered through the church. While the priest eulogized, Will gazed around spotting the people he knew, some local pols and a few senators' aides. The Governor was there, a Republican sticking out in this Democratic stronghold, and a half dozen members from the House, also from Pennsylvania. In a deep corner up front he spied Carol Macowiac, newly appointed by the same Republican governor to serve out Maloney's term. She'd been given the seat to spite the Democrats, but also the recent Republican candidate Shenck, whom the governor despised for running against him in the primary two years ago.

Next to Macowiac sat Nelson, his head bowed in deep thought, probably about his future, Will supposed.

The priest introduced Maloney's brother, which was the only way Will would have known that they were related. He must favor the other side of the family, thought Will. A short, lean figure of a man, when he opened his mouth, a cold air rippled up Will's back. The voice might have been Maloney's own except for the solemn strain as it told simple stories about the late congressman in childhood and early adulthood, finally building to an almost defiant ending.

"Make no mistake, my brother was no saint floating high in some esoteric ether. He was a man with both feet spread flat on the ground and his sleeves rolled up ready every day to take on the hard work of seeing to it that our people got a fair shake. And while he was alive, God bless him, we did."

He left crying fiercely, to be replaced by Patterson. Will cocked his head to listen closely.

"I'm going to read to you a list of the laws that Mike Maloney put in place. Not all of them, we don't have the time, even though he did, always, have enough time, for eighteen years. That was the kind of representative he was, a tireless worker. And this is how he made our lives better."

Will lowered his head and stared into his hands folded on his lap. Maloney, you're gone, and I'm left here wondering how I can put the pieces back together. He wished now that he'd spent more time working on the others during the past few months. But between his problems with Eileen and one crisis after another with Maloney, including the almost complete absence of Julie's help, matters just seemed to have run away from him. He simply didn't have enough fingers to stick into all of the holes in the dike, even if he could reach them.

Forster had made it plain that he was looking past him, now. So, he might as well write off Eileen despite the bit of thawing he detected in her. A reflex, he thought, she wavered reflexively before finally severing her feelings for him. She was gone, and he figured she was gone with Harry. Who else could it be? Who else had the ambition she admired, the promotion almost in his pocket, and knew when her birthday was, to boot? No, it must be Harry, and tomorrow, the two of them would be winging their way to California.

He couldn't blame her, or Harry for that matter. Harry was well-suited for her. And he no longer was. That was okay, he supposed, because he was so tired. But when she was gone, his heart would be so broken.

Outside of the church, Maloney's oldest, Mike Jr., stopped him.

"You know the way to the cemetery? I'll drive you, it's not easy."

Chapter 35.

With Mike Junior at the wheel, they climbed out of Williamstown toward the top of the mountain. They wended their way in and out of back roads toward an opening in a stand of trees.

In his early thirties, the young Maloney favored his mother's fair skin and light brown hair, though he was big like his father. Will wondered if Mike Jr.'s severe demeanor expressed mourning or the anger he shared with his mother at his father.

"I didn't see your mother in church."

The son shook his head, "She's in no shape to come, off her head most of the time. We're not even sure she knows, not that it matters much. He's been dead a long time to her, and her to him. Nope," he said, concentrating on a hairpin turn, "things aren't going to change much around here."

"Unhuh."

They drove on for a while until Mike Jr. said, "You know, he talked about your dad now and then."

"He did?" Will said.

"Yeah. He really liked him."

"I didn't know he knew him that well."

"During his first term. But evidently, your old man made a large impression."

They pulled into a small parking lot on a steep hill above the cemetery. The young Maloney put the car in park, engaged the hand brake, and swung around to rest his arm on the back of his seat.

"So, what was it like?" he asked.

"What was what like?"

"Being around him so much."

Will shifted back slightly. "I wasn't around him all that much."

"More than me."

"No, no way. If you want to know what his day-to-day life was like, Nelson would be a better person to ask."

The son made a sour face. "That little turd, I wouldn't ask him for the time of day. He was the one who screened our calls, you know."

Surprised, Will said, "You really tried all that hard to see your father? I heard otherwise."

Mike Jr. shrugged, "When I was younger. Then we stopped. What was the use? That's what we thought then, anyway. I feel different, I suppose, today. A little."

He jumped out of the car but leaned back in the open door. "The youngsters down in Washington tell how you were always on them to go see him, though. They're glad you did now. It was good of you, that's why I offered to drive. You can find your way to the house from here? Fine, see you there."

He slammed the door shut and strolled down the hill to the open grave where mourners had assembled around the coffin, which was on a bier to one side.

In his turn, Will threw dirt and allowed Mike Maloney to slip into the earth, out of his life, and soon enough, he knew, out of his thoughts. He trudged back up the hill and paused to look over the rugged valley below, spotted with snow and made hazy by smoke mingled with clouds. A cruel day for burial, he thought, then laughed harshly at himself for his lugubrious melodrama.

Most of the other cars had left, back to Maloney's for a reception, which Will was debating whether or not to skip. He pushed his hands deeper into his raincoat pockets and sighed as he looked out at the view, remembering the similar vista in Maloney's triumphant commercial. Gradually, he noticed a figure in front of him, sitting on a wooden beam bordering the small parking lot. A woman, he could make out, in a beige winter coat with a scarf pulled over her hair, vaguely familiar. Carol Macowiac.

He stepped down to her.

"Hello, Ms. Macowiac."

She turned her face up to him, a plain but not unattractive woman with alert, green eyes. Will introduced himself and said, "I just wanted to congratulate you on your appointment."

"ComCon? Oh yeah, one of Maloney's stalwarts. I hear you're the ones who came up with the money for that bogus TV spot."

Will shifted his feet uncomfortably. "Uh, yeah, well I guess that doesn't matter now."

"They shot that ad right over there on that hilltop. You see it?" she said, pointing it out.

"Yes. But you more or less won afterall."

She grimaced, "It's a pretty lousy way to win if you ask me."

"Yeah, it is," Will said.

She swung her head back. "You would think so, huh. Because of what he did for ComCon. I guess that puts you in a bind, right?"

"That's not the only reason," he said. "I miss him, too. After a while, Maloney got to you. At least, in retrospect."

"Unhuh," she said, giving him the gimlet eye. "But you did lose a major supporter, didn't you? And now ComCon's out to lunch. I'm the new rep from this district, and you guys were instrumental in trashing my campaign. I guess that's pretty bad news for you, huh?"

"Could be," Will said, ready to leave.

"Let me see if I can make it worse. Patterson told me that he intends to offer Maloney's seat on the committee to me in memory of Maloney and his district. Oh, I won't have any seniority, mind you," she hurried to say, "They'd never give away clout like that even if they could. But every little bit helps. I'll still have one vote," and she shrugged, "that could break a tie."

She stood up, brushing herself off. Up this close, Will could see that her coat was old, embedded with the dirt of time that would not yield to any amount of brushing. Its open flaps showed her black dress to be equally aged, in some areas worn gray to white, making him wonder if she went to that many funerals.

"So, I guess you could say," she locked eyes with him, and hers suddenly transformed into fiercely polished agates, stunningly forceful as she said, "that you, ComCon, and the horse you rode in on are, well, screwed."

His mouth tightened as he thought silently, You have no idea.

"As well as I can screw you, anyway, right?" She continued eyeballing him hard for a second, then said, "You should be so lucky."

She abruptly stepped back and turned away, saying, "Relax, Mr. Day, I'm not going to exact revenge on ComCon. Oh, don't think I'm above it, believe me, I'd like nothing better than to sit on you guys, with your smug attitudes and dirty dealings. But what good will it do me? I'm in office now, and I want to stay there long enough to get something done. I can't do it as a one-term congressperson, or less than a term, in fact, for that matter. I've already alienated the other good old boys who backed Maloney in the election --- it never would have been close if he hadn't kept shooting himself in the foot with his carrying on. So, to those guys, ComCon was a hero saving Maloney with the ad money. And in the next election, you can be sure that they'll find a new Mike Maloney to put up against me to get me out."

331

Turning her head away, Macowiac said sourly, "So, you see, it's in my best interests to support ComCon when I can, to show the bigs that I'm not just an intractable political zealot." She looked at him as she went on in an admonishing tone, "You see, you can't go on believing all the campaign rhetoric. Just because I ran against Maloney doesn't mean I wanted to undo everything he's done. He saved this district's economic butt over the years. The problem is that he didn't see beyond cutting the same old deals in the same old way."

She swiveled to point at the new, white stone buildings on top of the adjacent mountains, "Those places can be down-sized or closed just as easily as auto assembly plants in Michigan. We need to train people here so that the worker can change when the jobs change. We need to bring job training as another industry to this area, along with making sure that it's part of the business of the big three up there."

"A growth area like that is software, Ms. Macowiac," Will said quietly. She looked back at him questioningly.

"Software development demands a dynamic posture that allows for a wide variety of applications. Take our QuarterMaster packages," he said, "We've had terrific success with the Coast Guard, and the potential is there for the other Service branches

"Which are all cutting back," she said.

"But they'll always still need sound supply lines, large or small. Quartermaster has that flexibility, and ComCon is also investigating expansion into private sector applications at this very moment."

Macowiac crooked her head, "Are you promoting me, Day? With Maloney just laid to rest?"

"Force of habit," he said, "and Mike would've appreciated it. He would have wanted it, for his people here -- your people, now."

She nodded, "Okay, then Mike would've said 'What's in it for me?'"

"Our support when you need it. A good word to the other members of the association. And, who knows? If ComCon can win enough contracts from the other branches, we might need a new production facility ourselves. We might anyway if we do go commercial. That facility could be built here. Who knows?"

"You going to give me fifty thousand dollars for my election?" she asked sharply.

Will pulled back. He couldn't believe himself, what he'd just said. Slowly, with pressed lips, he shook his head, "No. That would be illegal," he said flatly.

Macowiac stared at him. "I don't know whether to take that as an insult or a compliment. Whatever. We'll be talking, Mr. Day."

She turned and walked away to her car.

In his own car, Will drew a deep breath. He slowly navigated his way down the winding road, thinking of how strange it all was even though in afterthought it all seemed like such a natural series of events, too. He felt a little ill, a small twist in his stomach, but he had something, too, to take back to Forster, even though it was a little thing. A little thing, he thought, but a lucky thing.

He passed Maloney's house, a tall, middle row home three streets off the main drag. Maloney used to tell him that a family's fortunes could be assessed by how close their home was to the main street. The poorest lived on the outskirts of town, either up the side of the mountain or down below, subject to water damage in bad storms. As family income increased, they could afford homes closer to the flatter land in the saddle. Maloney's father had been a miner who moved closer to town center when he'd been promoted to foreman. Even after his election, Maloney himself stayed in the family house, for political reasons, he'd said.

The narrow street was parked full on both sides. Will found a place four blocks away back up the grade. He loped down to the corner and turned on to Farragut Street, searching for the fifth house on the right side. On a clear day, sunlight would bathe the front porch at this hour, explaining the robust growth of flowers in the boxes on the wooden railings. The house was a large, three-story place with brown shingles up and down its sides. A small grass lawn grew on the right side of the concrete sidewalk, which was covered with bright green outdoor carpeting. The front shades had been pulled down, and the mourners so crowded the home that they spilled out onto the porch, clutching their drinks near their breasts as they held their suit coats close against the late autumn chill.

Will smiled at them grimly, nodding as he pressed by through the door. The front room was jammed with people standing, and milling. Older mourners filled the old couches and easy chairs facing the heating element sticking out of the fireplace, which had been taken out of service decades ago. He'd been to the house once or twice before, which made familiar the high ceilings and the narrow rooms running front to back like an old Pullman railroad car. Deeply varnished woodwork added to the effect, including the staircase that ran up the left wall. People stood at various levels on the steps, talking quietly, nursing drinks, and biting into sandwich halves.

He took his overcoat off and draped it over his arm. He started to work his way through the crowd, taking care not to knock over the occasional table covered by browning linen doilies. Upon them were groups of tiny, colored glass animals, a few Hummel sculptures, and family photographs that showed the kids in tepid hues the way they'd looked thirty-five years ago. Mike himself looked younger in the photos than at any time Will had known him, closer back then to his own age, although the styles seemed so dated, historic. Angie beamed with happiness and anticipation out of the old prints, as if she was wondering how her children would grow. At times like this it was so obvious, he knew, to speculate about who might be looking at old photos of Eileen, the kids, and himself at some future date when he wasn't around. But he couldn't help thinking the thought.

Mary Ellen, Mike Jr.'s wife, spotted him and came up immediately, saying as she grabbed his arm, "Hi, Will, thanks for being here. Come on into the kitchen. I'll get you a drink and fix you a plate."

A very pretty, dark-haired woman, Mary Ellen struck Will as a person who fretted herself bone thin, always worried about something. She brought him into the kitchen, bigger than he expected, where several of Mike's other kids stood or sat with people he didn't know. Most gave him a glance, then returned to their conversations. A couple stepped up to him, Jim and Noreen, two of the three who lived in Washington.

"Hello, Mr. Day. It's really good to see you," the young man said, then awkwardly, "I mean, considering." He was fair-skinned with cheeks so ruddy they looked like they'd been pinched, framed in a wreath of shaggy, pure black hair. Tall and angular, he towered over his sister, also fair, but with freckles and auburn hair.

"Thanks for coming, Mr. Day," Noreen said, reaching up to grasp his neck and bend him down for a kiss on the cheek, "and thanks for everything you did for Daddy and us." She caught herself before crying, leaned back and gave him a radiant smile, her eyes glistening with sadness.

"I didn't do so much," he mumbled.

"Here's a plate, Will," Mary Ellen said, "and a glass, the good stuff. Dad says – said -- you don't drink much, but when you do, you like the best."

"Thanks," he said, "I guess today's a good day for it."

"Here, come sit," she said.

"Sit here, Will,"

Will turned to find Nelson rising from a seat at a table in the corner of the kitchen. Opposite to him was Congressman John Patterson.

"That's okay, I can stand," Will said.

"No, no, have a seat, I'm finished, anyway, and I've got to go."

"Well," Will said, hesitating.

"Please sit, Will," Patterson said, "I'm glad to see you."

Will sat down and took a small taste from his glass.

Patterson folded his hands on the table and said, "This is a sad day."

No glass or dish was apparent in front of the congressman, and his black, beautifully tailored suit looked impeccable, his shirt seeming almost as fresh as it must have been when he'd put it on in the morning. Patterson was average in height and slender, fit in a way for a man of middle years that bespoke either the habit of a former career serviceman or the genetic luck of an actor. Only a small purse of flesh beneath his chin denoted age of any sort. His hair, charcoal on top tapered into gray at his temples, cut close though deliberately longer than military style. His deep colored eyes shone like black water in moonlight, and his mouth meandered across his face like an old river, every twist and turn hinting at digressions made over time.

"You were very eloquent today, Congressman."

"It wasn't hard to do, even for a son of a gun like Mike. He was a worthy man."

Will nodded soberly.

"I can't lie to you, though, Will, his time had come one way or another. Maybe it's best it turned out this way."

Will stared at Patterson, and he went on, "Oh, for God's sake I didn't want Maloney dead. For God's sake. But he was compromising the committee's impact, the goals. He got himself into such messes that he had to promise favors that totally went against his own beliefs – and mine, I'll admit freely. One folly after another, honest to God."

Patterson lowered his eyes in thought, swinging his head slowly back and forth as he remembered. He lifted his eyes suddenly to Will's.

"That was neat work, by the way, what you did with that Sloan affair." He saw Will's surprise and added, "Nelson told me, just now. Very cute, very inventive. Imagine what you could do deploying your resources in positive situations."

Will slumped slightly, embarrassed and discouraged all over again. If Patterson, the new chairman of the committee was chiding him, then all of the Macowiac support or that of any other rep in the world couldn't help him.

"I'm serious, Will."

Will's eyes snapped up. Then, he leaned back, not sure he wasn't being set up for more abuse.

"Oh, don't keep looking at me that way," Patterson said, slightly exasperated. He glimpsed at his wristwatch and said, "I've got to go. Walk me out, will you?"

Surprised, Will followed him as he made his way through the house, saying goodbye to Maloney's family, hugging the women and grasping the men's hands with both of his in sincere handshakes. He waved to others on the stairs and patted the backs of those in the living room as he went, occasionally pausing to exchange a word, or agreeing to meet later.

They stepped off the porch to the middle of the sidewalk, where Patterson stopped and turned back to Will. At the curb, Will could see Patterson's long black car waiting, the engine running.

"Look, Will, you're a good man in a squeeze. Don't let this get you down. No one is to blame, not you or anybody else at

ComCon. Maloney wouldn't have survived the ethics hearings, true, but no one wanted him to die over it. If we'd had an inkling, any hint at all that this would happen, we would've thought of something else. I just want you to know that; you and the other people back at ComCon. There's a new order now and I fully expect you to play an important role. Keep that in mind. I'll be in touch."

He shook Will's hand, probing him with his steely eyes, then left for his car. As it pulled away, Will watched, still standing by himself on the walk in front of Maloney's house.

He'd had too much to drink and it was late. The good Scotch had crept up on him as he sat in the kitchen eating his corn beef and cabbage while reminiscing with Maloney's children – the ones who would talk to him. But, during all that time and now, as he drove in the dark, his mind stewed over Patterson's words.

At first, when Patterson had told him not to blame himself, Will had thought that he meant it wasn't his fault for not stopping Maloney from leaving the bar drunk to drive home. As Patterson continued, Will's self-pitying guilt was driven away by amazement as the truth unfolded. He couldn't believe it except for the sentence rolling over and over again in his mind: They would have thought of something else.

Why? he asked himself, Why? Again, and again, why would anyone at ComCon want Maloney out? Sure, Maloney had trouble at night, but he'd been a team player, most of the time indulging the association and ComCon's requests. So, why set him up now?

"No one was to blame, not you or anyone else at ComCon."

Did that mean that Patterson had tipped off Sloan about the fifty grand illegal contribution? If so, who at ComCon had told him? Evans had threatened to, but the way he acted when Sloan called him didn't match the scenario. So, who else? Harry? It would have been awfully risky, since he controlled the funds.

Forster himself? It wouldn't be beyond him, the way he enjoyed scheming. And he seemed bent on retiring, so what did he care?

Eileen. Julie had sworn that Eileen didn't know about the money, but Julie could be wrong about that or lying to save his feelings. But why would Eileen do it anyway? What could she gain from it?

He forced himself to consider one possibility: including him out. If she had chosen Harry, she might also want to ensure that he was the crown prince. And Harry would be hard to connect to the money. Instead, Will thought, her estranged honey would be the logical casualty.

Will sighed. This kind of thinking was making him sick. He loved Eileen completely, so how could he imagine such things about her? If they were true, how could he go on wanting her back so much? Why was he willing to do anything for her love if he couldn't stomach the idea that she could do him like this? Why couldn't they love each other the way they had instead of letting these matters interfere? ComCon was only supposed to be a job, for God's sake. Yet, look what it's done to us. What does any of this have to do with defending democracy? What does it have to do with bettering the lives of poor people, black people, and so many women and children? Not a damn thing, he thought.

For God's sake, I used to be a fair, middle-of-the road radical. Why am I doing this?

He couldn't think of any answers, but he knew that he would go on fighting for her. And Patterson had handed him the key, Macowiac, too, in a supporting role. Now, he could go back to Forster flush with success. Patterson wanted him involved, he'd report, a major coup worthy of the new company's vice presidency. A major coup, flush with success. Yes, flush, he thought.

He decided that he couldn't drive any further. He pulled into a Howard Johnson and booked a room for the night. It was safer, he thought. From the time that he parked the car, entered the room, took off his clothes and climbed under the covers, he hid from himself as best as he could the real reason for stopping. He was safe now from erratic driving, true. Mostly though, he didn't have to go home to sleep next to Eileen the night before she left for the West Coast, and maybe forever.

Chapter 36.

In the morning, Will showered, but skipped breakfast, anxious to get on the road as soon as possible. He already decided to drive straight to ComCon, telling himself that he did not want to chance missing Forster with a stop at home. He kept a clean shirt and an extra shaving kit at work in case of emergencies on the Hill. They would come in handy now for a crisis on the home front.

This was it, he decided as he cruised through deep mountain cuts. This was his best chance to get the promotion, and maybe a second chance with Eileen. Patterson and Macowiac had opened a door for him, but he had to strike fast before something changed again. Still, the opportunity was stunning, a complete reversal. He was excited, but in a way that felt more like danger than joy. Too unexpected, he thought, too much at stake.

And here I am dancing on your grave, Mike, he said to himself. But of all people, you would understand, and you might even do a little turn yourself dead or alive.

He arrived at ComCon at ten, famished. As he walked into the lobby, he asked Kelly if she wouldn't mind calling the deli in the industrial park for a bagel and some coffee.

"Sure," she smiled brilliantly, "Cream cheese? Anything else?"

"No, that's good, thanks. Is the big guy in?"

"Yes, just about an hour ago. He looks like he's dressed to play some golf, though." After she said it, she seemed puzzled by her observation considering the wintery weather outside.

"Unhuh," said Will, "Okay, thanks."

So, he had been right to hurry straight here. A good sign, his instincts were back in order.

He loped through the long corridor past a few curious heads turning to follow him as he banked left into his office. He grabbed the spare Dopp kit and a clean shirt from the credenza. Just as he was about to head to the bathroom, the deli delivery man appeared. Will wolfed down the bagel, speed-dialing Forster's office at the same time. When he heard the connection, he pushed a piece of bread to the side of his mouth.

"Hi, Randy," he said, "can I see him? Fifteen minutes? Good, I'll be down."

He raced to the bathroom, shaved, and changed his shirt. The suit looked rumpled, but he couldn't help that. What the hell, he thought, most of his suits looked slept in half the time anyway. He brushed his hair back from his brow, did a final survey in the mirror, breathed deeply, and said, "Here we go, Willy Boy. Waterloo or Babaloo, it's up to you."

He tucked the Dopp bag out of sight up on a shelf and walked out, turning toward Forster's office.

When he arrived, Randy, Forster's longtime secretary, smiled at him, "Hi, Will. How are you?"

"Okay," he said firmly. "How about you? The kids?"

She said, "Driving me nuts. You know the drill, I love them to death but sometimes I wish they were dead – not really, though."

"I hear you," Will said, smiling distractedly. "Is he free now?"

"Yeah, just go on in."

He walked into the office and saw that Kelly had been wrong about golfing. Forster was wearing a Polo shirt, true, but also white duck trousers and boat shoes. He was about to take off back to the Caribbean. Will was twice lucky to see him now, although Forster did seem a bit agitated, probably just about to leave when Will had called. But Forster put his impatience aside immediately, saying in a welcoming tone, "Hi, Will, good to see you. Sit down, sit down."

He gestured to the same leather couch where Will had sat so long ago when Forster had told him about the promotion possibility. How long was it really, just a few months? Will remembered fidgeting then, cringing when he'd heard he was a candidate. He also recalled the other occasion, when Harry and he wheeled out their respective plans for saving ComCon, and how lame his had sounded, even to himself. Now, here he was again, this time a genuine supplicant for the vice president position for reasons completely foreign to those Forster might believe. Yet, Will wanted the job now and was ready to tell Forster whatever he wanted to hear to get it.

"So, how was the funeral?" Forster asked, sitting opposite Will, one arm draped across the back of the couch.

"Remarkable," said Will. Forster frowned slightly, puzzled, and Will continued, "I mean, it was a very nice, sad affair for Maloney, a great turn-out as you might expect, by his family and constituents. And of course, Congress. Maloney's brother made a strong speech, very moving. And Patterson did a great job, truly understated eloquence."

"Patterson, huh?" Forster said.

"Yeah. Carol Macowiac was there, too, you know?"

Forster nodded soberly.

"That's why it was remarkable." Will leaned in, grasping his hands low between his knees, staring hard at Forster's eyes. "Jim, I talked to Macowiac up there, and Patterson, too. They both made firm commitments to support ComCon. They said that they wanted to work with me to ensure we're not forgotten in the budget markups. Jim, this means that ComCon is in better shape now than when Maloney, God rest his soul, ran the house committee."

Forster smiled, "So, Macowiac is on board." He shook his head with a little laugh.

Will pulled back, his turn to be confused.

Forster glanced at him and said, "This is terrific news, Will. I'm happy to see you back in charge. I'm impressed that you were able to think about what we needed with such a clear head under the circumstances. I know that when I leave, ComCon will be in good hands, people who care. That means a lot to me, Will. I won't forget it."

Will felt warmth envelope him. Maybe Forster's reaction wasn't so strange after all. It wouldn't be strange if he had made his decision about executive vice president already, and this news about Patterson and Macowiac confirmed his choice. Tingling still, Will took the plunge.

"Well, as long as we're talking about ComCon's future, Jim, I'd like to make sure that you know that I'm wholly committed to the company's ongoing success. I want to reaffirm to you that I am keen, enthusiastic about the prospect of becoming ComCon's executive vice president. Putting it plainly, Jim, I want that promotion. And I think that I would do a hell of a job at it, too."

Spoken, the words sounded ludicrous to him. So Will stared at Forster with what he hoped appeared to be eyes steely with conviction and good faith. Somewhere, he heard that touching your nose meant that you were lying, so he resisted the temptation and kept his hands folded between his knees, waiting for Forster to respond.

"Oh," Forster said. He turned his head away, then stood up. Turning back, he said, "Will, there's just no easy way to say this, Will, so I'll say it flat out. I've already given Harry the job."

The house of cards and dreams in Will's mind tumbled to the deck. Even as he heard the words he wondered when he knew, before they were said or after? Was it body language that caused such dread or some prescience from the past, a past life? Whatever, he knew for sure now and his hopes, his dreams were all done.

"Shit," he said with a long sigh.

"Aw, Will, don't take it that way," Forster said, grabbing him lightly by a shoulder. "This isn't any kind of judgement or condemnation. I just think that Harry has a more expansive perspective on things, that's all. But you've done a hell of a job yourself, Will, a hell of a job. Both Harry and I know it, and we want you to stay happy on the team. We both agree that you should be a vice president in your own right for all that you've done for ComCon. Certainly, this latest coup with Macowiac proves that. Of course, there'll be a significant raise."

"Vice president," Will said to his still folded hands, "but not executive vice president." He twisted his fingers around, turning the skin white from pressure. Then he looked up.

"Was I ever really in the running, Jim? Did you ever seriously consider me really?"

Forster lifted his hand away from Will's shoulder and started toward his desk. "Will, you never persuaded me that you were truly interested. You seemed . . . ambivalent to me. You missed meetings, you were preoccupied with Maloney's problems when an overview would have been more appropriate."

"You mean like working on Patterson?"

Forster walked behind his desk, "He's a powerful man, no question, now one of the most powerful."

"And Harry has that kind of perspective, that overview." Forster didn't answer; answer enough, thought Will. "I wasn't really in it at all, was I? Just a way to prod both of us to shape up ComCon."

Forster again didn't respond. Instead, he picked up his phone and spoke into it inaudibly.

Will rose. "Let me ask you one more question, Jim. Does it surprise you that Harry gave Maloney fifty thousand dollars so that he could win his election?"

Forster's expression turned stony, and Will went on.

"Oh, yeah, Julie told me about the secret fund, she's that much loyal."

"What are you saying, Will?"

"I'm asking if you knew that Harry gave Maloney the fifty thousand dollars for his commercial?"

"I understood that Julie secured funds for his campaign."

Will paused thoughtfully, rubbing his chin. "You're right. It was Julie who gave Maloney the money, not Harry. Harry gave away the rest of it."

"Listen, I have a car picking me up for the airport in just a few minutes. We can discuss this more if you want when I return."

"Sure," said Will, "but I'd like to know if you approve of Harry involving himself in public affairs like this?"

Forster sighed, and Will found himself studying his features, the sun freckles on his forehead, the cracks down his neck that he knew would be pure white if the skin were spread wide, wondering where the difference lay between them as men, one in power, the other powerless. What kind of thoughts did this man think?

Forster said, "I appreciate Harry's initiative, yes. I would expect an executive officer to know what's going on throughout the company."

"Yeah," Will said, "I'm sure you would."

Impatiently, Forster said, "Just what are you after, Will?"

"I'm just looking for a little moral motivation here. That's all I'm after, I guess."

Chapter 37.

He would pack later, he thought. Tomorrow? No, too late; they might lock up his office. He would need to remember to pick up his Dopp bag in the men's room before he left. Most of this crap could stay, though.

He sat slumped in his chair, his knees propped against the desktop. How could things go from bad to good to terrible like this so fast. And seem like a lifetime of pain? There was no future now, only suffering from this recent past that became a new present again and again as he relived it in his head. This was grief, he thought, this was self-pity he had earned. Or someone had earned for him, bestowed upon him. Job, you have it all over me with your boils and lost children. But God healed you and gave you new children. And how could you love new children, you asshole, as though the others never existed? My God, I'm going to lose my children and my love, and I'll never get them back.

He bowed his head into one hand, covering his eyes.

He felt someone's presence and looked up.

Eileen stood just inside the door, staring at him with concern bordering on alarm.

"Will? Are you all right?"

He smiled sickly. She was magnificent in a dark suit with white pinstripes worn over an ivory silk blouse, a patterned gray scarf knotted at its collar. She wore blue hose to match the suit, and dark blue shoes with a short heel. Her hair was swept back away from her temples. She leaned slightly forward as if ready to help him if needed. An illusion, he thought.

"Are you okay?" she said.

"I'm dead."

Eileen nodded, "It must have been hard, Maloney's funeral."

He pressed his lips into a bloodless line and shook his head, "Yes, it was hard. What are you doing here? I thought you would be winging your way to California by now."

She shook her head, "Of course not, not after Maloney's death. Tomorrow's Thanksgiving, you know. Anyway, there's been a change of plans."

"Sure. I can imagine why."

"Yeah? How come?" She sat down in the chair opposite his desk.

"Oh, come on, Eileen, you're not telling me you don't know?" Her face was blank, so he continued, "Harry got the job. Harry's the new executive vice president. Forster just told me."

"Oh," she said quietly.

"Yup," he said, "I blew it. I know you're thinking it, so let me say it for you, loud and clear. I fucked up any chance I had to get it. You were right all along."

"I'm sorry, Will."

"Yeah," he said, turning a near sob into a hiccough, "me too."

He gazed up at her morosely, his eyes a thick glaze of moisture. He blinked and tried to regain control. "Aw, what the hell. I was never in it anyway from the very beginning. Forster as much as told me. It was Harry all the way. Forster likes his initiative."

Eileen said nothing. She sat straight in her chair, each hand propped on a knee, as though posed, he thought, to accept some kind of penance. For what? he wondered. What was she admitting?

"Relax, Eileen, I don't have any axes to grind. I don't want you to be unhappy with me. I know I disappoint you, and I'm sorry, but I'm just not the kind of mover and shaker that you'd like. I'm not Harry. I'm a PR flak who'd rather be a poet. If you want to change things between us, well," he swallowed, "I'm not going to make it hard for you."

Her eyes stayed fixed on him without any change in expression at all.

He sighed again, and said, "I'll make it easier. It doesn't make any difference if you know now, anyway."

He told her about Julie funneling Maloney the fifty thousand dollars. He laid out the rest of it for her, the bogus foundation-sponsored forums, the receipts, everything, painting himself with relish as a buffoon for not knowing. He enjoyed inflicting self-pain for failing so at the same time he was doing his best to free her from him.

But she didn't appear repulsed. At first, she seemed surprised, then intrigued, then startlingly angry. Well, angry at him maybe.

"So, that's it. I never could have been the boss, Eileen, I don't have it in me. To tell you the truth, I'm glad it's over," he said, then whispered into his breast, except for losing you.

He found himself staring at his hands again, pulling at his fingers once more while avoiding her eyes. Finally, bravely, he lifted his head.

She had moved back into the chair, resting her hands on the arms now, observing him with blank features. Cool, he wondered? She sat that way for some time. A short time in reality he supposed, but much longer in the darkness of his present universe. Nothing will break this trance, he thought, until finally she did.

"Will," she said quietly, "I'm sorry."

He exhaled slowly, at length, trying to expel all oxygen in body to stop all thought. "Yeah," he said at the end of his breath, "me too."

"I'm sorry that you had to go through this by yourself."

He nodded, pulling at the skin beneath his chin, "I've learned a lot."

"Yes," she said. She fell silent, mulling inward. He used the quiet time to take her in with his eyes, the familiar features that had become remote in such few short months, the slight lines and marks in her face he came to know by second nature. All those old things about her new again, right in front of him as he'd seen them for twenty years. Now distant and cherished.

She broke his revery, "So, you're saying that Harry was running a slush fund for ten years, or even longer?"

"Apparently."

"Through Julie?"

"Yeah, I guess."

"Julie? Jesus!"

"I take it then, you didn't know about this?"

She stared at him in disbelief, then erupted, "Hell no I didn't know!"

He flinched back in his seat saying "Sorry."

"Why would you think I knew?"

"I don't know," Will said, flushing slightly. As a diversion, he threw a hand into the air, then let it fall. "You always seemed more on top of this stuff than me. I became more paranoid, I suppose, since things kept happening."

"Well, thanks a whole lot."

"Yeah, kind of twisted, I guess."

Eileen stood up and circled the space in front of his desk. "So, did Forster know about the fund?"

"He wouldn't admit it directly, but I checked him on it regarding Maloney's commercial. I told him that Harry had okayed the fifty thousand, but he corrected me, saying that it was Julie's call. That makes me think he very well knew who was giving out what."

"Of course."

"And he seemed to know that Patterson would support ComCon. It was Macowiac who surprised him."

Eileen smiled, "Macowiac, that is rare. You're amazing, Will."

He reddened again and said quickly, "She volunteered, Eileen, believe me."

"Oh sure, but I'd bet it'd be hard to say who was the pitcher and the catcher. You're a natural talent, you know that?"

And with a thrill he suddenly realized that Eileen was standing in his office going over everything with him despite knowing he'd been a clueless jackass throughout. He shook off the sensation. Hold on to reality, Will.

"Patterson; now what would he get out of ousting Maloney? He already won the committee chair." She turned to him. "What do you think?"

Will shrugged, "Maloney was a force no matter what. The night he died he told me if they kept dumping on him, he was going to name names. Maybe that's what Patterson and the others had in mind, divide the old guard Democrats so they wouldn't unite to block new policy. You know, the way the Republicans did for the past two years?"

She nodded, half paying attention as she dwelled deep in thought. She turned away, then back to him. "What about the receipts? Are they still in Julie's desk?"

"I don't know."

"Let's go check."

They walked out together, and as he opened the bottom drawer, he could feel her posed above him, he could smell her perfume. So familiar, absent for so long it still made his heart ache.

"Gone." He caught his breath, working to control a sudden, senseless panic that she might think he made it all up, that she'd scorn him, leave him.

"Damn," Eileen said. "Do you think Harry got them?"

"No," Will said, "I think it's more likely that Barry Evans picked them up. Harry wouldn't care; nothing leads to him."

She trailed him back into his office, "Unhuh. So, you said there were other receipts?"

"Yeah, nickel and dime stuff – a thousand here, fifteen hundred there. For all I know, they might be gone now, too. But I stashed away carbons from a bunch of them."

"That's good. That's something."

Her mind seemed to race off again, leaving him standing staring at her, too abashed to fly any kites of hope. As he watched, he noticed her demeanor change gradually. Her usual crisp, forward-looking expression spearheaded by her sharp alert eyes had metamorphosized into a grave mood tinged with sadness, aging her.

Eileen noticed him, and said, "So, what were you going to do?"

"Pack."

She looked at him softly and said, "That's premature, don't you think?"

"No," Will said firmly, "I don't."

"Oh."

Silence filled room. He shifted his weight to lean a shoulder against the wall.

"Anyway, you came to see me for something?" He almost laughed asking the question, as though he were chiding the axeman at his own execution: Can we pick up the pace here a little bit?

She seemed to penetrate him with her eyes. "Yes. I wanted to," she said, faltering, "to talk to you . . . about deciding things."

"Oh," he said. "I thought everything had been decided."

She swung her head, "No." She walked over to him and embraced him, pinning his arms at first, then working hers under his to hug him closer, harder.

He stood still, stunned. Recent dreams recurred, of her coming to him and hugging him, he resisting at first, then giving way to love desperate beyond passion, a hunger for her that dismissed his cries of anguish that it was wrong, wrong. Wrong, but he didn't care, he loved her so. Waking in the middle of so many nights during the past few months, waking and finding her as good as gone. Then, the real pain followed.

But she held him now for real. She moved his arms up around her, and he could feel the delicate bones of her back again, the warmth of her body, the small rounding of her breasts, the slight press of her thighs, her neck within reach of his lips.

Deflated at first by what he had longed for, past what it could really feel like, without thought he lowered his head and kissed her on the nape of her neck. Then he squeezed her, almost crushingly, both of rage and relief.

He eased up and held off. Eileen pushed her face into his and kissed his mouth. She tried to kiss him passionately, but Will found himself clumsily missing. He pulled back.

"Excuse me but isn't this some form of sexual harassment?" he said.

She snuggled up to his breast, "Call it sexual caressment."

"Oh."

They stood holding each other silently. He found the slightness of her body a new wonder, amazing.

"I came to tell you why I canceled the trip to California. This was the reason," she said.

"I see."

"So," she went on, "do you want to go home now?"

He felt a needle of pain shoot straight through him. "Will you think less of me if I say yes?"

"Not at all," she purred.

Abruptly, she began to pull away. He stiffened.

"Listen, I've got to do one thing before we go, right away."

"Unhuh."

She spun away to leave the office, "I'll be right back," she said.

"Sure," he said as he watched her back quickly down the hall.

"And don't pack yet," she called back.

He watched her recede down the hallway until she disappeared around the corner.

He walked back into his office and started to search for a box. Finally, he emptied one full of old files. Let his successor sort through them, he didn't care. He opened the top drawer of his desk and began to select things to leave and things to take home. He paused then. Home?

Chapter 38.

Sitting behind his desk, Harry saw through his office doorway Eileen heading toward him. As she entered, he called, "Did you tell Will about the change, your change of heart?"

She didn't reply as she stopped directly in front of his desk. She slammed her hand on top. "What's this hidden account about, Harry, secret for ten years?"

Harry hesitated, mouth open. Then he shrugged and said, "I inherited it from Miller."

"And you used Julie to carry the water during all that time?"

"Miller assigned her to deliver it before. The continuity seemed natural."

"So, now she's taking the heat for Maloney's fifty grand?"

"I had nothing to do with that," Harry said, holding up one of his large pale hands. "She did that on her own. She screwed up the amount and the timing; too much, too fast. Anyone would've been curious."

"And you never told Will about it?"

"Considering his sensitive nature, it didn't seem like a good idea. He was new. How was I to know if he found it problematic? For all I know, he might've handled it the same way if he started here first."

"But he didn't, did he? That's what it was all about, right? The new guy pressing you for top dog? How fair is that? Unfair enough for you to make a little deal with Patterson, to call Paul Sloan, to get Maloney dumped just so that Will would look bad?"

"For crying out loud, Eileen," Harry said, "that's pretty farfetched. You think I would risk ComCon going down the tubes just to torpedo Will?"

She drew back, her face a scathing look of skepticism.

"Eileen, I like Will, a lot. I want him to stay on."

"Sure you do. Well, fat chance, Harry. Didn't you know that after being his friend for all these years? He's ready to pack up and go now. It's ironic, isn't it, you feeling threatened by him. The only reason he tried to get the promotion at all was because I was on his neck about it. Oh, it would've been problematic, all right, he never would have put up with it except to protect Julie, and for me. Isn't that a laugh, Harry?"

Harry stood up and came around the desk to take Eileen's hands. "I thought it would work out for all of us."

"Oh, bullshit," she said, jerking her hands away. "And what about me, Harry? Was the bum rush you put on me part of the plan? I'd be so distracted and down on him, sure. But wooing me would make sure I wouldn't see this coming? Was that what all your undying love was about?"

He appeared stung. "I meant everything," he said. He paused. "It doesn't matter, though, does it?"

Eileen didn't answer. She said, "Tell me the thought never crossed your mind that together Will and I would be tough to handle. Tell me it straight for once, for God's sake."

Harry stared at her momentarily, starkly. He relaxed his features. "You mean, how much do I love you? I do love you, absolutely" he said evenly, "but I didn't think it would hurt, either, if you didn't take too active a part in ComCon's reorganization."

"And you didn't see anything wrong with this, no conflict of interest by you?" she said loudly.

He stared at her unblinking, then said, "I didn't see this as being mutually exclusive."

"Well, thanks for clearing that up!" she yelled. She wheeled around and stalked off.

Long after she'd gone, Harry said forlornly to the empty office, "You're welcome."

Will finished packing a box, just two-thirds full. A few pictures still needed to come off the wall. Other than that, there wasn't much to show after ten years. Perhaps symbolic, he thought, of why he hadn't been promoted. He just didn't have that much invested in this place. He folded the flaps of the box closed just as Eileen returned.

"That son of a bitch," she said.

"Who?"

"Harry. He's a real shit."

"Oh? Why?" Will said.

"Why? Why? Is that a rhetorical question or philosophical?"

"Never mind," he said, returning to his box.

"You packed."

"I did."

"You didn't listen to me."

"Why start now?" he said.

"Good point. Well, you may be packed and ready to go, but I'm not. I don't want to leave, but if I end up going, I won't travel lightly."

"No?"

"No. Let's get to those receipts."

In the evening, in the dark, in bed, they talked.

"Do you think it could work?" he said.

Eileen sighed, "I don't know. It depends upon a lot of factors, not just what we know, but what kind of fight we're willing to put up with, how many rounds."

"Well, one way or the other, it's going to change things around."

"Oh yes."

He rolled over in the dark and stared at her silhouette revealed by moonlight. After a while, he said in the dark, "What would you do, Eileen, if you didn't have ComCon?"

He heard her reply in the dark.

"Oh, I don't know," she said, "though I might be about to find out."

"What would you like to do?"

She thought for a moment, then said, "I'd like to run my own company. Really, from the ground up. You know that idea about conversion into the private sector? Well, I'd like to do it. I'd like to see if we could, you know, go out there into the real world to compete and do it. God, that would be great! Only this time, I'd call the shots, all of them."

"Gosh. That sounds like fun."

She leaned over to him, squeezing him tight, "Oh, what do you know? You know nothing."

"I know goodness great gobs of nothing," he said. As she laughed, he went on, "But I do know a possibility for you to do what you want."

"Yeah? How?"

"Let's just say that it's time you have a little meeting with Eldon."

"Eldon? Why Eldon?"

"He has something to show you. And I think you'll want to see it."

"Eldon, huh? No kidding?"

"Nope. I wouldn't kid you."

They grew quiet. He wondered if they would make love again. The first time, they'd exercised passion solemnly. She was contrite and tried to show it. He felt uneasy the entire time, on edge as though all of this would be taken away again at any time – as though she might take it away.

Before, they were never reverent about love. He could remember caving in one time, gasping as he collapsed, "I'm having a heart attack."

"You can't be having a heart attack," she said, "we're married. It's only guys fooling around with other women who have heart attacks."

"Yeah, but when we make love, I fantasize that you're another woman."

She hit him, of course, hard in the shoulder. He had a bruise in the morning.

Ironic, now, isn't it, he thought. He shook his head; there's a sickness to love.

"Well," she said, breaking the silence, "I guess you know what you'll be doing."

"Oh, I don't know," he said. "I feel like I've been spinning my wheels in mud. Back and forth."

"Oh, come on!" she said, punching him lightly on the shoulder. "Don't give me that You're going to be a great poet."

"Eileen, what are you saying? You have no idea whether I'll be anything."

"Sure I do," she said. "You won me back, didn't you?"

And she drew nearer, pulling the blanket around so that she could press closer. He felt her soft body at his shoulder as he asked, "What do you mean? I thought you changed your mind because of what was happening to me at work."

"No!" she said, "It was the new poem you wrote for me."

His mind drew a blank. "New poem?"

"Sure. I saw it on your computer before you filed it." And she quoted, "'The trees are giving up their leaves . . ..'"

She continued, and as he listened, a slowing sensation overcame him, a feeling like some animal staggering around after being shot by one of those anesthesia rifles. Recognition paralyzed him as she finished.

359

"'A natural act, unlike, Eileen, when I lost your love.' Only you didn't lose my love," she said, hugging him hard, "I just lost track of why I love you."

Jesus. Mike's poem.

He found himself smiling sickly in the dark as though she could see him. She'd fallen back in love with me, he thought, because of Mike's poem, his first poem, which I stole. She has no idea whether I can write poetry or not. It's good enough for her that I wrote her that poem. Which I didn't.

Jesus, he thought. She loves me again for this, and I can't tell her the truth. Ever. He shook his head, love is sick.

Chapter 39.

Will peered into his mug, watching the swirling coffee slow and stop. His third cup. He hadn't slept last night, even after Eileen had dropped off. Too used to insomnia, he supposed. Or maybe it was the prospect of the future, still unknown as far as he was concerned, certainly uncertain.

Mike came down to the kitchen, nodding silently as he passed Will on his way to the refrigerator. He reached inside for a bagel and stuffed it in his mouth. He grabbed his backpack and headed out the door to catch the bus.

"Have a nice day, son," Will said softly after Mike closed the door.

Eileen walked in and spotted Will leaning against the counter. She moved next to him and gave him a warm kiss.

"How are you?" she said.

"I don't know," he said, immobile. "My brain is shot."

"Oh? Is that just today or for forever?"

He looked at her somberly and said, "There's no way of knowing."

Laughing, she said, "Well, I hope it's just temporary. We need to get going."

He sighed, "Eileen, you better understand one thing now. I'm through with this shit forever."

"I know, I know. You feel that way now, but let's wait and see what happens. They owe you something other than a wave goodbye. And they owe me a lot, not the least of which my being the one who brought them you. So, bear with me on this."

He sighed, "All right."

"Okay. Are you ready?"

"I suppose. No breakfast?"

"Later. The edge will do me good."

She grabbed her car keys from the hook, then thought again. "Do you want to drive?" she asked him.

"No. I might fall asleep."

"Okay." Then, she said, "Don't worry, I'll go easy on you."

As she drove, he tried to organize in his mind the blur that had been the weekend for him, the long holiday weekend. They'd spent Thanksgiving afternoon examining the receipt carbons he'd squirreled away. Then, he and Eileen grabbed Mike and drove to Washington to pick up Julie. They headed to a restaurant in Pentagon City, where they ate white meat carved with an electric knife from a turkey breast. Eileen explained to Julie when she asked, that Mary had decided to stay at school for Thanksgiving, to study for a logic exam. Eileen went on to say that she thought the real reason was that over the past two years, Mary had eaten Thanksgiving dinner with her old boyfriend Alan's family. She trailed off about Mary avoiding the pain when she noticed Julie's eyes falling, unseeing, to her lap.

After dinner, they stood outside an arcade, talking, while Mike played video games. They dropped Julie off and drove back home. They called Miami to page Forster, then headed upstairs.

Will fell spread-eagle on the bed without undressing. He stared at the ceiling as Eileen moved around him. He must have dozed off, for he started suddenly when he felt her settle near him, naked.

"My God," he said, "don't you ever get tired?"

"It's been a long time," she said as she pulled at his clothes.

Has it? he almost said, but instead he groaned.

362

"What were you thinking of in your little revery world, some great artistic thing?"

"Oh, yeah," he said wryly, "I was dreaming that I was an art terrorist in Florence wielding a Uffizi, you know, the terrible automatic weapon that fires fine art objects. Spraying the wall with row after row of Botticelli's, ducking Da Vinci's."

She sat up. "You know, you're a nutcase."

"Oh, is that the way you feel about me, and all men – we're just a case for our nuts, merely a repository for reproduction? You're not seeing us for ourselves, as sensitive, feeling being –"

"You left out caring," she said.

"We don't care."

She punched his shoulder, then hugged him fiercely. He smiled slowly at the ceiling.

They had heard Friday morning from Forster's service that he would be back in the office on Monday. They had done as much as they could, which left him watching meaningless football games during the day and staring into the dark at night.

"So, what's this emergency all about, Eileen," Forster said. "What's so serious that you have to drag me all the way back up here from Miami? All the way back from St. Croix, for God's sake?"

"Oh, it's plenty serious, Jim. I'd say that ComCon's future rides heavily on what's said today. Maybe even your boat."

He frowned, then said, "Go ahead."

The four of them sat in his office, Harry on one of the couches, Will opposite him. Forster sat in his desk chair, swiveling back and forth just enough to serve notice that he didn't consider this meeting worth his complete attention. Eileen sat on the edge of the green leather next to Will, ready.

363

"This has to do with fairness, Jim. It might even be about righteousness."

"Get to it," Forster said shortly.

"I'm talking about the executive vice president position," she said, "that you gave to Harry."

Forster glanced at Harry, who's face revealed nothing.

"So?" Forster said, "You're complaining about this? For Will?"

"Will's perfectly capable of presenting himself on this. But I think it has more to do with our shared responsibility as senior officers of ComCon. So, I'd like a few things clarified."

"Such as?"

"Such as how could you give Harry the nod when he's been administering an illegal slush fund for more than ten years, leaving ComCon with more exposure than at a nude beach?"

All eyes again turned to Harry, who continued to sit implacably.

"Come on, Eileen," Forster said, "not this old story again." But Will noticed that he had stopped swiveling.

Forster raised his hands and chopped in front of him with each word, "There is no slush fund, there never was a slush fund. Everything's been on the up and up, except for the Maloney affair, which is completely attributable to a lovesick assistant. Who is the only liable party, here, I might add. Hell, she worked for Will, he's the one who carries the responsibility if anyone does. Give him the vice presidency? I could have fired him considering this mess and all the others he and his hero Maloney created for us."

"That's crap and you know it. Harry's been calling the tune since Aaron Miller retired. You remember Aaron, he passed out the bucks all those years before, when Will wasn't even at

ComCon. No, this goes back, way back, a long time. You're the one, Jim, you've been handing it out since Day One. Will's the only person who gave you a semblance of respectability, which, of course, you used as cover for business as usual."

"Nonsense. That's an incredible fabrication, Eileen."

"Oh really? You should know, you're the resident expert at telling lies."

"I'm not telling lies," Forster said, "I'm just—"

"Offering alternative truths?" Eileen said.

"All right, that's enough," he said, rising in his chair. He sat back, then said evenly, "What is the purpose of this assault, Eileen? What do you expect to get out of this? I've already given Harry the job, and after today, you'll have to do some potent back peddling to hang on to your own place. So, what do you want? What's the bottom line on this?"

"Why, it's a matter of principal, Jim."

"Principle? You're talking about principles?" He started to laugh, when Eileen stopped him by saying, "I'm talking about the money kind of principal, Jim, not values."

Forster stilled. "Money."

"Yes, that principal. Do you think there's an interesting etymological twist to this, Jim, two almost diametrically different meanings for the same word? Then again, principle is always connected to money, isn't it?"

Forster gripped his hands together on his desk. "So, you want more money. A large raise, I suppose?"

Eileen laughed, "Oh, please, Jim, Will and I aren't staying here. It's too dangerous after all of your illegal contributions. I'm talking start-up capital."

Forster opened his mouth wide, then said, "You're out of your mind. I'm not giving you one red cent, especially since you have nothing on me."

"Oh, really? What about this security information foundation so conveniently set up by ComCon?"

"Utterly legal. Even if there was some question about the sponsorship offered, none exceeded the legal limit."

"Collectively? Even when the invited," she hooked her fingers on both hands into quotation marks, "experts didn't appear?"

Forster paused and sat back in his chair. "That's open to interpretation, of course." He smiled, and said, "You know, you're not the only lawyer I know, Eileen."

"No," she said, "but I'm the best. We're not going to court on this, Jim. We're going to the feds, under the False Claims Act. You know the one, when employees go to the government with proof of malfeasance by their employer? The employees get anywhere from ten to fifteen percent of whatever damages the company pays. My guess is that they'll get a good thirty million out of ComCon, so Will can claim at least four and a half million. That's ample seed money for the enterprise I have in mind. Of course, if not, I'll be happy to contribute my fee to ComCon's sole, last poet," she said grinning as she flipped her thumb in Will's direction.

The room became completely silent. Will shifted his eyes back and forth from Harry to Forster, waiting for their reaction, delighted in how much he was enjoying himself.

Harry suddenly appeared winded, but Forster grew livid.

"Jesus Christ!" he exploded, shooting up from his desk to hammer the top with his fists. "You ungrateful bitch! You would try to fuck me after all I've done for you? God, you're unbelievable evil!" he shouted.

She relaxed back on the couch, not saying a word. Will gazed at her with unadulterated admiration. After all these years, he knew Eileen's capabilities front and back. But the rare time he was able to see her exercise them still left him marveling in slack jawed amazement.

"You don't have a chance," Forster snapped, "There's no proof, only innuendo. I'll bury you before you even get out of the gate."

"Nice mix of metaphors," Eileen murmured. "We do have proof, Jim." She reached into her briefcase and pulled out a waft of papers, "Receipts from the famous information forums cum speakers bureau, pre-'89 that is, going all the way back to Aaron's day."

Forster slouched further into his seat. "Hah. They won't prove a thing. All the amounts are within proper limits. You've got nothing." Then he snarled, "Even if your wild story seems to have something to it, there's no way Harry could be connected. Julie gave Maloney the money, she's the logical conduit. Neither I nor Harry sanctioned any of it. You'll be setting up Julie and Will, for prosecution, not ComCon."

"Oh, come on, Jim, no one's going to believe Julie dreamed up a slush fund all by herself. Everyone will know that she got her cues from a higher-up."

"There's no written record, only the receipts for tax purposes. The finger still points at Will, Eileen. The Feds will think you're trying to save his ass with this whistle-blowing stuff. In fact, now that you've disclosed this pattern, I believe I'm going to have to discharge him for jeopardizing ComCon and National Security in this fashion."

Will detected a change in the timber of Forster's voice in his last sentence. Eileen smirked, saying, "Don't worry, Jim, we're not recording this conversation. We don't need to. Oh, did I forget to mention the third party in our suit? Julie's coming forward, too. Her testimony and the fact that the receipts predate Will's time here pretty much gets him off the hook I would think. Wouldn't you? For Julie's cooperation, she's getting no jail time or any fine either. That's how damning a witness she is, that and her attorney of course. By the way, she too will be tendering her resignation."

"God-damn it, Eileen!" Forster bellowed.

Harry stood, raising his hands to calm Forster without looking at him. "Eileen," he said in a gentle voice, "it seems like you and Will have reached an extreme position prematurely. Jim is right when he says he expected more loyalty from you. It is also true that we want to keep both of you happy and working at ComCon."

Eileen opened her mouth, but Harry continued before she could speak. "Now, we know that you're not happy at all with what has transpired. I personally am very sorry, very sad about this. Truly. If I could, I would like to have seen it all in our rearview mirror to make us and ComCon whole again, like before."

"Impossible," said Eileen.

"Out of the question," barked Jim. "You'll never work here again, Eileen."

"Our choice, Jim, and you can consider yourself lucky on that count. The Whistle-Blower Protection Act says we can work here for as long as we want while still twisting the screws on you."

Forster reddened even more, but Harry forestalled him again with a gesture, "All right, we've had enough acrimony. And your leaving is your decision, although I'm sure that Jim would reconsider, once he's had a chance if you like to." He gave her a questioning expression, but Eileen shook her head firmly, no.

"All right, Eileen," Harry said. "But do we need to destroy what all four of us have built over the years? The kind of revenge that you're after?"

She waved him away with her and.

"What about you, Will," Harry said. "Do you have an opinion on this?"

Surprised, Will hesitated, then said, "I have no opinion. Just common convention."

Harry pulled back. "Okay. But I don't think any of us want to see several hundred or more people abruptly on the street. Most of them are our friends as well as our colleagues. So, what will it take to solve this situation? Will? Eileen?"

Will saw no break in Eileen's stone face, her head lowered, the little smile gone. She leaned forward.

"Five million a piece. And you go to the government yourself with full disclosure."

"Jesus Christ, this is a solution?" yelled Forster.

"It's better than if we go. If we tell them, you'll lose thirty million to start. If you tell them, you can negotiate both a lower penalty and a payment schedule predicated upon your good faith in coming forward."

"They'll send us to fucking jail!" roared Forster.

"Not necessarily, and especially not if they need you to pay them. Debtor's prison went out of style centuries ago. If you work it right, you might even get a few more contracts out of the deal. No one ever said that QMIV was a bad product, just expensive. You know, it's the old story, you owe the bank a million dollars, they're at your mercy."

"Holy shit," Forster said. He sat down. He turned to Harry, who stared at him. "Can we think about this?"

Eileen shook her head, "This is a one-day offer, gentlemen."

Forster lowered his eyes to his desktop as he whispered, "You are the best, Eileen." He gnawed at his lower lip, then said, "Suppose we give you the money as a bonus, with the understanding that what has been said here today, stays here?"

Before Eileen could answer, Harry broke in, "No, Jim. That would be illegal. That would be wrong. Am I right Eileen?"

She sat back again, as if scaling back from Defcon 2 or 3, Will thought.

Harry stared at Eileen. Finally, he said, "I think we might reach an accommodation."

Eileen waited until Forster finally nodded his assent.

"Excellent," she said. "Three checks, two for five million made out to Will and myself each, one for a million to Julie. By the end of business today."

Pained, Forster nodded his head.

"Fine," said Harry. "Oh, before you go, Eileen, and I know that you're leaving ComCon, that's understood. But would you consider handling the negotiations between us and the government?"

Eileen smiled openly as she said, "No thanks. I have other business to attend. But it was charming of you to ask, Harry. How can you be so charming to everyone all the time?"

Harry shrugged, "By not being sincere about anything."

Everyone stood to leave except for Will. Forster saw him and said, "Well, Will, you're a big winner after all, thanks to Eileen. So, what do you think of all this?"

The others stared at him, standing and waiting. He studied each of them for a second in turn, then back again, until the feeling inside finally bubbled out. He started to laugh, deep, warm, fun laughter. Forster's expression became stern, Harry smiled at first, then looked puzzled, still half-smiling. Eileen smiled broadly at Will, warmly.

And Will laughed on.

Epilogue

Me-who?
Well, I like to eat, sleep, drink
and be in love.
I like to work, read, learn
and understand life.
— Langston Hughes
Paper for English B

The doorbell rang, and before Will could stir, Mike yelled, "I'll get it!"

He ran to the door and opened it. On the front steps, a person stood, a girl, vaguely familiar and growing more so as he stared at her.

"Sandy?"

"Hiya, Mike."

"Sandy, you're back?"

She nodded, "For the holidays, just like everybody else."

She was different. She seemed older, quieter, more serious, and . . . thinner.

"Sandy," Mike said in amazement, "you got skinny!"

Sandy shook her head, "Yeah, the food sucks up there. But I also wanted to. So, are you eating now?"

"No, not yet."

"Do you want to go for a walk?"

"Oh. Sure, I guess. Do you?"

"Yeah, if your parents don't mind."

Mike grabbed his coat from the hall closet, stepped outside, and shut the door behind him. "They don't mind."

They started down the walk, past the other houses lined with out-of-state cars and naked trees. She looked straight ahead, but he couldn't take his eyes off her. He admitted to himself that even though she was thinner, she still wasn't beautiful, not like Karen. But he was so glad to see her.

"So, how are you, Mike? How's school?"

He laughed, "Pretty much the same. My grades have gotten a little better, but not enough to please my dad. He's treating me like a slave, making me sit down with him every night for hours to do my homework."

"No, really? How can he stand it? What does he do while you're doing that?"

"I don't know. Write poetry, I guess. He's really gotten big on that. Quit his job and everything to do it. He's going to start teaching at St. Holden's Academy this winter."

"Unbelievable. He won't make the time of day there."

"Yeah, I guess. But Mom and Dad don't seem to be bothered. She's not working at ComCon anymore, either." He paused, then said, "They're getting along better."

"Cool," said Sandy.

They strolled on silently for a while until they came to a low brick wall separating the walk and adjacent lawns from the parking lot of a church. Sandy sat down, and Mike put a foot on the wall and leaned on his knee.

"So, whatever happened to Karen," Sandy said, idly examining the dry leaves at her feet.

Mike laughed and said, "Nothing. I tried everything I could think of, but she never cared. Did you hear, I tried to bribe my class into electing me to Student Council?"

"No! You really tried that?" Sandy said, turning to him.

Mike dropped his eyes sheepishly. "Yeah. They all laughed at me and told Mr. Kirchner. He called my folks, and that's when I started my life sentence in the house."

"Ouch. I wonder which is worse, house arrest or banishment?"

"House arrest, believe me. My dad almost drove me crazy. He made me write papers over and stuff. He made me write a poem, told me to try it out on Karen."

"Did you? Did she like it?"

"She laughed, too. Showed it to her boyfriend Kirk, and he circulated it around school," he said with a sigh. "I was the big joke again. So, I quit on her. I don't know what I saw in her in the first place."

"Nothing except she's drop-dead gorgeous."

Mike smiled wryly, "There was that."

He swiveled around and sat on the wall next to Sandy. He picked up a stick and began to worry it between his fingers. "So, what about you, Sandy. How's school away been for you?"

"Hard. I really miss home. A lot. I miss my mom and dad, you know? Yeah, even Dad and don't laugh. When I thought about it, I was sorry that he felt, like, so bad about me. I didn't mean anything like that, you know? I just wanted to feel . . . good. About myself, you know?"

"Yeah," he said, "I know."

She shifted around, then said, "Anyway, I wanted to do things different. I studied, and that was really hard," she said rolling her eyes. "But I got okay grades, and you know what? My parents said that I could come back home this semester. It's a goddamn miracle."

Mike couldn't believe it. Suddenly, he figured out that he really missed Sandy and that he was really looking forward to her return.

"Sandy, that's great! It's really great," he said fervently.

"I know," she said. She stared at him soberly, "You know, I really missed you. We've always been friends since we were little kids. I'm happy coming back, too, but I don't want to have to worry about stuff from back then. I want my folks to be happy I'm home. It felt good, you know? So, I'm not going to do the shit I was doing before. You understand? I mean, what happened with us, you know?"

Mike felt a ripple go through him, that warm hungry feeling he had staring at Karen, the one he knew so well. He felt glad, too, that he would have Sandy to shoot the shit with again. So, if that was what she wanted, the other thing could wait. Maybe.

"Sure, Sandy, whatever. I'm really happy to see you."

With his forearm above him pressing against the living room picture window, Will watched them return. Eileen passed him on the way to the kitchen.

"You see that?" she said.

"Yup. What can we do but hope for the best?"

"Easy for you to say now, pal."

"Count your blessings, dear, and go see to your guests."

She wandered off to sit next to Eldon, his wife, his four daughters, and Julie. Mary sat across with her new boyfriend Mark. A nice enough young dude with a crew cut that made Will long for Alan of all ironies.

Mary was healed as fast as that. In charge again, she had announced her new major, criminology.

"What's that?" Will said, "How to commit a crime? Oh, yeah, Rule Number One: First, become a cop."

"Daddy!" she fake howled.

She was all right for now, anyway. He turned back to the window in time to see Mike lounging on the walk before the front stoop. He and Mike were doing well, too, since their trip to the mall, the standing upon which they were able to make their pact. Will wouldn't tell Eileen about the sneakers in the wires if Mike wouldn't tell her about his plagiarized poem. Mike seemed puzzled wondering what poem, but he didn't care enough to ask. And his pops continued to urge him to write more. Maybe he would, someday. Maybe he would get good grades someday, too.

Will felt a little bit more confident in his own poetry, too. *Marching with the Ants* had been chosen for an anthology. He'd been thrilled to death until he received a host of letters and brochures offering to sell him the book and the audiotape.

Chinese Restaurants had been accepted by a small local literary magazine, and he had parlayed both notices into the job at St. Holden's. It was a little position, but it gave him a place to continue his learning curve, and there was so much to discover—Gary Snyder, Paul Zimmer, Renee Ashley, Miller William—and journals, like *Hellas*, and *Contemporary*

Literature, and books of criticism swinging from *The Top 500 Poems* to *Can Poetry Matter?* There were places to go, New York for Poets House and the Nuyorican Poets Cafe, and what about San Francisco, Europe, and whatever they called Persia these days? Hell, they even had a word that meant "relating to poetry," "Pieria," after the ancient Greek Muses they worshipped.

Nineteen thousand a year. Wow, he'd said to Eileen, good thing we hung on to this house.

"Oh, yeah," she said sarcastically, "It'll be worth a lot if we need to remortgage it for the business."

"Well, look at it this way, Eileen," he'd said. "It's not costing us much, and who knows? If I keep publishing this way, maybe I'll bring in some money for the business."

"Yeah, right. Poetry."

"Hey, it's got to be worth something, right?" he said, leering at her.

"Listen, buster, don't be so cocksure of yourself."

With that, appearing exaggeratedly concerned, he slowly lowered his eyes to his crotch. She punched him and laughed, falling against him.

Will had to wonder, though, if it would have worked out this way without ComCon ponying up ten million bucks? Since they'd been out of ComCon, Eileen could think of nothing other than her new business with Eldon. Already they were at each other daily. Eldon wanted *Paral-Leige* to have infinite capacity, while Eileen tried to contain costs, a new concept to those with government-only contract experience. Lately, virtual reality had entered the picture. And a million could go fast, maybe more with enough arguments about how to shape reality. Eileen was endlessly happy though and entirely devoted to Will.

If she had recreated her love for him, it would take longer for him to do so for her, he thought. She had done a lot of damage. Anyway, all she needed was to reinvent a love she lost on her own. Not true, he thought; he contributed, no question. Still, he had to overlook, to forget his sense of betrayal. He also feared the future from now on.

Will rolled his eyes up at the sky, gray, typical for the season, always igniting in the mind speculation about the prospect of snow. Sooner or later, Will knew some would fall. Covering the Earth gently perhaps, like freshly pulled bread wafting in the air. Snow would turn evergreens white and larger, and the wind would muss the snow like a dreamy ocean. Or a blizzard would come from a sky spitting snow like salt grains stinging the cheek, brutally. Yes, he thought, the weather would turn nasty soon enough, and they would all have to endure it, one more season. But the nice part would follow, Spring. There, out in the woods, fiddlehead ferns would sprout and unfold, and wild raspberries would make a brief appearance, catch them if you can. That was the guarantee that made winter tolerable, he thought.

He stared out at Mike, who leaned over from the waist to kiss Sandy, then quickly turned toward the house. The door banged open as he burst in with arms spread wide while crying, "Let's eat!"

Everyone laughed, and Will smiled. The future scares everyone for sure. He sighed as he surveyed the smiling, chattering faces at the table. And he said to himself, if I can just make it through the rest of my life, I'll be all right.

Acknowledgments

I started writing this book 30 years ago, borrowing much from what occurred where we lived, just five minutes outside the Beltway surrounding our nation's capital. Other matters took priority, family life and gainful employment, then other writing projects. When I returned to this novel recently, it was amazing to see how the same differences driving politics then still resonate today. One glaring difference, of course, is the higher stakes now since not much has been resolved in the interim three decades. Now, the Earth is at stake and both foreign and domestic differences at full tilt. Perhaps this story can add a somewhat better focus

Any value of this book evolves from those who help me move it along. Jim O'Donnell tops the list as an invaluable editor, to whom I've dedicated this book. His good advice and edits have galvanized me for more than half a century. He defines completely the title "my brother from another mother." Ta', Jim.

Of course, the usual suspects have played their parts, my brothers and sisters. George again helped with his gentle suggestions that I've followed faithfully. Lucie once again has been a wonderful spirit lifter, while Anne and Ellen never fail to lift me in unknown waters.

My beloved editor and sweetheart Ivey enhances every story with sound advice and suggestions. Our wonderful daughter Molly launches each book with an inspired cover design. And our sweet son Conor weighs in always with goodwill and humor.

These contributors make telling stories a great ride; I thank all of them and love them all.

About the Author

Dan Wallace worked in book publishing for 37 years, most of them at Gallaudet University Press. In 2014, he turned to writing full time. He has written seven novels that include *Tribune of the People: A Novel of Ancient Rome* and *Run West: A Novel of the Civil War*, and *Through Noise and Silence*, a speculative fiction story about the future. He also wrote a novel about a former rock and roll star who hopes to make a comeback in *Malachite Eyes* described on the next page. He has completed three short story collections and also writes poetry and essays that can be read online at his writing exchange *In the Wallace Manner* (inthewallacemanner.com). He lives with his wife Ivey, who is also his editor-in-chief, in the Washington, DC, area.

A 1970s Rocker's 1990s Comeback

Tom Weatherly made it big on the 1970s charts with his signature song *Malachite Eyes*. He lived the good life; money no object and occasional benefits from fulsome young fans. Respected as a rock'n roller, 20 years later he found himself to be a pop star in memory only. And he wanted more.

Reviving his band the Weatherly Experience with his longtime pal Don, he finds the young new players to be a handful. At the same time, he feels compelled to contribute to others in need, both as a matter of conscience and a good move for his comeback. While entertaining youngsters in Marbury House, a "safe haven for children," he meets Norah Kealy, the likes of whom he's never known before.

Malachite Eyes
ISBN 978-1-7353006-6-5 trade paperback
ISBN 978-1-7353006-7-2 Kindle E-Book
Wylisc Press, Silver Spring, MD
wyliscpress@gmail.com

A Spectacular Speculative Novel

In a world swept by waves of cataclysm and grace, Mick Morris crests them with ease. Founder of the Stanley Institute, he deftly juggles its quantum physics research, commercial development, and government limits with admirable aplomb, now going on for fifteen years. What could possibly go wrong? Mick's daughter Meg soon finds out.

As CEO, she guides the Institute in search of the next, great QP solution to unlock astonishing possibilities in spectacular realities. But obstacles large and small impede her, from mundane office issues to mortal danger both domestic and foreign. She and her stalwart companions Carla and Ev hold their own despite all risks. But their world is running out of time.

Through Noise and Silence travels fantastic pasts and futures on Earth and distant planets. By way of far reaches through the ethos to universes and dimensions unknown, it is a trip well worth the taking.

Through Noise and Silence
ISBN 978-1-73530064-1-7 trade paperback
ISBN 978-1-7353006-1-8 Kindle E-Book
Wylisc Press, Silver Spring, MD
wyliscpress@gmail.com

Historical Novels by Dan Wallace

Publishers Weekly—Wallace's epic novel triumphs with a vivid historical account of ambitious elite Roman politicians and generals.

Library Journal— This thoroughly researched novel is as dramatic and gory as any swords-and-sandals epic and demonstrates how educational historical fiction can be. A wide cast of characters including soldiers, senators, slaves, mothers, and wives expand the reader's understanding of life in this time.

Midwest Book Review—A deftly constructed, exceptionally well written, and consistently compelling read from beginning to end, "Tribune of the People" is a truly impressive novel of the old Roman Empire by Dan Wallace. This is the stuff from which block-buster movies are made!

The US Review of Books: Professional Book Reviews for the People— Wallace's epic tale vividly depicts the opulence and grandeur of the ruling classes while simultaneously detailing the sights, sounds, smells, and squalor of those not born to wealth or position. His battle scenes pulse with excitement as he couples the weapons, tactics, and strategies of war with the carnage they wreak. No less compellingly does he describe the deceit and scheming in the porticos of power as well as the intrigue and hidden agendas in intricate familial relationships. RECOMMENDED.

The Historical Novel Society—A most timely novel; the characters are engaging and well-formed and the story well told. The novel gives you a feel for ancient Rome in the last years of the Republic.

Tribune of the People: A Novel of Ancient Rome
ISBN 978-1-7335725-0-7 trade paperback
ISBN 978-1-7335725-1-4 Kindle E-Book
Wylisc Press, Silver Spring, MD
wyliscpress@gmail.com

In the winter of 1861, East Tennessee mountain boy Billy McKinney finds himself marching with the Rebels to engage the Yankees at the Cumberland Gap. He never wanted to fight for the South because his preacher taught him that slavery was wrong. Mostly, though, Billy fears getting killed. In his first battle, he charges through a storm of gunfire and cannon shot amid a driving, icy rain. All around him his friends fall, their mouths bubbling bloody webs of agony. Terrified, Billy decides to run. In his mad dash, he meets up with four runaway slaves led by Bev Bowman. They take him along on their flight, though as prisoner or partner remains to be seen.

Run West is a compelling story of survival in a time of anguish and conflict that no one could escape.

Run West: A Novel of the Civil War
ISBN 978-1-7335725-2-1 trade paperback
ISBN 978-1-7335725-3-8 Kindle E-book
Wylisc Press, Silver Spring, MD
wyliscpress@gmail.com

Mainstream Short Stories

A young West Virginia girl trained as a boxer by her father strikes up a troubling, long-distance friendship. Hoping to live the dream, a master plumber crosses the ocean to compete for a fantastic prize. In a small city museum, an ambitious curator crosses paths with two aspiring artists at an avant-garde exhibit. Humiliated after dropping a fly ball, a disillusioned boy's love of the game hinges on the actions of an old major leaguer. A young woman considering her tenth school reunion reminisces to decide.

These stories comprise an array that mine the country's cultural history during the past half century. Each offers vivid characterizations of common people and places as pieces in the puzzle of an ever-changing world. Insights abound in this wide-ranging collection well worth reading through and through.

Blossom Gold and other stories
ISBN 978-1-7335725-6-9 trade paperback
ISBN 978-1-7335725-7-6 Kindle E-book
Wylisc Press, Silver Spring, MD
wyliscpress@gmail.com

City Stories

Summoned to jury duty, a divorced carpenter finds himself neck-deep in a Philly mob case. In the high-stakes urban real estate trade, a young agent makes his move to join the heavy hitters. A housecleaner seeks a unique form of justice for her upscale clients only to run into unlikely speed bumps. Tired of his mundane work buying microchips, a computer tech road warrior stops in Las Vegas for twenty-four memorable hours.

These stories and their companions cast stark light on various characters striving to succeed in circumstances singular to life in urban settings. Far removed from the natural world, people are the game and currency is the currency. For many of those shaped by society's strictures, survival defines success. This collection reveals in striking fashion the means an assortment of individuals use to work out their own formulas for success in the city.

Jury of Peers
City Stories
ISBN 978-1-7353006-0-3 trade paperback
ISBN 978-1-7353006-1-0 Kindle E-book
Wylisc Press, Silver Spring, MD
wyliscpress@gmail.com

Science Fiction Stories

Travel through space with provisional immortals as they panhandle for treasure amid a million iotas of galactic trash. Reserve a front-row seat for truly heroic Olympic feats performed on the Moon. Land on a desert planet where an eternal being chances the immolation of her gray matter forever. Follow a troubled blue-collar worker as he experiences an ultimate epiphany. Join an ambitious researcher who risks his own consciousness by delving into the depths of the permanently comatose. Track the progress of professional sports in ever-shifting environments.

Explore these and other alternate human prospects in this enriching, eclectic collection of stories. Each offers an original perspective on a broad spectrum of the probable and the possible. Together, they deliver an extraordinarily entertaining spectrum of what the future might hold.

Garbage in Space: Speculative Stories
ISBN 978-1-7335725-8-3 trade paperback
ISBN 978-1-7335725-9-0 Kindle E-book
Wylisc Press, Silver Spring, MD
wyliscpress@gmail.com

www.ingramcontent.com/pod-product-compliance
Lightning Source LLC
Chambersburg PA
CBHW061511020726
47502CB00006B/2022